THE BADLANDS JUST GOT WORSE

"You are insane! As mad as a hatter! I have never seen you before in my life and you have never seen me!"

Virgil Black shrugged his wide shoulders and abruptly released her, saying, "It won't work, baby. Pretend to be anyone you please, but we both know damned well who you are."

Furious with him, the shaking princess stooped down, picked up a rock, and sailed it forcefully at him.

Virgil Black stopped, lifted a hand, touched his ringing ear, and slowly turned to face her. "Do that again," he warned, "and you *will* regret it."

"I doubt that!" she answered, but stepped back. "You ever try to kiss me again and *you* will regret it!"

"I doubt that," he said confidently.

Books by Nan Ryan

You Belong to My Heart
Burning Love
Desert Storm
Outlaw's Kiss
The Princess Goes West

Published by HarperPaperbacks

THE
PRINCESS
GOES
WEST

THE PRINCESS GOES WEST

Nan Ryan

HarperPaperbacks
A Division of HarperCollinsPublishers

HarperPaperbacks
A Division of HarperCollins*Publishers*
10 East 53rd Street, New York, N.Y. 10022-5299

ISBN 1-56865-888-5

For
Pat Bost Lamar
My adored aunt who always makes me laugh

1

The Small Central European Kingdom
of Hartz-Coburg, Spring 1880

"You wake her."

"No," said the royal exchequer. "It is *your* turn to wake her."

"*You* are to wake her," repeated Montillion, the princess's facto-tum. "Once she has had breakfast, I will speak to her about the press-ing matters at hand."

The exchequer's ruddy face screwed up into a terrible frown, and he vigorously shook his head. "I implore you, Montillion, do not make me go into the lioness's cage this morning. I've a weak heart, and any undue stress is likely to—"

"Enough of this squabbling." On hearing the familiar argument, the lord chamberlain, head of the royal household, had emerged from his study. "Montillion, either send a servant or else kindly go up your-self and wake Her Royal Highness."

"Very well," Montillion said irritably, surrendering to the inevitable.

There was, he well knew, no one he could call on to awaken Her Royal Highness, the fiery princess Marlena. All the palace servants staunchly refused. Even an aging lady's maid had begged off, some years ago, after being struck one morning with a piece of marble stat-uary thrown by the irate princess.

The poor old dear hadn't been badly hurt—a small superficial cut on her forearm followed by purplish bruising and soreness—but she had marched straight into the old king's chambers, showed him the wound, and announced that she would *never* again awaken his spoiled royal offspring. Sympathizing, the king had assured the distraught lady's maid that she would not be called on to perform such hazardous duty again, and furthermore she could rest assured he would harshly reprimand his misbehaving daughter, the spoiled princess.

Now resignedly climbing the palace stairs on this sunny May morning, Montillion shook his silver head sorrowfully. The old king was gone. That patient, caring, good-natured sovereign who had reigned over this small central European kingdom had passed away six short months ago at the ripe old age of eighty-one. His wife, the queen, had preceded him in death by more than a decade.

And so it was that the sleeping twenty-eight-year-old widowed princess Marlena was to ascend to the throne. Her crowning had been delayed for two reasons—a lack of funds and a royal request from her Dutch cousin William the Third to wait until after his own coronation.

Unless—Montillion reminded her daily—the crown princess accepted a marriage proposal from a wealthy, titled suitor, she would be sent to America on an extended bond tour, long arranged by the house of Rothschild, to raise money for her near-bankrupt kingdom. It was up to her. Marry immediately—or go to America.

A spirited, bossy young woman with a temper to match her flashing green eyes and ginger-red hair, the princess had no wish to sail to America, tin cup in hand.

A gala ball that very evening at the cliffside castle would afford her an opportunity to choose a proper husband from any one of several invited prospects.

Sheltered all her life from any and all unpleasantness, the pampered princess favored neither option open to her. She would have much preferred spending the season in exciting London, attending balls and parties with the smart set, including her dear cousins, England's royals.

But even though the widowed redhead concerned herself mainly with the pursuit of personal pleasure, she was—to the bone—a blood royal, and as such, would do her duty. In fact, it had been to please her late father that Princess Marlena had, at age seventeen, married a middle-aged British duke. The distinguished duke, being old enough himself to have been her father, indulged and coddled the princess, catering to her girlish whims, demanding little, allowing his beautiful child bride to order him about as if he were a smitten school boy. Cedric Primrose, duke of Hernden, had been constantly careful not to annoy his tempestuous young bride and risk exposing himself to one of her terrible temper tantrums.

The widowed king, the kingdom, the princess, and her adoring prince consort might well have all lived happily ever after if not for the prince consort's untimely death. The first son and heir to a vast fortune that would have saved Hartz-Coburg, Cedric fell quite suddenly ill and expired two days later. Rather unfortunately for Hartz-Coburg, he preceded his wealthy, aged father in death, thus leaving his young widow and her kingdom without a farthing.

Pondering what might have been, Montillion reached the castle's second floor landing. Mentally girding himself for the unpleasant task before him, the faithful factotum threw back his shoulders and walked briskly down the long carpeted corridor beneath gilt-framed portraits of the departed royal line who had once dwelled in the old cliffside castle and ruled over the tiny Hartz-Coburg kingdom.

The last of the royal line was very much alive and sound asleep inside her chambers.

Standing before the princess's closed door, Montillion fished his gold-cased watch out of his dark vest pocket and noted the time: 10:32. He had ordered the princess's breakfast to be brought upstairs at precisely 10:35 A.M. Montillion drew a deep breath, raised a gloved hand, and rapped lightly on the solid mahogany door. He did not wait for an answer from within but went quickly inside and crossed the silk-walled salon to the open double doors of the royal bedchamber.

He glanced across the spacious room to the big white-and-gold hung bed. And, despite himself, he began to smile. A head of sleep-tangled bright ginger-red hair was swirled about on a satin-cased pillow, and an unseen face, a fair, youthful-looking face of great beauty was burrowed deeply into the pillow's feathery softness.

Montillion crossed the shadowy bedroom thinking how sweet, how youthful she looked in slumber. More like a fourteen-year-old girl than a twenty-eight-year-old monarch. But she wasn't fourteen. She wasn't a child. She was a grown woman who was, by common consent, one of the great beauties of Europe. She was the heir apparent. A princess of the blood. And it was up to her to save her kingdom.

Montillion moved to the front windows. He drew apart a set of heavy velvet drapes, instantly flooding the room with brilliant sunshine. A sound came from the bed—muffled, unintelligible—and the princess burrowed deeper into the pillow.

"Your Highness—" Montillion's voice was soft, modulated as he neared the bed, "it is past ten in the morning. Time for you to rise."

No reply. No indication she had heard him.

"Princess Marlena, I have ordered your breakfast and—ah, yes, here it is now," he said, turning to smile at the anxious servant bearing the tray and motioning her forward.

Without glancing at the princess, the uniformed servant placed the silver tray—as indicated by Montillion—at the foot of the huge bed, turned, and scurried out of the room. When she was gone, Montillion said in a slightly louder voice, "Please, won't you wake up, Your Highness." And then louder still, "Princess Marlena, it is time to get up."

Roused at last, the highly annoyed princess hissed, "I am *not* getting up! You get out!"

"I'm going nowhere until you are up and we've had a talk," said Montillion, clasping his gloved hands before him. A satin-cased pillow, aimed in his direction, came flying from the bed. He nimbly side-stepped it. The tossed pillow was followed by dire threats and vicious scoldings, to which Montillion paid no mind. He began pouring hot black coffee into a gold-trimmed china cup.

The angry Princess Marlena, struggling up and onto her elbows, her wild red hair spilling forward and covering her frowning face, yawned and muttered, "Coffee! Where's my coffee? If you must wake me in the middle of the night, might I at least have a cup of coffee!" She groaned then, flopped over onto her back, sat up, pushed her tangled hair off her face, and looked at her factotum through narrowed emerald eyes.

He said simply, "Good morning, Your Royal Highness."

She did not respond to his greeting. She began to make little mewling sounds that meant her pillows were to be fluffed up and arranged against the tall headboard. Montillion lost no time in doing her bidding. Soon the princess was comfortably propped against the pillows and sipping her coffee.

Montillion drew up a lyre-backed chair, sat down, and, without preamble, reminded her—again—that unless she accepted a marriage proposal from a wealthy, titled suitor right away, she must go to America on the extended bond tour.

Shaking her head no to the offer of a piece of buttered toast, Princess Marlena made a sour face. "I have no desire to marry again," she said, as much to herself as to Montillion.

"Very well. We shall go to America and—"

"No," she interrupted. "As distasteful as the prospect of matrimony is, it is not as abhorrent as the thought of going to America to beg."

"I couldn't agree more, Your Highness."

"I will choose a proper suitor and rush him to the altar." A touch of wistfulness in the depths of vivid green eyes, she said resolutely, "It is the least I can do for crown and country."

"Spoken like a true princess," said Montillion, smiling for the first time all morning. "Perhaps at this evening's ball you will find your Prince Charming."

It was Princess Marlena's turn to smile. "As long as he is very, very wealthy, he doesn't have to be all that charming."

*   *   *

The princess had made up her mind.

She would marry again.

At this evening's ball, she would choose from several prospects. With matrimony her motive, the princess decided to dress for the occasion with males in mind. She chose from her immense wardrobe a gown of shimmering lavender satin with a bodice that was cut as low as a proper princess could dare wear out in public. She would have the royal hairdresser sweep her long, ginger hair up off her neck and arrange the luxurious locks into neat curls atop her head.

The princess was entirely confident in her ability to make the gentleman of her choice propose before the evening ended. She was used to reducing men to nervous adoration by her mere presence. Besides, she knew how to treat men. Badly.

They couldn't get enough of it.

As twilight descended over the huge stone castle atop the highest peak of the mountain kingdom of Hartz-Coburg, the princess dressed for the ball, then examined herself in a standing, gold-framed mirror. She was pleased with her reflection and certain of her lethal feminine charms.

But she was more than a little melancholy that picking a new prince was necessary. How she wished it could have been different, that her kingdom had no need of such a sacrifice. She wished it were as it had been in the old days. She had been a child of immense privilege, raised in a lovely isolated world that had shielded her from harsh realities.

At one time this tiny mountain kingdom, located high on the Swiss frontier, had boasted the natural resources of diamond veins, coal mines, and marble quarries. Money had been plentiful. Life in the kingdom had been marvelous. A constant stream of well-heeled visitors arrived daily at the old castle. It was said that the king, her dear father, hosted the most exciting soirees on the Continent. Those glittering affairs had been attended by European and British royals, sheiks and maharajahs, pashas, and wealthy Americans.

But, alas, those golden days and silver nights had ended. The vast marble quarries had been flooded, and the rich veins of coal and diamonds had finally been exhausted. The great sums of money they had produced, spent. Times were hard. Her monarchy was unquestionably in desperate straits.

She would, the princess privately pledged, do her duty. Save the kingdom. Choose for herself a rich husband at that evening's ball, which had been planned for just that purpose.

*   *   *

That was the princess's noble resolve.

But as the evening wore on and the suitors wore on her, the princess knew she could not bring herself to marry any one of them. The viscount of Bailey—one of the wealthiest aristocrats in all Europe—was practically drooling to win her hand. But the middle-aged, rotund royal was boring and lazy, and servants at his country castle whispered that the viscount sat around his chambers with his trousers undone over his protruding belly, belching loudly and scratching unselfconsciously.

After only one agonizingly long and awkward dance with the portly perspiring viscount, Princess Marlena marked his name off the list.

The young, blondly handsome Lord Willingham was a graceful dancer, had impeccable manners, and was definitely easy on the eye. But gazing up at the winsome lord's classically handsome face as they danced beneath the sparkling chandeliers, the princess knew she would never be comfortable married to a man whose fair fragile beauty surpassed even her own.

Clamoring for dances were other wealthy marquesses, earls, and barons from which to choose a prince consort, but they were all too similar. Richly dressed sophisticated gentlemen of grace, breeding, and polish.

But not so much as a hint of fire, passion, or virile masculinity in the lot of them. To spend the next forty to fifty years married to one of these pale, blue-blooded fops seemed tiresome indeed to the lively princess.

At seventeen she had been such a child, she had thought nothing of marrying a man she hardly knew. It had been her father's strong wish that she wed the duke, and she had agreed without entertaining any doubts. But she was no longer a child. And the king was no longer alive.

When finally the tedious evening ended and the last of the crested carriages transported lingering guests down the steep winding road from the castle, a tired, disheartened princess Marlena summoned her factor, Montillion.

Meeting his hopeful gaze, she shook her head and admitted she hadn't accepted a single proposal, of which there had been many.

His face gone pale with disappointment, he said anxiously, "But Your Highness, you know there is but one alternative."

"Well, fetch me the royal tin cup," she said resolutely. "We will go to America!"

2

It was morning when Her Highness, Princess Marlena of Hartz-Coburg, and her entourage boarded the royal yacht for the long voyage across the ocean.

But it was nighttime in America.

At just past midnight in the wild gambling town of Las Cruces, New Mexico, a pretty young woman stepped onto the foot-lighted stage of Main Street's rowdy, smoke-filled Silver Dollar Saloon.

The woman was a pale-skinned beauty with large emerald eyes and ginger-red hair and a voluptuous body. Her ample curves were daringly accentuated by the revealing green satin costume she wore. She carried a white ostrich feather, which she used, skillfully, to tickle and toy with those lucky enough to be seated ringside.

She sang with a distinct accent as she smiled and strutted about the stage, teasing and flirting, to the delight of the crowd-packed saloon. Billed as the Queen of the Silver Dollar, she was, in every way, quite the crowd pleaser. Warbling a song with risqué lyrics, she played coyly to her enthusiastic audience, which was made up mainly of shouting, whistling, applauding men.

One man in the noisy saloon neither shouted nor whistled nor applauded.

Seated alone at a table against the far back wall, the silent, unsmiling man sat drinking his whiskey, his hooded eyes fixed on the red-haired woman on the stage. The man was a tall, lanky, black-haired native Texan with squint lines around his piercing blue eyes; a straight, prominent nose; and a hard mouth, around which often flickered the merest shadow of mockery.

His name was Virgil Black.

Black was a thirty-four-year-old loner who took his women like he took his whiskey: straight, with no buildup and no chaser. A hard-as-nails veteran Texas Ranger with a gun on his hip and a star on his chest, Captain Virgil Black had earned a reputation for his many feats of derring-do. Tales of his numerous exploits had been told and retold until his name was recognized by almost everyone in the vast deserts of the Southwest.

It was said that in his fifteen years as a Ranger he had, on more than one occasion, single-handedly stood off bands of Indians and fought more than his share of Mexican marauders and border bandits. Nobody knew how many men Virgil Black had killed, but everyone wondered when Black's own number would come up.

It was, they whispered, overdue.

Texas Rangers rarely lived as long as Virgil Black. Half were killed in their first year. The lives of those who went into the service were not considered good for more than a year or two.

Captain Virgil Black had beat the odds. He had looked into the face of death many a time and spit in his eye. It was the opinion of those Rangers who served with Black that the hardened captain had survived so long because he didn't much care if he lived or died.

A quiet, brooding, dark, and dangerous-looking man with steely muscles that matched his steely stare, Captain Black was said to be trigger-happy and coldhearted. Some even thought he belonged on the other side of the law.

Desperadoes feared him. Women desired him. Nobody knew him.

Nobody, save one retired Ranger: William "True" Cannon, the proud silver-haired Confederate war veteran whose life Virgil had saved more than a decade ago. The two had since become like favorite nephew and uncle. They were each other's only family.

On this warm May evening in the crowded, smoke-filled saloon in Las Cruces, Ranger Black was alone. As usual. On special assignment, Black had ridden up from Ysleta headquarters outside El Paso, to track down a daring desperado who was wanted for murder.

Earlier in the day, Black had captured his man. Tomorrow he would escort the prisoner back to Texas. But tonight he sat in the Silver Dollar Saloon, relaxing, a half-full bottle of bourbon in one hand, a shot glass in the other.

His prisoner safely ensconced in the Las Cruces jail, Virgil Black was doing some hard drinking as he gazed with mild interest at the red-haired entertainer onstage. He coolly stared as the seductive young woman came to the lip of the small stage, bent over, and tickled a grizzled, dark-bearded old cowboy with her white ostrich feather.

Bending from the waist, flashing a naughty smile, the Queen of the Silver Dollar allowed the appreciative gents an eyeful of the pale, abundant cleavage swelling above her low-cut green satin bodice. The audience loved it. They loved it even more when the lithe, lusty dancer shook her bare shoulders about, causing her breasts to dance and jiggle and threaten to spill completely out of her dress.

There were riotous hoots and whistles, and eager hands grabbed at her. Smiling provocatively, the Queen of the Silver Dollar adroitly sidestepped outstretched hands, tantalizing her eager admirers with what they were welcome to look at but could not touch. As she played to the excited men, the redhead pointedly glanced over their heads to the back of the shadowy saloon where a dark, unsmiling man sat alone at a tiny table.

Virgil Black raised his half-full glass of whiskey in silent salute and acknowledgment. The Queen of the Silver Dollar raised her hand to her scarlet lips, kissed her fingertips, and threw him a kiss. Then she spun about, showing her back to her panting audience. All came roaring to their feet when she reached down, grabbed the hem of her green satin skirt, and saucily tossed it up over her shoulders, allowing them a fleeting glance of her soft, rounded derriere covered only by skimpy satin tights with lace ruffles on the shiny seat.

It brought down the house.

Every man in the saloon was on his feet screaming for more.

Except Virgil Black.

Unmoving, he continued to sit at the table and drink his whiskey. His intent, at the moment, was to finish his bottle of bourbon and then sleep it off in the redhead's bed.

There was no doubt in Virgil Black's mind that he could, and would, do both. He didn't consider himself to be arrogant. Quite the contrary. To him it had always been a bit of a mystery why women fell so easily into his arms. All women. Not just the kind he found in saloons, but those who were supposedly respectable.

He could only surmise that all the accommodating women he had known would have behaved exactly the same way with any other man. To his way of thinking there was nothing special about him, yet females of all ages couldn't wait to give themselves to him. He had yet to desire a woman who had turned him down.

So Virgil Black was not the least bit surprised when after the show, the shapely, ginger-haired Queen of the Silver Dollar fought her way to his table through the mobs of men shouting to her, wearing an inviting smile on her scarlet-painted lips.

"I've heard about you, *Herr Kapitan* Black," she said in a distinctive, perhaps affected, foreign accent and saucily sat down on his lap.

A faint, half-mocking smile touching his hard mouth, Virgil Black poured the last of the whiskey into his glass, leisurely downed it, wiped his mouth on the back of his hand, and asked, "Just what have you heard?"

She smiled flirtatiously and said, "That you're lightning fast on the draw with that big gun on your hip, but—" she paused, leaned down, placed her gleaming red lips close to his ear, and whispered, "you can keep that awesome weapon in your trousers aimed, cocked, and ready to fire all night long."

"Want to find out?" was his cool reply.

She squealed and giggled and instantly shot up off his lap. Reaching for his hand, she said, "Come upstairs with me, *Kapitan* Black. We'll have us a real good time."

Virgil Black rose to his feet. At six foot three, he towered over the five-foot-five-inch Queen of the Silver Dollar. She tipped her head back, looked up at him, possessively clasped red-nailed fingers around his hard biceps, and said, "My goodness, you're so tall. So big." She fluttered her long eyelashes and licked her red lips. "Is everything about you . . . big?"

Virgil slowly raised a lean, dark hand, wrapped long fingers loosely around the back of her bare neck, and staring directly at her full-lipped mouth, said, "Everything's in proportion." His icy blue eyes flashed dangerously then, and he added, "Or will be once you get your hands on it."

"Oh, *Kapitan!*"

Anxious to get this big, handsome Ranger upstairs to the privacy of her room, the red-haired entertainer took his lean brown hand and led him hurriedly through the crowded saloon to the staircase on the far left side of the room. At the base of the stairs, she stopped him, took a couple of steps up, and turned to face him.

"Carry me?" she asked coquettishly.

"Why not?" was the Ranger's flat reply.

He slid his strong fingers around her small waist, and she immediately put her hands atop his broad shoulders. Effortlessly, he lifted her up in front of him, and she eagerly wrapped her stockinged legs around his trim waist. Virgil Black locked his hands beneath her shapely bottom and ascended the stairs. While she laughed with joy, hisses and boos and shouts of jealousy followed them from below.

Once inside her gaudily decorated room, Black lowered her to her feet and reached for the lowriding bodice of her tight green dress.

"No, wait," she scolded, smiling as she slapped his hand away. "Let us change roles, *vat* do you say? Instead of you undressing me, I first undress you."

"Suit yourself, Red," Black drawled as he shrugged wide shoulders. "So long as we both wind up naked."

"Oh, we will. I promise."

With that, her hands went to the buckle of his gun belt. Before she could get it undone, the ever-cautious Texas Ranger removed the heavy Colt .45 from its leather holster and laid it out of harm's way on the marble-topped chest behind them. The redhead drew the gun belt slowly from around his hips and tossed it aside. She touched the silver star on his chest, then her nimble fingers went to the buttons of his starched white shirt. Virgil Black removed the silver star, placing it beside his weapon, while she unbuttoned his shirt.

Yanking the long shirt tails up out of his black twill trousers, she swept the opened shirt apart, leaned to him, and gave his dark, naked chest a warm, wet kiss. Quite adept at what she was doing, the Queen of the Silver Dollar had, within a few short minutes, completely undressed the tall Texas Ranger. His clothes, gun belt, and boots lay on the carpeted floor, and he stood, a bare brown hip against the marble-topped chest, Adam naked. She hadn't yet removed so much as her high-heeled dancing slippers.

She played with him, teasing him and tempting him, circling him, kissing his smooth clefted back and his bare, hair-covered chest and his drum-tight belly. Finally she took him in her soft warm hands and toyed enticingly with him. Soon, awed by the size and hardness of the throbbing flesh she held, she was murmuring, "You were right, *Herr Kapitan*. Everything *is* in proportion." She stared down at him with widened emerald eyes, adding, "You are even bigger than I'd supposed. I am impressed."

"If you plan on staying impressed," came his low, flat rejoinder, "you'd better get undressed and into that bed."

She nodded happily, gave his pulsing shaft one last gentle squeeze, and said, "Give me a little time to freshen up for you. I'll be right back, I promise."

Virgil Black nodded as she hurried away and into her dressing room, assuring him she'd be "only a minute." His aching tumescence bobbing on his belly, he walked to the bed, turned back the spread, and stretched out on the clean white sheets. He waited. And waited.

His erection starting to wither, Virgil Black put a warm, gripping hand on himself, closed his eyes, and attempted to envision how his pretty red-haired companion would look without her clothes. He tried to imagine how she would feel when she was naked in his arms.

But try as he might to keep himself in a state of hot arousal, the tired Texas Ranger was swiftly losing it. He was exhausted from too little rest and too much to drink. And she was taking too long to freshen up.

He passed out.

Inside her small dressing room, the Queen of the Silver Dollar had stripped off all her clothes. She took a refreshing sponge bath so she'd be nice and clean for the handsome Texas Ranger. She undid her hair and brushed it out so that it would spill around her bare shoulders. After dabbing her most expensive perfume between her full breasts, behind her ears and knees, and on the insides of her thighs, she slipped on a slinky robe of shimmering white satin trimmed with white ostrich feathers. She tied the robe's sash at her waist, then purposely pushed the feather-trimmed lapels wide apart so that her full breasts would be half-revealed.

Sliding her bare feet into a pair of white satin house slippers, she eagerly hurried out to join her Ranger.

Her smile quickly turning to a frown, the Queen of the Silver Dollar sighed with bitter disappointment when she saw that the lanky, naked Ranger was sound asleep. Miffed, and frustrated, she paced back and forth for a few uncertain minutes, before kicking off her house slippers and removing her satin robe.

Naked, she crawled in next to the sprawled Ranger. She snuggled close, pressing her bare, soft body against his hard length while she leaned over his face and licked at his lips, murmuring, "Come on, handsome, *vake* up."

She ran her hands over his hard muscled frame. She tickled his broad chest. She pressed wet, tongue-probing kisses to his hard belly. She cupped his groin warmly, caressed his flaccid flesh in an all-out attempt to make it spring to life. She did everything in her power to awaken the sleeping Ranger and his magnificent body. But to no avail.

Exasperated, she finally got out of the bed, went through his trouser pockets, and took some cash, paying herself for what was promised but never delivered. Then she sighed wearily, blew out the bedside lamp, got back into bed with Virgil Black, and fell asleep.

When the Queen of the Silver Dollar awakened late the next morning, the handsome, hard-faced Ranger was gone.

New York City was in a royal tizzy over the visit of Her Highness, Princess Marlena of Hartz-Coburg.

The elegant presidential suite at the Waldorf-Astoria Hotel had been engaged for the royal party, where, on the morning of her arrival, fresh-cut flowers were placed in all the suite's spacious rooms and the hotel's nervous staff fussed over the smallest of details in an effort to ensure the total comfort and privacy of their illustrious guest.

The city's foremost families fought for the privilege of hosting glittering balls and lavish dinners for the princess. There were far more hostesses anxious to fete the visiting royal than the proposed length of her stay allowed, so the arguing ladies finally resorted to a democratic lottery. Those who won an evening were elated; the losers, extremely disappointed.

On a bright sunny morning in early June, the royal yacht steamed into New York Harbor right on schedule. Swarms of admirers, crowding Hudson River pier 51, waited expectantly, hoping for a glimpse of the arriving royal.

As the yacht slowly maneuvered into its appointed berth in the busy harbor, the object of their interest was inside her satinwood-paneled stateroom, dressing for her initial appearance in New York.

Princess Marlena was terrifically tired from her long journey. First there had been the exhausting train ride in the royal railcar across the mountains to the seacoast city of Bremerhaven where the royal yacht was moored. Then the lengthy and frightening voyage across a storm-tossed ocean, which had on more than one occasion made her wretchedly seasick.

Weary and suffering from a slight headache, she would have liked nothing more than to slip unnoticed into the city and the blessed privacy of a quiet hotel suite where she could lie down and rest. But rest would have to wait.

First impressions were, the princess knew all too well, lasting ones. And so she chose, from the many wardrobe options presented for consideration by her lady-in-waiting, a freshly pressed, tastefully tailored traveling suit of heavy linen, the hue of which was a deep emerald green that brought out her eyes. To compliment the simple elegance of the stylish linen suit, she chose a delicate lace-trimmed blouse with a tall, tight-banded collar that felt as if it would surely choke her to death. The high-throated blouse and heavy linen suit would, she knew, be uncomfortably warm in the sweltering June heat of New York. But decidedly attractive. She could, for one short hour, endure a measure of discomfort.

When she was dressed, Princess Marlena placed a wide-brimmed straw hat atop her ginger-red hair, which had been carefully swept atop her head. She thoughtfully studied herself in the mirror and, focusing on her ears, made an unhappy face. Why, she had wondered a thousand times, couldn't she have had her mother's ears instead of her father's? The queen's ears had been absolutely perfect: small, well shaped, and lying close to her regal head. The king's ears had not been overly large, but they protruded noticeably, and she, to her profound dismay, had inherited that unwanted family trait of the house of Ballarat. Her ears were as small as her mother's, but they stood out a fraction too much from her head. She was extremely self-conscious about them.

"Do you think these Americans will notice my ears?" she worriedly asked her hovering lady-in-waiting, a favorite cousin of the princess's.

"The only one aware of your ears is you, Your Highness," said the baroness Richtoffen, right on cue. She shook her graying head, adding as she always did, "There is nothing wrong with your ears."

Unconvinced, Princess Marlena sighed and reached for her white kid gloves. Drawing on the gloves, she crossed to the stateroom's closed door. There she paused, smoothed down the skirts of her green linen suit, bit her lips to give them extra color, and took a deep, spine-stiffening breath.

When she exited the royal cabin, Montillion met her with raised umbrella, but Princess Marlena waved it away. "They will want to see my face."

"Yes, of course," said Montillion, bowing slightly, tossing the umbrella aside and escorting her to the yacht's railing. There, smiling broadly, he extended his arm full length and made a wide sweeping gesture, indicating the huge crowd anxiously awaiting her appearance.

Princess Marlena stepped up to the railing and into sight. Shouts of joy immediately rose and quickly grew to a din as she smiled and waved to the masses below.

It was the same throughout Manhattan. So many people had turned out to see the princess, it took four hours for her to travel the few miles from the pier to the Waldorf-Astoria Hotel.

Throughout, Princess Marlena sat in the slow-moving coach with her back absolutely straight—never touching the seat. All along the route she smiled and waved and appeared to be as fresh as the first rose of spring. No one who saw her could have suspected that she was hot and miserable and had a headache and a backache.

Graciously enduring the ordeal, she reminded herself that she *was* royalty and that the future of the crown was at stake. She had been assured by her Rothschild advisers that there had been no problem arranging and executing a potentially successful bond tour. They had confidently predicted that in the heavily populated Northeast—where many prosperous Hartz-Coburg immigrants lived—she would be able to raise great sums of money rather quickly. With any luck, she'd be returning home at summer's end with sufficient funds to drain and reopen the flooded Hartz-Coburg marble quarries. The much-sought-after pink stone with its ocean-blue veins would again satisfy the demands of worldwide construction.

Judging by the size and enthusiasm of the crowds that had turned out to see her, her advisers had been right. This happy thought lifted the princess's spirits, and her smile became broader and more dazzling.

Nonetheless, the princess could hardly hide her relief when the gleaming black coach finally drew up before the Waldorf-Astoria's canopied entrance. She was literally counting the minutes until she could get inside the suite, strip off her hot clothes, and sink down into a cooling tub.

The carriage wheels had barely ground to a stop before a high-hatted doorman rushed forward. Montillion motioned him back to the luggage coach pulling up alongside the servant's coach, which was directly behind the royal carriage. The doorman nodded, put a whistle to his lips, blew one sharp blast, and a half-dozen uniformed young men rushed out of the hotel and began unloading the luggage.

In all there were eight large steamer trunks, thirty-five leather valises of various shapes and sizes, and a couple of velvet suede cases containing gifts that the princess had brought along to give to the people in service to her while in America. The cases were filled with pens and studs and rings and bracelets, all bearing the Hartz-Coburg royal crest.

The royal party began alighting from the carriages. Only a few of her most trusted traveling companions had come to America with the princess. The princess had been advised, and had agreed, that to be accompanied by too large a retinue would be unseemly in view of the fact that the purpose of her visit was to raise money.

So her small entourage consisted of Montillion, her trusted factor; the baroness Richtoffen, her dear cousin and lady-in-waiting; Doctor Hondrich, the royal physician; and Hantz Landsfelt, a large, muscular Bavarian equerry who served as protector and bodyguard and baggage handler.

The tired princess was swiftly whisked from the carriage and escorted across the red-carpeted entrance into the hotel's grand lobby. She was spirited through the lavish lobby with its waxed mahogany and painted paneling and emerald-green ferns. Within minutes she was being directed into a spacious top-floor corner suite.

Ignoring the vases of fresh-cut roses and baskets of fragrant fruit and the beckoning view of the city from her private balcony, Princess Marlena tore off her straw hat, removed her kid gloves, and was already unbuttoning her green linen suit jacket as she headed straight for the bedroom.

Collecting articles of clothing carelessly dropped by the princess, the baroness Richtoffen followed Her Royal Highness into a huge white bath where a gleaming porcelain tub was—as requested—filled with steaming water.

The princess, pausing directly beside the tub, turned to the baroness and held out her arms. The baroness Richtoffen quickly undressed her charge and helped her into the waiting bath.

While the princess lolled in the soothing tub, the baroness—with the help of two hotel maids—unpacked her mistress's extensive wardrobe. Montillion appeared shortly to advise the baroness Richtoffen of the princess's agenda. Her schedule had been purposely kept free on this her first afternoon in the city so that she might rest. That evening she was to be the guest of honor at an important dinner hosted by one of New York's most influential families, the William K. Vanderbilts.

"See to it the princess naps this afternoon," Montillion advised. "She mustn't be cranky tonight. She must look and feel her best."

As dusk descended over the magical city, Princess Marlena, dressed in an elegant gown of ice-blue satin complemented by diamond-and-sapphire earrings and necklace, had never looked, or felt, better. As she lovingly fingered the glittering diamond-and-sapphire necklace that had been her dear mother's, she was glad that she had kept it. Most of the kingdom's precious jewels had, of necessity, been quietly sold, but she could not bring herself to part with these particular gems that had been the king's wedding present to his young bride.

Arriving at the Fifth Avenue mansion of the William K. Vanderbilts at exactly eight thirty, the glowing princess was ushered into the vast Italianate palace where she was warmly greeted by her proud hosts, William and Alva Vanderbilt. For the next half hour she stood in a reception line with the Vanderbilts as two hundred handpicked, well-heeled dinner guests filed by, curtsying and bowing and exclaiming how thrilled they were to meet her.

It turned out to be a lovely, lovely evening.

The princess liked the Americans. They were warm and witty and highly entertaining. She had such a good time, she stayed on at the mansion long after the seven-course dinner had ended. She was not the only one. Protocol demanded that the other guests stay until the princess departed, but none minded. They were totally charmed by the beautiful young princess and enjoyed themselves immensely.

What had been planned by the thoughtful hosts as a brief hour-long dinner, after which the travel-weary princess might be excused to return to her hotel for much-needed rest, turned into something altogether different. Alva Vanderbilt, the beaming hostess, seeing how lively the guest of honor was, suggested moving on to the ballroom for a bit of dancing. The idea was met with genuine enthusiasm by all.

Inside the mammoth white-and-gold, parquet-floored ballroom, eager gentleman quickly lined up for a dance with the princess. An orchestra, in full evening dress, magically appeared. Chilled champagne soon flowed freely. Laughter and gaiety filled the massive room.

No one had more fun than the visiting princess. She turned about on the polished dance floor, never noticing the low discussions taking place on the fringes of the crowd, nor the worry-creased foreheads of those gentlemen who were deep in conversation. She was unaware of the growing unease shared by the majority of her fellow guests. She had no idea that a single one was concerned with anything more pressing than where they would lunch tomorrow.

It was past three in the morning when the exhausted princess finally walked into her hotel suite's spacious bedroom, yawning sleepily. Her lady-in-waiting, napping in a chair with a book on her lap, immediately came awake and hurried to meet her young mistress.

Holding out her arms, the sleepy princess said to the baroness Richtoffen the same thing she said every night.

"Undress me."

When the sun rose over the big eastern city of New York, it looked the same as ever. The tall buildings still rose majestically to meet the clear blue sky. The early morning quiet was as serene as ever. The city's wealthiest had not yet awakened to learn what had happened.

At ten A.M., Montillion got the shocking news with his first cup of black coffee. The latest edition of *The New York Herald* splashed the bulletin in heavy black headlines. NEW YORK STOCK MARKET CRASHES!

His heart hammering, Montillion hurriedly took his wire-rimmed glasses from inside his suit pocket, set them on his nose, hooked the ear pieces over his ears, and anxiously read of how vast fortunes had been wiped out overnight.

By eleven A.M. news of the market's crash had spread like wildfire across the island of Manhattan. Worried people poured into the streets, shouting and pushing .and asking themselves what would become of them. Frustration-fed arguments broke out. Fistfights ensued. Carriage traffic couldn't move on crowded thoroughfares. Frightened wild-eyed horses neighed and whinnied and reared. Mounted police, blowing whistles and shouting warnings, couldn't contain the mobs on the verge of hysteria. Panic in the streets.

The deafening noise awakened the sleeping princess. Alarmed, she got out of bed, drew on a silk wrapper, and hurried into the suite's sitting room. Montillion stood at a front window, looking down at the crowd.

Princess Marlena hurried to him, caught his arm. "Montillion," she asked, "what is that horrible noise?"

Turning away from the window, he looked directly at her and replied, "The sound of an empire collapsing."

4

The bullet whizzed past his head and made a high pinging sound as it struck the rising wall of sandstone directly behind him.

Crouched behind a fallen boulder, Captain Virgil Black ducked a little lower, picked up a large pebble, and sailed it firmly into a spindly sun-blistered mesquite a few yards away.

A volley of shots followed immediately, stripping leaves and bark from the gnarled tree. Virgil Black let out a loud groan, as if he had been hit. Instantly there was chattering in rapid Spanish as the two assailants foolishly scrambled up out of their hiding place.

Gun drawn, hammer back, the Texas Ranger came quickly to his feet. "Drop your guns and gun belts, then put your hands over your heads, *amigos.*"

The younger of the two Mexican bandits lifted his gun instead, then yelped in fright and pain when Virgil shot it out his hand.

"Maybe you're having trouble with your ears. I said, 'Put your hands over your head.' *Comprende?*"

"*Sí, sí, Capitán,*" the older bandit said, his short arms raised high while the younger man hurriedly unbuckled his gun belt.

"Now, kick your weapons away," ordered Black. Both men obeyed, but the one whose gun hand was powder blackened and bleeding slightly muttered under his breath how he would get *venganza* on the cruel gringo *capitán.*

"While you apparently have a serious hearing problem, *amigo,*" Black said, addressing the young hothead, "mine is perfect. You can forget any foolish plans for vengeance. And, you can take that knife out of your pants, drop it to the ground, and kick it away."

"Knife? I have no knife and I—" A bullet from Black's raised revolver ended the sentence and kicked up dust an inch from the Mexican's scuffed left boot. Eyes wide, the young bandit anxiously slipped the long, sharp-bladed knife up out of its leather sheath and tossed it away.

"*Gracias,*" said Black, and whistled for his battle-trained saddle horse.

Shaking his great head and whinnying, the coal-black stallion came out of a rocky draw and moved straight to his master. Virgil Black took a coiled lasso from behind the saddle and walked down to the two bandits, warning them to keep their hands in the air. He bent, picked up the Mexican's discarded knife, cut two short, equal lengths of rope from the long lasso, and tied the hands of the two criminals.

His blue eyes squinting against the sun, Black addressed the younger man, "Know how far it is back to El Paso?"

Dark eyes snapping with anger, the bandit shrugged, and said, "Four, five miles."

"Six," Black corrected.

Then he walked down a slight incline to where two saddled horses were tethered. He untied the horses, took off his sweat-stained hat, and slapped them on the rumps, sending them galloping away.

He returned to his captives. He took a cigar out of his gray chambray shirt pocket, stuck it between his lips, and lit it, cupping his hands around the tiny match flame. He puffed the smoke to life and, never taking it out of his mouth, said, "Let's go to El Paso, *amigos.*"

The pair looked at him. They looked at each other. They looked back at him, incredulous.

Shaking his head, the younger man said, "How can we go to El Paso? You have run off our horses."

Black rolled the lit cigar to the left corner of his mouth. "You will walk."

Two hours later Captain Black rode down the dusty main street of El Paso with his two dirty, hot, thirsty prisoners stumbling along behind him, a long length of rope wrapped around their bound hands and tied to Black's gun belt. People spilled out of saloons and stores to point and laugh, but Virgil Black had no pity for the humiliated pair. Any lowlife thieving coward who stole from a poor widow woman with four young children to raise deserved a hangman's noose as far as he was concerned.

Captain Black delivered the pair to the El Paso County jail. He handed them over along with the little drawstring bag of money they had stolen from Widow Thompson's modest Stanton Street home where she took in washing and ironing.

"We're much obliged to you, Captain Black," said the guard on duty as he slammed the barred doors on the prisoners. "Let me buy you a drink to show our gratitude."

"Not necessary," said Virgil. "I need to be getting on back out to head-quarters." He looked at the incarcerated pair hugging the steel bars and glaring at him. Pointing a lean forefinger at them, he warned, "You ever cross my path again, I won't be so kind and understanding. *Comprende?*"

"*Sí, sí,*" said the older man, nodding anxiously.

Virgil Black turned and walked away, the silver spurs on his boots jingling. He stepped out onto the jail's wooden porch, looked up the street, then down. He reached for the worn suede gloves stuffed into his back pants pocket. He drew on the gloves slowly, then stepped down off the porch. He unwound his mount's long leather reins from the hitch post and climbed into the saddle. He backed the stallion away, turned him east, and put him into an easy canter for the four-mile ride to the Ysleta Ranger headquarters.

"We got trouble. Indian trouble."

That was the greeting from his superior when Virgil Black reached headquarters just as the scorching summer sun was setting behind the blue-purple Franklin range of the Rockies. Black had no need to ask which Indian was causing the trouble. He knew.

Victorio.

A name that struck terror in the hearts of travelers and settlers and ranchers across the vast Southwest.

The Apache chief had quit the reservation more than a year ago. In the autumn of '79 he had taken 125 warriors and a hundred women and children and headed for Mexico. The old Apache's knowledge of the mountains and the location of water, grass, and wood was unparalleled. And his ability as commander made him formidable and dangerous to Americans and Mexicans alike.

Choosing a stronghold high up in the Diablo Mountains, the fero-cious and cunning Victorio had, from his eagle's nest, an unobstructed view of the country all around for twenty or thirty miles. He could see the wagon trains as they moved from El Paso del Norte to Chihuahua. He could spot details of blue-coated soldiers paroling the border. He could spy on dozens of remote horse and cattle ranches scattered across the southwest desert.

When least expected, he rode down from his mountain hideout to kill and burn and steal livestock.

Black dropped down into a straight-backed chair across the scarred desk from Captain George W. Baylor.

"What's the red devil up to this time?" Black asked.

"He's back in Texas. The Mexican government notified General Grierson at Ft. Davis. Grierson notified me."

Nodding, Black said simply, "When do we leave?"

"At sunrise tomorrow," said his commanding officer. "Grierson's instructions are for us to scout toward Eagle Springs, try to pick up the Indian trails."

At dawn Baylor, Black, and a dozen handpicked Rangers set out for Eagle Springs. Two days later they came upon a place where U.S. troops had fought the Apache. Dead cavalry horses littered the landscape. Bullet marks dotted the rocks, as well as fresh blood of the soldiers.

The Rangers rode on.

Soon they came to where the Indians had ambushed a stagecoach. The vicious Apache had killed the driver and passenger, then mutilated the dead by stuffing torn letters from the mail sack into the wounds of their victims.

"Damn that Victorio," muttered one of the sickened Rangers. "Why couldn't he just kill them? Why does he have to be so god-awful cruel?"

Taking a shovel from one of the supply horses, Captain Virgil Black calmly began digging a grave.

He said flatly, "It could have been worse. Last time he and his band were fleeing Texas after a rampage, one of his most feared young braves stopped long enough on this side of the Rio Grande to dunk a poor sheep-herder's head in some hot tallow he had been rendering."

"Must have been Chief Thunderfoot," put in one of the other Rangers. "They say young Thunderfoot is even meaner than old Victorio. And that is mean."

"Amen."

5

"It's not fair! It just is not fair," Princess Marlena raged in disbelief.

"Your Highness, where is your compassion?" Montillion gently scolded. "Think of those whose fortunes have drastically dwindled because of this sudden market plunge."

"Oh, I know, I know. And I am sorry for them, truly I am," said the princess, pacing worriedly back and forth. "But I don't see why the market crash had to happen now, of all times."

"Unfortunate," Montillion had to agree. "Most unfortunate."

A long pause. Then the disappointed princess reasoned, "With this unexpected calamity, we will be unable to raise the money we need. Is that not a fact?"

"I'm afraid that the market crash changes everything," Montillion admitted. "Those who are now quite worried about their own diminished fortunes and uncertain futures will not likely be predisposed to prodigious foreign investments."

"No. No, of course not," said Princess Marlena. "We have come all this way for nothing, spending money we did not have to make the journey. All our well-laid plans have been for naught."

"Come, come. We are not defeated yet, Your Highness," said Montillion, smiling in an attempt to lighten her mood. "This unexpected setback means only that . . . ah . . . well . . . that we revise our plans somewhat."

"Revise our . . . ? How can we?" Princess Marlena's well-arched eyebrows lifted questioningly.

"There is a way," said Montillion.

As if she hadn't heard, she murmured, "We were all so confident we could raise large sums here in the Northeast."

"A great disappointment," said Montillion.

"Be home by late summer in time for the season with enough money to drain the flooded marble quarries."

"Early fall is still quite possible."

"Make the quarries productive again," she said wistfully.

"And so we will."

"Save the kingdom and its subjects. I had so hoped that . . ." The princess stopped speaking, shrugging her slender shoulders.

"Yes, I know," said her factor. He drew a quick breath and pressed on, "If we are to raise the funds for our insolvent kingdom, we must go out west."

"Go out west?" She stared at him, incredulous. "Are you insane? In case you have forgotten, I am the princess royal of Hartz-Coburg!"

"I haven't forgotten, Your Highness."

"I? Go west? Never!" she announced decisively. "Never, never, never! You cannot expect me to travel to the wild and uncivilized frontier." Making a face, she added, "Why, there's no one out there but dirty miners and wild cowboys and dangerous outlaws and blood-thirsty savages." She laughed sarcastically. "I can well imagine how much money we'd raise among their kind." She wrinkled her royal nose.

"You might be pleasantly surprised," Montillion hastily informed her. "I am told that the upper crust of Denver, Colorado, are really quite cultured." His thin gray eyebrows raised thoughtfully when he added, "Tons of gold and silver have been taken out of the Rockies over the last few decades. Vast fortunes have been made. The city's population boasts a high percentage of millionaires—some from Hartz-Coburg."

Unconvinced, the princess shook her head, causing her unbound red hair to whip around her shoulders. "That may well be, but it changes nothing. I simply will not go and that is final!" She jabbed a thumb toward the middle of her chest and told him loudly, "*This* princess does not go west!"

The princess went west.

After further gentle, but relentless, persuasion from her stalwart factotum, the out-of-sorts princess Marlena finally agreed to go as far west as Denver, Colorado.

And not one mile farther.

But as her royal railcar rolled into the Queen City of the Rockies, the princess was overwhelmed by the warm, enthusiastic welcome she received from the enormous throngs crowding Denver's Union Depot. Many of the rich and prosperous had turned out to pay homage and, at a Brown Palace bond rally the next afternoon, proved to be exceptionally generous. So generous, in fact, the pleased princess changed her mind about traveling farther west. Bond sales, higher than her expectations, were gratifying.

After only twenty-four hours in the city, she summoned Montillion and excitedly told him that she would be more than willing to go on to other western cities.

Montillion was delighted. He wasted no time setting up bond rallies and banquet dates for Her Highness in Fort Worth, Dallas, San Antonio, and finally Galveston, where they would board the royal yacht for the return voyage home.

Exhilarated from her successful week-long visit, Princess Marlena stood on the open platform of her royal railcar and waved good-bye as the train left Denver at sundown. She stayed on the platform long after Union Station and the exuberant crowds had been left behind.

As the train snaked southward, Princess Marlena gazed fondly at the majestic snow-dusted peaks of the towering Rockies bathed now in the purples and pinks of the setting summer sun. The awesome Rocky Mountains reminded her of her beloved Alps. Seeing the huge monoliths of stone reaching to meet the quickly darkening Colorado skies, she could almost pretend that she was at home.

Texas, she felt sure, would be very different from home. But hers was a curious nature, and she was looking forward to seeing America's largest state.

The gathering dusk soon drove the princess inside where she was served a late light dinner. It was then, while dining, that the princess got a glimpse of her face in one of the narrow strip mirrors of the royal rail coach. She was shocked and horrified to see that the whites of her eyes had turned yellow.

She dropped the heavy sterling soup spoon. It clattered into the gold-crested china bowl, splashing beef-and-barley broth onto the white tablecloth.

"Summon Doctor Hondrich!" the frightened Marlena cried out, rising so quickly her chair toppled over backward. Her trembling hands flying up to her face, she screamed, "Something terrible is happening to me!"

By morning when the train was just outside Raton Pass, Princess Marlena's entire face was the color of a lemon peel. When she tried to eat a bit of breakfast, she experienced excruciating pains in her lower stomach.

Dr. Hondrich, as he had done repeatedly throughout the long

night, went again into the royal bedchamber to examine his patient. Hovering just outside the door, Montillion and the baroness Richtoffen waited anxiously. Both jumped when the door abruptly opened and Dr. Hondrich stepped out.

"The princess has," announced the royal physician, "come down with a case of yellow jaundice."

"Dear Lord in heaven, no," murmured Montillion and the baroness in unison.

"There is no doubt in my mind," said Dr. Hondrich firmly. "She must have at least three weeks of total rest and quiet."

"But the bond tour . . ." Montillion lamented. "Advance word says they are certain to love her in Texas, and we have not sold nearly enough bonds. Anticipation is presently high. A delay would be disastrous."

The physician sympathized. "I know, but there are times when providence changes our—"

"Doctor Hondrich, you must understand, the house of Rothschild advance man has set firm dates for the sales rallies and—"

"Be that as it may," interrupted the physician, "I am warning you that unless the princess has rest, quiet, and the proper diet, well—" he shrugged and added gravely, "jaundice *can* kill."

A soft sob escaped the lips of Baroness Richtoffen. Dr. Hondrich laid a comforting hand on her thin shoulder and said, "Do not worry. We will not allow anything to happen to Her Royal Highness." He smiled then, and urged them to action. "Now, go in to your mistress and offer her the comfort she so desperately needs."

Nodding, the worried lady-in-waiting slipped into the royal bedchamber, closing the door behind her.

"A shame about the bond tour," Dr. Hondrich sympathized with Montillion, "but it simply cannot be helped."

Ever resourceful, Montillion rubbed his chin and replied thoughtfully, "Perhaps there's still a way to keep the dates . . . to address the rallies . . ." He stopped speaking. His eyes flashed and the downturned corners of his mouth lifted. To the puzzled physician, he said, "I have a new plan."

"A new plan?"

"I shall inform the engineer to change our route at once! Instead of going directly to Fort Worth, we will take the ailing princess to Cloudcroft, New Mexico. It's a remote mountain village nestled high in the cool pines, less than a hundred miles from here."

"What on earth would be the purpose of that?" The physician

frowned. "The princess would surely be better off in Fort Worth than—"

Shaking his graying head, Montillion interrupted, "In Cloudcroft there is an abbey of Benedictine nuns who operate a small sanatorium. Don't you see, it's the perfect place for the princess to recuperate in privacy and total secrecy." Excited, Montillion rushed away, with a warning to the physician that no one must know.

"But how can we possibly keep it quiet?" Dr. Hondrich trailed after him. "With her tour cut short, the parades, the rallies, everyone will . . ." The doctor sighed. "And it's the princess alone that the Texans want to see."

"And see her they shall," said Montillion.

"But," the doctor flushed, "the deadly jaundice . . ."

"The bond tour will proceed on schedule," said Montillion, enigmatically. "Leave everything to me."

6

"And I can assure you, we will make it well worth your while," Montillion said, addressing the satin-robed, red-haired saloon performer.

"Why me?" she asked, yawning sleepily.

It was the middle of the afternoon, but the red-haired entertainer had been sleeping when Montillion walked into the near-empty saloon and asked if he might be granted a brief visit with the Queen of the Silver Dollar. Told she was resting and could not be disturbed, he had calmly informed the ham-fisted man tending bar that he would wait.

And he had.

Finally, at just past three o'clock, a door opened on the wide second-floor landing above, and a woman shouted irritably, "Where's my breakfast?"

"Keep your shirt on," the bartender bellowed back. "It's comin'."

Montillion quietly slipped upstairs behind a dour-looking girl carrying a covered breakfast tray. Outside the saloon singer's door, he smiled at the servant, took the tray from her, and said, "I will take care of this."

Relieved that she wouldn't have to endure the abuse of the singer/actress who was beastly until she'd had that first cup of coffee, the serving girl nodded eagerly and hurried away. Balancing the tray on a gloved palm, Montillion knocked.

"It's open. Come on in."

He entered the gaudily decorated room and blinked. The shades were pulled against the hot June sun, and it took a moment for his pupils to adjust.

"And just who the hell are you?" came a voice from out of the shadows.

Squinting, Montillion spotted a young, very pretty woman seated before a vanity mirror. She wore a robe of shiny black satin that was carelessly open over her crossed, shapely legs.

She twisted about, glared at him, and, supposing he was a newly hired kitchen servant, said, "Well, what are you waiting for? Pour my coffee!"

Smiling, Montillion obeyed. Then as the ill-tempered entertainer sullenly sipped the strong, black coffee, he introduced himself and hurriedly told her why he had come to see her. And as she listened, her eyes began to widen, her interest piqued.

When he quickly explained that all she had to do was imperson-ate the ailing princess for two or three weeks, she asked again, "But why me?"

He smiled and handed her a small framed tintype. "As you can see, you bear a striking resemblance to the princess—and you speak English with an accent." Before she could say anything else, Montil-lion quickly told her everything she needed to know.

Frowning, she started to speak.

"You will simply," he continued, "take Princess Marlena's place on the remainder of the bond tour in Texas. You will, of course, be gen-erously rewarded for your services, and you will have the total support of the royal entourage. I myself will patiently tutor you so that any Texan who meets you will not doubt for a second that you actually are the crown princess of Hartz-Coburg."

The Queen of the Silver Dollar finally pulled her robe together over her bare crossed knees, and said, "What about clothes? I have some stunning theatrical gowns, but—"

"You are very near the size and build of the princess." Montillion paused, studying her carefully. "Well, perhaps you weigh a few pounds more than she. Her royal ceremonial wardrobe may be a trifle snug on you, but with a few alterations it should work well enough."

"I suppose I wouldn't be allowed to tell anyone that—"

"No."

She frowned. "Just one person? There is this particular gentleman who is my—"

"Absolutely no one."

"Absolutely no one," she repeated to herself, pondering.

The Queen of the Silver Dollar continued to frown with indecision as she asked herself, What about Robert? He wouldn't know what had hap-pened to her. He'd be sick with worry. Or would he? How long had it been since she last saw him? Two weeks? Three? God, he was a selfish bastard. And arrogant. He assumed that she was his, body and soul. That she wouldn't look at another man. But he was wrong. She would have done a whole lot more than *look* if that big, handsome Texas Ranger hadn't fallen asleep on her a few nights back. And it would have been Robert's fault. He supposed he could neglect her for as long as he chose, and she'd be waiting patiently any time he walked into the saloon, ready and willing to do anything he asked of her. Well, he had another thing coming, the pompous English cad!

Green eyes suddenly flashing, she said to Montillion, "You actually think we could fool all those—"

"You are an actress, are you not?" Montillion quickly challenged.

She immediately rose to the bait.

"One of the best," declared the spirited young woman who—when in her cups—liked to boast that her mother was none other than the renowned stage actress Lola Montez, and that her father was of European nobility. Wasn't the annual "anonymous remittance" proof of it?

Montillion quietly studied the lovely young woman, noting the ginger-red hair, the emerald green eyes, the small, well-shaped, but distinctive, slightly protruding ears.

Smiling, he said, "I'm sure you are. Now you've a chance to prove it."

"Monty, you've got yourself a deal," she said decisively. "Let's shake on it!" She thrust out her hand and told him, "The name is Roberta Ann, but you can call me Robbie or Red or Queenie."

Montillion took the offered hand in his gloved one, shook his graying head sternly, and corrected her. Bowing slightly, he said, "You are now Her Royal Highness, Crown Princess Marlena of Hartz-Coburg, and that is what I shall call you."

Robbie gaily giggled.

Montillion learned to his pleasure and relief that the comely dance hall singer was a quick study. Innately intelligent and anxious to play this, the most important role of her acting career, she listened, learned, and tirelessly practiced being a princess. She was determined to make anyone who met her believe that she was Princess Marlena of Hartz-Coburg.

As promised, the pretty impostor had the support of the entire royal entourage. The real princess—sick, jaundiced, and miserable in Cloudcroft—was shocked and distraught when she was told that her royal party would not be staying with her at the remote sanatorium. To her dismay, Princess Marlena learned that she was to be left alone in the care of the nurturing nuns. She would, she was assured, be perfectly safe and comfortable there with the dedicated sisters. When she was quite well, Hantz Landsfelt, her burly bodyguard, would return to Cloudcroft to fetch her. He would then escort her to Texas, where she would take her rightful place on the tour.

Had she felt the least bit better, the outraged princess would have thrown a temper tantrum at such high-handed decisions being made without her consultation, and she would have demanded that her lady-in-waiting, at least, stay behind with her. But she simply hadn't the energy to scream and threaten.

So, while the real princess was safely, secretly stashed away in the remote sanatorium high in the Sacramento Mountains of New Mexico, the eager impostor was set to play her part with consummate grace and ease.

Coaching her every minute of the day as the royal train made its way across the high plains of Texas, Montillion was well pleased with his pupil's amazing progress. She was a natural. By the time they reached Fort Worth, he was confident of the Queen of the Silver Dollar's ability to convince everyone that she was indeed a royal princess.

Captain Virgil Black was disheveled and dead tired when he and his fellow Rangers rode into Ysleta headquarters after two weeks on the trail. He was unshaven, and alkali dust flecked his itchy black beard. His tanned face was shiny with perspiration, and his sweat-soaked shirt stuck to his back. His squinted blue eyes were bloodshot from staring at too many heat-undulating horizons, and his back ached from too many hours in the saddle.

Silent and sullen, Captain Black rode alongside his commanding officer, George W. Baylor, to whom he had said little in the last three days. None at all today.

The exhausting seventy-five miles they had ridden since dawn was not solely responsible for Black's fatigue and morose mood. It was that the entire two-week campaign had been fruitless. In his opinion, it needn't have been.

The Rangers had successfully tracked the cunning Victorio and his band of ruthless renegades from the Hawkins stage station down into the rugged Big Bend country of Texas. At the Ranger station at Fort Davis, they were joined by a half-dozen more Rangers and a fully armed detail of soldiers from the fort. The combined forces had numbered more than one hundred men.

The contingent had chased the elusive Apache chief all the way to the border. At the muddy Rio Grande, they had come upon forty head of stolen cattle, mired in the sand. From these hapless animals the heartless Indians had cut chunks of beef and left them in their misery.

Without waiting for the command, Black had immediately drawn his rifle and started firing. Others followed suit, and within seconds the suffering beasts had been mercifully killed.

But before the gun smoke had cleared, General Grierson had turned to Captain Baylor and said, "My men and I have to turn back here. Federal troops do not have the authority to enter Mexico."

Captain Baylor nodded. "We'll turn back too," he said regretfully. "To follow Victorio with so few men would be sheer suicide."

A bitterly disappointed Virgil Black had had to bite his tongue to keep from hotly protesting the decision. Why in hell couldn't Grierson bend the army's rules a little? What difference did it make which side of the river they were on? If they killed or captured the murdering Victorio, would anybody really give a tinker's damn that it had happened on the wrong side of the border? Damn it to hell, the crafty old Apache chief and his warriors were so close, they were probably watching, laughing at the stupidity of the white man's laws.

"I know what you're thinking, Virgil," Captain Baylor said, reining his mount alongside Black's.

His firm jaw clenched, his narrowed eyes staring fixedly across the muddy Rio Grande, Black hadn't trusted himself to speak. After a long, tense moment, his commander sighed wearily, turned his head, and gazed wistfully across the border.

He said, "I, too, am sorry we couldn't have tried a round with old Vic."

Black's head snapped around. "Let's do it, Captain. We've been chasing this bloodthirsty red bastard for—"

"No." Baylor was firm. "Perhaps you don't care whether we make it home or not, but I do. I have a family to consider. My wife is too young to be made a widow."

Virgil Black exhaled heavily. "Yes, sir."

Now as he rode wearily into the Ysleta compound after the failed campaign, he was still half-despondent, half-angry. Had he been in command, he would have bent the rules just as he had so many times before. The marauding Apache didn't go by the book, so why should the U.S. Army and Texas Rangers?

A muscle twitching in his ridged jaw, Virgil Black tiredly dismounted as dusk began to settle over headquarters.

"Captain Black, Captain Black." A young Ranger came running out of the main building.

Affectionately patting his winded stallion's foam-flecked neck, Virgil Black lifted his head. "What's up, Logan?"

"British Bob!" said the young ranger excitedly. "He's been apprehended! They caught him in a Juárez saloon this afternoon and brought him in. He's here, here at headquarters. And it's just as you suspected—he has an accomplice. A female accomplice. We haven't got her yet, but we have him. Isn't that great?"

Virgil Black ground his even white teeth in frustration. For months he had been tracking the bold bank robber who had hit banks all over southern New Mexico and west Texas. The thief Black referred to as British Bob was an Englishman whose full name was Robert Alfred Campling. Campling was noted for his finely tailored clothes, his courtly manners during holdups, and his uncanny ability to elude the authorities. Now the "gentleman robber" was finally in custody, and somebody else had claimed the satisfaction of capturing him.

This, Black decided, wasn't his day.

"Yes, Logan," Virgil Black said finally, "just great."

7

At sunup, sixty-seven-year-old Confederate war veteran and retired Texas Ranger William "True" Cannon stood on the porticoed flagstone porch of his small salmon-hued adobe. Hands in the pockets of his gray trousers, a slightly stooped shoulder resting against a rough cedar support pole, True Cannon watched unblinking as a coldly angry Captain Virgil Black rode away into the summer dawn.

True Cannon knew Virgil was quietly furious. To a man like Virgil who regarded danger as the acme of life, it was an insult to be sent after a helpless woman. He didn't blame Virgil for being mad as a hornet.

Virgil Black was, in True's opinion, the epitome of the proud and fearless Texas Ranger of legend. He was constantly on the prowl, whether alone or in the company of a score or more.

Los Tejanos diablos—the Texas devils. That's what the Mexicans called the Rangers. They had a special name for Virgil Black: *los Tejano sanguinario*—the blood-thirsty Texan.

Fear was totally foreign to Virgil Black. He thrived on taking risks, lived to put himself in peril. True suspected Virgil's remarkable courage was attributable less to a strong sense of duty than to the fact that he didn't have much to live for. No wife. No children. No family of any kind.

True was the closest thing Virgil had to a family, and they were not related. It troubled him to know Virgil didn't particularly care whether he lived or died.

But he understood.

He understood about not caring.

And about caring too much.

Back when he himself had been a strapping, healthy young man, he had also been a daredevil. It wasn't until he met, then married, the most beautiful girl in Tarrant County that life became so sweet, so precious. He actually started looking before crossing the street. Then, nine years after the wedding his cherished young wife finally became pregnant with his child, and his joy was unequaled.

Until that nightmarish summer day when his frail, darling Betsy had gone into early labor and he had lost both her and his child.

True Cannon swallowed hard, remembering that horrible hot August afternoon as vividly as if it were yesterday.

After that, after he lost Betsy and his boy, he hadn't cared much about anyone or anything. He'd been half-glad when the War Between the States broke out; had signed up with Hood's Brigade the minute he heard the news. He came through the bloody four-year battle with only minor wounds, rode home to Texas, and joined the Rangers so he could fight the Comanche and the Mexicans.

True Cannon smiled recalling the chilly autumn afternoon more than a decade ago when young Ranger Virgil Black had saved his life. The boy's ability to penetrate enemy defenses was downright uncanny. Virgil had managed to slip into the Palo Duro Comanche camp to rescue True, the only Ranger left alive after a bloody skirmish, who was being held and tortured. Virgil quietly slit the throats of the braves guarding True and whisked him away before the sleeping savages knew what was happening.

True owed his life to Virgil Black. He owed him a whole lot more. The two of them had become the best of friends, the nearest thing to family either of them had. When Virgil was at Ysleta near El Paso, he stayed at True's adobe, which was less than a mile from headquarters. Lived there, really.

It was the only home Virgil Black could remember ever having.

Maybe someday Virgil would have a home of his own. Maybe he would meet the right woman, fall in love, and find out just how good being alive could be.

True watched until the younger man's shiny black stallion was out of sight, then turned and went back inside thinking that as put out as Virgil was with this latest humiliating assignment, at least it wouldn't last long. It was simply a matter of traveling the sixty miles up to Las Cruces and bringing the woman in.

When Virgil had come in the previous night after two weeks on the campaign trail, he had told True that the notorious bank robber British Bob had been apprehended in his absence. Said that under intense questioning the bank robber had implicated an accomplice. A woman accomplice. Said she had supplied him with strongbox and safe keys stolen from drunken bank and stage guards. She was, British Bob had confessed, a pretty Las Cruces entertainer with ginger-red hair and large emerald eyes.

Virgil, sitting in on the interrogation, had spoken without thinking, "The Queen of the Silver Dollar."

"You know her?" British Bob's dark eyes flashed with jealousy.

"Nope, not really," said Virgil. "I've seen her perform and—"

"You know who this woman is then?" Captain Baylor interrupted.

Twisting uncomfortably in his chair, Virgil said, "Sure, same as everybody else, but—"

"Then you will bring her in, Captain."

"But, sir, I—"

"That's a command, Black, not a request," Baylor said with quiet authority. "Go home. Get a good night's rest, then leave for Las Cruces at first light. Take the train up. I'll expect you and the woman to be back here within forty-eight hours at the most."

"Yes, sir."

"What do you mean 'she's gone'?"

"Exactly what I said," the frowning bartender sputtered, attempting to pull free of the lean dark fingers tightly clutching the collar of his shirt. "The Queen of the Silver Dollar left a couple of weeks ago without telling anybody where she was going." Struggling, half-choking, the bartender coughed. "Will you let go of me!"

Virgil Black released the red-faced man. "You don't have any idea where she went?"

"I just told you, I don't know. Nobody knows. One afternoon she didn't call down for her breakfast, so we went up to check on her. She was gone." He shrugged beefy shoulders.

"Didn't leave a note, didn't—"

"Nothing. Just disappeared."

Virgil Black exhaled. "Okay. If you see her, if you hear from her, you leave word for me at the telegraph office. I'll be checking in regularly for messages." He turned and walked away.

"Sure," the bartender called after him. "Why? What's she done? She actually been robbin' banks?"

Black made no reply.

Annoyed with himself that he'd had the pretty red-haired thief within his grasp a couple of short weeks ago and had let her go, Virgil Black was anxious to put out the word that the Queen of the Silver Dollar was wanted for armed robbery.

He headed for the telegraph office. He had to alert the authorities in all surrounding New Mexico and Texas cities within a hundred-mile radius to be on the look out for the missing red-haired entertainer.

"Mornin', Clarence," Virgil greeted the balding, narrow-shouldered telegrapher. Clarence nodded. Virgil said impatiently, "I need to get out a bunch of wires pronto."

Clarence crossed his skinny arms over his sunken chest. "Oh? Wouldn't have anything to do with the disappearance of the Queen of the Silver Dollar, would it?"

"As a matter of fact it does. So if you'll—"

"The word on the street is that she's wanted for armed robbery. That why you're looking for her?"

"We're wasting precious time, Clarence. Send wires to—"

"Sorry, Virgil. Can't send any telegrams today," the telegrapher told him, shaking his balding head. "The lines are down."

"Jesus Christ," swore Black.

"But you're in luck," Clarence smilingly informed him. "The last message to come over the wires before the lines went down was a tip that a woman fitting the description of the Queen of the Silver Dollar has been spotted in Cloudcroft."

The words were hardly out of his mouth before Virgil Black was turning to walk away.

"Hey, wait a minute," the telegrapher called after him. "Don't you want to know what . . . come back here. Where you going?"

Over his shoulder as he walked out the door, Virgil said, "Cloudcroft."

The aging sister crossed herself as she walked slowly down the long, stone-floored corridor.

Silently she prayed for the Almighty to give her the strength and the patience to endure a few more trying hours in the company of Her Royal Highness, Princess Marlena of Hartz-Coburg.

Sister Mary Elizabeth could hardly wait for the bossy young woman to leave the abbey so that life within the walls could return to normal. How she yearned for the peace and tranquillity she had come to take for granted and to treasure. It was astonishing that the presence of just one slender, red-haired girl could so upset the quiet routine of the entire sanatorium.

When she was first brought to the remote hillside haven, Her Royal Highness had been far too ill to cause any trouble. Sworn to total secrecy and put in charge of the sick princess, Sister Mary Elizabeth had tenderly cared for the poor, miserable young woman whose pretty face had been the exact hue of a bright yellow lemon peel.

So deathly sick she could barely lift her head off the pillow, the princess had been genuinely frightened and therefore dutiful, clinging desperately, gratefully, to the hand Sister Mary Elizabeth offered throughout the long, sleepless nights. Comforting the pathetic, sick soul, praying for her recovery, Sister Mary Elizabeth had sat with the princess hour upon hour, talking softly to her, soothing the suffering girl for whom she soon developed a natural affection.

And then the ailing princess had gotten better.

That is, her health had improved.

But not her disposition. As soon as a faint hint of roses appeared in her sunken cheeks and her dulled emerald eyes brightened a trifle,

Princess Marlena became an unruly handful. Each day thereafter the princess grew a little stronger, and much more demanding.

Strong-willed, childish, used to getting her own way, and accustomed to having orders obeyed at the snap of her fingers, Princess Marlena had attempted to bully and boss Sister Mary Elizabeth about as if the sister were a personal servant. Sister Mary Elizabeth had resolutely resisted and had caught the sharp edge of the princess's tongue for her trouble.

At age seventy-one, the sister was far too old, wise, and disciplined to argue with the overbearing young royal. She simply stood her ground, refusing to be anyone's puppet or lackey. Biting back the stinging words she longed to hurl at the spoiled sovereign, Sister Mary Elizabeth simply ignored the princess when she angrily shouted from her room that she was hungry. She wanted her dinner immediately. She was bored and needed company. Come in and sit with her. Now! Right now! She wanted to go outdoors again and lie in the sun on the back terrace. To take a short stroll around the grounds. Would someone kindly please take her outside? She wanted her bath. At once!

Sister Mary Elizabeth was painfully aware that, although a bride of Christ and a dedicated keeper of the faith, she herself was all too human. She knew it was so because she purposely made the princess wait for anything she haughtily demanded. She personally saw to it that the pampered princess had to wait for her bath until all the other patients had been bathed.

If the arrogant royal was stubborn and unreasonable, well so was Sister Mary Elizabeth. And she knew it. So the sister prayed for forgiveness and for strength, and admitted to herself that she could hardly wait for the princess to leave.

Today was the day.

Thank heaven.

Princess Marlena's bodyguard had arrived in Cloudcroft the previous evening. At shortly before noon today he would come to the sanatorium, collect the fully recovered princess, and escort her to the train depot where the two of them, at straight up noon, would board the southbound train to Texas.

"Sister! Sister Mary Elizabeth!" the princess's unmistakable voice echoed down the silent hallway. The princess was calling out from her room. Shouting really. Not to be ignored.

The sister rolled her eyes heavenward. She drew a deep breath, crossed herself, lifted the brooch/watch pinned to her stiff white wimple, and checked the time. Nine o'clock. Telling herself she could surely sit on a straight-edged razor blade for three short hours, she headed for the princess's room.

"Kindly quit shouting, Your Majesty," the sister scolded when she stepped inside the princess's room. "There are those who are quite ill, and you are disturbing their rest."

To the utter shock of Sister Mary Elizabeth, the princess, looking prim and pretty in a simple summer dress of crisp cotton poplin, said, "Oh, I forgot. I am sorry. I apologize." She dashed forward, threw her slender arms around the tiny stoop-shouldered sister, and hugged her warmly, confessing as she did so, "I have been an awful nuisance, haven't I? Say you'll forgive me? Please?"

Instantly disarmed by this unexpected flash of girlish charm and total honesty, the sister lifted her short, brittle arms, wrapped them around the taller, younger woman, and patted the princess's back.

"Of course, I forgive you, child," said the sister, her kind heart suddenly filled with affection for the princess.

"Thank you, Sister." Princess Marlena pulled back to look down at her. "Thank you so much for everything," she said with naked sincerity. "I shall never, ever forget you."

Sister Mary Elizabeth gazed up at the beautiful young woman who had so totally disrupted the serenity of the sanatorium. The sister realized, with surprise, that she was going to miss the princess, despite all the trouble she had caused.

Sister Mary Elizabeth reached up and touched the princess's rosy cheek and, with a smile, admitted, "I shall miss you, too. It won't be the same here without you."

Virgil Black was the first passenger to step down off the morning train when it pulled into Cloudcroft's tiny depot at shortly after nine. Stretching, flexing his long legs to get the kinks out of his tight muscles, he rolled his tired shoulders, causing the fabric of his starched white shirt to pull and strain across his back.

He turned and walked down the long line of railcars. He stopped before the third car from the caboose, slid back the heavy plank door, leaped agilely up into the hay-strewn car, and hurriedly lowered the unloading platform.

"Well, what you waiting for?" he said to his dancing, whinnying stallion, Noche. "We're here. Let's go take a look around."

Without benefit of bridle or rope, the big black carefully picked his sure way down the wooden platform. Virgil, saddle and gear thrown over his left shoulder, followed. Side by side, man and beast made their way to the livery stable where—Virgil had promised Noche—a healthy helping of oats and a refreshing rubdown awaited him.

His horse turned over to the stable keeper, Virgil Black walked up the street to the High Country Saloon. The smoky saloon was half-full even though it was only just past nine in the morning. Inside, Virgil stepped up to the bar, motioned to the barkeep, bought a round of drinks, and, looking up and down the polished bar, stated his reason for being in Cloudcroft. He tossed the bartender the wanted posters. He said a reward would belong to any man who provided the lead resulting in the apprehension and arrest of the fugitive Queen of the Silver Dollar.

"If you see her," Virgil said in his slow Texas drawl, "don't approach her. Don't let her know you've spotted her. Come straight to me. Let me handle it."

The habitués nodded and began to talk among themselves, questioning each other as to whether or not they could have seen the pretty saloon singer in Cloudcroft. Virgil felt confident that his stay in town would be a brief one. It was a small mountain municipality. Everybody knew everybody. Nothing went on there without a goodly number of the population knowing about it. A stranger—especially a beautiful red-haired female—would stand out like a sore thumb in this remote mountain hamlet. With any luck he'd be on the southbound noon train, the Queen of the Silver Dollar in custody. This time tomorrow the Queen would be cooling her heels in the El Paso jail. And he would be back at Ysleta headquarters, ready for a real campaign assignment.

9

It was twenty of twelve when the princess's burly bodyguard, Hantz Landsfelt, helped Her Highness down from the hired carriage at the Cloudcroft train depot. Her ginger-red hair carefully concealed in a long lace shawl draped around her head, the princess, determined to keep her identity a secret, looked neither to the left nor the right. Nor did she look the least bit royal. She might have been any young woman waiting for a train.

The princess nodded and took a seat when Hantz Landsfelt said he would check to see if the train's departure would be on time. Realizing how important it was that she attract no attention, Princess Marlena sat quietly, patiently waiting. Anxious to board the train.

After hearing Hantz Landsfelt's glowing reports of how successful her stand-in had been on the bond tour, the half-jealous princess was more than a little eager to take her rightful place before the impostor got any foolish ideas.

And, before their shared duplicity could be found out.

Gripping the lace shawl closely under her chin, the princess looked up expectantly when Hantz Landsfelt, a frown on his florid face, returned.

"What? What is it?" she asked, puzzled.

"Bad news, I'm afraid, Your Highness," he told her regretfully. "I've just learned that yesterday afternoon a band of renegade Apaches tore down the telegraph lines."

"So?" She shrugged with disinterest. "We've no need of sending telegrams. Montillion and the others know full well we are on our way to meet them in San Antonio."

Hantz Landsfelt exhaled heavily. "Well . . . ah . . . now . . . it seems that this morning . . . ," he cleared his throat nervously, "the savages blew up the railroad trestle a few miles down the mountain. It happened only minutes after the morning train passed over the trestle on its way up the mountain. The telegrapher says it's more than likely that the Apaches have blown up portions of the tracks all the way down the line." He paused, waited for the outburst he knew was coming.

For a long moment, Princess Marlena didn't fully grasp the meaning of what he had told her. Then, with a flash of understanding, she realized exactly what this news meant.

Speaking quietly, she said, "Are you telling me that the noon train will not be running on schedule today? That we will be getting a late start?"

Hantz Landsfelt grimaced. He leaned down and whispered, "Not merely late, Your Highness. The train will not be running today. We won't be getting out of Cloudcroft at all. Not until the tracks have been repaired."

"Oh? And how long will that take? An hour? two?"

He shook his head. "It could be days before—"

Princess Marlena shot to her feet so swiftly, the lace shawl fell to her shoulders. Her voice lifting, she said, "But we must get to Texas! We can't wait around here forever! You just go right back over there and tell them that they had better get those tracks fixed immediately!"

"Shhh," Hantz warned, glancing nervously about, concerned that she would attract attention.

"Don't you shhh me," she said angrily, her emerald eyes snapping with impatience. "And don't just stand there. Do something!"

"Be reasonable, Your Highness," he entreated, fearful she would make a terrible scene. "There is nothing I can do and—"

"Then I shall do something!" she again interrupted, brushed past him, and headed for the ticket window. The lace shawl fell forgotten to the floor. Bright New Mexico sunlight, streaming in through the tall depot windows, set her ginger hair aflame.

She caused quite a commotion. People turned to stare. The ruckus alerted a reward-hungry cowhand. He stared openmouthed at the upset young woman and then he began to smile. He had, like many another lucky man, spent more than one happy drunken evening in Las Cruces's most famous saloon. He recognized this angry redhead who was so anxious to get out of Cloudcroft.

The Queen of the Silver Dollar!

Trapped right here in the Cloudcroft train depot. There was, he had learned a couple of hours ago, a reward on her head. She and that British beau of hers were wanted in Texas.

The grinning cowhand slipped unnoticed out of the waiting room. He ran as fast as he could toward the High Country Saloon, hoping the tall Texas Ranger would still be there. The cowboy's heart raced when he spotted the Ranger, not a block away, standing on the wooden sidewalk outside the stage station, talking to one of the drivers.

Virgil Black listened, then shook his head in frustration. The stage driver had just told him that the long wooden railroad trestle, three miles south of town, had been blown up.

"Must've happened just minutes after the morning train cleared the trestle," said the driver.

Virgil knew immediately who was responsible. He knew as well that the Apache wouldn't be satisfied with wrecking only one railroad trestle. If he were a betting man, he would bet everything he owned that the red devils had blown up portions of the tracks all the way to the Border.

As if the stage driver had read Virgil's thoughts, he said, "You know the Apaches, Captain Black. Eight to five they've destroyed track clear to El Paso."

"Sure enough," said Virgil, absently tapping his Stetson against his twill-trousered thigh. Then, "Jesus Christ! No train service. No wire service. The way my luck's going, the woman I'm after probably slipped out of town last—"

"Captain Black, Captain Black," shouted the out-of-breath cowboy as he came rushing up. Pointing excitedly, he sputtered, "She's here! She's here! The woman you're looking for! She's down at the train depot right now throwing a hissy fit because the train's not running."

Virgil Black nodded. He put on his hat, pulled it low on his forehead, turned, and walked away.

"Hey, wait just a damned minute, Ranger!" The cowboy hurried after him. "What about my reward?"

"Go to the livery stable," ordered Black calmly, never slowing his pace. "Have my horse saddled and bring him to the near side of the depot. Leave him there. Put your name and address in my saddlebags, then get lost. And keep your mouth shut," warned Black. "You'll get the reward. *If* it's her."

Virgil Black walked with a sure, determined stride directly to the train depot. He stepped inside, scanned the room, and immediately caught sight of her. She was hotly reprimanding a stunned railroad conductor. Her ginger hair, pulled back from her face, flamed in a shaft of alpine sunlight. She tossed her head angrily, and Virgil got a good look at her ears. Small. Well shaped. But protruding slightly.

Virgil Black calmly bided his time. Sinking back into the deep shadows, he leaned against the wall, long arms crossed over his chest, and watched her every move. The crowded depot began to empty as thwarted travelers gave up and went back to their homes or to the hotel. The red-head continued to berate the railroad employee until a stockily built man, clearly urging her to calm down, took her arm and drew her away from the ticket window.

Virgil had a hard time repressing a smile of wry amusement. The angry Queen of the Silver Dollar sure hadn't allowed any moss to grow under her feet. Already she'd taken up with a new man. Poor old British Bob. He would be heartbroken.

Virgil pulled his hat lower over his eyes and turned aside so she wouldn't see his face, as her muscular companion led her out of the depot waiting room. Virgil counted to ten, then followed the pair out onto the now deserted platform. He waited near the doorway as the solidly built man stepped down to the ground and walked up the tracks, obviously searching for a carriage for hire.

There were none.

The woman now stood alone on the platform. Virgil Black moved in to take advantage of the unexpected opportunity.

His eyes pinned to the heavily muscled man attempting to hail a carriage, Virgil stepped up beside the Queen of the Silver Dollar, took her arm, and said in a low, flat voice, "Sorry, Red. I've got to take you in."

Princess Marlena's head snapped around in stunned surprise. Speechless, she looked up to see a tall, dark, hard-faced stranger whose sky-blue eyes, glinting from beneath his hat brim, instantly shifted to her. When he began to draw her to him, the startled princess promptly came to her senses.

Attempting to free her arm from his firm grasp, she commanded, "Get away from me! You let me go!" He did not obey. Frantically she looked around, shouted, "Hantz! Hantz! Come quickly. Help me!"

Hantz Landsfelt turned, saw the princess struggling with a tall stranger, and came running, his eyes round with alarm.

"You there," shouted Hantz Landsfelt, throwing back his suit coat and drawing his revolver. "Unhand her at once or I'll fire!"

Virgil Black's reply was a flat "No, you won't. Stay where you are, my friend. This woman is under arrest. I'm a Texas Ranger and I'm taking her into custody."

"Taking me into . . . Are you insane!" screeched the princess, struggling furiously against him.

"You're taking her nowhere!" shouted Landsfelt, but he hesitated to shoot, afraid he might hit the princess. Shoving the pistol into the waistband of his trousers, he leaped up onto the platform with the agility of a much trimmer man, bellowing like an angry bull. He lunged at Black with the full force of his muscular body.

Never releasing his hold on the now-screaming princess, Virgil deftly sidestepped the charge and threw a well-placed, lightning-fast left upper-cut. The powerful, unexpected blow caught Landsfelt directly under the chin and knocked him flat on his back, stinging and stunning him badly. By the time he could clear his head and get to his feet, Virgil had snatched the clawing princess down off the platform. Hurriedly he carried her, kick-ing and screaming, around the side of the depot, lifted her up onto his sad-dled stallion, Noche, and swung up behind her.

"Oh, God, no! No!" Landsfelt choked, staggering on weak rubbery legs toward the mounted pair, again drawing and aiming his pistol, deter-mined to save the princess. "Stop!" he ordered. "Come back here! Let her go! Let her go!"

"There are no wants or warrants on you," Virgil Black told the frantic man, and calmly backed the stallion away, "but Queenie here is a thief, and she is going to jail."

Virgil then yanked on the reins, wheeled the stallion about, and whisked the frightened princess away with a helpless Hantz Landsfelt running wildly after them, terrified of firing his weapon, lest he strike the princess. Out of breath, lungs laboring, Landsfelt stumbled, fell, got up, and ran again. But he was no match for the fleet-footed stallion. Soon he was left far behind.

Battling frantically against the long arms imprisoning her, a terrible thought quickly flashed through the princess's mind.

The impostor! The woman who was taking her place on the tour was a fugitive from the law! Dear God in heaven! The stand-in Montillion had chosen was a common thief! And now, this big Texas lawman thought that she . . . that she was . . .

Angry now as well as frightened, the princess began shouting loudly, telling him that this was all a terrible mistake. That he had her confused with another woman. That she was no thief! She was visiting royalty!

"You stupid, misguided fool," she screamed, attempting to make him understand. "You have the wrong woman! I am not who you think I am!" In her furious struggling, she managed to free one hand. "You're not lis-tening to me!" she accused, and reached up, intending to rake her long punishing nails down the smooth tanned skin of his cheek.

Virgil swiftly grabbed her wrist before she could do much damage, but with her middle finger she managed to scratch one long furrow down his jaw, drawing blood. And she continued to shout, "You let me go! I command you to release me at once! I tell you I am not the woman you're seeking! I am Crown Princess Marlena of Hartz-Coburg!"

But Ranger Captain Virgil Black wasn't buying it.

The ginger-red hair. The flashing emerald eyes. The distinctive ears. The exaggerated accent. He had the right woman. She might have lost a pound or two since last his arms were around her, and she was well scrubbed and fresh faced instead of covered in heavy stage makeup. And she wore a simple cotton dress instead of a skimpy satin costume. But Virgil was not fooled. This was the woman he had carried up the stairs at the Silver Dollar Saloon.

"Are you deaf? Can't you hear me?" she shouted into his face, "I am a royal princess!"

Deftly untying the pale blue bandanna knotted around his throat, Virgil raised it to his jaw and carefully blotted away the droplets of bright red blood.

He looked directly into her furious green eyes and said, "Sure you are, Princess. And you're going to feel right at home in your new palace. The El Paso County jail."

10

Hantz Landsfelt continued to run after the galloping stallion in a futile attempt to save his frightened mistress. Winded, choking, his face beet red, the helpless bodyguard was beside himself with worry. *He* had allowed the royal princess to be snatched away from right under his nose! *He* alone was responsible for her safety and well-being, and *he* had failed her.

Bolting wildly down the dusty street, leaving the buildings of Cloudcroft behind, Hantz Landsfelt tripped and fell once more. His breathing so labored it was deafeningly loud in his ears, he lay on the ground for a second, panting, regaining his strength, wondering what to do next.

He was up in an instant, running back toward town. On weak, rubbery legs he sprinted straight to the sheriff's office, only to find it closed, the door locked, the shades pulled.

Frantically he looked around, saw an old-timer, halfway down the wooden sidewalk, seated in a barrel chair tipped back against the wall of a dry-goods store, whittling. Coughing and wheezing, Hantz Landsfelt trotted down to him, bent, grabbed the lapels of the startled old man's jacket, and yanked him to his feet.

"Where is the sheriff?" Landsfelt's voice was loud, booming. "I must speak to a lawman at once!"

The aging local wrenched free of Hantz Landsfelt's big hands, shoved him away, bent and picked up his dropped pocket knife and the whistle he was whittling. He eased gingerly back down into his chair, looked up at the big, red-faced man standing over him, and said, "I reckon whatever it is you need to say to the sheriff will have to wait till tomorrow." He took up his whittling again. "Sheriff Jackson's gone fishin'. He won't likely be back before tomorrow."

"Tomorrow? I can't wait un . . . Where did he go fishing?"

The slight little man lifted bony shoulders in a shrug. "No way of knowin'. Lots of good trout-filled streams up here."

Hantz Landsfelt slammed his open palm against his forehead. He turned and hurried away, not knowing where he was going. Then he caught sight of the stage office two blocks down the street. Yes! That was the answer! He'd grab the next stagecoach out of Cloudcroft! Surely by the time he reached Las Cruces the telegraph wires would be back up and he could send a telegram to Montillion! And he could inform the authorities!

Landsfelt rushed into the stage office, looked about, and was surprised to find it empty. He hurried to the counter to buy a ticket on the next stage to Las Cruces. And learned why the waiting room was empty.

"The stage to Las Cruces," he said, still laboring to breathe, his big chest heaving. "When does it leave?"

"Three thirty this afternoon," said the slender, bespectacled man behind the counter. "That be a one way ticket, mister?"

Landsfelt shook his head. "Forget Las Cruces. When is the next stage out of Cloudcroft?"

"Going where?"

"Anywhere! Doesn't matter. I don't care where!"

"Well, now, that would be the three-thirty stage to Las Cruces," the man said, a teasing twinkle in his light eyes, as if he had said something humorous.

Landsfelt was not amused.

Frustrated, frantic, he knew he had no choice but to wait. He could go down to the livery stable and buy a saddle horse. But it wouldn't do him any good. He didn't know how to ride. He had never been on a horse. So he was forced to wait. He paced nervously back and forth, back and forth, realizing with every step that the Texas Ranger was carrying the princess farther and farther away.

After what seemed an eternity to Hantz Landsfelt, the time finally came for the stage to depart. There were two other passengers traveling to Las Cruces. A couple of slow-moving, white-haired old ladies. Landsfelt rolled his eyes, silently counted to ten, and stepped forward to assist the brittle-boned ladies in boarding the coach. They were grateful. One tried to give him a coin from her worn reticule. He declined.

The bearded driver stuck his head in the coach and said, "Looks like it's just the four of us today, folks. The young man who normally rides shotgun didn't show up. Don't know where the devil he is, beggin' your pardon, ladies." He patted the heavy Colt .44 on his hip, and added, "No need for worry though. I don't anticipate any trouble, but I'm always ready. Now sit back and enjoy the ride."

Three hours into the journey down the steep, treacherous mountain pass, a dozing Hantz Landsfelt was awakened by the sudden sound of gunfire. He bolted upright, looked at the two frightened, twittering ladies, and drew the revolver from the waistband of his trousers. He peered cautiously out the stage window.

In the pastel gloaming of the setting sun he saw a half-dozen masked mounted gunmen swiftly surrounding the slowing coach. A bullet whizzed past his ear. He jerked his head back inside and ordered the little old ladies onto the floor. He heard the driver yelp in pain, knew he'd been hit.

He was aware that if he tried to shoot it out with the bandits, somebody would get killed. He didn't want the blood of the little silver-haired ladies on his hands. So, at gun point, hands raised above his head, Hantz Landsfelt climbed down out of the coach, as ordered. He and his two terrified traveling companions were robbed of their valuables.

Then the coach's six horses were unharnessed and set free. Leaving Landsfelt with two feeble old ladies and a wounded stage driver afoot in a high mountain pass beside the useless stagecoach.

Miles from the nearest town.

Physically defeated, but still defiant, Princess Marlena, seated across the saddle, enclosed in the long arms of the stone-faced Texas Ranger, clung tenaciously to the saddle horn. Despite the fierce aching in her back, she sat ramrod straight, determined she would not collapse against the broad chest of her stubborn abductor.

She abhorred the thought of touching or being touched by this mean-looking Texan who was so inflexible and pigheaded he wouldn't listen to reason. She had explained everything to him over and over again! Had told him exactly who she was. Had told him of her untimely illness. Had told him of the pretender who was taking her place on the bond tour.

It had done no good.

All her reasoning and revelations had fallen on deaf ears. She may as well have been talking to the wind. There had been no response. He hadn't said a word or even nodded his head. He had continued to lope the stallion across the high mountain meadows, hardly glancing at her. Taciturn and withdrawn, displaying no emotion.

The princess was angry, but she was also frightened.

She was afraid of both the dark-visaged man and his huge black stallion. Never in her twenty-eight years had she been on the back of a horse. Her kingdom had owned some of the finest horseflesh in Europe, but the well-trained creatures had been used only to pull the royal carriages. She had never had any desire to be a horsewoman. Now here she was, high up off the ground, on a snorting, thundering beast that might well toss her over its head any moment.

And her only protection from the big four-legged devil racing wildly in and out of the towering pine trees was the big, two-legged devil astride him. An unapproachable man with a dark, strong face. A face too hard, too strong for pure beauty. But a lean, chiseled face as darkly bronzed as an Indian's with a high, intelligent forehead, a straight nose, soaring cheekbones, sensual but cruel-looking lips, and a pair of deep, piercing blue eyes that were sullen and brooding. A harshly masculine face that compelled and arrested attention. She couldn't keep from covertly sneaking peeks at that harshly handsome face, despite continued efforts to keep her eyes off him.

The princess had finally—after what seemed an eternity atop this tirelessly running stallion—become too exhausted to raise a hand and strike at her stone-faced abductor another time. There was no fight left in her. She had expended every ounce of her energy. Her arms were now so weak and tired, it was all she could do to hold on to the saddle horn.

Her throat was raw and aching from screaming, but she continued to threaten in low, hoarse tones. "You will *not* get away with this," she rasped, her red-rimmed eyes flashing with a mixture of fear and anger. "I'll have you flogged until there is no flesh left on your back! I'll order you tossed into the deepest, darkest dungeon beneath the castle and throw away the key! I'll see to it you are hanged in the town square before all my cheering subjects! I'll call for a firing squad to—"

"I get the general idea," Virgil Black finally interrupted, his hard-planed face expressionless. "Now, why don't you give it a rest before you lose your voice entirely."

"Oh, you would like that, wouldn't you?" she croaked. "You'd revel in silent obedience from me, but let me assure you that . . . I . . . I—" her voice cracked, she swallowed painfully, then swallowed again, "I . . . I will not be quiet! Never, ever! I shall curse you with my last breath!"

"Your last breath may come quite soon if you don't pipe down." He glanced warningly at her, then back at the trail ahead. "Red, you know as well as I do that the Apaches could be within earshot."

"Indians? Don't be ridiculous," she scoffed. "Even in Hartz-Coburg everyone knows that the American Indians have been placed inside little villages and told to stay there."

"Telling an Apache to stay on the reservation is like telling you to be quiet." Again he glanced at her, and Princess Marlena flinched involuntarily as his icy gaze touched the tangled locks lying around her face. "If you want to hang on to all that red hair, you had better be still."

The princess opened her mouth to protest, but shut it without speaking. What was the use?

It was early afternoon.

The two of them had been atop the black stallion since the noon hour when Virgil had snatched her off the depot platform. Indifferent to her distress, he had galloped the big stallion for a full mile before reining him down into a more comfortable lope. Now as they crossed one of the many verdant mountain meadows high up in the pine-cloaked Sacramentos and the princess had finally fallen silent, Virgil Black said, "That's better, Red. Why don't you lie back against me and get some rest. We've a long, hard ride ahead of us."

"How long?" she asked, refusing to release her grip on the saddle horn.

"We've only ridden about six or seven miles, so we have another hundred and thirty-five miles to go," he said. "Barring any unforeseen problems, we should be in El Paso in four, maybe five days."

Princess Marlena was horrified. Four days before anyone would know what had happened to her! Four days before this terrible mistake could be cleared up. Four days before she would be released to join the bond tour.

It might as well have been a lifetime.

Her throat too sore to continue trying to speak, the distraught princess made mean faces at the uncaring Ranger until she grew so weary she could no longer hold her head up. The effort was too great. She was too exhausted.

Her head finally bowed, her chin sagging down onto her chest. Her back was aching painfully. Her eyes were burning. Her throat was hurting so that she would barely swallow.

So the bone-weary princess put up only a brief show of obligatory resistance when Virgil Black laid a gloved hand on her shoulder and gently urged her back into the curve of his bent arm. The stiff fingers of her left hand opened and came uncurled from the saddle horn, fell to her lap. Her head drooped against the support of his muscular shoulder. She slid a weary arm around his back and clutched at the white cotton fabric of his shirt, admitting to herself she was so impossibly tired, she would have willingly rested in the arms of Satan himself.

Her stinging, watering eyes slipped closed. She sighed softly and her entire body relaxed. She snuggled her cheek close against the flat muscles of Virgil Black's broad supporting chest. She licked her dry lips. Her eyes fluttered half open. She looked up, and an unsettling shudder surged through her slender body.

His darkly handsome face was as impassive as a stone statue, but his eyes—those incredible indigo eyes—were fastened on her face, a strange, sardonic light shining out of their deep blue depths. Somewhere in her groggy brain, a warning signal sounded.

She *was* in danger.

Great danger.

Instinctively she knew that being thrown into the El Paso County jail was likely the least of her worries. This tall, lean, virile Ranger of Texas posed the biggest threat of all. He was nothing like any of the men she had known back home. She didn't know how to handle him. And she didn't trust him. Not for a minute. She would have to be on her toes at all times.

But even as those worrisome thoughts nagged, Princess Marlena knew she was drifting helplessly toward slumber, and there was nothing she could do about it. She simply had to have a short nap, then she'd watch him. She inhaled deeply, closed her eyes again, and nestled her face closer against his chest. The last thing the princess heard was the heavy rhythmic beating of the Texas Ranger's heart.

"... *off to London in June,* the races at Goodwood, yachting at Cowes, and then, of course, the German spas in July."

Montillion spoke in low, conversational tones, continuing, as he did anytime there was a free moment, to inform and enlighten his attentive charge. He was repeating himself, he knew. He had told her all of this before. But he would tell her again and again until he was certain she would not forget a single detail. It was imperative that she be so well versed in every aspect of royal life that there would be no chance she would falter, not even under the most intense questioning.

It was nearing dusk in Dallas.

The last dying rays of the setting summer sun spilled in through the open balcony doors of the lavish Adolphus Hotel rooftop suite. A gentle breeze stirred the sheer curtains.

Montillion relaxed in an easy chair near the mirrored vanity where the lovely woman he had chosen to play the part of the royal princess sat obediently still on a velvet stool, listening intently, while Baroness Richtoffen put the finishing touches on her upswept ginger-red hair.

The Queen of the Silver Dollar, in her role of royal princess, was even better than Montillion could have hoped. From the minute she stepped down from the royal train in Fort Worth, she had demonstrated incredible acting ability. Their five-day stay in the seat of Tarrant County had been hugely successful, the banquets and rallies attended by the city's elite. Hartz-Coburg bond sales had been brisk.

Six days ago they had left Fort Worth and traveled the short thirty miles to Dallas. The reception they'd received here had been as warm and rewarding as that in Fort Worth. And as profitable. Bond rallies had drawn huge crowds of monied tycoons eager to invest. And nightly parties and banquets had brought out the city's glittering aristocracy.

Tonight was to be their final night in the city. At dawn tomorrow, they would board the royal train for the long journey south to San Antonio.

Montillion was well pleased.

"You must remember, at all times, that the princess royal was reared from birth in the hermetically sealed atmosphere of privilege," Montillion continued to educate and instruct. "She had a German nursemaid, a Swiss dresser, and a French tutor." He fell silent for a moment, shook his head, and, as if thinking out loud, said, "She never had the normal exchanges with other children. Therefore, she never learned the need for patience and unselfishness. As a child she never had to deal with sacrifice and challenge, was never called upon to cope with others' feelings." Montillion again paused thoughtfully for a moment, then stated, "However, you must never forget that a monarch's personal and public character are revealing qualities." He stopped speaking.

"Not to worry, Montillion," the glowing, elegantly gowned Robbie Ann said, turning slightly to favor him with a full-lipped smile, not the least bit offended that he had told her these things over and over again. "I shall be so very regal no one will suspect that I'm not Her Royal Highness."

Convinced, Montillion smiled back at her. Dressed for the evening's glittering gala, she did not look like what she was—an actress of easy virtue. She was stunning. Regally beautiful in a long graceful gown of ice-blue chiffon. The gown's tight bodice was cut so that her smooth ivory shoulders were attractively framed, but her full, rounded bosom was modestly covered. The princess's sapphire-and-diamond necklace graced her pale, delicate throat. Her oval face was naked of paint and powder save for a hint of berry-stain color accentuating her full lips. Her exquisite emerald eyes were lined with a double row of thick silky lashes that were so inky black they had no need of further emphasis.

"I am finished. You may rise now, Your Highness," said the baroness, playing her part with the pretty young woman she had so carefully dressed and coiffured.

The queenly, ginger-haired beauty stood. Montillion came to his feet, offered his hand. She took it, and together they retired to the suite's spacious sitting room. There Montillion, totally dedicated to the success and welfare of his charge, told her, "This evening should be a fairly easy one for you. The governor's carriage will arrive at eight thirty. You will be driven just down the street to the Baker Hotel. Dinner is to be served at precisely nine o'clock, and you will be seated between the mayor of Dallas and the Texas governor. After dinner, the dancing will begin at ten. Everyone will be dying for a dance with you, as usual. But you may, if you feel tired, leave anytime after eleven, explaining to your hosts that you must rise early tomorrow for our departure." He paused and graciously inquired, "Are you up to such a full evening?"

"Am I up to it?" she repeated, a wide smile stretching her full lips "Are you teasing me? I absolutely adore attending these soirees and meeting all these rich, glamorous people. I could do this for the rest of my life!"

A slight warning frown flickered across Montillion's face. He looked her straight in the eye and—for the first time ever—called her by a name other than Your Royal Highness. "Robbie Ann, my dear child, your enthusiasm is admirable and refreshing, but you must remember, at all times, that this extravagant existence you are now enjoying is only temporary. You are a great actress. You are playing a role in a show that will soon close."

Robbie Ann's wide smile slipped slightly. "I know. Yes, I know." She sighed wistfully. "It's going to be hard to give all this up."

Montillion nodded knowingly. He understood fully. What young woman wouldn't love having everyone agreeing with her, clinging to her every word, granting her every wish. Who wouldn't relish being constantly treated with awe and deference? Who couldn't fancy gliding through a gracious, gilded life as if surrounded by some bright mystical nimbus?

A knock on the suite's heavy carved door drew Montillion from his reverie.

"The carriage is here, Your Highness," he said in a loud, clear voice.

"My gloves, Montillion," said Robbie, with a mere hint of pomposity.

He handed her the gloves, then whispered, "Curtain going up, my dear. Break a leg."

Princess Marlena had been asleep for more than an hour, but it seemed as if it had been only a few minutes when she was jolted awake by the sudden sound of a gunshot.

Before she could scream, a loud, masculine voice shouted from a few yards away, "Identify yourselves or prepare to meet your maker!"

"Put the shotgun down, Cecil," Virgil called out, "and come on out here."

"Ranger Black? Virgil? That you?"

"None other," shouted Virgil Black to the man who had not yet shown himself. "What's the matter with you, Cecil? You're jumpy as an old woman." Virgil lifted the princess from the saddle, deposited her on the ground.

"What are you doing?" she asked, blinking up at him. "Why are we stopping here where some lunatic is shooting at us?"

"To buy you a horse," he replied in a low, level voice.

She frowned, looked around, and saw a weathered log cabin tucked in among the pines. Beyond the house was a plank corral.

"I do *not* want a horse, thank you very much!" she said irritably, still jittery from the gunfire.

Virgil dismounted, stood close beside her. "Why, I thought you'd be pleased, Red. Surely you don't want to ride all the way to El Paso in my arms."

"Well, no, of course not, but . . ."

The cabin door flew open. "If you had a lick of sense, you'd be nervous too!" came a booming shout as a rangy, raw-boned man with salt-and-pepper hair and a mouth too full of teeth came hurrying toward them. "That really you, Virgil?"

"In the flesh." Virgil turned to smile at the rancher.

Cecil Watson reached them. Clasping Virgil's hand in a strong grip, he said, "You're not here to arrest me, are you, Captain Black? Why I haven't even cheated at cards in quite a spell."

Smiling, Virgil said, "Then I guess I'll let you up this time." Cecil's attention shifted to the princess. Virgil put his hand on her arm, drew her forward, said, "Cecil, this is Red. She and I are taking a little trip together, and she needs—"

"Help me, please," the princess anxiously interrupted. "This dimwitted Ranger has me confused with someone else and he will not listen to reason! You see, I am Princess Marlena of Hartz-Coburg and I—I—" She stopped speaking. Her head snapped around. She caught Virgil Black shaking his head and rolling his eyes as if to say she was delusional. She looked back at the rancher. He was grinning broadly, leaving little doubt that he didn't—wouldn't—believe a word she said. She sighed in exasperation and told them both, "I *am* Princess Marlena of Hartz-Coburg and you are a pair of fools who can both go to blazes!"

Cecil Watson chuckled merrily, clapped his hands, and said, "You're a mighty fiery little thing, whoever you are."

Virgil Black spoke. "As I was saying before being so rudely interrupted, Red needs a nice, gentle horse. Think you can help us out?"

"Got just the mare," Cecil said, grinning, "A big dappled gray with great stamina. So docile a child would be safe on her, and as smart as they come." His twinkling eyes on the princess, he said, "Wanna come have a look at her, miss?"

"I most certainly do not!"

"I'm sure the mare will be perfect," Virgil said. "Why don't you go on out and get her saddled while Red and I go inside so she can change clothes."

"Mighty fine," said Cecil Watson, nodding as he turned and headed for the corral.

"Change clothes?" the princess repeated acidly. "I can't very well change clothes, now can I? *You* left all my luggage at the train depot, remember?"

"I'll loan you some of mine."

He turned to unstrap his gear from behind the cantle.

Her hands went to her hips. She said, "I would rather go naked in a blizzard than to wear anything that belongs to you."

"Suit yourself," he said calmly and restrapped the gear.

"I shall. And furthermore," she told him, grabbing his arm, turning him to face her, "I have never been on a horse in my life and have no intention of learning to ride now and you can not make me."

He said nothing, just looked at her with an unexpected flash of mocking humor glinting from his eyes as if he knew he could make her do most anything he wanted. She felt a premonitory twinge at the troubling thought. This man, she felt certain, would have control of any situation in which he was involved. Would he have control of her as well?

No. No, of course not. After all, he *was* a man. Men had always been drawn to her like wasps around a lump of sugar. This tall Texas Ranger might suppose he was so rugged and impenetrable that nothing could get to him, but he was wrong. He would fall victim to her charms just like all the others.

Then it would be she who was in control.

She watched in silence as Virgil Black unbitted the stallion and allowed him to dip his great head to the full water trough and drink contentedly. In minutes the rancher, Cecil Watson, was leading the saddled gray mare toward them.

As he came, he said, shaking his head, "Now it ain't my place to ask why the two of you are ridin' through the high country like you are." He paused, hoping Virgil would volunteer the reason. Virgil said nothing. Cecil continued, "But I am obliged to warn you, Virgil, that it's not safe to have a woman with you out on the trail." He stopped, grinned at the princess, and added, "Especially such a pretty one."

"You think she's pretty?" Virgil said in a flat Texas twang, glancing pointedly at her, his blue eyes glacial. He shrugged wide shoulders. "I never noticed."

The princess shot him a wilting look.

Cecil grinned broadly, clapped Virgil on the back, and indicating the long raw nail scratch on Virgil's dark cheek, teased, "Looks to me like you did notice and she set you straight pronto." He roared with laughter, then sobered and said, "I'm serious now, Virg, about it not bein' safe. All them really bad thieves and thugs are back in New Mexico. J. J. Harlin, Saw Dust Charlie, Billy the Kid, Little Jack, the Cutter. Even the Pockmarked Kid."

"So I hear," said Virgil.

"Not to mention the Apaches," Cecil went on as if Virgil hadn't spoken. "They say that young, crazy chief Thunderfoot is so bad that when he gets his hands on a—"

"We'll watch our step," Virgil cut in, not giving Cecil the opportunity to say more.

He, like Cecil, had heard the grizzly, stomach-turning stories of what the wild young Apache did to defenseless white women. Thunderfoot was, it was said, like a cruel cat with a mouse. He enjoyed playful torture. He relished subjecting his helpless female victim to hours of sexual degradation, then he would set her free. Only to pounce on her again when the poor suffering soul thought she'd gotten away.

"Why don't you two spend the night here?" Cecil offered. "Leave in the morning."

"Thanks, but we better be getting on down the trail," said Virgil, counting out some bills, paying the rancher a fair price for the mare and saddle. "There's still a good three or four hours of sunlight."

Nodding, Cecil stuffed the money in his shirt pocket, took the long leather reins of the dappled gray, and handed them to the princess. She looked at him, made a face, looked at Virgil with mean, snapping eyes, and shook her head forcefully.

"I am not riding this big ugly beast!"

"You'll have to forgive Red," Virgil said to Cecil. "She didn't get her nap out and she's a little cranky."

In the blink of an eye he turned to her, put his hands on her waist, and lifted her up onto the gray. Perched precariously on the saddle, she protested loudly when Virgil, without so much as a by-your-leave, turned her about. Then casually lifted one of her legs up and over until she was seated astride, her stockinged knees exposed by her high riding skirts.

Her face red with humiliation and anger, she said, "I demand to at least have a sidesaddle! I cannot ride astride in a dress!"

Concerned with her dilemma, Cecil Watson apologized. "I'm sorry, Miss. I don't have a single sidesaddle on the place."

Virgil was not so sympathetic. Holding the reins of her mare, he swung up onto the back of his stallion. "I offered to loan you clothes more suitable for riding, but you refused." He leaned down, extended a hand to Cecil Watson. "Much obliged to you, Cecil. Come on down to Texas for a visit real soon."

"I will. I surely will," said the smiling horse rancher. "And you give old True my regards."

"Will do." Virgil pulled his hat brim lower, reined the black around, and put him into a trot.

Her emerald eyes now wide with fright, her skirts blowing up into her face, Princess Marlena clung to the saddle horn and silently cursed the big bullying Ranger of Texas who was no part of a gentleman.

When her fear lessened a little as she became more accustomed to being alone atop a cantering horse, she glanced up at the Ranger to be sure he wasn't looking at her. He wasn't. He was keeping the black a few feet ahead of the mare. His back was to her, his eyes on the trail.

So she reluctantly tore one hand from the saddle horn and attempted to push her dress and petticoats down over her knees. But as soon as she managed to cover one leg, the other would be exposed from midthigh to ankle. Frustrated, she kept jerking the skirts back and forth, this way, then that. She sighed. She groaned. She ground her teeth. She huffed and puffed.

And she felt her rising anger reach the boiling point when, without ever turning his head or glancing over his shoulder, the Ranger said in that irritating, slow Texas drawl she so despised, "Relax, why don't you, Red. After all, I've seen your knees before."

"I am not speaking to you!" she hissed.

He shrugged, reached into his breast pocket, shook a store-bought cigarette out of a crushed pack, and lit it.

"I don't like you, Ranger Black," she told him hotly.

"Few do," he said, then warned, "Better hold on tight now." He eased his grip on the reins, and the black's stride lengthened into a gallop. The dappled gray swiftly changed her gait to match that of the stallion's, and the princess had no choice but to hang on for dear life. Skirts and hair flying, she cursed her callous companion with every frightened breath she drew.

The sun had completely disappeared behind the towering peaks of the Sacramentos when the pair finally stopped for the night. Choosing a narrow meadow partially concealed by tall pines, shimmering aspens, and scrubby cedar, Virgil drew rein. Turning in the saddle, he searched the small shadowy valley for the snow-fed brook he heard tumbling over the rocks. He dismounted, glanced at the weary princess, and was satisfied she wouldn't try to get away. Leaving her there atop the gentle gray, he swiftly made his way through the trees and momentarily came upon the roaring stream. Clean, clear water surged so swiftly down the rocky bed, it splashed white and noisy over its banks.

Virgil returned to the clearing.

When he lifted the princess down off the mare's back, she was so tired she hardly knew what she was doing. Obediently she sat down on the soft grass while the Ranger unsaddled the horses. Warning her to stay put he led the thirsty stallion and mare down to the stream and watered them. In minutes he returned and ground-tethered the horses. Then he built a small fire of piñon twigs and cooked supper.

Far too hungry to turn him down when he offered her a tin plate filled with decidedly unappetizing food, the princess took it and ate every bite of the beans, beef, and bread.

After the meal, Virgil lit a cigarette and poured himself a second cup of strong black coffee. But the princess, so drowsy and exhausted she hardly knew what she was doing, rose unsteadily to her feet and moved toward Virgil Black.

So accustomed was she to being waited on hand and foot, she walked directly up to the seated Ranger, her arms outstretched, and sleepily issued the order she had automatically issued every night of her life since she learned how to talk.

"Undress me."

12

"Sure baby."

In one fluid movement, Virgil tossed his coffee into the fire, flicked his cigarette away, came to his feet, and reached for her. Catching the sleepy princess off guard, he wrapped a long arm around her narrow waist, drew her swiftly into his embrace, bent his dark head, and kissed her.

When his warm smooth mouth closed over her soft open lips, her eyes popped open in shocked surprise, and she came fully awake. But she didn't immediately push him away. Her heartbeat accelerated crazily and she felt breathless at his touch. Of their own volition, her widened eyes soon slipped closed again.

The unexpected kiss had the startling effect of a great bolt of lightning shooting through her, searing her trembling mouth. Burning its way down into her body. Numbing her addled brain. Instantly disarmed by the incredible kiss that was, strangely, an irresistible blend of fierceness and tenderness, she hadn't the will to end it without delay.

Swaying helplessly into him, she trembled against his tall, hard body as he forced her teeth apart. And she shuddered helplessly at the aggressive probing of his tongue.

Her knees were dangerously weak. Her breath was painfully short. Her head was spinning dizzily. She was so completely conquered by his blazing kiss, she had no idea that as his lips moved on hers and his tongue stroked fiery pleasure inside her sensitive mouth, that he had begun undressing her. His deft fingers were hurriedly undoing the tiny buttons down the bodice of her blue summer dress. She didn't feel the cool night air on her exposed flesh. She felt only the heat of his mouth on hers, his lips expertly molding her own to more perfectly fit his, his sleek tongue seeking out the inner recesses of her tingling mouth.

Finally he ended the devastating kiss, but his lips stayed on hers when he said again, "Sure, baby, I'll undress you." He nudged a bent knee between her legs as he promised, "We'll take up right where we left off."

Then he kissed her again, drawing her closer against his tall, ungiving frame, aggressively insinuating his hard muscled thigh between her legs in a shockingly blatant gesture of intimacy. She made a fleeting little sound of censure, but his arms only tightened around her. He deepened the kiss, and her soft, pliant body quite naturally sought the heat and hardness of his.

Shocked by his bold behavior, even more shocked by her own, the princess was impotent against the sensual onslaught. This tall Texan was kissing her as she'd never been kissed before, and for a long, shameful moment she was totally powerless against him. Momentarily suspended in that wonderfully thrilling state of escalating sexual excitement, logical thought had slipped away, unseated by simple, basic need. She was swept away by a primal hunger she'd never known was a part of her. Helplessly she responded to Black's burning caresses before finally managing to regain her temporarily lost senses.

A little of her equilibrium returning, she tore her kiss-scorched lips from his and began to fight him. Struggling to free herself from his embrace, she scolded in a voice shaky with emotion, "Are you mad! You let me go you—you—maniac!"

His tone flat, even, Virgil said, "Ah, come off it, Red. What is it really? You still miffed because I went to sleep on you?"

Continuing to struggle within his arms, she shouted, "You are insane! As mad as a hatter! I have never seen you before in my life, and you have never seen me!"

Virgil Black shrugged wide shoulders and abruptly released her. "It won't work, baby. Pretend to be anyone you please, but we both know damned well who you are. You're a beautiful thief and you are going to jail, just like your accomplice, British Bob."

Backing away from him, she shook her head. "I know of no one called British Bob."

"Well, he sure knows you, and the ungentlemanly coward ratted out on you." He turned and walked away.

Confused by her frightening emotions, furious with him for causing her distress, the shaking princess stooped down, picked up a rock, and sailed it forcefully at him. The well-thrown pebble caught him on the right ear, breaking the skin, drawing blood.

Virgil Black stopped, lifted a hand, touched his ringing ear, and slowly turned to face her. "Do that again"—his dark face struck by the bright moonlight seemed to be chiseled from the most resistant stone— "and you will regret it."

"I doubt that!" she answered confidently, but took a defensive step backward.

"Trust me." He blotted the blood from his ear with the kerchief he had used earlier on his nail-scratched jaw.

"You ever try to kiss me again and *you* will regret it!"

"I doubt that." His blue eyes flashed menacingly in the moonlight.

She opened her mouth to utter a stinging retort, but thought better of it and said nothing. She watched in angry silence as the Ranger nonchalantly spread a blanket on the ground near the dying fire, stretched out, covered himself to midchest, folded his hands beneath his head, and closed his eyes.

Nonplussed, Princess Marlena moved tentatively closer. "Just what do you think you're doing?" she asked, standing above, her hands on her hips.

Virgil cocked one eye open. "Going to sleep," he said. "I suggest you do the same."

The princess looked about, frowned. "Where shall I sleep? I see no blanket spread for me. No pillow. No—"

"You're more than welcome to join me," Virgil interrupted, tossing back one side of his blanket.

"Never!" she huffed. "I would gladly sit up all night before I would lie down next to a rude, ruthless, ill-bred commoner like you!"

She turned away contemptuously and walked toward the low-burning campfire, sat down, and thought how she would wait until the Ranger was asleep, then she'd take both horses and flee. Leave the cocksure bastard afoot! That's exactly what he deserved.

A long, chilly, silent hour dragged slowly by.

The fire had burned so low only a few glowing embers remained. It was cold in the mountains at night, even in mid-June. Princess Marlena was shivering. She sat hugging herself, her teeth chattering. She would freeze if she waited much longer. She drew a shallow breath and slowly rose to her feet.

And froze where she stood when the Ranger said, in that flat Texas drawl, "Don't take a step. You're not going anywhere." A long tense pause, then, more softly, "It's cold, Red. Come here and get warm."

The princess fervently wished that she had the fortitude to say no. But she did not. She was, for the moment at least, beaten. Dead-tired, impossibly sleepy, chilled to the bone, she gave in. Saying nothing, she started toward him. He again threw back one side of the blanket. Despising herself for being weak, the princess reluctantly lay down beside him, carefully making sure not to touch him.

She turned away from him, drew the shared blanket up over her shoulders, and closed her burning eyes. Then gasped and sputtered her outrage when the Ranger's arm came around her.

"Shhh," he cautioned, drawing her back against his hard muscled chest, fitting his long, lean body around hers, spoon fashion. "Behave now. Go to sleep."

The princess didn't go to sleep.

Not for a long, long time. Never in her life had she slept with another human being. Not even when she was married to the duke of Hernden. Not once had she allowed Sir Cedric to spend a night in her bed. Every night of her life she had gone to sleep alone and awakened alone. No way in the world would she sleep tonight. It was totally impossible. Out of the question.

The princess was horrified by the realization that she was lying in the arms of a ruthless Texas Ranger who was taking her to jail. She was even more horrified by the way her heart misbehaved when his muscular arm suddenly tightened around her. She stopped breathing entirely when his large tanned hand with its long, tapered fingers spread, settled possessively on her stomach.

She shivered involuntarily. And it wasn't from the cold.

This man in whose arms she now lay was decidedly dangerous in his potent virility. She had never known such a ruggedly masculine man, and she recognized, with a shiver of icy fear, the very real threat he posed. An animal, sexual threat as old as time itself, but one that was totally novel to her.

Instinctively, the princess knew that she would have to be constantly on guard against this strange man. Which was a first for her. She had spent her life in the company of some of the most handsome and sophisticated gentlemen in Europe, but had never felt threatened by any of them.

This Ranger was different. This Ranger was dangerous. This Ranger must *never* get the chance to kiss her again.

The sudden, vivid recollection of his hot, aggressive kisses brought a warm flush to her cheeks and a strange tightness to her nipples. And she couldn't keep from wondering—imagining—just what kind of lover he would be.

At that moment Virgil sighed deeply in his sleep, and the princess felt his warm, moist breath on her neck. Her own breath caught in her throat. Tingling from head to toe, experiencing new and disturbing feelings from simply lying in this sleeping man's arms, the princess squirmed and shivered and knew she wouldn't sleep a wink all night.

*   *   *

"Kiss me, baby," he coaxed huskily, "Kiss me like you've never kissed any man before."

Naked, he lay stretched out on his back in the brilliant mountain moon glow, his long, lean body gleaming a dark golden bronze against the vivid velvety green of the soft meadow grass. She too was unashamedly naked, her body as pale as the puffy white clouds that sailed high above them. Enclosed within his powerful arms, she lay close beside him on the downy cushion of grass.

"No," she murmured, stretching lazily, "you kiss me. Kiss me and tell me how much you want me."

"Anything you say, baby."

He rolled agilely up onto an elbow, leaned down, and kissed her open, responsive lips. She felt the fire lick of his tongue burn through her naked body, heating the blood that raced through her veins, starting a gentle, rhythmic throbbing low, low in her bare belly.

She started to lift her slender arms, to put them around his neck, but she hesitated, deciding against it. Instead she raised her arms above her head, stretched them to their full length, let them drop upon soft grass, clasped her wrists together, and sighed.

She would do nothing. Make him do everything. She would pretend to be a perfect, naked goddess to be worshipped, and he her handsome, devoted slave.

Knowing innately what she wanted, he gladly gave it to her. He kissed her temples, her eyes, her ears, her mouth. And as he kissed her, he stroked—with gentle fingers—her bare yearning body as carefully as if it were made of priceless porcelain while he murmured sweet words of devotion and told her how he idolized her.

For a long time, he was extremely tender, extremely gentle, paying humble homage to the pale pliant flesh, literally worshipping her with his hands and mouth. Adoring her. Revering her.

Then came the best part.

By now she was on fire for him, so aroused she was feverish. So she gave a great sigh of pleasure when—like a magician waving a wand—he ceased being the docile slave and became her forceful master.

Commandingly he pushed her legs apart and came between. He loomed just above then, filling the entire scope of her vision, the sleek, steely muscles in his bare, broad shoulders a silent testament to his strength and masculinity. His deeply tanned face, struck by the dazzling alpine moonlight, was hardened by passion and strikingly handsome. His inky black hair was appealingly tousled and falling over his high forehead and his changeable blue eyes had darkened to a deep navy hue. Awesome heat shone from their bewitching depths, and she trembled beneath his fixed stare.

His full lips were parted and his quickened breath was loud in the mountain quiet. He was naked against her and she was feverish with desire. He knew it. He lowered his lips to hers, pressed a kiss to them, and whispered, "You want me, baby?"

"Yes," she breathed, "oh, yes."

He raised his head and looked at her with those smoldering eyes. "I'll make you mine, baby. You'll never want anyone else." He tangled a hand in her wild ginger-red hair, bent his head, and kissed her, his lips opening hungrily on hers.

Her arms came down from over her head. She was trembling violently now. Her hand stole beneath his arm and moved over his back, feeling the muscles surge and bunch under the hot smooth skin. Her fingertips drifted tentatively along his ribs and down to his hard, muscled waist.

His lips left hers, moved to the rising swell of her breasts. His silky black hair ruffling against her chin, he bent and kissed her aching breasts, and her heartbeat accelerated wildly. She whimpered with joy when he raked his teeth back and forth across the rigid nipples. And she gasped with heightened pleasure when his warm, wet mouth fully enclosed her left nipple and he sucked on it as if it were some sweet treat.

Her eyes closing against the brightness of the moonlight, she sighed and gasped and wriggled. And she moaned with rising anticipation when she felt him place the throbbing tip of his heavy tumescence just inside her.

Her anxious hands gripping his corded waist, she heard him say, "Open your eyes, baby. Look at me."

She meekly obeyed.

And, looking straight up into his mesmerizing eyes, she cried out in pain/pleasure when he thrust himself firmly into her, penetrating deeply. She uttered a single cry of shocked joy that became a low moan as she surged up to meet the driving fire that filled her.

Continuing to look into his eyes, she lay there in the moonlit meadow in the middle of the night, being expertly pleasured by this magnificent master of love. It was exquisite. Unlike anything she'd ever known or imagined.

"Oh, yes, yes," she murmured breathlessly as he thrust forcefully into her, stretching her, filling her, making her wild and giddy with sensual delight.

The joy swiftly escalated. The passion blazed out of control. Her pleasure became so intense it bordered on pain.

And then, she felt a new kind of pleasure beginning. A sensation she'd never experienced. She had never felt this way before. As if something were about to explode inside her.

"Yes, yes." She tossed her head about. "Yes, please . . . ohhh . . . yes . . . yes . . ."

"Yes?" he repeated, gently shaking her shoulder. "Yes?"

"Yes . . . yes . . . ," the princess again murmured breathlessly, still submerged in the beautiful dream.

"Exactly what is it you're saying yes to, Red?" his low, provocative voice finally pierced the lingering mist of the lovely fantasy.

The princess awakened.

Her eyes opened to see Virgil Black, unshaven but wearing clean clothes, crouched on his heels above her. The rising sun was behind him. Flustered, her heart hammering, she glanced at him, then away, feeling herself color hotly with shame and embarrassment. Hoping he wouldn't notice.

"You blushing, Red?" he asked.

"Certainly not!" The princess glared at him.

"You were dreaming," she heard him say.

"No!" she denied too quickly. "I was not."

A half smile curving his lips, he accused, "Yes you were. You were dreaming of me."

"Dreaming of you?" she repeated, as if incredulous, tossing the blanket aside, and hastily sitting up. She made an exaggerated face of repugnance. "That would be no dream, Texan. That would be a horrible nightmare."

13

His wicked smile made the princess instantly furious. Furthermore she was appalled by the suggestive way he was crouched there on his heels with his knees wide apart, practically in her face, the fabric of his black trousers straining across his groin.

Her emerald eyes snapping with displeasure, the princess impulsively reached out, flattened her hands on his shoulders, leaned into him, and pushed with all her might. His dark face a sudden study in surprise, Virgil toppled over onto his back. Smiling with triumph, she rose quickly to her feet with intent to flounce away and sweep grandly toward the campfire.

"Owwww, ohhh," she moaned, when she tried to walk and found that her legs were so sore she could not even stand.

She felt herself falling and looked around expectantly, assuming he would catch her. He did not. Although Virgil had agilely shot to his feet the second his back touched the ground, he stood and watched her fall without making a move to come to her aid.

"You insensitive bastard!" she shouted, as she lay there on her stomach, her weight braced on outstretched hands. "Are you blind? Couldn't you see that I was falling?"

"I saw," he said, his thumbs hooked into the cartridge belt circling his slim waist, his booted feet apart.

"You saw?" she repeated. "You saw and did nothing!" Like a thwarted child, she bent and banged her forehead on the grassy ground in angry frustration, beginning to cry. "I am in wretched pain and you do not even care, you black-hearted viper!"

Virgil knew exactly what was wrong with her. "A little sore, are you, Red?"

Tears streaming down her cheeks, the princess rolled over with effort and sat up. Sniffing, she said, "My legs and my back are killing me. I cannot walk, much less ride that miserable gray mare today, so you can just forget about traveling. This is all your fault, and I hate you with every breath I take for causing me this terrible agony and not even caring!"

Unconcerned, he said, "Relax, I have something that will fix you up, good as new."

"You have?" She was skeptical, sure she would suffer forever. She struggled to stand.

"Stay where you are," he advised, and she nodded.

She watched as he rummaged through his gear, picked out a black tin of something, and came back to her. He unstrapped his gun belt, tossed it out of her reach, and sat down beside her.

"Lift your skirts," he commanded.

"Certainly not!" she spat, incensed. "If you think for one minute that you will *ever* be allowed to—to—"

She stopped speaking when, ignoring her protests, he nonchalantly reached down and flipped her wrinkled blue skirt and lacy white petticoats up over her knees.

She automatically started to fight him, but he easily caught both her hands in one of his, drew her up so that her face was only inches from his own, and told her, "If you want to suffer all day, that's fine with me. But, ready or not, we are riding away from here within the hour. I can make you feel better in fifteen minutes. It's up to you."

"Wh-what are going to do to me?"

"Rub down your sore, aching legs with a restorative salve," he said. "And, when your legs are feeling better, I'll work on your back."

Still skeptical, she said, "You're not just trying to—to—"

"Seduce you?" He shook his dark head. "You'll know it when I am. Now take off those stockings and lie down."

"Shut your eyes," the princess commanded.

"Not a chance," he told her. "Get those stockings off or I'll do it for you."

She exhaled indignantly, pushed her saucy satin garters down over her knees, then rolled the stockings down to her feet.

"I'll do the rest," he said. "Lie down."

Too miserable to argue, she stretched out on her back, placing her folded arms beneath her head. She watched from narrowed eyes as the Ranger slid the rolled-down stockings from her feet and stuffed them into the breast pocket of his black shirt. Without asking permission, he pushed her lace-trimmed underpants up until they were bunched high on her pale thighs. He then dipped his middle finger into the tin of salve and rubbed it into his palm. He warmed and softened the thick ointment in his hands and then carefully placed his hands on her.

The princess quivered involuntarily at the first bold touch of his warm, surprisingly soft hands on her exposed flesh. She had to bite her lip to keep from whimpering. Unself-consciously he rubbed the mint-smelling ointment over her shins and knotted calves. She cried out in pain when his long, tapered fingers punished the aching muscles, massaging firmly, kneading and stroking the soreness away.

Shortly she was reluctantly admitting—to herself, not to him—that he had talented fingers. She closed her eyes and gave herself up entirely to his magical hands, allowing every muscle in her body to slacken. She idly thought how she could lie there forever while those strong smooth masculine hands rubbed away the awful soreness from her limbs.

But just as that thought occurred, those powerful hands glided up above her knees. Any measure of relaxation she had experienced ended abruptly. She felt her entire body tense with the first upward stroke of his fingers on her left thigh. She slitted her heavily lashed eyes open just a fraction and felt her heart slam against her ribs.

He was seated on the ground facing her, his intense gaze riveted to her bared flesh. Dressed today all in black—black shirt, black trousers, black kerchief, black boots—he looked more like an outlaw than a Ranger. His shirt was the yoked kind that cowboys wore, but one side of the yoke was unbuttoned. The flap of the unbuttoned yoke hung open, exposing a thick growth of jet-black hair on his dark-skinned chest. The shirt's long sleeves were rolled up, revealing muscular, suntanned forearms.

His trousers were a hard finish black twill that fit his slim hips and long, lean legs so snugly it was almost indecent. He sat now with one leg cocked outward and resting on the ground, the other bent at the knee and raised, booted foot flat on the ground. Unaware of her perusal, he continued to touch and rub and knead the sensitive flesh of her thighs. The princess finally allowed her gaze to glide down and watch him at work.

It was a mistake.

The sight of those strong, deeply tanned hands moving so seductively on her milky white thighs was powerfully erotic. As each long, tapered finger vigorously pressed and squeezed, she grew a little more breathless, a little more disturbed. Those incredibly arresting hands moved higher and higher and she watched, through barely opened lashes, in fascination and excitement, her body tingling as it had in last night's pleasurable, but troubling dream.

Had the dream been a prophecy of what was actually to happen? Had this stone-faced, black-clad seducer of unsuspecting women only used her soreness as an excuse to break down her defenses? Had he known that he could easily topple the ramparts of her reserve with this intimate touching and stroking.

"That's enough!" she suddenly burst out, levering herself up onto her elbows. "Stop! Stop it now."

"Ready to start on your back?"

"No, no, that won't be necessary. My back is fine and—"

"It is no such thing," he disagreed. "Turn over, Red. Let old Doc Black and his magic potion have a go at it."

"Absolutely not." She shook her head. "I've had quite enough of your pummeling. I do believe you deliberately hurt me."

"How can you say that when your legs feel so much better?" A hint of a knowing smile stretched his full lips. "Don't they?"

"Well . . . yes . . . yes," she admitted, amazed at how the soreness had left her legs. "But, still . . ." She anxiously rose to her feet, afraid to let him touch her anymore. Standing above, she looked down at him and said, "Where shall I have my morning bath?"

"The same place I had mine," he told her, draping a forearm over his raised knee. He inclined his dark head. "That brook you hear tumbling over the rocks is not more than a hundred yards away and well concealed by the dense cedars and pines bordering it."

She nodded. "You won't follow me? Spy on me?"

Virgil lifted a hand, idly rubbed his nail-scratched jaw. "You overestimate your feminine charms, Red."

Insulted, she accused, "Do you actually suppose I don't know that you are attracted to me, Texan?" She laughed, incredulous. "I know. Believe me, I know. Why, you would take me in your arms right now and . . . and . . ." She swallowed hard. "If you had the opportunity."

Virgil abruptly rose to his full, impressive six-foot-three-inch height above her. Smiling easily, he hooked a finger into the open-necked collar of her blue summer dress and said, "Sure, I would, Red. You owe me one, remember?"

"I owe you nothing!" she said, slapping his intrusive hand away. "I am going down to that stream to take my bath, and you better not come near me!" She turned and walked away.

"Wait," he called after her. "Don't you want to take—" He stopped speaking. He was going to offer her a towel, but she was too headstrong to stop, so to hell with her. Let her dry off as best she could.

Virgil stood there watching until she was out of sight. Then he shook his head and exhaled heavily. This was going to be one long, tiresome journey.

He returned to the campfire and poured himself a cup of strong black coffee. He sat down cross-legged on the ground and lit a cigarette. Physically, he felt fine. He'd had a good night's sleep.

His thoughts drifted back to when he had awakened with the dawn, eased away from the sleeping Queenie, and built the campfire. When he got it going, he had gone down to the snow-fed stream, stripped to the skin, and bathed away the grime and dirt of the trail. The cold, clear water had been bracing, exhilarating.

It was not until he had been ready to get out of the water that he realized he hadn't brought a towel or any clean clothes with him. Shivering when he emerged and stood on the rocky banks, he had debated. Should he put his soiled clothes back on or return to camp unclothed and risk finding his pretty prisoner wide awake and staring at him? Then he had smiled to himself. So what if she saw him naked? She had seen him naked before.

So he had gathered up his dirty clothes and boots and returned to camp as the summer sun was rising over the mountain rim. He had found her still fast asleep, making funny little mewling sounds in her slumber, smiling foolishly, and thrashing around. She was obviously dreaming, and it must have been a very pleasurable one.

Smiling, wondering who it was that filled her dreams, he had stood naked before the fire, allowing the shooting flames to dry the beaded moisture from his bare, lean body. He turned his back to the warming campfire and stood facing the dreaming woman who slept not twenty yards away.

Her ginger-red hair was appealingly tangled, a strand curled caressingly around her cheek. Long dark lashes fluttered restlessly over closed emerald eyes. Lips, as soft and pink as a baby's, were slightly parted over gleaming white teeth. All at once she moaned softly and her tongue came out to lick her top lip.

Virgil felt his belly tighten, his body surge. He was half-tempted to go to her. Crawl naked in under the blanket with her and kiss her into an easy submission before she had fully roused from her dreams. Be a nice way to start the day.

He groaned, wrapped a restraining hand around his half-hard flesh, and turned quickly away. He wouldn't take unfair advantage. Not even of a jaded criminal like the Queen of the Silver Dollar. He wouldn't have to. She would eagerly fall into his arms before they reached El Paso, he'd stake his life on it. When it came to women, he had yet to be wrong. They invariably behaved as expected. And he always obliged himself of their generously offered charms. But with every meaningless tryst, his innate distrust of women was strengthened.

It had been while he was dressing by the fire that he heard her cry out in her sleep.

"Yes, yes," she had murmured, and he had gone over and shaken her shoulder to awaken her. "Yes, please, yes," she had whispered.

Remembering, Virgil began to smile.

Then a sudden piercing scream startled him out of his reveries.

His dark face immediately frozen into rigid lines, he was up in a heartbeat and grabbing his Colt. Before the spine-tingling scream ended, he was sprinting headlong across the open meadow toward the pine-hidden stream, praying he could reach her in time.

He expected the worst.

That kind of bone-chilling scream from a helpless woman brought back horrible images of things he had seen when he was a young man. The sickening sight of a naked white woman's bruised and battered body after a band of Comanche had raped and tortured her for hours before killing her as her family was forced to watch. He could still see the poor abused woman, the horror of what she had lived through fixed in her sightless, staring eyes.

Virgil ran faster.

He crashed through the dense pine forest, his heart squeezing painfully in his chest. Envisioning her pinned to the ground by a big renegade Apache astride her, a knife to her throat, Virgil bolted through the trees, his blue eyes flashing with fury.

Gun raised and cocked, he was ready to kill or be killed.

14

Virgil exploded from the trees onto the rocky bank of the rushing brook. Eyes deadly, trigger finger poised, adrenaline pumping, he took in everything in one alert, sweeping glance. He saw her immediately. He saw no one else. She stood in waist-high water in the middle of the stream, her arms crossed over her breasts.

"Where are they?" he called out anxiously as he looked up and down the stream's rocky banks. "Are you hurt? How many are there? Did you see where they went?"

"Who?" the princess asked innocently, staring at him as if he had lost his mind. "Who are *they*?"

His narrowed gaze shifted swiftly back to her. "The Apaches!" he said passionately. "Or the outlaws. Or whoever it was that frightened you so badly."

The princess frowned at him. "I saw no savages or bandits." She tilted her head to one side. "For goodness sake, what would make you think I did?"

Virgil Black's eyes instantly darkened to a deadly hue. His tone, when finally he collected himself enough to speak, matched his eyes. "There was no one here? Nobody hurt you or scared you half to death? You saw no one?"

"Not a soul."

Virgil silently counted to ten. He slowly lowered his Colt, drew a deep, calming breath, and stuck the weapon in the waistband of his trousers at the small of his back.

Then with exaggerated politeness, he nodded and asked, "Would you mind telling me just exactly what is was that you were screaming about?"

"The water, of course!" she was more than eager to explain. "I had no idea it would be so icy cold and I—"

"Damn it to hell." His voice was hard as steel. "Do you mean to tell me you were screaming like a gut-shot panther because the water was a little chilly?"

"A little? It is absolutely freezing! *I* am freezing!" And she was. She was shaking violently, her teeth were chattering, and she blamed him for her discomfort. "You might have at least warned me."

"I will warn you now," Virgil said calmly. "You ever scream like that again for no good reason, I'll *give* you a good reason to scream. You got that?" Before she could reply, he said, "Get out."

"No!" she sank back down into the frigid water, gasping as it rose to lap at her bare shoulders. "Not while you're standing—"

"Now!" he said with such authority it stunned her. And removing the silver star from his chest and shoving it into his pocket, he began unbuttoning his black yoked shirt.

"All right, all right," she said, having no wish to further anger him. "My clothes, please. They are right behind you. If you will be so kind as to bring them directly down to the water's edge and then leave, I will get out."

His black shirt now unbuttoned down his dark chest, he shrugged out of it, hooked it on his thumb, and said, "I'll turn my back. You get out of the water and put on my shirt."

"Certainly not! I shall wear my own clothes."

"No," he coolly corrected, "you will not. Today you are wearing clothes more suitable for a long, hard ride." He dropped the shirt to the rocks below and stood there looking at her for a long moment, unmistakable challenge flashing out of his piercing blue eyes. At last he spoke. "Now, get out before you catch a cold." He pivoted about. His back to her, he walked the few steps to where she had gotten undressed. He collected her discarded clothing and underwear, tossed them over his right shoulder. He stuck her soft kid slippers into the back pockets of his black trousers.

Watching him suspiciously, afraid any second he would whip around and catch her naked and defenseless, the princess anxiously paddled to the stream bank, got out, and, trembling furiously from the cold, her flesh covered with goose bumps, snatched up the black shirt and slipped her arms into the too-long sleeves. Her teeth chattering violently, her wet, bare body shaking like a leaf in the wind, she struggled to button the yoked shirt but made little progress.

The shirt's sleeves kept falling down over her hands no matter how hard she tried to keep them pushed up. And her cold wet fingers were so stiff she had trouble with the shirt's buttons.

How he was aware of her difficulty, she didn't know, but he said over his shoulder, "Need help?"

"No, thanks," she snapped. "I am almost finished."

"Liar," he said, turning to face her. "I'll do it."

"Don't you dare come a step closer!" she threatened, shaking her head and frantically holding the long-tailed shirt together with both hands.

He came a step closer. He walked right up to her, brushed one of her hands away, and began deftly buttoning the shirt's yoke over her bosom. Her face flaming, she had no choice but to stand there before him and allow him to button the shirt.

"There," he said when every last button was buttoned. "Let's get you back to the fire so you can warm up."

Automatically tugging at the shirt's long tails which reached well below midthigh, she nodded, said, "My slippers?"

"You won't need them," he replied, and before she realized his intent, he swept her up into his arms and started back to camp.

She shrieked with surprise and, grabbing his neck with one hand, felt around beneath herself with the other to make sure that her bare buttocks were not exposed. Relieved to find that the black cotton fabric securely covered her bottom and was caught and pulled tight by his supporting arm, she let out a breath and draped her other arm loosely around his neck.

She was, of course, quite annoyed with him for being so high-handed. All the same, the fierce animal heat of his lean, hard body was unquestionably comforting. She was so incredibly cold and he was so amazingly warm. She was tempted to bury her head on his shoulder and snuggle closer against his broad, bare chest.

Afraid he might misinterpret such an innocent gesture, she held herself stiff and as far away from him as was possible under the circumstances.

"Jesus Christ," he said suddenly, glancing down at her face, then back up at the trail, "don't you ever relax?"

"Why, yes, I . . . certainly. I—I don't know what you mean."

"Yes, you do," he charged. He tightened his hold, pressed her closer. "You're stiff as a poker, Red. Let yourself go. Hell, I'm not going to bite you." She laughed nervously, said nothing. And wanting him to know that she was not the least bit afraid of him, she ordered herself to relax. She released a small sigh and let her tense muscles slacken. "That's better," he told her.

Maybe for him.

Not for her.

Despite all her best efforts to remain completely calm, the princess felt her heartbeat immediately quicken from the more intimate contact. Her right breast, covered only by the damp shirt, was pressed flush against his muscled chest, directly over his heart. She could feel his heart's steady, heavy beating against her soft flesh, and a tiny tremor of unwanted excitement shot through her.

"Still cold?" he inquired, feeling the shudder.

"Y-yes," she lied.

Believing her, he drew her closer still, tucking her head beneath his chin, lifting her higher against his chest. As he weaved through the tall pines and over the thick underbrush, Virgil kept his eyes fixed on the trail. Taking care to avoid any low-hanging limbs, he seemed to have forgotten her entirely. Which gave her the opportunity to covertly study him.

The princess eased her head from beneath his chin, moved it out to rest on his shoulder, and, from beneath lowered lashes, cautiously raised her eyes to his face. Gazing at him, she noticed, and not for the first time, the absurdly long black eyelashes that swept upward from his hard blue eyes. His thick, naturally arched black eyebrows were presently knitted together as if he were in troubled thought. His straight, well-shaped nose gave him an almost arrogant appearance. And his mouth, with the full, wide lips now firmly closed, had a sinister, dangerous look, made all the more so by the heavy growth of day-old black stubble surrounding it.

The long scratch on his left jaw, made by her scraping fingernail, was an angry red, and his left ear, where she had struck him with a rock, was both cut and bruised. The superficial wounds added to his menacing demeanor.

Looking at him up so close sent a little shudder of alarm racing through her, and the princess quickly lowered her eyes to his tanned throat. Although he wore no shirt—she was wearing it—the black silk bandanna was still knotted around his bare throat.

He should have looked quite silly, shirtless with the black silk kerchief tied around his neck, instead he looked roguish, devil-may-care, scarily appealing. She was at once repelled and attracted. And she wished, above all else, that she were more fully clothed and therefore less vulnerable. He knew that she was naked beneath his shirt. Suppose he decided to take advantage of her? What would she do? What *could* she do?

She hazarded another quick glance at his face. He was looking straight ahead, not at her, never at her, his disinterest evident. Princess Marlena realized, with a twinge of disappointment, that taking advantage of her was likely the last thing on his mind. This was rather puzzling and a totally new experience for her.

He did not behave like any of the men she had known. He was certainly not panting after her, hoping for a kiss or a kind word. If she had spent twenty-four hours alone in the wilds with any other man on earth, she would have, by now, had him wrapped around her little finger.

The princess had the distinct feeling that this granite-faced Texas Ranger had never and would never be wrapped around any woman's little finger. Not even hers.

Virgil stepped out of the trees and into the bright mountain sunshine. Blinking, shutting her eyes against the sudden change in light, the princess was relieved they were back at camp. She could hardly wait to get some clothes on.

Virgil carried her straight to the campfire, set her on her bare feet.

"Thank heaven for the fire," she said. "I am *soooo* cold."

He nodded, left her there. She stretched icy hands to the shooting flames and felt the welcome heat lick at her bare thighs. Shortly Virgil returned, carrying a pair of faded Levi's jeans and a collarless pullover blue shirt over his arm.

He said, "I'll break camp and saddle the horses while you get dressed." She looked at the clothes. She looked at him. "What shall I do with the shirt I'm wearing?"

"Give it back," he said, absently rubbing his washboard abdomen where his low-riding trousers fell away from his hard waist. "If you ever considered anyone other than yourself, you might realize that I'm a shade chilly myself."

15

Stung by his accusation, the princess felt compelled to defend herself. A protest quickly rose in her throat. "I will have you know that—"

"Save it for somebody who'll believe it," he cut her off. "Get your pants on and be ready to ride." He turned and walked away, leaving her glaring at his broad, bare back.

Moments later he returned with the saddled horses and saw her standing motionless, staring into the dying fire. She was dressed in his faded jeans, which hung precariously on her hipbones. The denim legs were rolled up several turns over her bare feet. The blue collarless pullover shirt with the tails outside the pants reached almost to her knees. She had taken the bolo tie he'd given her to use for a belt and instead had secured her wild ginger hair at the back of her neck. Her face, clean and smooth and totally devoid of the heavy paint and powder she wore onstage, was near perfect. There was one imperfection to her fair good looks. A minor one. With her hair pulled back from her face, her slightly protruding ears were more noticeable than usual.

Struck by how cute and youthful she looked in his clothes that practically swallowed her, Virgil felt obliged to again caution her about the many perils she would encounter should she be lucky—and foolish—enough to escape him.

"Red, we need to talk," he said, dropping the horses' reins to the grass and stepping up beside her.

Arms crossed over her chest, chin tilted imperiously, she refused to turn and look at him. "I have nothing to say to you, Ranger."

"Then let me amend," he said. "I need to talk to you."

"Really?" she replied sarcastically, "I can't believe you'd want to converse with someone who thinks only of herself."

Virgil exhaled with irritation. "If I hurt your tender feelings, I'm sorry."

"No you're not." She whipped her head around and looked up at him with blazing emerald eyes.

He shrugged bare shoulders, reached for the black shirt she had discarded on the ground. He picked it up, thrust his long arms into the sleeves but left the shirt unbuttoned.

"Okay, I'm not," he said, reached out, took hold of her upper arms, and turned her to face him. "I have something to say and you are going to listen."

"Why should I care what you have to say?" She attempted to wrench herself free of his strong grasp, and failed.

"Hold still," he said, refusing to release her. She made a face, turned her head away, and gazed off across the meadow. "And look at me," he commanded, giving her a gentle shake. Her snapping green eyes returned to his face. He said, "You should care because it concerns you. It is important that you listen and pay close attention."

"Then say it and get it over with," she replied, chin jutting pugnaciously.

"You think you've met every kind of man at the Silver Dollar, but—"

"Just what is this Silver Dollar?"

"Jesus, don't be coy with me, I don't have the time. And don't interrupt me again," he warned. "What I'm trying to tell you, Red, is that no matter how many rough, rowdy men you adeptly handled at the saloon, you are no match for the trigger-happy bandits, Mexican outlaws, and renegade Apaches roaming these mountains and the deserts below. You're a very pretty woman, and I'd hate to think what would happen if you fell into the wrong hands." He paused, waited for her to speak.

"Are you finished?" she asked, bored with this latest revelation of the perils of America's West.

"No, I'm not. The Apaches are the most dangerous, the worst of the lot. They are ruthless, pitiless. They subject white captives to unspeakable acts of torture." Her eyes changed slightly, as did the expression on her face. She was listening now and he knew it.

He pressed on. "Surely you've heard that scattered bands of renegade Apaches are again off the San Carlos Reservation. For weeks now they've been terrorizing ranchers and farmers throughout New Mexico and Texas. One of the renegade bands is led by a fierce young giant called Chief Thunderfoot." Virgil glanced pointedly at her hair, flaming now in the early morning sunshine, then back at her face. "If Thun-

derfoot gets so much as a glimpse of your wild red hair . . ." He shook
his head, left the rest unsaid.

Princess Marlena nodded to appease him, but she wasn't terribly
frightened by his warnings. He wanted to scare her so she wouldn't try to
slip away from him. Well, it wouldn't work. Yesterday she hadn't been
thinking clearly. She had been too frightened and confused to contemplate
escape. Today was different. She felt more like her old self again.
Confident. Ready to take matters into her own hands. She was sure that
she could now handle the gentle gray mare by herself. It seemed simple
enough. She had watched the Ranger. Had noted the way he reined his
mount about with no apparent trouble. She could do the same. And she
would. Starting today.

Then she could escape the Texas Ranger.

The minute the opportunity presented itself, she would be gone. She
would take her chances against Thunderfoot and the Apache. At least they
wouldn't be dragging her off to jail.

She nodded earnestly and told Virgil in a soft, little girl voice, "Why,
just the mention of the Apaches is enough to frighten me half out of my
wits."

"Good," he said, dropping his hands from her arms. "You should be
frightened. Stay that way." He shook a long finger in her face. "And stay
close to me at all times. Do *not* get out of my sight."

As sweetly as possible, she replied, "I won't. You can trust me,
Ranger."

"I'm sure I can." His blue sardonic eyes mocked her, letting her know
he *didn't trust her at all.* He stuffed the long tails of his black shirt down
inside the waistband of his snug trousers. "Still, if you don't mind," he
said, buttoning his shirt, "I'll keep a pretty close eye on you."

Struggling to tamp down her rising temper, Princess Marlena smiled
engagingly at the tall, dark Texan. "Mind? Why I'm relieved to hear it."

He grinned an evil grin, nodded. "Remember this, Red, I'm always
prepared for whatever happens," he said. "That's my motto. "*Semper
apparatus.*" It's Latin. Means 'be prepared.' "

"I know that," she said condescendingly. "I studied Latin for four
years."

He gave no reply. Just reached into his back pockets, retrieved her kid
slippers, and went down on one knee before her. When his long tapered
fingers swiftly wrapped around her left ankle and he lifted her bare foot,
the princess almost lost her balance. She automatically reached out,
grabbed at his shoulders, felt the muscles flex beneath her hands. He slid
the slippers onto her feet, rose, and said, "*Vamanos, pues!* Know what that
means?"

Refusing to answer, she took a step backward, putting some space between them.

"It means, 'Let's go.'"

When he put his hands to her waist to lift her up onto the saddle, the princess announced casually, "I will take the reins of the mare today."

"You'll do nothing of the kind." He ignored the expression of disappointment that quickly clouded her face. "Today we ride most all the way down out of the mountains," he told her. "Where we now stand is at the eight-thousand-foot level. By sunset we'll have dropped five, six thousand feet. The trail down is steep, narrow, and treacherous. I'll handle both horses. You just hold on and stay in the saddle. *Comprende?*"

She refused even to look at him.

She sat astride the gray mare, her jaw set, wondering how she could possibly escape when he insisted on controlling her mount.

Virgil Black knew what she was thinking.

"Believe me, Red, before an hour has passed, you'll be glad I'm leading the mare."

The princess remained stubbornly mute, but he was unbothered by her silence. With the gray's long leather reins in his left hand, Virgil swung up into his saddle, and the responsive black stallion immediately went into motion. Virgil tugged gently on the mare's reins, and she moved forward to follow the stallion.

By the time they reached the far side of the wide, high country meadow, the newly risen sun had disappeared. Thick ground clouds had rolled in from the north, obliterating the tall pines and aspens ahead. Squinting, the princess could hardly see the dark horse and dark rider directly ahead of her. Clinging to the saddle horn with both hands, she wondered at him. Surely, if what he had said was true, if the trail was a steep and perilous one, it would be foolhardy to ride down it in the dense fog. She expected him to pull up any minute and say they would wait until the clouds burned off.

"Ranger," she called out shortly, "shouldn't we stop and wait for the sunshine?"

"No," he said evenly from out of damp, swirling mists. "That could be hours."

"So? You said yourself the trail is quite perilous," she reminded him. Her voice raising, she threatened, "See here, if you put my life in jeopardy, you will—"

Interrupting, he said, "Noche could make his way down the mountain blindfolded. As long as you do as I say, you'll be safe. Let me do the worrying." She opened her mouth to say more, but before she could speak, he said, "Not another word."

The princess ground her teeth in frustration, then made mean faces at the Ranger's back. She couldn't recall anyone ever telling her to be quiet. And she didn't like it. Not one bit. Who did this arrogant Texas lawman think he was telling her—Marlena, crown princess of Hartz-Coburg—to shut up? *Nobody* could tell her to shut up!

"Just who do you think you are? You strut through Texas with a gun on your hip making up the law as you go! Well, nobody tells me to shut up!" the princess shouted at the top of her lungs. "You hear that, Ranger? *Nobody!*"

The words had barely passed her lips before a dark form emerged from the impenetrable cloud forest, and the startled princess found herself being snatched down out of the saddle. Blinking in surprised alarm, she saw, through the thick swirling mists, the chiseled, unshaven face of the Ranger looming just above her own. He was close. So close that without touching her she could feel the physical emanation from him.

"I have," he said in a low menacing voice, "had just about enough of your nonsense."

She put up her chin, despising the sudden trembling in her limbs, knowing that if he moved any closer and touched her, she would no longer be able to conceal it.

"Get away from me!" she threatened hotly.

"Obviously you are a slow learner," he said, and moved aggressively closer. He stood so close his thighs brushed against hers and she wanted to die, knowing that he now knew her legs were quivering. "*I* give all the orders here. This is not a democracy. Nor is it the Silver Dollar Saloon where you're the Queen. You have no vote here, no say in any of the decisions made. Think of me as a dictator. *Your* dictator."

His hands at his sides, only his trousered thighs touching hers, he had her pinned against the gray mare. The annoying Texas drawl pronounced, he said, "You understand?"

Her temper flared. "I understand. Now perhaps you can understand this!" she said, and impulsively raised a hand to slap him hard.

But he was too quick for her. Her grabbed her wrist, forced her arm down, and shoved it behind her back.

"Perhaps you can understand this," he said, urging her up onto her toes against him until his dark, unshaven face was scant inches from her own. "If you act up again," he promised in a quiet deadly voice, "I'll hand-cuff you."

"You don't scare me one bit," she said with more assurance than she felt. "You wouldn't dare!"

He pressed her even closer, so close she gasped. "Try me."

"Maybe I will." She struggled to free herself.

"What are you waiting for?" he challenged coolly. "Go ahead."

"Oh, you'd like that, wouldn't you?" she said, refusing to be intimidated.

"No." He loosened his hold on her. "But I'm beginning to think you would."

While she hotly protested such an outlandish idea, Virgil picked her up, set her back atop the gray mare. She continued to talk a mile a minute, threatening him, scolding him, assuring him she wanted *nothing* to do with him. Finally he laid a hand on her trousered left leg, just above the knee, and squeezed gently until she finally fell silent.

"That's better." He patted her knee almost affectionately. "You behave, I'll behave." She sighed loudly, grudgingly nodded. "Good. I'll say it again. We have a long, hard journey before us."

16

Virgil Black had no idea, when he made the simple statement, just *how* long and hard a journey. A long and hard journey of discovery had begun for the pampered princess and the world-weary Ranger captain.

The princess, cherished and coddled from birth, was, by her own admission, headstrong and spoiled and selfish and demanding. And why not? From infancy she had thought first and foremost of herself and no one had ever objected. On the contrary, they had encouraged it. So naturally she had taken worship as her due, had thoughtlessly treated everyone as a loyal subject meant to do her bidding. Before coming to America, she had never, in her twenty-eight years, met the man or woman who was not eager to please her, to grant her every wish. Growing up in such a privileged, hothouse environment had molded an adult with the mature body and alluring beauty of a woman who was, in many ways, as naive and demanding as a child.

The princess couldn't hope to understand the Ranger's behavior. She had not yet learned that Virgil Black was not the kind of man to do anyone's bidding. As hard and ungiving as the harsh Texas deserts he called home, Black was a rugged loner who had raised himself by himself. A lonely child, he had grown up to be a cynical man who expected and was given nothing. He had made his own way, in his own way. He had spent his entire adult life outwitting bandits and thieves and cheats and liars.

He respected few men. Fewer women. The women Virgil had known were not ladies. And the ladies he had occasionally met, turned out to be mere women once he got them alone. He treated them all the same. They *were* all the same to him. He had made love to many women, but he had never been in love. And he was certain he never would be. More than one discarded lover wept that Black's heart, like his well-honed body, was as hard as marble. Others said he had no heart. And perhaps he didn't. Or maybe he had purposely hardened his tender heart when he was still a boy so that no one could ever hurt him again.

Virgil Black kept his own counsel, shared his innermost thoughts and feelings with no one. He asked no quarter. And he gave none.

Nobody understood him.

Certainly not the self-absorbed princess Marlena of Hartz-Coburg. To her, the tall, dark Texas Ranger was an enigma. She had attempted to analyze his conduct and had found him to be a complete paradox. Try as she might, she could not fathom what was going on in his mind, couldn't read what emotions—if any—lay behind those icy sea-blue eyes. A naturally curious woman, she couldn't help wondering how he felt about her.

On the one hand, he treated her badly, ordering her about and acting as though she were a common prisoner who was nothing but trouble to him. On the other hand, he had, last night at bedtime, swept her up into his powerful arms and kissed her, obviously yearning to make love to her.

From past experiences, she had learned that any man who kissed her with even half the passion he had shown was helplessly in love with her. Could it be? Was the stone-faced Ranger already falling in love with her? It was certainly not out of the question. It would not be the first time a man had fallen so quickly in love with her.

But then, if that were the case, why was he so mean and hateful to her? Why did he refuse to acknowledge her when she made a small request or a sensible suggestion? Why did he ignore her when she issued a mild command? Why didn't he try a little harder to please her? to woo and win her favor?

It was all so confusing, it gave her a headache. None of it made any sense to her. *He* made no sense to her. She had failed to convince him she was actually a visiting princess. He was inflexible in his certainty that she was a common thief. That being the case, how could he possibly be falling in love with her?

Well, what was the difference? She didn't care if he loved or hated her. She didn't plan on staying around him long enough to find out. She would escape him the first chance she got.

But for now, as the two of them wound their way slowly through the dense pine forest, she was grateful for his presence. He had told her that she would be glad he was leading her mare. He was right. She was. Although she would never have admitted it to him.

The ground clouds were so thick, she could hardly see her hand before her face, and she was growing increasingly nervous. Just being atop a horse was enough to make her jittery. Especially in these mountains. Although she loved the towering Tyrol of home, she had been, from childhood, afraid of heights. She had kept her eyes tightly closed anytime the royal coach transported her down the winding road from the cliffside castle.

Now, with thick, rolling mists swallowing her up, she was terrified the snorting, blowing mare might step into nothingness and the two of them would plunge off a craggy, fog-shrouded peak to their deaths.

Ducking tree limbs and squinting madly to see, the princess was suddenly plagued with a new worry. How she would ever find her way down out of the mountains if she were left there alone. It was such a disturbing thought, she quickly decided that she would, before she attempted any escape, question the Ranger at length about their proposed route to El Paso. She couldn't just take off with no idea where she was going or how to get there. And, she would definitely wait until they were down out of the mountains to make her getaway.

In less than half an hour the clouds began to lift and dissipate. Soon, welcome shafts of slanted sunshine pierced through the thick pine branches. The princess gave a great sigh of relief. She impulsively leaned over and patted the mare's sleek neck.

As she straightened, they emerged from the dense forest into bright, blinding sunlight. Virgil drew rein, bringing both horses to a swift halt. The princess's eyes widened in disbelief, then quickly closed in horror. They were on an overhanging lip of rock high above a wide flat valley. She was sure that the horses' hooves were but a few short feet from a sheer dropoff.

She didn't scream. But it wasn't because he had warned her about screaming. She was simply too frightened to make a sound. Paralyzed with fear, the princess couldn't move, couldn't speak.

Unaware of her distress, Virgil slouched comfortably in the saddle as if he were in a rocking chair at home. His hooded eyes riveted to the striking scenery, he wound the reins loosely around the saddle horn and reached into his breast pocket for a cigarette. He struck a sulfur match with his thumbnail, then cupped his hands around the tiny flame and lit the cigarette. He drew the smoke deep into his lungs, then slowly released it.

The cigarette dangling from the corner of his mouth, his eyes squinted against the brilliant alpine sunshine, he continued to gaze out over the magnificent vistas before them.

Virgil liked it up here. Liked the sting of the wind on his face.

Liked breathing the rarefied air of the high altitudes. Liked drinking in the breathtaking views afforded by this vantage point.

Without realizing he was doing it, Virgil had chosen to exit the pine forest here so that he could show his pretty prisoner this very special spot. Some of the most magnificent scenery in all New Mexico was visible from this high mountain promontory and he wanted her to see it.

Four thousand feet below, the wide Tularosa Basin stretched all the way to the vast Chihuahuan Desert and the Border. A parched desert with almost no water and no shade, the barren basin lay between two high mountain ranges: the towering Sacramentos on the basin's eastern edge where they were now, and across the wide valley, the San Andres and Oscuros, deep blue shadows looming large on the western horizon, rolling southward to El Paso.

Virgil inhaled deeply of the cool, clear air and turned his head to see if she was enjoying the splendid sight as much as he. Expecting her to be at least a little awed by the dramatic panorama spread before them, he frowned when he saw that her eyes were closed.

"Jesus," he swore, disappointed and irritated, "you sleepy?"

"N-no," she choked.

"Then why the hell do you have your eyes closed?"

"Afraid," she managed weakly.

"Afraid? Of what?"

The princess swallowed with difficulty, and her racing heart tried to pound its way out of her chest. "Of . . . falling off . . . this . . . cliff."

Virgil stared at her. "You afraid of heights?"

"Y-yes."

"*You* are afraid of heights." It was statement now, and his tone was cynical. "You, the royal ruler of a mountain monarchy?" He shook his head. "I don't believe it."

"Believe anything you like!" She was on the verge of tears, "But get me down off this beast and away from the edge of this precipice!"

"As you wish, Your Majesty," Virgil said mockingly. He took one last drag off his cigarette, snuffed it out in the palm of his gloved hand, flicked it away into the wind, and swung down from the saddle. But when he stepped up beside her and saw how she was trembling, he softened a little. Laying a gentle hand on her trousered thigh, he spoke in a low, comforting voice. "It's all right now, Red. I'm here. Right here. You're safe. Just let go of the saddle horn, and I'll help you dismount."

Her throat aching with fear, her eyes still closed, she nodded, reluctantly released her hold on the saddle horn. When she felt his hands firmly enclose her waist, a shudder of relief raced through her. Still afraid to open her eyes, she anxiously grabbed at his shoulders and didn't release him even when he set her on her feet. Instead, her arms slipped anxiously around him, and she clung to him as though she would never let him go, pressing her face against his chest, shaking and sobbing. Realizing just how frightened she was, Virgil didn't tease her. He drew her close and held her, soothing her with soft-spoken words of reassurance.

"I've got you now," he said in a low whisper. "I've got you, baby. I won't let you fall." The princess nodded against his chest and dug her fingertips into his back. He continued talking, consoling her with the calming cadence of his voice. "There's no need to be frightened. You're safe here in my arms." He tightened his arms around her. "It is so beautiful up here, Red. Have you ever been here before?" No answer. But the fierce trembling was subsiding, she was beginning to relax against him. "If you haven't, you really should have a look." She hugged him more tightly, buried her face. He raised a hand, stroked her gleaming ginger hair. "Tell you what, you can stay right where you are. I'll just turn you in my arms so that you can have a quick look. What do you say? Think maybe you could open your eyes if I promise not to move?"

"How close are we to the edge?" was her shaky reply, the words muffled against his chest.

"Not that close, but we can move back even farther." With that he began to walk slowly backward, bringing her with him. When he stopped, he told her, "Now we're a long way from the edge. I wouldn't lie to you. Open your eyes and see for yourself."

Reluctantly lifting her head, the princess allowed him to slowly turn her about so that she was facing the same way he was. His arms remaining around her, his jaw brushing her temple, he coaxed, "Look, Red, from here you can see for a hundred miles."

The princess cautiously opened her eyes. He hadn't lied to her about being back away from the cliff's edge. They were standing a good ten yards from the rocky rim. The horses had followed, were now behind them at the edge of the trees, contentedly cropping grass.

Feeling more secure, the princess cautiously eased out of Virgil's arms. But she wasn't ready to completely let go of him. Standing close beside him, she clung tenaciously to his shirtsleeve as she gazed out at the breathtaking vistas. Awed by the dazzling beauty of the place, she blinked, lifted a hand to shade her eyes, and stared at the hazy blue mountains on the horizon, then lowered her gaze to the wide, desertlike valley far below. Her fingers gripping Virgil's shirtsleeve, she peered in childlike wonder at a faroff strip of the basin at the base of the distant western mountains. She couldn't believe her eyes. It was covered with pristine white snow! How very odd, she thought, that snow would have fallen on the warm flat land when there was none here on the mountains where they were.

"Look!" she exclaimed excitedly, "there's snow way down there in the valley!"

Virgil chuckled. "That's not snow."

"Not snow? But it must be, it's—"

"It's sand."

"Sand?" She looked up at him with questioning eyes. "But it's as white as—"

" Sugar," he finished for her. "Yes, it is. The White Sands of New Mexico. They stretch north and south for miles. You'll see when we get closer."

"We are going to ride all the way down there?"

He nodded. "By sunset we should be almost down to the desert floor."

For a long moment he said nothing more, nor did she. They stood side by side on the high, stark rimrock as a golden eagle left its perch in the stony battlements above and wheeled gracefully on a rising current of air. They watched until the eagle disappeared in the clear blue sky. Then Virgil, smiling, pointed to a jutting rock ledge a few hundred feet down the mountain. An old tawny mountain lion lay sunning himself on the warm sandstone. As if the lion felt their eyes on him, he lazily rose, yawned, stretched languidly, then slowly padded away.

Enchanted, the princess watched until the big beautiful cat had gone completely out of sight. She sighed and took a deep breath of the clear, crystalline air. In the quiet she could hear the whisper of the wind in the trees and the bubbling of the stream rushing down its rocky bed. She could smell the fresh fragrance of the pines and the clean, unique scent of the tall, rugged Texan beside her.

The pair continued to stand there together on that rocky, windswept summit as Virgil pointed out well-known landmarks. Listening, nodding, the princess automatically swayed closer to him, her gaze following his pointing finger.

". . . and up to the north, Tres Rios. Three Rivers. The little village of La Luz down the mountainside. San Nicolas Pass across the valley to the south. Chalk Hill over there at the eastern edge of the White Sands and . . ."

As the princess listened to his deep-timbred voice, a rare feeling of contentment washed over her. She had completely forgotten, for the moment, who she was, who he was, where they were, and why.

Then she caught herself.

She snapped out of the rosy glow and was instantly upset and angry with herself for so foolishly falling under his spell. Naturally she took that anger out on him. She turned, glared up at Virgil, and interrupting him in midsentence, said, "You cruel, insensitive bastard! You did it on purpose, didn't you?"

Astonished by her quick change of mood, Virgil squinted in puzzlement. "Did what? What the hell are you talking about?"

"Brought me up here!" She flung out her arm and made a wide sweeping arc. "Led my mare out onto the very edge of this dangerous cliff! You wanted to scare me! I know you did!" Her teeth gritted, she doubled up her fist, and, before Virgil discerned her intention, hit him squarely in the stomach.

"Owwww," he groaned, and his breath came out in a *whosh* as he bent over slightly from the waist, a hand gripping his midsection.

Realizing immediately that she had actually hurt him, the princess attempted to dance out of his reach. She wasn't quite quick enough. He managed to grab the tail of her borrowed blue shirt. She screeched as he reeled her in.

"Ohhh!" she cried out in pain, when he slammed her roughly against his tall frame. "You're hurting me!" she shouted.

She struck out at him in a fury, and heard him yelp when the tip of a slender finger somehow connected with his right eye. His hand automatically shot up to cover his stinging, watering eye, and he cursed under his breath. But he didn't let go of her. Momentarily blinded in one eye, he kept the other eye open and on her. With one firm hand he held her to him and let her continue to flail away before finally crushing her in his big arms.

"I'm hurting you?" he said, incredulous, holding her tight, refusing to let her go, his burning eye still closed and watering. "Christ, I've been with you less than twenty-four hours and you've scratched my jaw, bloodied my ear, punched me in the belly, and almost put my eye out."

Struggling against him, she said, "My, my, so the big bad Ranger's afraid of a helpless little female." She again tried to pull away.

"No," he drawled. "I'm afraid of crazy people."

It was as if he had thrown kerosene on fire. Highly insulted, she blazed with new anger. "I'm glad I hurt you!" she exploded. "That's nothing compared to what you deserve! If I get half a chance, I'll . . . I'll . . ."

"You won't," he cut in, continuing to hold her in a viselike grip as she thrashed about.

"Don't bet on it, Ranger!"

"Let's ride," he said, abruptly loosening his hold, turning and heading for the horses, pulling her along by her shirt front. "I'd like to get you to El Paso while I'm still in one piece."

17

She stood alone on the wide stone balcony.

The summer sun had not yet risen, but the dim gray light preceding it now seeped over the sleeping city. A steadily brightening glow of pale pink streaked the eastern sky. Within minutes the huge orange disk would climb above the earth's curve and cast its blinding radiance over the old river city of San Antonio.

And over the elegantly gowned young woman who was on the hotel balcony.

A gentle breeze off the San Antonio River lifted loosened tendrils of ginger-red hair and softly rustled the many flounces of shimmering feuille-morte taffeta. The woman lifted a pale hand, gently swept a raised flounce back down into place, off her bare ivory shoulder. But she did not immediately release the ruffle. She ran her fingers over the satiny silver-white fabric and sighed.

Montillion had told her that the exquisite silver-white gown—one of the finest of the Princess's many ceremonial gowns—was a Doucet, delivered straight from the rue de la Paix to the Hartz-Coburg castle. When she had looked blankly at him, he had said kindly, "The dress came from Paris, my dear. You'd do well to remember in case one of the wealthy Texas ladies should ask."

The Queen of the Silver Dollar was glad he had told her because at that night's gala, not one, but a half-dozen ladies had admired the silver-white ball gown and inquired about its designer. With total ease and confidence she had replied, "Why, it's a Doucet. He's simply my favorite French designer. So talented, knows instinctively which fabrics and colors best enhance one's looks."

"Do you suppose he would consider designing some dazzling ball gowns for me?" asked Mrs. Maggie Travis, a plump, pink-cheeked matron who was among San Antonio's Old Guard.

"Now, Maggie, I was planning to engage the noted French designer," said a dark-haired, statuesque woman in black lace who was reportedly one of Texas's richest young widows.

And so it went.

While the ladies had twittered over renowned dress designers, the gentlemen had eagerly gathered around her like bees around a sweetly pollinating spring flower. She was, as she had been at every event in Fort Worth, Dallas, and here in San Antonio, the undisputed center of attention.

It had been wonderful.

Every thrilling moment of it. Like a lovely dream from which she never wanted to awaken. These past two glorious weeks had shown her precious glimpses of the privileged life she had surely been meant to lead.

A splendid existence with all the royal trappings. Catered to and waited on hand and foot. Not expected, no, more than that, not even allowed to dress herself! For each and every bond rally or banquet, she was very carefully dressed by the capable lady-in-waiting, the baroness Richtoffen. And, no matter how late she returned from a lavish soiree, the baroness, dozing in a bedroom chair, awakened to undress her and tuck her into bed.

Montillion, dear resourceful Montillion, was constantly at her beck and call. Ever patient, ever kind, he consistently treated her as if she actually were a royal princess. With his encyclopedic knowledge regarding every facet of a sovereign's life, he had never once made her feel stupid when she asked a foolish question. On the contrary, he encouraged her to quiz him on anything about which she might be unsure. And she loved listening when he described—in such fine detail she could actually picture it—the beautiful little mountain kingdom of Hartz-Coburg and the three-hundred-room castle perched on the cliffs.

Montillion and the baroness were both so solicitous and supportive, they had successfully imbued her with the confidence to convince anyone she met that she was Her Royal Highness, Princess Marlena of Hartz-Coburg.

So comfortable had she been playing the part, there had been occasions when she forgot—for an hour, sometimes longer—that she was not actually the princess. It seemed so real, so right. All the attention, the admiration, the adoration; it should have been hers.

Thinking back over the past two wonderful weeks, the Queen of the Silver Dollar smiled as she attempted to recall the number of marriage proposals she had received. It was impossible. She had lost count well before they reached San Antonio. Such, she supposed, was the glorious, everyday life of a princess.

She sighed wistfully.

It was over.

All over.

Last night's sumptuous wine supper and the following midnight ball at the Alamo Hotel was to be her last official appearance. There were, of course, more rallies, banquets, and parties planned for the days ahead.

But she would not be attending.

Montillion had told her that today—early in the afternoon in plenty of time to make the four P.M. bond rally—the real princess, now recovered, was scheduled to arrive in San Antonio.

All at once, to her surprise and dismay, Robbie Ann felt her eyes misting with tears. She was shocked at herself. She'd never been the sentimental sort, had wasted little time yearning for what might have been. Now here she was standing on a Texas hotel balcony crying because she was destined to nothing better than a return to her post at the Silver Dollar Saloon and—sooner or later—a reunion of sorts with her neglectful lover, British Bob.

Lost in troubled thought, she started when Montillion's well-modulated voice, coming from just behind, said, "Child, it's daybreak, why aren't you in bed?"

Not wanting him to see her tears, she didn't turn around. She blinked anxiously and said, "I—I was just about to come inside."

The concerned factotum joined her at the balcony's stone railing as the rising sun cleared the horizon. "What are you doing out here alone?" he asked, placing a square hand atop hers on the railing. She smiled, but didn't trust herself to speak, or even to look at him. Frowning with worry, Montillion reached up, gently cupped her chin in his hand, turned her face toward him, and saw the diamond drops of tears matting her long dark lashes.

"Oh, my dear, child," he said, understanding immediately. "You're sad, of course."

"Sad? Why should I be sad?" she said, smiling ruefully, "Just because I've turned back into a pumpkin. That's no reason to be sad."

"This is all my fault," he said, his brow creased with care.

"No. No, it's not," she said, taking the clean linen handkerchief he quickly offered and dabbing at her eyes. "The fault is mine."

Silently remonstrating himself, Montillion shook his graying head

THE PRINCESS GOES WEST

and said, "None of the blame is yours, child. I should never have done this to you."

She smiled bravely. "You should never have done what? Given me the best two weeks of my entire life? Don't be ridiculous. I'm very glad that you did." But even as she said it, fresh tears welled up in her eyes.

"No," he was unconvinced, "it was a terrible mistake. It was wrong. I never considered your feelings when—"

"I was eager to play the part of the princess," she cut in, "and I'm happy to have been given the opportunity. Really. After all," she managed a weak smile despite her tears, "it was the best role of my career."

Tenderhearted, Montillion was deeply touched. He placed a fatherly arm around her slender shoulders and said, "If it helps any, I want you to know, you are an exemplary princess."

"*Was* an exemplary princess," she corrected.

Patting her bare arm affectionately, he sighed wearily and said, "Child, at times we all question our lot in life. I, myself, have wondered why it couldn't have been me who sat on the throne of the Hartz-Coburg kingdom instead of the old king."

"You have?" she looked up at him, surprised that he would have ever entertained such a disloyal thought.

"I have," he admitted with a self-mocking laugh. "But not often. Generally I am most content with my station in life. I am needed in my position and that is reward in itself. Besides, consider, if you will, all the duties a sovereign *must* perform. They have no choice. Think of the countless strictures placed on them. And the constant worry over the financial health of their kingdom. Their entire life is spent in service that surely must seem, at times, like a never-ending prison sentence. They have little freedom. Even when they choose a mate, it is generally done for the good of the crown. Love has little or nothing to do with royal marriages. A monarch listens not to his heart, but to his head." Montillion fell silent, hoping what he'd said helped soothe her hurt a little.

Feeling better, her old spunk quickly resurfacing, Robbie Ann said, "Shoot, Monty, if I were the princess, I wouldn't mind marrying some titled rich man to save the crown. And I wouldn't even care if he was twice my age. I've always had a fondness for older men." Thoughtfully she added, "Maybe it's because I never knew my father."

Montillion cleared his throat needlessly and quickly changed the subject.

18

"Excuse me, Captain," the princess called out, "I think it's time we stop to rest."

"When I want your opinion, I'll ask for it," Virgil said over his shoulder. "Until I do, keep it to yourself."

Her face flushing beet red, she said irritably, "You know, I hate to say this, but—"

"Then don't," he cut her off.

Irritation turned to anger. She shouted at the top of her lungs, "You are the meanest man I have ever had the misfortune of meeting!"

"That's me," replied Virgil, unruffled "I'm one *muy malo hombre."*

It was nearing noon.

The entire morning, beginning with the early dawn scuffle, had gone much the same way. The princess, unable and unwilling to change the habits of a lifetime, attempted, at every turn, to boss the taciturn Texas Ranger around.

Big mistake.

Virgil Black was not accustomed to any woman supposing she could tell him what to do. And he sure didn't cotton to it. Few people got under his skin, but this overbearing female he was transporting to a Texas jail was beginning to annoy the hell out of him.

"Herr Kapitan," she tried again after a few minutes, her voice soft and modulated, "I realize I'm getting on your nerves, but I—"

"I have no nerves," he said, concluding the conversation.

The princess sighed, genuinely bewildered by his indifference. She was beginning to realize that—for the first time in her life—she didn't have the upper hand here.

He did.

Damn him.

Just her dismal luck to be apprehended by the only lawman on earth who would not listen to reason and could not be easily distracted. Not even by her. Captain Virgil Black was, it was becoming crystal clear, totally single-minded in his resolve to deliver her to the El Paso County jail. Never mind that he had the wrong woman! She had given up on setting him straight. What was the use of wasting any more breath in futile attempts to convince this big, dark, sullen Texas Ranger that she was *not* the thief he thought her to be.

For several minutes, the princess said nothing more to Virgil. But she made sour faces at his back and she silently vowed that he would pay dearly for the misery he had dealt her.

The mounted pair had spent the sunny June morning descending down out of the rugged high country. Following the rail bed, they had made sure, slow, steady progress. They had wound their way down twisting, treacherous mountain trails, rapidly losing altitude.

Squinting his eyes now under his pulled down hat brim, Virgil studied the perilous terrain cautiously. Keenly alert, he tirelessly searched ahead for spots of risky footing or unexpected drop-offs or impassable places along the plummeting switchback trail.

It wasn't just perilous topography that had his rapt attention. He was careful to check every jutting cliff, every narrow shoot-off canyon, every towering, thick branched tree and scrubby brush for lurking danger of another kind. Renegade Apache and armed outlaws were a far bigger concern to Virgil Black than the hazards of the coiling, curving path.

A seasoned veteran of Texas's foremost peacekeeping force, Virgil had trained himself to be constantly on the lookout for even the smallest signs of trouble. Nobody was better at noticing fresh hoofprints, even in rocky regions. Or spotting the remnants of a campfire someone had tried to conceal. Or at picking up clues from nothing more than a broken tree branch or a dislodged boulder.

Detecting no evidence of intruders, Virgil reined the surefooted stallion onto a narrow stretch of railroad right-of-way and out onto a wooden trestle high above a rocky ravine. He was still leading the dappled gray mare.

To this, at least, the princess had no objection. She didn't really want to take over the reins until they had lost most of the altitude. The rough, uneven ground they'd covered so far had dropped so quickly in spots she had a bad case of the jitters. Her anxiety escalated when she saw that they were heading onto a high wooden railroad trestle. When, nearing the trestle's center, the Ranger abruptly drew rein, halting the stallion and the mare on a dime, the princess was at first puzzled. Then she saw his reason for stopping, and she shuddered involuntarily.

This trestle, like the one just three miles out of Cloudcroft, had been blown up. A portion of the wooden structure—directly before them at the trestle's center—was missing.

"What shall we do?" she asked, looking about, seeing no way out of their predicament.

Virgil turned in the saddle, fixed her with those riveting blue eyes, and said calmly, "Jump it."

"Jump it?" she repeated, incredulous, and her well-arched eyebrows immediately knitted. Staring at him, she shook her head forcefully. "You're teasing me, of course. That's it, isn't it? A tasteless prank. You've a warped sense of humor, Captain Black! You obviously take perverse pleasure in frightening the daylights out of me."

"I've got to hand it to you, Queenie," Virgil said with bland innocence. "You've figured me out, all right. Yes, indeedy. Fact is I've been really hoping that the Apaches had blown this trestle up so I could give you a real good scare." His jaw flexed then, and pinning her with icy-blue eyes, he added, "Never in my thirty-four years have I met a more self-absorbed human being. Jesus, you think the entire world revolves around your beautiful ass."

The princess gasped, horrified by his crude language. "Why you crass bastard! You can't . . ."

"I can," he calmly interrupted, "anything I like." She started to speak, he stopped her with a raised hand. "Listen to me, Red. This is not some game we're playing here and I'm not trying to frighten you. There is absolutely nothing here to be afraid of. Nothing. The segment of trestle that's missing is no more than ten to twelve feet. The horses can easily jump it."

"Noooo," she murmured, her rounded eyes quickly narrowing. "I will not do it! There must be another route."

"Sure, there is," he told her. "Look below. We can swim the horses across. But we'll have to be very careful. The water's moving pretty fast."

The princess hazarded a glance at the boiling, rushing water far below. Tree limbs and debris, swept into the surging stream, flashed by in the swelling, splashing torrent.

"We would drown," she declared, her voice shrill.

"A possibility," he agreed. "So we are going to jump."

"Oh, dear God." She breathed shallowly and her face paled.

Virgil took pity on her. "You can ride over with me on Noche."

Comforted a little by the prospect, she asked, "What about the mare?"

"She'll follow the stallion across. Don't worry about her making it." He pushed back his hat brim with a forefinger. "What do you say?"

She nodded but stayed where she was, too scared to move.

Virgil exhaled heavily and swung down off the black. In three long strides he was to her and plucking her out of the saddle. When he set her on her feet and released her, the nervous princess didn't move away from him. She stood as close as she could while he looped the mare's reins around the saddle horn and tied them.

Virgil patted the mare's sleek neck and murmured soothingly into her pricked ear, "You can do it, girl. Noche will lead the way. All you have to do is follow him." The mare whinnied and tossed her head.

Virgil turned abruptly and found the princess practically standing on top of him. Frowning, he took her hand in his and led her to the stallion. She was puzzled when he dropped her hand and mounted the black first. But when he leaned down, reached for her, and drew her up behind him, she understood. She might be a hindrance if she were seated in front of him.

The princess started to put her arms around him, but stopped herself. Instead, she gripped the saddle's cantle and pressed her denim-clad knees close to the stallion's belly, hoping she could hang on when the big beast leaped the chasm.

Virgil reined the big black around in a slow, tight semicircle and walked him off the trestle. The mare followed docilely on the stallion's heels. When they reached the place where the railbed widened just before the wooden trestle commenced, Virgil again reined the stallion around.

Over his shoulder, he softly inquired, "Ready, Red?"

She swallowed anxiously and said, "Promise I won't fall to my death!"

"Promise," he said. Then, "But you better put your arms around me and hold on tight."

She gave no reply but hurriedly wrapped her arms around him, clasping her hands together over his hard waist. She felt him shift in the saddle as he touched his big-roweled spurs lightly to the black's powerful flanks. Then her head snapped back from the swift motion as the stallion went from standing stock-still to a thundering gallop, rushing headlong onto the wooden trestle. The gray mare raced after him.

The princess flattened herself as close to the Ranger's back as she could, closed her eyes tightly, and pressed her cheek against Virgil's muscular shoulder. Her heart drumming in tempo with the stallion's clattering hoofbeats, she offered up a quick, brief prayer to the Almighty.

Get me through this and I'll be a saint for the rest of my days!

In a matter of seconds she felt the powerful black's hooves leave the wooden trestle as he leaped into the air. It seemed to her that they hung suspended over the abyss for a tortuously long time before she finally felt the welcome jarring of her body against the black's rump and the Ranger's back as the stallion landed loudly on wood. The mare's hooves struck seconds later.

Virgil immediately reined the stallion down and said over his shoulder, "You can open your eyes now, we're on the other side of the trestle."

"My eyes are not closed!" she said indignantly, wondering why he had to constantly be such an insulting know-it-all.

"My mistake," he said, his tone of voice indicating he knew better.

Princess Marlena, gritting her teeth, swiftly withdrew her arms from around him. "I want to get down now," she told him haughtily.

"As you wish," Virgil said, turned halfway around in the saddle, crooked a long arm around her waist, lifted her as easily as if she were a small child, and deposited her on the trestle.

She stood there looking up at him, waiting for him to dismount and put her on the mare's back. He stayed in the saddle, fished in his shirt pocket for a cigarette, stuck it between his lips, and lit it. Then took his own sweet time drawing the smoke deep down into his lungs and leisurely releasing it.

Virgil blew a perfect smoke ring and said, "Any possibility you can mount the mare all by yourself?"

The minute he said it, he was half-sorry.

She stood directly below, looking suddenly small and vulnerable. Her emerald eyes were the questioning eyes of a child, and faint traces of terror were still clearly written on her pale, lovely face. The jump over the ravine, while not actually dangerous, had genuinely frightened her. She was, he realized, still badly unnerved.

Squinting at her, Virgil felt his chest suddenly tighten. A twinge of guilt, the kind to which he was a stranger, momentarily plagued him.

Maybe he had been too hard on her. He had, he realized, treated her with scant civility. He wondered why, but had no answer. Seized with remorse, he purposely softened his expression, climbed down out of the saddle to stand facing her, and said almost apologetically, "Can I give you a hand?"

But his tranquil tone and kind offer came too late. Tired of his insults and insensitivity, the princess stiffened her backbone, lifted her royal chin, and said, "You can't give me anything!" She took a step backward, spun on her heel, and stalked away, saying, "Nor can you *take* anything from me, Captain Black!"

19

Princess Marlena managed, after a couple of failed attempts, to mount the mare on her own. When she was securely in the saddle, she tossed Virgil an I-don't-need-you look and began untying the reins from the saddle horn.

"No, you don't." In the blink of an eye he was beside her, easily wresting the reins away from her. "Like it or not, you are my responsibility, and I aim to deliver you unharmed to the authorities."

"You'll never get me to El Paso!" she told him hotly. Virgil didn't bother to refute the statement. Disappointed by his lack of reaction, she said with scathing authority, "I am warning you—"

"Don't warn me," he casually cut her off, gazing at her dispassionately.

He looped the mare's reins over her head, and the gray nickered and nudged his shoulder, wanting him to pet her. He didn't. He led her up alongside the black, climbed into the saddle, and they set out once more.

The princess ground her teeth in growing frustration. He always got the last word. Worse, nothing she did or said seemed to penetrate his invisible shield of steely armor. He possessed the power to upset her with just a word or a look, but she couldn't seem to get his goat no matter what she did. He effortlessly kept her off-balance and unsure of herself while he projected an unwavering attitude of cool confidence. Lord, how she longed to see him slip the sanguine pose and reveal something of himself.

The hell with him! No. She wouldn't give him another minute's thought.

The princess took her eyes off the Ranger's black-shirted back and looked around. What she saw pleased her. The steep rocky ground abutting the ruined railroad trestle had turned now into a sloping grassy meadow. Her slender shoulders relaxed. She sighed with relief. The worst part of the journey was behind her. There could be nothing ahead that would be half as dangerous as jumping the wide, gaping void beneath the blown-up wooden trestle.

Thank heaven.

Not a half hour later the princess learned, to her horror, how wrong she had been. Jumping the trestle had been nothing compared to what lay just ahead. They had rounded a bend and come upon a high, windswept ledge so narrow they didn't dare ride out onto it. They had to walk and lead the horses. The ledge was barely wide enough for a horse. Below, a drop of more than a thousand feet awaited the misplacement of a foot or a hoof. White as a ghost and sick with fear, the princess tried not to think what it would be like to have a kid slipper slide and give way. To feel herself falling to the rocks below.

To make matters worse, a fierce wind was now blowing with gusts so strong she was sure she would be blown off the ledge to her death. After ten spine-tingling minutes of edging slowly along the high ledge's travertine twists and turns, the princess's stomach churned when, despite his warnings not to, she looked down. She was instantly dizzy, clammy, and unable to move.

Virgil, following closely on her heels, knew what had happened. Angry with her for disobeying and putting all their lives in jeopardy, he turned slowly to the stallion he was leading and spoke to him in low, soft tones, warning him not to make a move. Then, carefully releasing the reins, Virgil, speaking in the same calming tone he'd used with the stallion, told her of his intent.

"I'm right behind you and I'm moving steadily closer. Don't be startled when I touch you. I am going to put my arms around you. Right now."

As he spoke Virgil stepped up to the paralyzed princess, slowly, carefully put his arms around her and drew her into his close embrace.

Against her sun-burnished hair he murmured, "Only a few more short yards to go, Red. Then, I promise you, the rest of the way is a piece of cake. The trick is to never look down. Pretend you're strolling along the sidewalk back in Las Cruces." He gently rubbed her back, patted it, held her trembling body next to his. "We're nearly there, baby, nearly there." He continued to hold her close and to speak to her in a low, comforting voice. But she was inconsolable. Quickly, he realized that she was not going to make it. She was incapable of taking one more step. She was stranded where she was. She couldn't go forward and she couldn't go back. He was left with no choice. He would have to carry her the rest of the way.

"Tell you what I'm going to do," he said as casually as if he was making pleasant dinner conversation. "I'm going to take your arms from around me for just one second. No more. See, like this." He did just that as he spoke. "Then, while I continue to stand here in this same spot, close to you, I am going to turn around so that we are facing the same way, with me directly in front of you. You can continue to hold on to me." He turned then, carefully, slowly, with her clinging frantically to him. "And now I'm going to take your arms and put them around my neck." He drew her arms up around his neck. "Good girl," he praised, as her slender body pressed as close against his back as possible. He told her of his intent again as he crouched down slightly, put his hands around the backs of her knees, and cautiously eased her up onto his back.

The rest of the trek along the high, narrow, windswept ledge was completed with the princess riding Virgil piggyback while he lead the stallion and the mare followed.

Virgil was totally focused. He *had* to get her to safety. He steeled himself to disregard the fact that her forearms, clasped tightly around his throat, were pressing on his Adam's apple, causing him to have choking sensations. Or that her firm thighs squeezed his ribs so tightly, he could barely breathe. Or that the heels of her small slippered feet, crossed at the ankle in front of him, were gouging into his groin so intensely, it was painful.

His quick mind, like his lean body, was well trained. He was able to put everything aside and concentrate solely on taking one well-placed step at a time. With the keen eyes of an animal, he examined every inch of the perilous path before him. And as he carefully placed his booted feet, one before the other, he promised, "We're as good as there. A few more steps. That's all."

When the danger was past, when the ledge widened at last onto a tree-studded slope, Virgil felt a sudden weakness in his legs. And, as sometimes happens after a protracted period of extreme stress, he started to laugh. The princess, finally releasing her choke hold on his throat, slid off his back and she, too, began to laugh.

They sank to their knees and, laughing uproariously, soon fell over onto their backs. They lay there on the shade-dappled grass and laughed and laughed.

Virgil regained his composure first. A wide grin splitting his black-whiskered face, he turned onto his side and watched her.

What a sight she was. Tears of laughter spilling down her flushed cheeks, she looked like a carefree schoolgirl. Her hair had come undone from the bolo tie and swirled like a copper cloud around her beautiful face.

Rocked again and again by great peels of laughter, she kicked her feet in the air and tossed about on the grass. One of her kid slippers had come off and lay on the ground near her knee. Her borrowed blue shirt had drifted up around her midriff and the too-large Levi's had floated down almost to the danger point.

Innocently unaware and uncaring that she was exposing so much pale flesh, she lay there on her back laughing hilariously, eyes closed, bare belly jerking with her convulsions.

Virgil's eyes, swiftly darkening, were riveted to her. He couldn't look away. Her bunched-up shirt afforded tempting glimpses at the bare underside of her left breast. Pale and luminous, it looked so soft and warm Virgil's mouth watered. His fingers itched to push the shirt's blue cotton fabric an inch or two higher, just enough for a quick flash of a pale pink nipple.

He licked his dry lips and let his smoldering gaze slide slowly down her body. She was so slender, every rib showed beneath the flawless alabaster skin. Her denim pants had slipped below one prominent hipbone and were snagged precariously on the other. Her pale, bare stomach was so flat it was almost concave. He focused on her navel. Like all the rest of her, hers was an appealing belly button. Equally appealing was the almost imperceptible line of wispy pale ginger hair descending from that cute belly button and disappearing into the waistband.

A vein pulsed in Virgil's throat.

He lay on his side, staring unblinkingly at her.

Not touching her.

Wanting to touch her.

Needing to touch her.

He had an acute craving to lean over, bend his head, and press his open lips to her pale belly. To kiss his way up to the warm underside of that half-exposed breast and nudge the shirt up with his face until his lips could close over a smooth, sleeping nipple.

But even that would not have been enough.

Not nearly enough.

He wanted to brush his bearded face back and forth in the shadowed plain between her rising hipbones. To place his mouth squarely over her navel and kiss it as if he were kissing her lips. To put out his tongue and trace that narrow little line of silky hair down to where it vanished inside her pants. To pull the denims down with his teeth until they were out of his way so he could lower his hot face and scatter teasing, biting kisses up and down the warm insides of her alabaster thighs.

Virgil was so caught up in his carnal fantasy, he didn't realize that she had stopped laughing and thrashing about. When she started frantically shoving the long-tailed blue shirt down to cover herself, Virgil, lost in lust, automatically reached out to stop her, saying hoarsely, "No. Don't."

"Don't? Don't what?" she asked, slapping his hand away and levering herself up into a sitting position. "What are you talking about?"

Her voice, slightly shrill, pierced his prurient reverie. He immediately came to himself and his bearded face flushed beneath his tan. Shaken, not wanting her to know what had been running through his mind, he sounded more gruff than usual when he said, "Finally finished laughing? Good. Now maybe we can get back on the trail."

Confused by his quick change of mood, the princess said, "Me? You were laughing, too!"

Virgil rose agilely to his feet. "I'm not laughing now."

The princess jumped up, got right in his face. "Let me get this straight. When you are laughing, it is perfectly okay, the right thing to do. But, if I am laughing, it annoys you. It seems to me that everything I do annoys you. You may not believe this, Captain Black, but I am trying very hard not to annoy you."

A muscle danced in his jaw. He was confused and angry with himself for wanting her. This uncharacteristic flash of burning desire half frightened him. He had always controlled passion; passion had never controlled him.

Virgil took a defensive step away from her. His lower belly still tight, his heart thudding against his ribs, he did the human thing. He took out his frustration on her.

"I know," he said coldly, "and that annoys me."

20

The afternoon passed quietly, uneventfully, with the two of them exchanging very few words. Determined she would be as stubbornly uncommunicative as he, the princess showed Virgil the same closed expression he showed her.

Their progress good, they dropped lower and lower down the mountain, the trail winding through the tall pines and scattered Douglas firs, past clumps of oak and over loose flat rocks. They were less than fifteen hundred feet above the valley floor when Virgil abruptly reined in and dismounted.

Curious, the princess watched him walk a few feet off the trail and crouch down on his heels. He was looking with interest at something. He stayed there for a long minute, then rose and came directly to her.

"I want to show you something," he said, and plucked her out of the saddle.

"Indians?" she asked, as she stared down at the odd assortment of things gathered together beside the road. Piles of rock. Knotted rawhide strings. Hieroglyphics scratched on boulders.

"Apache messages," Virgil told her. "This is the way they keep in touch with each other."

"What are they saying?"

He shrugged. "Don't know. What I do know is we have to be very careful from here on out." He looked directly at her. "You understand me?"

"I am not dimwitted, Captain," she declared.

"Good. Then you know better than to get out of my sight."

*   *   *

On they rode.

Finally, as the burning summer sun was dropping behind the blue-purple peaks of the distant Oscuras, they stopped for the night. While Virgil unsaddled the horses, the princess examined the campsite. The spot he had chosen was a nice flat plateau, studded with cedars and carpeted with grass. On one side of the grassy mesa, a narrow stream splashed down from above.

Princess Marlena, casting a glance at Virgil, leisurely crossed the plateau, reached the front edge, and peered cautiously down. And sighed, her shoulders relaxing. No dangerous drop-off here. Just a long sloping hill covered with loose gravel and scattered patches of sparse underbrush. Nothing to be afraid of.

Shading her eyes against the sun's glaring gloaming, she gazed out at the valley which they were sure to reach early tomorrow. And then . . .

The princess emitted a sudden loud shriek of surprise as, moving her right foot slightly, she slipped on a pebble. Instantly she found herself hurling headlong down the rock-strewn hillside. She managed to stay on her feet, but couldn't stop herself from speeding down the incline.

Virgil heard the shriek and came running. She was already halfway down the hillside when he plunged anxiously over the edge and chased after her. His legs longer and more powerful, he caught up to her within seconds but knew if he reached out and grabbed her, they were both sure to fall and roll the rest of the way down the hill. If that happened, she might be badly hurt.

He raced on past her while she shouted, "Stop me! Stop me!"

Almost to the bottom, Virgil managed to plunge a stiffened left leg into the loose shale, twist his body slightly, and bring himself to a swift halt. He dug in his heels and got his balance. Then he turned quickly, arms outstretched, ready to catch her.

The round-eyed princess slammed directly into him running full force, managing somehow, to get him in the ribs with a sharp, punishing elbow. Virgil let out a muffled yelp, but ignoring the pain, he enclosed her in his protective arms and kept her from falling.

"You all right?" he asked, then gritted his teeth in agony.

"Yes, yes I believe I am," she said, not thinking to ask if he was hurt.

"Well, I'm not," he said, releasing her, putting his hand to his left side.

"You're not?" She automatically reached out to touch him. He grimaced and she snatched her hand away. "What is it?"

"A rib," he told her.

"Oh, dear me," she said, looking up at him. "I do hope you didn't break it."

"I didn't," he said, face tight. "You did."

"I?" she said, offended. "Why must you blame everything on me?"

"You got me with your elbow, Red," he said. Then, "Maybe the rib's just badly bruised."

"Is there a physician close?" she asked.

His face etched in pain, Virgil said, "You will be the doctor."

Not sure what he meant, she said, "Such nonsense. I am no physician, and I have never tended a sick or injured person in my life."

"There's a first time for everything," he told her. "Now, you'll have to help me here. Get me back up the hill."

The princess exhaled. "How? I can't possibly—"

Interrupting, Virgil said, "Step in here real close to me. That's right. Now, drape my arm over your shoulder—no! Jesus Christ not that one!" He grimaced as she yanked on his left arm, the upward motion pulling painfully on the injured rib.

"Sorry," she said and moved quickly to his right side, drew his long arm over her slender shoulders, and wrapped her hand around his wrist.

"Now, put your arm around my waist," he instructed.

She put her arm around him, hooked her fingers around his belt, and looked up at him.

He said, "What are you waiting for?"

Nodding, the princess struggled manfully to get him back up the rock-slippery hill. He was so much bigger than she, it was all she could do to support him as he leaned heavily on her. A couple of times she had to stop to get her breath. Once she stumbled on loose rocks and almost fell, but quickly righted herself.

With effort they reached the camp with just enough light left to see. One-handed, Virgil unbuttoned his black-yoked shirt, pulled the long tails free of his trousers with his right hand, and sat down on the ground. The princess, a few feet away, was bent over, hands on her knees, gasping for breath.

When her breathing slowed and she straightened, Virgil said, "This shirt comes off over my head."

"Yes," she said, "I know. Why are you telling me this?"

Needing her help, he labored to conceal his frustration. In an even voice, he said, "You'll have to help me get it off."

"Oh, yes, of course," she said, stepped closer, leaned down and gripped the shirt's long tails. She peeled the shirt up his torso and heard him groan as he raised his arms so she could take it off. Tossing the shirt aside, the princess sank to her knees before him. "What will you do now?"

"Nothing," he said. "*You* will do everything."

She shook her head. "I can't. I have no idea how to do the kind of things that occupy the time of ordinary people. You see, I've never learned because it simply was not necessary. Why, I never even dressed myself until . . . until you . . ." She lifted her shoulders in an unapologetic shrug and admitted, "When it comes to tackling mundane tasks, you'll find that I am really quite useless."

His reply was, "You're fairly intelligent. Surely as intelligent as my stallion, Noche. I trained him. I'll bet you can be trained."

"Are you comparing me to a horse!" she said, outraged.

He replied, "Kindly move around behind me."

The princess stayed where she was. "I will not."

"Get behind me!" he ordered, and she, startled by his biting tone of voice, anxiously obeyed. "Now, carefully examine my back. That's where a broken rib can be most easily located."

Puzzled, having no idea how to search for a broken rib, the princess laid her hands on him. He had, she noticed immediately, a beautiful back. Perfectly shaped with wide muscular shoulders tapering down to a surprisingly narrow waist. His skin was smooth and deeply tanned, as if he had lain naked in the sun. And he was warm to the touch.

"Press your thumbs in the flesh on either side of the spine," Virgil directed, his tone now low, soft. The tip of her tongue caught between her teeth in concentration, the princess did as instructed. "Now, pressing with your thumbs, run them very slowly down my back, one on each side."

"Oh, Virgil," she said, using his name for the very first time, "I've found it! Right here, under my left thumb, a rib is protruding more than the others and . . . and . . . the one just below it feels like it is slightly prominent as well."

Nodding, he said, "I believe the actual break is in front. Come around and have a look."

The princess moved around directly in front of him. She put out her hands, and he guided them to where he thought the break was.

"Right there," he said, and she gasped audibly as her fingers found where one rib stuck out at an angle under his chest wall. He winced when she touched the spot.

"That's it," he said, lips thinned.

"What shall I do? I don't know—"

"There's a supply kit in my saddlebags. Get it and tape my ribs."

This time the princess didn't hesitate. She was up instantly and rushing to the saddlebags. Then back in a flash and falling to her knees before him. Following his instructions, she got out the roll of tape and then she was forced to reach inside his trouser pocket for his knife. She could feel her cheeks burning as her fingers searched for the knife. She didn't dare look at him. After several awkward pats and feels, she snagged the knife's end, and withdrew it so rapidly, the lining of his pocket came out with it. She didn't bother with stuffing it back in. Nor did he.

With a smooth mother-of-pearl case, the pocket-knife looked harmless enough until—complying with his orders—she eased the blade out and up. It glinted in the sun's dying red rays.

With Virgil patiently guiding her, the princess cut several long strips of the wide tape and carefully laid each one on the grass, with the sticky side up. He told her when she'd cut enough, and she closed the knife, laying it and the roll of tape aside. She raised her eyes to meet his.

"Now, you stretch those pieces of tape, one at a time, around me, starting at the backbone and pulling them as tight as you can get them in front. Think you can do that?"

"I shall try." She picked up a long strip of the wide tape and went to work.

"Yes, that's it," he commended as she pulled tape after tape as tight as she could get them around his back and halfway across his naked torso.

When the task was complete, the princess sank back on her heels and admired her handiwork. And, she admired the broad, symmetrical masculine chest with its appealing growth of curly jet hair. When she'd drawn the tapes tight, her knuckles had brushed the crisp raven hair, and the recollection now sent a thrill of strange excitement surging through her. She wondered how it would feel to lay an open palm against his warm muscular chest and twine some of that crisp curly hair around her fingers.

"Is something wrong?" Virgil's voice startled her, and she felt herself blushing.

"No. No," she said with a nervous laugh, "I . . . I was just thinking that . . . that when you take the tape off," she pointed, indicating the top piece of tape, "it is going to . . . to . . . yank out some chest hair."

"I'll cross that bridge when I get there," Virgil said. "Right now I'm in enough pain to keep me pretty well occupied." He gave her a hint of a self-deprecating smile and said, "Now, don't you think it's about time we have a bite to eat."

She looked at him. She looked around. "You haven't built a fire, so how can we—"

"No fire tonight, Red," he interrupted.

"Why? How can we possibly fix the evening meal without a fire? And how can we sleep tonight? Already it's getting cold. We *must* build a fire."

"Have you forgotten already what we saw on the trail not two hours ago?" He shifted his weight a little, grimaced, put a spread hand to his taped ribs, and said, "The Apaches. If we build a fire, they might see it."

"Dear God," she said, looking anxiously around, "will they kill us as we sleep?"

"Nope," he assured her. "We're safe enough tonight. The Apaches are unique, different from all other tribes. They rarely attack at night. They believe that the soul of a warrior killed at night must wander forever in darkness."

"If they won't attack at night, then I don't see why we can't have a campfire."

"If they're close by, a fire would alert them to exactly where we are. They wouldn't kill us tonight, but come morning they'd be waiting to ambush us." He paused, then added, "If, by any chance, you were attempting an escape a while ago when you went barreling down that hill—"

"I was not! I slipped and—"

"Let me remind you again that if the Apaches get us, I will likely die a quick, merciful death. You, however, will not. You're pale and you're pretty. Just the kind of woman the hostiles—"

"You have made your point, Captain," she cut him off. "I don't wish to hear more." She quickly changed the subject. "Now, I am quite hungry. Surely you mean to prepare us at least a cold supper of some kind."

"No, I don't. I mean for *you* to prepare us a cold supper."

"Me! Out of the question! Haven't you heard one word I said? I do not know the first thing about fixing meals. Hot or cold. I am, whether you can be convinced of it or not, a royal princess!"

"Well, Your Majesty, unless you want to go to bed hungry, you'll fix us something to eat."

"Oh, very well."

The princess grumbled to herself as she filled two tin plates with cold beans and beef jerky and stale bread. When they had finished eating, she really made her feelings known when Virgil told her to take the dirty dishes down to the stream and wash them. She did so, but as she crouched there on her heels in the gathering dusk dipping the tin plates into the water, she really let him have it. She expressed her feelings about him candidly, speaking loudly, on purpose, hoping he would hear every unkind word she said.

He did.

But it didn't particularly bother him.

When the princess returned carrying the clean tin plates and utensils, she was nonplussed to see that the Ranger had spread his bedroll and was retired for the night. Stretched out on his right side, blanket pulled up to his bare shoulders, he appeared to be fast asleep.

Her delicate jaw ridging with resentment, the princess raised the tin plates high above her head and released them. They clattered loudly to the ground.

Virgil calmly cocked one eye open and said, "If you're going to see how much noise you can make, you may as well build a fire." He yawned then, and said, "Better come on to bed before you freeze."

Princess Marlena's hands went to her hips. "If you think for one minute that I am ever going to lie down beside you again, you are an even bigger fool than I thought!"

"Suit yourself." His eyes closed again.

"I always do," she said, walked over, and unceremoniously yanked the blanket off him.

While Virgil drew the bottom blanket up over himself, the princess walked a good twenty yards away from him, spread the blanket, lay down, and pulled it around herself. She sighed and stretched and attempted to get comfortable. It wasn't easy. The ground was hard, and with the sunset had come a deep chill to the air. She knew she was going to spend a cold, miserable night. She consoled herself by thinking it would be the last one. Tomorrow she would get away from Black. She didn't know exactly how, but she would manage to escape. By this time tomorrow night, she would, with any luck, be sleeping in a soft, clean bed somewhere.

Her eyelids growing heavy, the plotting princess watched swallows dart about and heard a muted cacophony of insect sounds. Hoping nothing was crawling on her, she finally closed her eyes. They came open again when a quick series of eerie yelps rang loudly in the night silence.

She sat up. "What was that?"

"Coyotes," said Virgil. "Or Apaches."

The princess, hating herself for being a coward, shot to her feet and snatched up her blanket. She hurriedly crossed the twenty odd yards to Virgil. Not bothering to ask permission, she stretched out beside him and covered herself with the blanket. Virgil eased the one side of the blanket up, moved closer to her, and spread the cover over them both.

In that low, flat Texas twang he said, "To what do I owe this—"

"None of your smart remarks, Captain," the princess stopped him in midsentence. "I am most definitely not in the mood."

21

The princess soon fell asleep.

Virgil did not.

He was, of course, plagued with pain from the broken rib. But it wasn't physical discomfort that kept him awake. At least not the physical discomfort caused by an aching rib. Nor was it the hard ground. Or the cold night air. Or the yelp of the coyotes.

The ginger-haired woman sleeping next to him was responsible. She was, he had learned, exasperating, domineering, selfish, stubborn, foolish, and more damned trouble than any woman he had ever known. Yet, oddly enough, she was also interesting, appealing, entertaining, exciting, and incredibly tempting.

She lay now on her side, backed up close against him, slumbering peacefully.

There was no peace for him.

Not with silky strands of her wild hair pleasantly tickling his face. And the sound of her soft, even breathing, which was causing her breasts to rise and fall directly above the forearm he had wrapped around her. Most disturbing of all was her denim-clan bottom pressed intimately into his groin. It wouldn't have been so bad had she never moved about in her sleep.

She moved a lot.

She fidgeted. She wiggled. She twisted. She curled.

And with every move she made, she unconsciously ground her shapely little bottom against his pelvis.

Gritting his teeth, Virgil felt himself surge and strain against the restraint of his tight black trousers. His heart hammered in his naked chest. Perspiration formed in his hairline and above his upper lip. He moved back away from her. Never waking, she followed, her body instinctively seeking the animal warmth of his.

Long agonizing minutes passed.

A torturous half hour dragged slowly by.

Virgil's burning eyes never closed. And his pulsing, fully formed erection never diminished; stayed up and hot and hard, rising involuntarily to seek the enticing cleft in her buttocks. In all his life, nothing like this had ever happened to him. If not for the fact that he was in actual pain, he would have laughed at the absurdity of it. Here he was so rock-hard and burning hot he was almost feverish.

And, for God's sake, this raging desire was for a loose-moraled dance hall entertainer in whose bed he had been not three weeks ago and had fallen asleep without laying a hand on her.

It made no sense.

He hadn't wanted this woman enough that night to stay awake. Now he wanted her so badly he couldn't go to sleep.

Virgil slowly, carefully withdrew his arm from around the sleeping princess. He scooted back from her and slowly, carefully turned over so that he was lying on his bruised side, facing away from her.

Bent on putting an end to his painful predicament, he silently began naming all the men with whom he had served in the Texas Rangers over the past fifteen years. Memory flashes of the close calls and wild escapades he had shared with some of those Rangers helped distract him. He focused his mind away from the here and now and ordered his body to follow suit.

At last, Virgil exhaled with relief. His erection had deflated. The fever in his blood had cooled. His heart rate had slowed perceptibly.

But, just as he grew pleasantly calm and began to feel sleepy, the princess turned in her slumber, flung her arm around him, and pressed herself against his back. The misery started again.

Her small, warm hand was spread on his naked chest, her fingertips innocently entwined in the thick curly chest hair directly over his thundering heart. Her soft, rounded breasts were crushed against his bare back, and he would have sworn he could feel her soft nipples hardening, nudging provocatively into his flesh. With their positions reversed, it was now her denim-clad pelvis and thighs cupping his hard buttocks. His muscles there involuntarily flexed, and it seemed to him that her slender body stirred in answer, her groin pushing aggressively closer so that he lost his breath entirely.

It went that way all night.

A prolonged, strangely erotic duel of sweet agony between a sleeping woman and a tortured man. Two healthy bodies sensually writhing together. One soft, pale, slender. The other hard, dark, and lean. But strength and power did not conquer here. When the dawn finally drove out the darkness, the soft, pale, slender woman was well rested.

The hard, dark, lean man was exhausted beyond belief.

"I was wondering," the princess said, flashing her most dazzling smile, "if perhaps today you would train me to ride the way you ride. I mean, you know, allow me to hold the mare's reins and show me how to use them. I believe I proved yesterday that I am quite capable of following instructions. Your ribs are taped nicely, are they not?"

It was finally morning.

They were preparing to set out on the trail.

The princess, rested, talkative, and cheerful, was optimistically planning how she'd make her escape as soon as the opportunity presented itself. Perhaps today would be the day. But she needed to know how to handle her mount.

The Ranger, tired, silent, and sullen, was pessimistically thinking that if he didn't get this red-tressed bundle of trouble to El Paso soon, something was going to give. The pressure from her presence was steadily building. After last night's torment—for which there had been no release—he felt like a human stick of dynamite with a very short fuse. This slender, pale-skinned dance hall singer could light that fuse far too easily. A lowered-lashed look, a huskily spoken word, a soft warm touch, and he might well detonate.

"Well, will you?" The princess tilted her head to one side.

"Will I what?" said Virgil, tightening the saddle cinch under the gray mare's belly.

"Let me take the reins this morning. Your ribs are hurting, I know they are. If you have to lead the mare, it will put a strain on them and the pain will get worse."

The saddle cinch tightened and buckled, Virgil straightened, looked down at her with squinted, skeptical blue eyes. "Why this sudden concern for my welfare?"

Sensing instinctively that he felt a hint of attraction to her, the princess moved a step closer, wet her lips with the tip of her tongue, laid her right hand lightly on his chest, and said, "I deserve that, I know. I've been selfish and worrisome and I'm genuinely sorry." She playfully walked her fingertips up his chest to his tanned throat and, smiling seductively, said, "People can change, Captain Black. If they are given half a chance."

Virgil narrowed his eyes and dropped his gaze to her lips. The princess was startled by the way her heart leaped. She thought for a second he was going to lean down and kiss her, and she wasn't certain she could resist.

Virgil didn't kiss her.

He wrapped long gloved fingers around her wrist and moved her hand away. "Don't flirt with me, Red. And don't pretend you are worried about my ribs." Her smile quickly changed to a frown. He continued evenly, "You may take the mare's reins today, but don't suppose you can get away from me. So don't try. Noche could overtake the mare in less than thirty seconds." He paused, fixed her with a cold stare, and added cryptically, "But, if I have to come after you, it might affect my congenial mood."

"You are not one bit funny, Texan!" She brushed past him and mounted the mare.

Wordlessly, Virgil looped the long leather reins up over the mare's head and handed them to her. Before releasing them to her completely, he said, "Do as I tell you and you'll be okay."

Refusing to look at him, she nodded almost imperceptibly. Virgil spent the first half hour of the morning's ride telling her how to make the mare go and stop by using the reins. When he was confident she had the hang of it, he fell totally silent. At first the princess tried to carry on a conversation but soon gave up. It was clear that he was in no mood for idle chatter. He was, she admitted with a small twinge of regret, in no mood for her.

She couldn't believe it. He had flatly told her not to flirt with him. Such insulting audacity! The gentlemen she had known had been thrilled and flattered if she so much as favored them with a cordial nod. And, when she "flirted" with any one of them, the gentleman in question was quickly beside himself with joy. What was this big Texas Ranger made of that he could not be swayed by her celebrated beauty and charm? What, she wondered, would she have to do to get his undivided attention. And why, for heaven sake, did she care whether or not she could get his attention?

There was no sensible answer. None. She had never in her twenty-eight years met such an unresponsive male. His indifference was insulting.

Casting sidelong glances at Virgil as they rode through the low foothills, the princess wondered if the imperturbable Texas Ranger ever got upset. Really upset. Oh, she annoyed him, all right, but only in the fleeting way a pesky fly bothered the horses. She had never really "gotten to him." What, she wondered, would it take for her to disconcert him? What would it take to make him lose that constant cool confidence? Did he ever completely lose his temper? Was there hidden fire behind those frosty sky-blue eyes?

The Ranger's mannerisms both annoyed and attracted the princess. Those often evasive, yet penetrating glances. The way he casually leaned in the saddle. His negligible eyebrow moving or the sneering curve of his lips. His low, soft vocal delivery, which exuded such firm, unshakable confidence.

Captain Virgil Black was, she suddenly realized with a flash of uncharacteristic insight, at the very prime of life. He had reached that moment of poised maturity when he exuded neither boyish exuberance nor an old man's tired cynicism. He was at his peak, both physically and mentally.

The princess cast another quick covert glance at the Ranger, slumping comfortably in the saddle, and shivered inside. With a three-day growth of dense black beard and those scary eyes, he looked like a lusty pirate. Cold, hard, dark, and dangerous.

And irresistibly appealing.

To her chagrin, Princess Marlena was strongly attracted to this mysterious, ruggedly male Texan who never fawned over her like the many titled suitors she'd known.

Perversely, his I-don't-give-a-damn behavior intrigued her. Made her long to attract—and hold—his attention. She again attempted to carry on a conversation with him as they rode knee to knee, descending now down into the wide valley. She talked about the tiny mountain kingdom over which she was to rule. She spoke affectionately of her dear, deceased father, the king. She repeated her oft-told story of how she had come to America on a bond drive, had fallen ill and could not perform her royal duties.

But to her many revelations she got only a nod of his head. And to her many questions—questions about his family, his life in Texas, his plans for the future—she got only monosyllabic answers. Answers which revealed nothing. It was apparent that he was not interested in talking to her. It was apparent that he was not interested in her.

By midmorning, they had left the foothills behind and were well into the eastern edge of the wide Tularosa valley. The terrain had changed dramatically, the cool verdant mountains having given way completely to a flat dusty plain. Only sparse vegetation dotted the valley floor, and the sun had grown noticeably hotter. Still, Virgil managed to locate a small trickling stream to water the horses and rest for a few minutes.

But Princess Marlena was not concerned with resting. She didn't care that the narrow stream's cold, clear water might be the last they saw for hours or possibly days. She was, by now, almost desperate to attract the Ranger's attention.

Unsuccessful, she finally attempted to anger him. She was determined to upset him. To get a rise out of him. To have him react to her in a volatile manner would be somehow reassuring.

It didn't happen.

She insulted him. She accused him of secretly desiring her. She threatened him. She said everything she could think of to make him lose his temper. Nothing worked. The Ranger continued to sit slumped with his back against a tree, totally relaxed, smoking a cigarette while she stormed back and forth in front of him.

Finally, as coolly as if he were saying "good morning," Captain Black lithely rose to his feet, dropped his cigarette, crushed it out with his boot heel, and unemotionally warned her to "behave yourself."

The princess was in no mood to behave herself. Determined to anger him, she shook her head as though disgusted and said, "You know, Captain, you are such a big bully and a yellow coward! Hard as nails with me, but scared to death of a few renegade Indians."

"That I am," he agreed, still unruffled.

Her hands went to her hips and she foolishly bragged, "Well, I'm not! I am not the least bit afraid of a handful of pitiful, starving Apaches."

Virgil shrugged wide shoulders and said, "Maybe you have no need to be. It's said the only human beings the Apaches spare are lunatics, whom superstition makes them leave alone."

That did it.

Thwarted, stirred up, her face went mean and she swung at him with an incoherent cry of frustration. Virgil was beside her quick as a flash. Immediately overpowering her, he controlled her body with his good right arm around both of hers. And he clasped his left hand tightly over her mouth. Struggling frantically against him, the princess tried to scratch his darkly whiskered face and to bite his hand.

For a long moment, Virgil said nothing. Did nothing. Just stood there effortlessly containing her while she impotently fought him. When finally she tired so that she could no longer lift her arms or even squirm about within his firm embrace, he loosened his restraining arm but continued to hold her.

They stood there, face-to-face, his arm around her, his hand over her mouth. When some of the raging fire went out of her flashing emerald eyes and he saw tears forming there, he took his hand away from her mouth. Bested, unhappy, the princess allowed him to gently press her head down onto his chest. The gesture made her cry. Why she didn't know. She never cried. She never had any reason to cry. The tears rolled down her hot cheeks and the sobbing princess wondered miserably if she were losing her mind.

Back on the trail the puffy-eyed princess was as mute as Virgil. She was confused by her emotions and frightened by feelings foreign to her; feelings she couldn't understand. She disliked this man intensely, and she would never forgive him for implying that she was a "lunatic."

Yet some foolish, feminine part of her still wanted the hard-faced Ranger to be attentive. To really notice her. To be aware of her as a woman. To be physically attracted to her.

To desperately desire her, so that she could turn him down cold!

If she could turn him down.

The princess stole a brief look at the Ranger. Her heart began to race when from out of nowhere came the thrilling thought that this tall, imperial-looking Texas Ranger with his aggravating, cocksure manner and forceful masculinity would make an excellent sovereign! He could rule a kingdom and its subjects with the same ease and nonchalance with which he had conquered these wild, god-awful deserts into which they were now riding. And, imagine the offspring he would sire.

Princess Marlena's face reddened at the guilty thought, and she was suddenly genuinely afraid. Afraid of this big, cold-eyed, black-haired, devilishly handsome Texan. Afraid of his rugged masculinity. Afraid of his unique ability to easily conquer her. Afraid as she had never been afraid of any man.

Afraid because she was absolutely fascinated by him. He was an exciting, mysterious man, and try as she might, she could not seem to forget how she had felt that first night when he took her in his arms and kissed her before she could stop him. Inwardly she shivered, knowing that if tonight he were to take her in his arms and kiss her, she wouldn't—couldn't—stop him.

That sobering knowledge convinced her she could wait no longer.

She *had* to escape today.

22

On a low, sunbaked mesa, in the Tularosa valley's wide corridor, an Apache warrior sat unmoving on his dancing, snorting mustang. Directly behind him, a dozen mounted Apache braves were silent. Totally silent.

None dared speak. None dared ride up alongside the young, sulking chief. Their volatile leader was in a black mood, had been in a black mood for weeks. Each long hot day that passed without a drop of rain made him grow more gloomy, more menacing.

The chief prided himself on his ability to make rain. He bragged how he had only to lift his arms to the skies and call for the rain to fall. A great downpour would follow. It always had.

However, to his great despair, he had, for long months now, been unable to make it rain. No matter how many times he stood under the cloudless skies and called for a cloudburst, nothing happened. Not a sprinkle fell on the dust-dry desert. Not a single dark cloud billowed up in the summer sky. Precious water holes were drying up, and there was no longer any gama grass for the horses.

His braves dared not mention his failure to bring the rain. To do so would risk his wrath. Nor did they dare mention what they knew was bothering him as much, if not more, than his inability to bring the rain.

They knew, too well, the danger this hot-blooded chief posed when he had been too long without that most favored prize that meant more to him than any other pleasurable diversion. More than stealing horses. More than burning out pesky settlers. More even than scalping blue-coated soldiers or the hated *Tejanos diablos*.

It was common knowledge that the big bronzed warrior, though married to three young, comely Apache, relished nothing quite so much as raiding a remote farmer or rancher's spread and finding a young white woman. A *pretty* white woman. He had no taste for sturdy, raw-boned, sunburned wives whose hard life showed on their plain, wrinkled faces. He shunned homely, calico-clad matrons with big, billowy breasts and spreading behinds. He paid no attention to any woman, pretty or plain, whose hair was dark like his own.

Discriminating in his taste, he searched ceaselessly for just the right woman. Young, but not a child. She had to be fully grown, totally mature, preferably between the ages of eighteen and thirty.

He, himself, had passed his twenty-fourth winter.

The sulking young Apache who sat astride his dancing mustang upon that barren New Mexico mesa was called Chief Thunderfoot.

Chief Thunderfoot was proud that his name struck cold fear in the hearts of all the despised white-eyes. His reputation grew with every surprise raid he led and every successful stage holdup and every white man's scalp he added to his war lance.

And, with each white beauty he claimed for his own personal prize.

Chief Thunderfoot was at the height of his physical prowess. His strength and endurance were legendary. He could run on tireless legs for twenty or thirty miles. He could snap a strong man's neck with one quick twist of his huge bronzed hands. It was rumored that he had once—on a dare—lifted a well-tied, blind-folded, one-thousand-pound mustang off the ground.

Chief Thunderfoot stood six foot six in his big bare feet, with wide, well-proportioned shoulders, a very deep chest, and long, muscular arms and legs. His forehead was very broad and high and his mouth was large. When his wide lips stretched in a rare smile of pleasure, strong white teeth flashed in his copper face. His nose was of the Roman order, too large and too broad for his face. His nostrils were expanded and seemed to pulsate when he was angry.

As he was now. Or, when he was electrified, as when he led a raid. Or, when he was sexually excited, as when he pleasured himself with a woman.

His large, lean body was nothing short of beautiful. But his big, broad face with its too large mouth and Roman nose was ugly. Menacing. Unsightly. Frightening. Chief Thunderfoot was aware that his looks alone scared people. That pleased him. Nothing was quite so satisfying as having cowardly white-eyes quake and tremble before him.

Naked now, save for the soft chamois loincloth covering his groin, Chief Thunderfoot's oiled chest and arms and legs glistened in the strong New Mexico sunshine. His thick raven hair, worn long, was held back off his ugly face with a white head band and fell around his bare, broad shoulders and down his back. Gusts of warm southerly winds lifted strands of the coarse black hair and blew them against his high cheekbones and into his flat black eyes.

He never noticed.

At the moment, he was absorbed. Consumed. Totally immersed in thought.

Those silent, nervous braves mounted directly behind him knew exactly what was on their young leader's mind. And they knew that until he found what he yearned for, there would be no rest for any of them. They had seen him this way before. It was like a vile disease that came upon him. A wild craving that had to be satisfied if he were to keep his sanity.

The sickness was upon him now. Had been upon him for many moons, growing steadily worse, causing him to behave ever more unwisely. When he was like this he took too many wild chances, thereby putting them all in danger. If he did not soon find that which he sought, he would become increasingly reckless until they might all lose their lives.

If they were to survive, Chief Thunderfoot *had* to have—very soon— a woman. A special woman. A young, beautiful white woman with whom he could spend a few enjoyable hours or days before he finally tired of her. A slender, fair-skinned beauty to make his blood run hot. A terrified, helpless human toy whom he could strip naked to admire with eager eyes and hold in his powerful hands. To tease and taste and take and torture until there was no life left in her.

Chief Thunderfoot suddenly raised his large right hand.

A responsive brave immediately kneed his paint forward, handed his chief an old pair of field glasses taken in a long-ago ambush.

Thunderfoot raised the glasses to his glittery black eyes and stared. Through the magic lens he spotted, far, far away, a small plume of dust rising from the eastern edge of the valley floor. Curious, patient, he watched and waited. While the gathered warriors began to fidget and squirm, their leader sat as still as a statue, peering through the raised field glasses.

While the braves looked at each other, shook their heads, and wondered if they were to stay there on this mesa in the hot morning sunshine forever, Thunderfoot continued to look through the glasses.

A full hour had passed when the young Apache's belly contracted and his broad, bronzed chest swelled. A smile of pleasure tugged at his wide lips. With his eagle's eyes enhanced by the magic of the lens, he saw what he hoped might be the prize for which he was searching.

Pleasant visions immediately filled his head. A brightly burning fire in the inky darkness of the hot desert night, it's shooting flames illuminating the pale, soft flesh of a beautiful naked female captive. He envisioned the fire's intense heat causing her bare, trembling body to grow so wet with sweat his big hands glided and drifted easily over her slippery flesh. All that pale, damp flesh, licked and pinkened by tongues of shooting orange flames.

And then, licked and pinkened by his own fiery tongue.

The princess's opportunity to escape came sooner than expected.

By early afternoon they had left the mountains far behind and were well into the dry, hot Tularosa Valley. The princess noticed that Virgil looked extraordinarily tired and sleepy. His sinfully long black lashes kept drooping down over his habitually squinted, sky-blue eyes. A couple of times she considered attempting her escape then and there.

But his warning words came back to her. *Noche could overtake the mare in thirty seconds.* She would wait until the time was right.

Her pulse fairly leaped with excitement when, upon reaching a small copse of scattered cottonwoods about one o'clock in the afternoon, he suggested they stop to rest. She was quick to agree. And when, stretching out in the sparse shade, Virgil admitted how badly he needed a nap and asked if he could trust her to stay put, she assured him that he could.

Sensing how uncommonly sleepy he was, the princess yawned dramatically and said, "I need a nap myself."

"Fine," he murmured, his eyelids already closing, "let's get an hour's sleep, then we'll push on."

"Shall I lie down next to you and—"

"No!" he answered too quickly, gruffly, his eyes opening. Needing an hour's rest, not more tiring torment, he suggested, "Why not stretch out there in the shadiest spot." Leaning up onto an elbow, he pointed to a place near—but not too near—him. So impossibly sleepy he could no longer stay awake, Virgil lay back down, cocking one eye slightly open to watch her.

She made a big show of sighing, yawning, and lying down, acting as if she could hardly hold her eyes open. Virgil exhaled heavily. He'd have to trust her. He *had* to have a few minutes sleep. He placed a spread hand on his black-shirted chest, gingerly checked his tightly taped ribs, and fell instantly to sleep.

Lying on her side facing him across the short distance of some forty feet, Princess Marlena's emerald eyes opened like a dozing cat, and she watched the reclining Ranger for several long, tense minutes. She could tell by his deep, even breathing that he was asleep. Still, she lay for a few more tension-filled moments, warily watching him, afraid to move.

Even in slumber he looked dangerous. Like a sleek, powerful animal, all coiled power and deceptive gentleness. As if she so much as moved, he would come instantly awake and pounce on her.

Princess Marlena stayed as she was for several more long, agonizing minutes. Finally she whispered his name.

"Virgil," she murmured ever so softly. "Virgil, are you asleep?"

No response.

Nothing but the continued heavy breathing, his broad chest moving up and down rhythmically. Her gaze slowly crawled up to his dark face, strikingly handsome despite the dense growth of black beard. Long jet lashes rested in spiky crescents on his high, slanted cheekbones. His sensual lips—slightly parted over straight white teeth—looked soft and warm and incredibly inviting. For one insane second, the princess was overwhelmingly tempted to scoot over close, bend down, and press a quick good-bye kiss to that beautifully shaped mouth. That marvelous male mouth that had sent jolts of such unbelievable pleasure through her when it closed so commandingly over her own.

She couldn't think about that. Not now. She had to remember that this darkly handsome man with such stunning blue eyes and exquisite lips was a heartless Texas Ranger who was taking her to jail.

"Captain Black," she whispered, "are you asleep?"

He was.

Her heart beating fiercely, the princess very slowly, very silently, eased up onto her knees, her unblinking eyes fixed on the sleeping Ranger's face. She pushed to her feet and held her breath. He slumbered on. She tiptoed away, heading for the still-saddled horses.

When she neared the stallion and mare, both began neighing loudly. Frowning, she put her finger perpendicular to her lips and tried to shush them. Her heart pounding, she looked anxiously around. Virgil was lying just as she had left him.

"Please, pleeeeease, be quiet," she whispered to the ground-tethered horses.

When she picked up the mare's reins, she considered taking the black stallion as well. That's exactly what she should do, she reasoned. Leave the Ranger afoot. That would give her plenty of time to reach the little settlement of Alamogordo, which he had promised was no more than five or six miles to the south.

The princess turned around and around. She wasn't sure which way was south. She looked up at the sky, but the sun was no help. It was still almost straight overhead in the cloudless sky. She lowered her eyes, blinking.

She would just have to make a guess. Maybe the stallion would know the way and he'd guide her.

That prospect soon died.

Mounted on the mare, the princess yanked hard on the stallion's reins, but Noche refused to budge. Well-trained and loyal, he was too smart to leave behind the only man who had ever been on his back.

Angry with the stubborn stallion and afraid he might wake the Ranger, Princess Marlena abruptly dropped his reins to the ground and whispered, "Well, then go to blazes, Noche. And take your dark master with you."

The black bared his teeth and tossed his great head.

The princess ignored him. Taking a guess at which way was south, she gently, but firmly, pulled the mare's reins to the left. The mare turned in that direction, just as Princess Marlena wanted, and walked away at a slow, comfortable gait. Behind them the black stallion reared his forelegs high into the air and whinnied loudly enough to wake the dead.

The princess hunched her slender shoulders, gritted her teeth, and made terrible faces, silently praying that the racket wouldn't wake the Ranger.

It didn't.

Virgil was so dead tired from the constant pain of his broken rib and the long sleepless night that he would have slept through a wild cattle stampede. He was sound asleep, and he stayed that way, as the nervous princess rode out of the stand of cottonwoods, crossed a long, shadeless plain, and finally dropped out of sight below the horizon.

Virgil slowly awakened by degrees. His blue eyes opened slightly, then slipped closed again. He drew a deep, extended breath. He lay there on the ground, yawning and stretching, in no real hurry to get up. He rubbed his eyes, opened them again, and leisurely turned his head.

"Jesus God!" he roared and bolted upright. Swallowing hard, he shot to his feet and looked frantically around. "Red!" he shouted loudly, "Red, where are you? Come here this minute! Red, answer me!"

No reply.

Just the mourning sigh of the hot winds rustling the leaves of the cottonwoods.

"Damn her to hell!" he muttered and hurriedly gathered up the gear.

Virgil slammed his hat on his head and tried not to think about what might happen to her. On legs weak with fear he hurried to the horses. And saw only Noche. Angry with himself, needing to take it out on someone or something, he grabbed the black's reins, jerked his great head down, and shouted into his ear, "Why the hell didn't you wake me?" The stallion neighed plaintively as if to say he had tried. "All right, all right, I'm sorry," Virgil apologized, as he swung up into the saddle. Noche immediately went into motion.

His whiskered jaw ridged with anger and fear, his eyes trained like a deadly weapon on the broad valley stretching before him, Virgil cursed the foolish woman responsible for his distress. How many times had he warned her that this was wild country where hostile Apache and Mexican *banditos* and ruthless renegades roamed at will. Hell, she should have known without having to be told. Everybody else in New Mexico knew.

He shuddered at the sudden recollection of having told her that the Apache might not bother her since they were afraid of lunatics. She might just be stupid enough to suppose they wouldn't harm her. God Almighty, why the hell hadn't he kept his mouth shut.

Quickly leaving behind the stand of cottonwoods, Virgil, leaning down from the saddle now, anxiously searching for tracks, spotted the mare's hoofprints. She was headed southwest. If he couldn't overtake her, his only hope was that she would safely reach Alamogordo.

Virgil carried no watch. He looked up at the sun and ground his teeth viciously. It must have been after three o'clock. She had at least a two-hour jump on him. He laid the spurs to Noche's flanks, and the stallion shot away. Squinting against the hot sun, Virgil glanced at the ground every few seconds to make sure he was still on her trail.

It was a searing hot afternoon in the barren Tularosa Basin. So hot that the air shimmered, rising from the hard-packed soil in undulating waves. Sweat trickled down Virgil's back and between his shoulder blades. It was uncommonly dry in the valley that summer. It hadn't rained in weeks and might not rain for weeks or months. There was hardly a hint of shade as far as the eye could see. The only vegetation was a few scattered mesquites and the hearty cholla cactus and the prickly pears.

Virgil clenched his jaw tight. She had taken no water with her. Out there it didn't take long to die of thirst. She'd be badly sunburned by the time she reached Alamogordo. If she reached Alamogordo. She had no hat, and as fair-skinned as she was, a few short minutes under this scalding sun would blister her unmercifully.

That worry was immediately forgotten when, yanking up abruptly on the reins, Virgil lunged down out of the saddle. His lips a thin, tight line in his darkly whiskered face, he crouched on his heels, stared unblinking, and saw that the gray mare's hoofprints had changed direction. Had turned due west.

Worse, other tracks joined hers. At least a dozen horses. And, none but the mare was shod.

Apaches!

His chest tightened, and Virgil felt as if he couldn't get a breath. He was back in the saddle in the blink of an eye and riding west. As good a tracker as any Indian, Virgil rode hell-bent for leather, praying he would not be too late.

Horrible images filled his mind's eye, and he couldn't make them go away. Too vividly he could see the pretty, pale-skinned redhead lying naked under some greased, grunting brave while the others watched and laughed and impatiently waited their turn.

Virgil felt as if he were going to be ill. The light lunch he'd had two hours ago was threatening to come up. He was, for the first time in his life, literally sick with fear. The thought of something terrible happening to her was unbearable.

Like a madman Virgil spurred the big stallion across the valley under the hot blazing sun and the near constant winds. His eyes stinging, his heart hammering, he rode at breakneck pace that caused the thundering stallion to wheeze and his big sweaty body to lather with thick white foam.

The tracks passed a couple of hundred yards below the little village of La Luz. Virgil never slowed the pace. No use wasting time asking for help. Every minute counted.

After nearly an hour of racing westward, Virgil finally drew rein. The big-eyed stallion gratefully slackened the pace and soon stopped. Virgil dismounted, carefully studied the tracks he had followed for miles. From where he now stood, the tracks led directly up and onto a high, flat mesa not fifty yards ahead. A secret Apache stronghold, he assumed, one of many scattered across this sparsely populated desert.

Virgil slowly rose to his feet, turned his head to the side, and listened intently. He could hear the low hum of voices. Male voices. He felt the blood congeal in his veins, and he was chilled to the bone despite the heat of the sun beating down on him. Knowing he would have no hope of saving her if he walked into the stronghold armed, Virgil unbuckled his gun belt and looped it around the saddle horn. He took off his hat, hung it atop the gun belt, and ran both hands through his sweat-damp hair.

He gently touched the stallion's shiny jaw and whispered softly, "Stay right here and rest up, old friend. I'll be back."

Virgil turned and walked away. The stallion stood dutifully still, not making a sound. Scaling the rocky-sided mesa as easily and as quietly as any Apache, Virgil neared the top in minutes. Terrified of what he would find, he reached the flat summit, climbed out onto an overhang of rock and, not daring to breathe, cautiously poked his head over and peered down.

His eyes widened and his mouth fell open.

More than a dozen Apaches were seated submissively in a circle around a slender, ginger-haired woman in too-large Levi's who paced at its center. Stunned, relieved, Virgil shook his head and smiled foolishly. Air filled his starving lungs.

She was unbelievable.

Strutting around, speaking with that fraudulent foreign accent, pulling her queenly Miss High-and-Mighty act on the Indians. And they were obviously enraptured. Clearly in her thrall, they stayed obediently silent while she lectured them as if they were misbehaving children. It was nothing short of a miracle.

Virgil saw her glance up briefly as a billowing white thunderhead materialized from out of nowhere and sailed high above the cinnamon-hued bluffs of the dry wash.

Virgil's gaze clung to her as she stepped directly in front of the biggest, ugliest Apache of them all. Virgil recognized the powerful giant. Chief Thunderfoot. One of the meanest hostiles alive. A crazed creature whose unspeakable torture of white captive women was legendary.

Virgil's heart thumped painfully against his injured ribs, and he almost choked when the princess, looking into the flat, black eyes of the gargantuan young chief, said in a clear, level voice, "So it is rain you want?" Thunderfoot, staring at her, nodded, entranced. The princess threw back her head, gazed up, snapped her slender fingers, and regally demanded rain.

Sprinkles soon peppered the upturned faces of the bewildered Indians. They began to smile and murmur about this fire-haired woman who could make rain.

The princess spoke forcefully, in distinctive tones, as if they were her servants, "Don't pretend you do not understand me! You are to escort me to the nearest city. Do you hear me?" She shook her finger in Thunderfoot's broad upturned face. "Alamogordo. You must take me to Alamogordo. Do you know where it is?"

Afraid any second the enchanted Apache would have a quick change of heart, grab her up, and brutalize her, Virgil Black slowly rose to his feet. He called out to make his presence known.

All heads turned.

All eyes immediately fell on him. He descended down through the gently falling rain into the nature-concealed camp with his hands raised over his head. The Apache, chattering and pointing, were all now on their feet.

Ignoring the woman, except to shoot her a quick "keep quiet" look, Virgil went directly to the towering six-foot-six Chief Thunderfoot. Speaking in soft, low Spanish, he explained to the massive Apache chief that "as you have just witnessed, the fire-haired woman has strong powers." He blinked as the raindrops peppered his face. "You do understand that it was she who brought you this rain."

Chief Thunderfoot looked from Virgil to the princess. He smiled and shook his big head, causing his loose black hair to dance on his bare broad shoulders. He rubbed the cooling rain over his naked torso, and in Spanish he told Virgil that he wanted this pale woman for his own. And he told Virgil exactly what he wanted to do with her.

Sickened, Virgil kept his face totally devoid of expression. Still speaking in soft, low Spanish, he said, "This is not possible. The woman belongs to me, and even if she did not, she cannot be used that way."

"You use her?" asked the chief.

Virgil reddened beneath his tan. "No. Never."

"Then you a fool," said Thunderfoot.

Dashing the rain from his matted eyelashes, Virgil reached out, took Princess Marlena's arm, and slowly drew her to him. Continuing to look up into the chief's broad face, he said, "Surely you can see that this woman is not like other women. She is a spiritual being who does not engage in physical pleasure. She has been kind enough to work her magic for you. Now she must go to other bone-dry areas and make it rain."

For a long tense moment the big Apache stood there totally silent, deep in thought.

Chief Thunderfoot truly believed that the pale red-haired one had brought the rain. He believed as well that since she was some kind of spirit woman, it would be wrong and dangerous to touch her.

He smiled suddenly, his wide lips slashing across his coppery face. Wishing he could have the pretty white woman but happy to have the much-needed rain, the big Apache allowed the two of them to leave unharmed.

Chief Thunderfoot even gave the princess a present. A necklace made of beads and human hair. At Virgil's gentle urging, she leaned over so the towering chief could place the necklace around her neck. Virgil thanked him and told the chief that their present to him was the gray mare and saddle. Frowning, the princess opened her mouth to contradict him; he tightened his hold on her, and she remained silent. Pleased with the gift, Chief Thunderfoot shook hands with Virgil, then reached for hers. He took her small hand in both of his own and held it, his glittering black eyes running admiringly over her face and body.

Virgil could tell by the expression in his black eyes what he was thinking. Then, warning her softly under his breath not to rush, not to run, Virgil led the princess back up the rocky embankment as the cooling summer rain continued to fall, soaking them, plastering their clothes to their bodies, their hair to their heads.

When they reached the rock summit overhang, they turned and waved in salute to the silent, staring Apaches.

24

His bearded, rain-wet face set in hard lines of fury, Virgil Black swept the princess to safety, racing due south atop the responsive black stallion. Thunder boomed and lightning streaked across the steadily darkening sky as the summer rain continued to fall in blinding sheets.

Enclosed in Virgil's long arms, the princess was draped across the saddle before him, her wet head on his shoulder, face pressed against his throat, arms wrapped around his waist. He hadn't said a word since he hurriedly lifted her onto the black's back, swung up behind her, and rode swiftly away from the Apache stronghold. But she could tell by the inflexible set of his jaw and the expression in the narrowed blue eyes staring straight ahead that he was angry.

She had no idea how angry.

Virgil's anger rose with each mile they covered. This unthinking woman had frightened him so badly his usual composure had been shattered. Never had he been so scared. Never had he been so mad. As the stallion put more and more distance between them and the Apache, Virgil's fear gradually dissipated.

But his anger blazed out of control.

Blindly furious with her, he spurred the big black toward a high shelf of rock rising from the valley floor. A few yards from the jagged walls and spires of rock, he abruptly pulled up on the reins. The startled stallion came to plunging halt. The princess lifted her head, gave Virgil a quizzical look. His blue eyes flashed with a kind of fire she'd never seen before. He shoved her roughly off the horse. Caught off guard, she lost her balance, fell to her knees in the mud. He dismounted, stood for a long moment towering above her, his booted feet apart, a muscle spasming in his whiskered jaw.

Then, looking mean and menacing, he leaned down and grabbed her. He yanked her to her feet with such quick force, her head rocked on her shoulders. His teeth bared like an animal's, he angrily tore the beaded necklace from her throat, tossed it away, and clamped his hands too tightly around her upper arms.

"You little fool," he finally spoke, and the sound in her ears was like the roar of a lion. A flash of lightning struck the rocks nearby. "Damn you!" he bellowed above the blast of following thunder. Intending to shake some sense into her, he shouted, "Jesus Christ, woman, you scared me half to death! Don't you know that . . . don't you . . . oh, God . . . God Almighty . . ."

His heart thundering, a vein throbbing on his high forehead, he abruptly drew her into his embrace and held her close against his heaving chest, relieved beyond words that she was unharmed, safe, here with him. But the feel of her soft, slender body pressed against his own quickly turned his anger and relief to desire. His hands, shaking slightly, rose to frame her upturned face. His lean fingers twined in her tangled wet red hair.

Before the startled princess realized what was happening, he lowered his lips to hers and kissed her forcefully. And he kept on kissing her as they stood there in the falling rain with the lightning flashing and the thunder cannonading.

Virgil kissed the astonished princess until she stopped trying to tear her lips from his and responded in kind. It didn't take long. In seconds she was kissing him back with a fire and a hunger that matched his own. In minutes both were ignited by a mutual burst of white-hot passion that could not, would not, be denied. Desire blazed out of control and demanded release. There was no going back. No stopping to think if this was the right thing to do. No questioning where it would lead once the deed was done. No wondering if they should discuss it first.

Like a couple of untamed animals they began anxiously stripping the clothes from the other. Fighting the rain that caused garments to cling to soaked flesh, the struggle was made all the harder because neither could bear to take their lips from the other's lips. Probing, sucking kisses continued as the difficult disrobing dance took place.

When finally both were naked to the waist, the princess glanced at the tape around Virgil's middle and remembered that he was hurt. Bracing herself back from him she looked up into his rain-wet face and said, "I forgot you were hurt. We . . . we can't . . . your ribs—"

"Are fine," he said and drew her back against him.

They sighed with pleasure and excitement as they kissed again and eagerly ran their hands over the other's bare, wet flesh. A flash of too-close lightning finally caused Virgil to tear his lips from hers. She moaned at the desertion and tried to pull his head back down.

"Wait, baby," he said, immediately lifted her up into his arms, and carried her toward the jagged wall of rock.

She didn't question him, just looped her arms around the strong column of his neck and pressed kisses to his wet throat. She was tracing the top of his bare shoulder with the tip of her tongue when she heard Noche neighing loudly. She opened her eyes, looked over Virgil's shoulder, and saw, through the falling rain, the black following them.

They reached the wall of rock. Virgil didn't stop to put her down but followed the ragged wall's perimeter southward for several yards. All at once, he ducked his dark head, stooped, and swept the princess inside a dry, dim cave with a smooth stone floor.

"Virgil," she said breathlessly, and the sound of his name on her lips made his heart pound. "Our own shelter from the storm."

Pleased, he leaned down, gave her a kiss, and lowered her to her feet. His hands cupping her bare shoulders, he said, "You cold, baby? Maybe we could get a fire going and . . . and . . ."

His words trailed away and both grinned wickedly, their eyes flashing with the shared secret. They had already gotten a fire going. A fire that was hotter than any other kind on earth.

"Come here." He drew her up onto her toes and kissed her.

The princess stood against her tall, lean lover, shamelessly pressing her breasts against his hair-covered chest. Her nipples felt as if they themselves were on fire, so sensitive were they to the touch of his warm, wet flesh. Her mouth open wide to his deeply penetrating tongue, she could feel his beard pleasantly tickling her cheeks and chin. She shocked herself by wondering how that ticklish black beard would feel if his lips were at her breast. The prospect caused her to shudder involuntarily against him.

The awakened princess was so caught up in his probing fiery kisses and the thrill of his chest against her swelling breasts, she hardly realized that he had unbuttoned her pants. She sighed into his mouth when she felt the rough fabric slip over her hips and down her thighs.

Virgil slowly released her lips, raised his head, and looked into her eyes. As his hands spanned her waist, he lifted a booted foot, snagged the pants with his toe, and sent them to the floor. Still looking deeply into her eyes, he gently lifted the princess off the stone floor. Her arms wrapped around his neck, she kicked free of the jeans. Now she was totally naked, save for her ruined leather slippers.

"Don't let me go," she said, as she put the toes of her right foot to the heel of her left slipper.

"Never, baby, never," he murmured.

When both slippers lay discarded on the cave floor and she was as naked as the day she was born, Virgil again lifted her up into his arms. His eyes a smoldering blue, he allowed his gaze to slide over every inch of her bare body. And, to her surprise and delight, she felt no shame. She knew her body was beautiful. She wanted him to look at it. She loved the feel of those burning eyes caressing her tingling flesh.

"Jesus, you are exquisite," he said, his voice low, husky.

"I'm glad you think I'm pretty," she said, her chest swelling with pride, her nipples standing out in darkening twin peaks of pure arousal.

"What I can see is perfect," he said, his Texas twang more pronounced than usual. "I want to see everything, baby. Say you'll let me."

"I'll let you," she sighed.

25

After that, everything that happened seemed to be taking place in a lovely, prolonged dream. A fiery, fulfilling fantasy.

The next thing the princess knew she was lying on her discarded pants, and Virgil was lying beside her. With the worsening of the storm outside, it had grown dramatically dimmer inside the cave. She blinked to see in the deep shadows, letting her gaze slide curiously down his body.

He was still wearing his tight black trousers. She half shocked herself when, burning hot from his expert kisses, she rolled up into a sitting position. Then smiling shyly at him, she moved her hands to the waist band of his pants and began unbuttoning the buttons.

He let her.

Virgil lay stretched out on his side facing her, weight propped on an elbow, cheerfully allowing her to unbutton his pants. He wished it were not so dark there in the cave so that he could better see her beautiful face and bare lovely body. She worked quickly, eagerly. When every button was undone, his thrusting masculinity was still restrained, but his hard brown belly and the dense black hair of his swollen groin were visible in the gaping trousers. Staring, her lips fell open and the curious princess became momentarily reticent.

Virgil picked up on the signal, rose, and quickly kissed her, leaving the opened pants just as they were. While he kissed her, he gently eased the naked princess back down onto her back. His open lips slanted across hers, he slid his tongue up under her top lip, ran it back and forth teasingly, then nipped playfully at her soft bottom lip with his gleaming white teeth.

She became aware of his hand on her breast and thought she might die of joy when his rough thumb rubbed back and forth across the stinging nipple. He lifted his dark head, gazed into her eyes as he gently caressed her breast. A flash of lightning struck nearby, and for a second, the cave was as light as day. Then came the darkness once more as the thunder echoed.

Virgil took her hand and drew it down to where the black trousers were parted over his belly. She gasped and touched him timidly. He lowered his face and kissed her eyes, her cheeks, her chin. When his lips trailed heated kisses down the side of her throat to her shoulder, the princess's breath grew short.

She grew a trifle bolder. Her hand, lying where he had placed it, now began to carefully explore the varied textures beneath her sensitive fingertips. The heavy black twill fabric. The crisp curly black hair. The hot smooth flesh. The almost frightening surging of that confined male flesh, the restrained power pulsing through her fingertips as if it were her own heartbeat.

Her hand momentarily stilled, and selfishly she temporarily forgot about his throbbing tumescence when she felt his mouth enclose her left nipple. Straining to see him in the darkness, she sighed and shivered and breathlessly murmured, "Yes, oh yes."

His lips tugging firmly on the pebble-hard nipple, Virgil swept his hand slowly down her slender, fever-hot body. He touched her caressingly from just under her arm down to her pale thigh. After a second's pause, his hand trailed leisurely on down to her knee. He wrapped his fingers around the back of her knee and urged her left leg up into a bent position with her bare foot flat on the stone floor. Then, ever so gently, he prodded the bent knee outward, cocking it to fall over toward to the floor, thus giving him easy access to that most sensitive part of her beautiful body.

While he licked her nipple and dragged his teeth over it, he laid his hand on her bare, flat belly. His thumb found her navel and toyed with it, brushing back and forth, pressing gently, playing harmlessly.

In a sweet daze of desire, the naked princess lay there on the floor atop her discarded denim pants in the private shelter of the cave. While the summer storm raged just beyond the cave's entrance a few short feet away, she gloried in the steadily escalating pleasure. A physical joy of a kind she'd never known existed. She moaned. She sighed. She murmured his name.

Virgil moved his hot face to her untasted right nipple. He pressed a tender kiss to it before opening his mouth wide and taking as much of the soft, round mound into his mouth as possible. The first strong pull of his lips at the nipple made her cry out with elation. At that instant a day-bright flash of lightning struck just outside, and she could clearly see Virgil's dark, bearded face clamped onto her pale, swollen breast.

His eyes were closed, the long dark lashes resting against his high cheekbones. His firm jaws were flexing as he suckled her. His heavy beard was pleasantly tickling her skin. Every nerve ending in her body thrumming with almost unbearable excitement, it was as if she were outside herself, watching. A fascinated voyeur. Seeing the two of them as well as feeling what he was doing to her.

The fleeting glimpse she got in the lightning flash might have been of a dark, dangerous, highly sexual predator feasting ravenously on a pale, helpless, shamelessly aroused maiden. A strange and disgraceful image, yes. But erotic beyond belief.

In her heightened state of arousal, the princess felt as though she would have allowed this big black-bearded beast to devour her if he chose to do so. She couldn't have stopped him. Didn't want to stop him. Wanted him to do anything and everything to her. For her. With her.

The stimulated princess soon realized that the scalding fire she felt in her nipples had spread to her lower body. When the next flash of lightning came she saw that Virgil's tanned hand was between her open legs, spreading the heat. Darkness returned and she could see nothing. She could only feel.

She felt his warm lips against her bare belly and his long, dark fingers caressing that slick, throbbing bud of flesh between her parted thighs. She couldn't believe the intimacy and the ecstacy.

His low masculine voice coming to her from out of the deep shadow, he said softly, "Feel good, baby?"

"Yes, yes," she choked. "Don't . . . don't stop."

The tip of his middle finger, slick with the fiery wetness flowing from her, slid around and around that tiny tingling button of flesh which was now—to him and to her—the center of the entire universe. Virgil let the tip of his finger glide up to the very beginning of her swollen cleft, he cupped her, then gently swept the soft flesh and ginger curls aside, bunched his fingers together, and slowly moved them back down until his middle finger slipped inside her.

She gasped, stiffened, as his loving hand pleasured her, his finger penetrating slowly, gently, his thumb again skillfully rubbing that fiery spot where she had just learned she most relished being touched. They stayed that way for a time, he caressing, thrilling, bringing her steadily closer to the peak of passion. She, lying on her back beside him, her left leg cocked outward, her bare bottom surging and lifting to meet his stroking hand.

When Virgil was certain she was as hot and as ready as he, he leaned down, kissed her open lips, shot to his feet, hastily took off his boots and socks, then gave his open trousers a forceful push, shucking them quickly.

Lightning flashed.

Princess Marlena saw him standing above, totally naked. She trembled. Tall and lean and tanned all over, he was the epitome of masculine grace and steel-muscled power. Beautiful. God-like. Awesome. His thrusting erection was almost frightening in its shocking enormity and promising potency.

"Sweetheart," he murmured, and came down on his knees between her legs. Carefully he lowered his body to hers, keeping his weight balanced on a braced arm.

He kissed her and whispered, "Let me love you." He captured one of her hands, drew it between their bodies, placed it on his pulsing erection. "*Help* me love you, baby. Help me."

Shocked, thrilled, the princess held and stroked that throbbing power in her hand for a long moment, not wanting to let it go, wishing she could hold him this way forever. She had no idea that Virgil was in sweet agony and terrified that if she didn't stop stroking him, he would climax before ever being inside her. He gritted his teeth. His belly contracted. He held his breath.

And then, for the first time in her life, Princess Marlena guided a lover's hard pulsating flesh up into her soft wet warmth. Both sighed when he easily slid in. Virgil placed a kiss on her lips as he began the slow, sensual movements of lovemaking. As it had been when she held him in her hand, Virgil could hardly keep himself from coming immediately. But he was determined he would wait for her.

He looked into her eyes and thrust slowly, deeply, going almost all the way in. Then pulling almost all the way out, leaving only the smooth, mushroom-shaped tip inside her. It had the effect he had hoped for.

"Please," she whispered, scratching his flesh with her long nails, pulling frantically at his biceps, wanting him back inside, needing him back inside.

He gave her what she wanted. He slid back into her and pumped leisurely, rhythmically, flexing the muscles in his bare buttocks, loving the feel of her gripping him, holding him. When she began to toss her head and arch her back and tilt her pelvis up to meet each piercing thrust, Virgil changed the pace of their loving. He rocked into her faster, hammered harder, drove deeper.

And she loved it.

Their rapid breaths and sighs and groans loud in the small enclosure, they went at it with total abandon. If he was an experienced, exciting lover, resolved to give her the ultimate in sexual pleasure, she was the eager, apt pupil, willing to learn what he could teach her, greedy to take all he had to offer.

The princess bucked and ground her hips and squeezed him tightly and thought she had surely fully attained carnal heaven. Until, that is, heaven really began.

When it happened, her closed eyes flew open in shock and fear. "V-I-R-G-I-L!" She gasped, "Oh, oh, I'm . . . Virgil, I . . . I . . ."

"I know, baby" His answer was a low caress as he pounded rapidly into her. "Let it come. I've got you, I'll stay with you. Give it to me, baby. Give it all to me."

As promised, he did stay with her while she frantically clawed at his shoulders and upper arms and murmured his name again and again. Helplessly, she writhed and rocked and shuddered in the throes of a wild, deep climax. And when she started to scream as the ecstacy became so powerful it began to verge on pain, he let himself go and joined her in paradise.

The princess bit his shoulder with punishing teeth when she felt the hot liquid of love spurting deep inside her. Virgil groaned with satisfaction and collapsed atop her, his face resting on her breast, his midnight black hair ruffling against her chin.

The princess smiled foolishly, wrapped her arms around him, and held him fast as their thundering hearts began to slow. Hoping he wouldn't move away immediately, she hooked her left foot around the muscular calf of his leg and placed a spread hand on his head to hold him to her.

To her delight he seemed more than content to stay just as he was, his bearded face on her breast, his hand on her thigh. Those magical moments following the fiery lovemaking were the sweetest she'd ever known. Princess Marlena realized now that she had never really made love before. Nor had she ever really been made love to.

This was the very first time.

The shattering climax she'd just experienced was her first one ever. She'd had no idea that this incredible zenith to which she had ascended was actually a part of lovemaking between a man and woman. A big part. The best part! Now she knew why the palace maids giggled and whispered about the joys of married life.

Smiling, sighing, stretching like a contented cat, the princess stared unseeing up at the low, rocky ceiling above, totally sated and totally happy.

For her, this uninhibited lovemaking had been an incredible awakening. She had known only one man intimately, her deceased husband. Early in their marriage, she had let him know she found lovemaking rather tedious. So she had been spared, save for an occasional late-night visit.

Now, here she lay, naked in the arms of a dark, rugged stranger. Their legs entwined, arms around each other, they lay directly in front of the cave's entrance where any passerby could see them. She didn't care. Let the whole world see.

She didn't want to move an inch from this magnificent lover with whom she had eagerly engaged in shocking sexual intimacy, the kind of which she had, until today, been totally ignorant.

And it was wonderful.

26

In the afterglow of lovemaking, a totally relaxed Princess Marlena realized that this was one of those rare moments that come but once in a lifetime. A sweet, precious interlude that she would never forget. The sights and sounds and smells surrounding her would, she knew, stay with her forever.

When she was an old woman with failing eyesight, she would still be able to see the craggy rock ceiling above her. And the lean, masculine body partially draped over hers. And the dark handsome head resting on her breast.

She would always be able to hear the pleasing sound of Virgil's deep, slow breathing mingling with her own. And the neighing of the nervous black stallion prancing back and forth outside. And the raindrops hissing against the dry, thirsty ground.

And, if she inhaled deeply, she would smell again the intoxicating odor of the rain on the desert. And the clean fragrance of the silky black hair ruffling her chin. And the subtle scent of sex. A scent that was as new to her as the glorious intimacy in which she had just participated.

Princess Marlena sighed softly.

She felt no guilt. No shame. After the wild passion they had shared, she was confident that Virgil Black was in love with her. It was not surprising. Every suitor she'd ever known had fallen in love with her after just one kiss. She had given Virgil Black much more than a kiss. She had given him her body and her soul. Surely, after taking both, he was mad about her.

Lying contentedly beneath her dark lover, the princess was unaware that she was still frightfully ignorant and innocent when it came to matters of the heart. And body. It never occurred to her that she might be mistaken about Virgil Black loving her. Such a possibility never entered her head. He loved her. She knew he did.

The princess *was* wrong.

Dead wrong.

"Sorry about that, Red," Virgil said finally, easing himself off her. "Guess I got carried away. It won't happen again."

Stunned, unable to believe her ears, the princess stared at him, speechless, for a long, uncertain moment.

When he rose to his feet, she nervously sat up. At last, she said, "But . . . but . . . why? Why are you sorry?" She swallowed hard and asked the real question. "Aren't you . . . in love with me?"

Leisurely hunching into his black trousers, Virgil paused with his hands on the fly's buttons. He shot her a glance of incredulity and replied with blunt honesty, "In love? With you?" He shook his handsome head and grinned. "Jesus, Queenie, you've got to be joking."

Horrified, hurt, the princess squeezed her legs tightly together and threw her arms up to cover her breasts. She sat there on the cave's stone floor shaking with emotion. She was temporarily unable to grasp what he was so callously saying.

She hadn't heard him correctly. That was it. It had to be. Not in love with her? That simply could *not* be true. She didn't believe it. It was too awful, too insulting to believe. How could this man with whom she had just shared such incredible ecstasy tell her that she must be joking about his being in love with her?

For a few agonizing seconds, her misery was so intense it was physical. Her naked chest felt as if it might explode from the burning ache there, and her bare stomach clenched spasmodically. She bit her lips to keep from screaming in agony. No one had *ever* hurt her like this. She had never suffered this kind of misery that left her dazed and defeated.

But she didn't stay overwhelmed long.

Her royal blood rose quickly to the surface, and her crushing pain was replaced with blinding anger. The princess snatched her denim trousers up off the floor, shielded her body with them, and shot to her feet to face him.

Shaking with rage, she shouted loudly, "You bloody bastard! You monstrous cad! You miserable excuse for a human being! You—you—"

"I'm all those things, Red," Virgil, nodding, agreed with her. "Always have been. I'm sorry, I shouldn't have—"

"No, you shouldn't have!" She was sobbing now, furious, heartbroken, and humiliated. "And you should be horsewhipped and hanged for it!" Tears pouring down her flushed cheeks, her tone was lethal when she warned, "If you ever touch me again, Black, I will kill you. And I am *not* joking about that!"

"Fair enough."

Irritated that this foolish woman was carrying on so over nothing, Virgil found the whole thing rather absurd. She was shrieking and sobbing as if she were a trusting young girl whose sweetheart had seduced her and then said he didn't love her. Utterly ridiculous. And tiresome. She was obviously one of those women who could turn on the tears when it benefited her. Or thought it would benefit her.

He exhaled heavily. "Please, Red, stop crying. I told you it won't happen again."

"No, it certainly will not, you heartless son of a bitch!" Her tear-wet eyes flashed with fury, and she continued to call him every bad name that came into her head.

"We're even now," he finally cut in, rankled by the continuing insults. And annoyed that she had the power to rankle him. No woman ever had. That startling realization compelled him to behave childishly. To give her a dose of her own medicine, to insult her.

He drawled in his flat Texas twang, "Yep, I finally got what I paid so handsomely for in Las Cruces."

"I have no earthly idea what you are talking about." She held the Levis against her shaking body.

Virgil rubbed his bare chest, shrugged wide shoulders, and said, "Have it your way, Red." He turned, crossed the small cave.

When he ducked his head to exit, she said angrily, "Where are you going? You come back here!"

Virgil straightened, looked at her. "In case you haven't noticed, the rain has stopped." The princess's head snapped around. She was stunned to see bright sunlight streaming in the cave entrance. He said, "Time to leave our little hideaway."

Holding on to the denim trousers for dear life, the princess looked about. "My shirt . . ."

"Is outside where you left it."

She looked puzzled. Then it came rushing back. The two of them standing in the falling rain, kissing, and stripping the shirts off each other. Lord, if she could only roll back time one short hour and change everything.

"Go get it, Ranger!" she arrogantly commanded. Virgil just looked at her. "Did you hear me? Bring the shirt to me at once," she ordered, as if she were speaking to a personal servant.

Which was not the way to get Virgil Black to do anything. Had she asked him sweetly, he likely would have brought her the shirt.

"Nope."

"Nope? What does that mean?"

"Get it yourself," he said, ducked his dark head, and slipped out the cave.

Foiled, wondering how she was supposed to get dressed when her shirt was lying on the ground outside, Princess Marlena turned her back to the cave entrance. She jerkily drew on the trousers, stepped into her slippers, and gripping the too-big waistband, turned round and round searching for something—anything—she could use to cover her naked torso.

There was nothing.

Sighing with frustration, she reasoned that if she released her grip on the trousers so that she could raise her arms to cover her breasts, the pants might slip down off her hips as she walked. But, if she held on to the trousers, she wouldn't be able to hide her breasts. In a quandary, the princess pondered the problem briefly. Then she came to a quick decision.

To hell with Captain Virgil Black!

She wasn't about to go slinking out there, cowering like a coward, mortified and trying to cover herself. She was, whether he believed it or not, a princess of the royal blood, and she would—just as she always had—carry herself like a royal princess.

Princess Marlena threw her head back and released her hold on the denim trousers. The pants instantly slipped down around her flaring hips and snagged there on her prominent hipbones. She threw her slender shoulders back, raked her hands through her tangled red hair, and crossed the cave. She drew a deep, restorative breath, and ducked outside.

His black shirt back on but unbuttoned, worn leather saddlebags draped over his left shoulder, Virgil stood beside the stallion, checking its front right hoof. The princess paused by the cave's entrance, anticipating the moment when he would become aware of her. As she watched, he took out a knife and worked at dislodging a pebble caught under the stallion's iron shoe. The chore completed, Virgil put away the knife, glanced up, and saw her.

His lips fell open.

He squinted, staring.

Once she had his undivided attention, the princess, with her pride again intact, swept regally toward him. Her dignity and self-assurance as much in evidence as the bouncing of her bare breasts with every step she took, she majestically approached. Virgil's eyes never left her. She noted a definite tensing of his tall, lean body and felt a quick surge of feminine vanity.

So she had no hold on his cold heart? The same could not be said for his hot body.

The princess walked directly up to Virgil, stopped not a foot away, lifted her slim arms, and swept her tangled red hair up atop her head. Holding it there with her arms raised, elbows bent, she flashed him a wicked smile, said, "Ah, the rain has certainly cooled everything off, hasn't it?"

She easily read the turbulence in his summer blue eyes, noted the quickening beat of the pulse in his throat. She slowly lowered her gaze and saw that his tanned fingers gripped the saddlebags so tightly, the knuckles were white while his free hand was balled into tight fist at his side. And, his stomach had contracted to such a degree, his waistband fell away from his hard, washboard belly.

A quick learner, the princess realized that he wanted her again. So, she inhaled deeply, knowing what would happen when she did. Her breasts rose and swelled, her stomach sunk in, and her trousers started to slide.

"Jesus God!" Virgil rasped as his hand shot out, clasped the waistband of her pants, and kept them from falling even farther.

"What's the matter, tall Texan?" she asked innocently, tipping her head back to look at him. Wetting her lips with her tongue, she purred, "Dear me, you're perspiring while I'm so cool and comfortable. Is something bothering you?"

His eyes murderous, he said gruffly, "Damn it, woman, you can't go around here without clothes."

"Oh? So you want me to put on the shirt?" She leaned in a little closer so that her unfettered breasts brushed briefly against his chest.

"Now!" he roared, and released her.

She smiled, hooked a finger through a belt loop so her pants wouldn't fall off, and said defiantly, "You want me back in that shirt, Captain Black, you go get it."

Challenge sparkled from her emerald eyes. She knew she had beaten him when, without another word, he turned and walked away. He was back in seconds, the dirty blue shirt in his right hand. Eyes narrowed, jaw ridged, he thrust it out to her.

But the princess refused to take it.

"Now what?" he said, at wit's end, half-tempted to turn her over his knee and give her a spanking, which was exactly what she needed.

"If you want me to wear the shirt, Captain," she said silkily, "you will have to put it on me."

She folded her arms across her bare midriff and drew her elbows in, a movement designed to provocatively squeeze her bare breasts together. She gave him a seductive smile.

But once again, as he had so many times since snatching her off the Cloudcroft railroad platform, the enigmatic Texas Ranger surprised the scheming royal princess.

His hot gaze touched her breasts briefly, then lifted to her face. Smiling lazily back at her, he casually stuffed the faded blue shirt into the worn leather saddlebags draped over his shoulder.

"It'll be cooler for you without the shirt," he said agreeably. "But I do hope you don't blister too badly."

He shook his head as if concerned, turned, and headed for the saddled stallion.

Shaken, wondering how she could have lost the upper hand so easily, Princess Marlena stood rooted to the spot not knowing what to do next. She watched as he tossed the saddlebags over the stallion's back. Surely he was only teasing her. A tasteless joke. Any second he would take the shirt out of the saddlebag and bring it to her.

He didn't.

"Ready, Red?" Virgil called as he swung agilely up into the saddle. "Noche and I are leaving now." He clicked his tongue to the stallion and the mount went into motion, walking at a slow pace.

A twinge of panic shot through the princess's bare breasts. The evil bastard might actually leave her here like this with no clothes, no water, and no horse! Damn him to eternal hell!

"Wait," she screamed, and raced toward him.

Virgil immediately drew rein, and the stallion halted on a dime. Virgil waited, noting with no small degree of satisfaction, that her haughtiness was now totally missing. But, God, she was a hardhead, so it might be wise to keep her off-balance for a while longer.

The princess reached him. Her arms now crossed over her bare breasts, she asked, "Please, may I have the shirt."

Virgil made a big show of scratching his bewhiskered chin as if in deep thought.

"No."

"No?" Her face screwed up into a terrible frown.

"That's what I said."

"Oh, don't be such an ass!" she exploded. "You can't expect me to go riding across the desert half-naked."

Virgil gave her a cold look and replied. "Ah, but I do."

And with that he leaned down, took her arm, and told her to step up into the stirrup. His tone made her respond at once. She raised her left foot, put it in the stirrup. Virgil immediately drew her up, wrapped a long arm around her waist, and held her like that, standing in the stirrup against him, for a long, uneasy moment. His bearded face at the level of her bare breasts, he devilishly puckered his full lips. The princess trembled involuntarily, her nipples tightening traitorously.

He grinned evilly, raised his knowing eyes to meet hers, and said, "Next time I tell you to put on a shirt, you'll do it."

"Don't bet on it."

Ignoring her reply, he quickly thrust her behind him in the saddle and laid his spurs to the stallion's flanks. The princess automatically grabbed at him to keep from falling. She heard his sharp intake of air and realized that she had squeezed his injured ribs. She squeezed harder, hoping to inflict pain. Her arms wrapped tightly around him, she leaned close, said into his ear, "You were right, Texan." Pressing her breasts against his back, she trilled, "It's much cooler without a shirt. You really should try it."

Bested, Virgil gritted his teeth and drew rein.

He reached into the saddlebag, withdrew the soiled blue shirt, and shoved it at her. "Put on the shirt."

"Say please."

"Please, goddamnit!"

"Why certainly," she purred, "anything you say, *Herr Kapitan!*"

27

In silence they headed eastward across the thirty-mile-wide Tularosa Basin. The brief rainstorm had passed as suddenly as it had come. The thirsty ground had quickly soaked up the water. Dust rose beneath the stallion's pounding hooves, and a blistering late-afternoon sun bore down on them.

Neither noticed.

They were each lost in their own troubled thoughts.

Try as she might, Princess Marlena couldn't forget what it was like to be held and loved by this handsome, hard-faced Texan, although he had made it crystal clear that it meant nothing to him. Unfortunately, the incredible lovemaking *had* meant something to her. His touch, his kiss, had stirred in her an almost frightening passion that she had never known existed. And now that she did, she would never be completely happy without experiencing it again.

The troubled princess, clinging to the cantle to keep from touching Virgil, flushed hotly at the vivid recollection of how she had cried out in orgasmic ecstasy. She had never experienced sexual gratification—not until this coldhearted, hot-blooded Texas Ranger showed her what it was like to *really* make love. Now she was afraid that every time she looked at him she would shiver and blush, recalling the things he'd done to her, the way he'd made her feel.

For Virgil the abandoned lovemaking had been enjoyable, but that was all. She was convenient. She was willing. He was aroused. So he'd had a mindless roll in the hay with the delectable Queen of the Silver Dollar.

End of story.

Granted it had been good. Damned good. And she had behaved as if she were totally lost in him. She had been genuinely responsive to his touch, his kiss. That wasn't entirely faked, he'd stake his life on it.

Then again maybe it was.

After all, she was a saloon singer/actress by trade who added money to her personal kitty by entertaining a few handpicked gents in her upstairs boudoir when her lover, British Bob, was not in town. God knows how many men's bare backs she had wrapped those long, silken legs around.

He was aware of her checkered background, so it plagued Virgil that now every time he looked at her, he wanted to take her in his arms again. Further, it scared the hell out of him to recall just how worried he had been when he awakened to find she had escaped. And how relieved when he found her with the Apache, alive.

His squinted blue gaze fixed on the ragged peaks rising on the distant southeastern horizon, Virgil couldn't stop thinking about how soft and sweet and hot she had been in his arms. He arrogantly assumed that he could have her again anytime he wanted her, despite her protestations that she would kill him if he ever touched her again. Eight to five said he could draw rein right there in the middle of the treeless Tularosa Basin, haul her down off the stallion, and make love to her under the burning sun.

He was tempted.

But he wasn't about to do it.

The reason? He was half-afraid. Half-afraid that if she again came into his arms she might take more than his body. Half-afraid that he might start to care more than he cared to. Half-afraid that he was in jeopardy of falling in love with this beautiful, ginger-haired outlaw who had likely slept with more men than he had fingers and toes.

The thought stung Virgil badly. The unwanted visions that drifted before his tired eyes made him uncommonly angry. Made him mad as hell. And, naturally, his anger was directed at this tempting woman who was solely responsible for his distress. Hell, he hadn't wanted this tiresome assignment in the first place! He was a Texas Ranger, for God's sake. He shouldn't be wasting his time dragging a worrisome female thief to jail. He ought to be down on the border with the rest of the frontier battalion, chasing dangerous criminals.

The hair suddenly lifted on the nape of Virgil's neck.

He swallowed hard and his chest tightened. It struck him that this slender woman was dangerous. Plenty dangerous. More dangerous than all the killers and thieves he had faced over all the years put together. She was, he realized with a shudder, capable of stealing something no Mexican bandit, or ruthless renegade, or hostile Apache could touch.

His heart.

And he couldn't let that happen. He was far too smart for that. His natural distrust of females had been fueled by a never-ending parade of delectable, deceitful ladies. He was yet to be proven wrong by a member of the fair sex. This particular Jezebel was just like all the others. Only more dangerous, more deadly. He would, from here on out, keep her strictly at arm's length.

The silent woman that Virgil meant to keep at arm's length was presently vowing to herself that she would *never* speak to the brutish Texas Ranger again, much less let him touch her.

Princess Marlena kept that vow for hours. Even when they stopped to water the stallion at a willow-fringed pond, she didn't speak to him. Didn't say a word.

Sullen himself, Virgil never noticed. He made no attempt to engage her in conversation. He didn't want to talk to her any more than she wanted to talk to him.

Without a word, Virgil crouched down on his heels, filled the canteen, and handed it up to her. She took it, quickly turned the canteen up to her parched lips, and drank thirstily. As she drank, Virgil stretched out on his belly, levered himself forward on braced forearms, and dipped his dust-flecked, bearded face into the clear, cool water.

The princess lowered the canteen, glanced at him. His eyes closed, lips open, he lapped at the water like a big sleek cat. Princess Marlena pressed the cool canteen to her hot, sticky throat and watched him, appalled and helplessly fascinated. Again and again his tongue came out from between his parted lips to dexterously lick up drinks of water.

Staring, the princess's own lips fell open and her breath grew shallow. She tried to look away, but couldn't. There was something staggeringly sensual in the way he was lapping and swilling and sipping the water.

Her pulse beginning to quicken, her cheeks coloring hotly, the mesmerized princess frowned with rising discomfort. Why couldn't he just drink out of the canteen like anyone else? And when was he going to get his fill? Did he mean to lie there lapping at the water for an eternity?

Virgil abruptly stopped drinking. But he didn't lift his head. He ducked it completely underwater and turned it rapidly from side to side, then stayed there, fully submerged. When several long seconds had passed and he hadn't surfaced, the princess grew alarmed. Surely he couldn't hold his breath that long. Nobody could. Not even Virgil Black. Dear Lord, he was drowning!

She dropped the canteen and anxiously stepped forward. But just as she reached out to grab at his shirt, Virgil's wet head broke the surface. The princess quickly jumped back, not about to let him know she had been concerned.

From beneath lowered lashes she watched as he levered himself up, sat back on his booted heels, and raised his hands to push his wet hair straight back off his face. Beads of water glistened in his black beard and clung to his long dark eyelashes. His soaked shirtfront was stuck to his skin, clearly delineating the steely muscles of his chest and even the tiny twin points of his chilled flat, brown nipples.

The princess felt faint. She was momentarily overcome with a strong desire to sag to her knees before him, sweep his soggy black shirt apart, lean to him, and kiss that magnificent chest until the heart beneath her lips pounded with passion.

Instead she turned on her heel and rushed away, cursing herself for her shameful moment of weakness. Determined that he would never know about it.

Breaking the silence, Virgil called after her, "If you're planning on a bath today, Red, now is the time and the place. There are no streams or brooks where we're heading."

The princess spun around to face him. "And if I take a bath here, just where did you plan on being?"

"You know damned well I have no intention of letting you slip away again."

"Are you saying that you intend to stay right here and watch while I—"

"That's exactly what I'm saying."

Her hands went to her hips. "I would go the rest of my life without taking a bath before I would allow you to spy on me!"

"It's your decision," he said, shrugging.

"Yes it is! Besides, what good would a bath do without a change of clothes? I am sick and tired of wearing your smelly things. I want my own clothes back."

"You should have thought of that before you went running off to join the Apaches."

"What does that have to do with it?"

"Everything," he said. "Your clothes and underwear were rolled up and packed behind the saddle on the gray mare."

She huffed. "And you had to go and give them the mare!"

She turned away once more, firming her resolve to speak no more. To never speak to him again for as long as she lived!

Without another word passing between them, they got back on the trail. The princess maintained her silence as the hot June sun lost its sting and began to slide toward the blue shadows of the San Andres rising behind them.

But, despite her best efforts, she found it next to impossible to keep quiet when all at once they rode into the luminous world of pearly sand that she had glimpsed earlier from the high country promontory outside Cloudcroft.

The dazzling white sands of New Mexico!

Staring in wonder at the huge swirling lake of ivory sand, Princess Marlena stayed still as long as she possibly could. Enchanted, she shaded her eyes with her hand and stared at the unbelievable sight surrounding them.

Glittering dunes and the bright sun formed black-and-white shadow patterns on the shifting sands. The princess gazed, enthralled at dunes that were miles wide, some rising to fifty and sixty feet above the floor of the basin. Virgil narrowed his eyes against the glare from the great hills of snow-white sand. The gypsum crystals, shining like millions of diamonds in the summer sunlight, were almost blinding.

But he had seen it before. Many times he had crossed this huge lake of pristine sand. He had no need to look now. He purposely lowered his heavy lids, let his thick, spiky eyelashes filter out some of the blinding light. Head bent, chin sagging slightly, he slumped comfortably in the saddle.

Half-dozing, he nearly jumped out of his skin when the princess, no longer able to contain her childlike excitement, suddenly shouted, "Captain, can we stop?"

Blinking, mentally shaking himself awake, Virgil said in a low, flat voice, "No."

"Please, oh please," she entreated, forgetting her vow to not talk to him. "This place is soooo extraordinarily beautiful I can't believe it's real. I want to stop and scoop up some sand to take back to Hartz-Coburg."

"We're not stopping."

"Only for a minute," she pleaded. "Just long enough to collect some of the sand for a souvenir. There is nothing like this in my kingdom and I really—"

Irritated that even at this late date she still refused to drop the royal princess pose, Virgil interrupted, "Your 'kinkdom.' What's that?"

"Kingdom! I speak perfect English!" she snapped, taking offense.

"Sure you do," he said in a bored, flat voice, "when you forget yourself and drop that fake accent."

"My accent is not fraudulent! I have told you a dozen times that I am—"

"Sure, sure," he cut her off.

Exhaling with frustration, Princess Marlena again fell silent. Clamping her teeth tightly together, she swore that these glittering white sands over which they rode would turn to snow before she again exchanged words with the rude Ranger.

When the sun had completely disappeared and a big early moon rose from behind the ragged peaks of the Organ Mountains, the princess still gazed with wonder on the silvery fairyland. In all directions the sands spread out in a ghostly glittering world of pure white.

When Virgil abruptly drew rein on the leeward side of a towering white dune where a stand of tenacious cottonwoods clung to the dune's shifting sands, the excited princess forgot herself again.

"Can we camp here tonight?" she asked, unable to hide her enthusiasm.

The idea greatly appealed to her. If they spent the night here, she could, whether he liked it or not, collect some of the beautiful white sand for a keepsake.

"We'll see," he said, noncommittal, sounding like a stern parent.

Her hopes were raised when he dismounted, then reached for her. She followed when he led the stallion through the sparse stand of cottonwoods.

"What? What is it?" she asked, when he shook his dark head.

"Water," he said. "There is none here."

"Oh, is that all? It doesn't matter!" She rushed the words. "The canteen is still nearly full, and I'm not very thirsty so—"

"I was thinking of Noche," he said, turning his head to look at her. "I don't suppose it ever occurred to you that the stallion *is* thirsty."

"Oh, well, yes, of course . . . I—" She looked all around. "Surely there's a stream where we can . . ."

"No," he said decisively. "We'll ride on. Once we leave the White Sands, we'll find water and make camp." Terribly disappointed, the princess said, "Well, can't I at least collect some sand?"

"We've nothing to put it in." He shook his head, dismissing her. "Come on. Time's wasting."

In the saddle again, the unhappy princess made mean faces at the back of Virgil's dark head. She wanted to cry when the great carpet of white abruptly ended and they rode out into the dismal dusty desert.

Less than half a mile from the eastern edge of White Sands, they made camp. It was, the princess decided, not such a bad place to spend the night. It was so dry and forbidding, nothing could live there. Which meant she could spread her blanket safely away from the Ranger and not have to worry about the danger of predators.

Except him, of course.

He was the most threatening predator in the entire desert.

The strained silence between them continued, lasted as darkness fell and the night fully came. Through unspoken, but mutual consent, they slept apart. That is, they spread their blankets away from each other. Neither slept much. Neither could fall asleep knowing that the other was lying stretched out in the moonlight a few short yards away.

So near but yet so far.

The moon had gone completely down before either of them finally went to sleep. At dawn, Virgil awakened as a few pale streaks of gray appeared above the eastern mountains. He rose silently, tiptoed over, and glanced down at the princess. And his breath caught in his throat. She was sleeping soundly, her ginger hair a blazing cloud around her face. She looked like a beautiful child whose fair good looks were slightly marred by days spent under a too harsh sun.

His long legs suddenly weak, Virgil noiselessly crouched down on his heels and studied her as if she were a fragile work of art. Her long lashes rested in feathery crescents on her sun-reddened cheeks. Her small well-shaped nose had a markedly defiant tilt to it, which he found tremendously appealing. And her mouth. God that mouth. The smooth, soft lips, partially open now over small white teeth, were exquisite. The bottom lip was pleasingly full, and the top was fashioned into a perfect cupid's bow.

Virgil licked his own lips as he gazed at hers.

Unbidden came the graphic recollection of how those lips had tasted when they made love in the rainstorm. The sweet, intoxicating scent of her came back to make his senses reel, his heart slam against his ribs.

He was almost grateful when a distraction suddenly presented itself. Something moved in his side vision. Virgil's head swung around. A scorpion sidled across the sand. It's tail raised, claws extended, it was heading directly for the unsuspecting woman. He glanced back at the princess's face. She hadn't stirred.

He rose to his feet, brought his heel down on the advancing scorpion, killing it instantly. He looked around for signs of other pests, pocket mice or kangaroo rats or lizards. Seeing none, he turned and hurried away. He had a little errand to take care of before she awakened.

Cursing himself for being a fool, Virgil hurriedly went through the gear, found a near-empty half-pint bottle of Old Crow whiskey, swigged down the last of the fiery contents, made a face, wiped his mouth, and set out toward the White Sands carrying the empty bottle.

He returned before she awakened. Again crouching down beside her,

Virgil boyishly held one hand behind his back, meaning to surprise her. He shook her gently. The princess's eyes opened to see him looming above, and for a sleep-dazed second she started to reach up, take his bearded face in her hands, and draw it down for a kiss.

But she quickly came fully awake.

"Get away from me!" she said hatefully, "and stay away from me."

"With pleasure," he rejoined, rising quickly to his feet, keeping his hand behind him. "Get the hell up, we're getting out of here."

28

"Her Royal Highness, Crown Princess Marlena of Hartz-Coburg."

A hush fell over the crowd as the announcement of her arrival was made by the uniformed page.

Robbie Ann, on the arm of her distinguished escort, paused at the ballroom's elevated marble entrance. She stood perfectly still, allowing the cream of San Antonio's Old Guard ample opportunity to admire her.

The ginger-haired actress, adroitly playing her part of the royal princess, was gowned in a stunning Paris creation of shimmering green silk. A rope of priceless emeralds graced her pale, exposed throat. The exquisite emeralds were not a part of Princess Marlena's jewel collection. There was nothing left of the royal gem collection, save the prized sapphire-and-diamond necklace and matching earrings that had belonged to the princess's mother.

This dazzling emerald necklace was an offering from her enchanted escort for the evening, the dignified Texan Andrew Forester. One of San Antonio's most powerful and richest citizens, the vain, silver-haired widower owned commercial real estate, banks, and cattle ranches throughout the vast state of Texas. Andrew Forester had eagerly volunteered to be the visiting princess's escort for the evening's gala.

The arrangements meticulously made and agreed to by all concerned parties, Andrew For-ester had, at that afternoon's downtown bond rally, maneuvered to get up close to the platform on which the waving, smiling princess stood.

Patiently waiting until he could catch her eye, he had shouted to be heard above the din, "What color is the gown you will be wearing this evening?"

"Green," she told him, mouthing the words soundlessly. "Emerald green."

He had nodded, smiled, and slipped away while she turned her attention back to the cheering crowd.

That evening, when the immaculately groomed Andrew Forester had shown up at the hotel to collect her, he was beaming broadly as if he had a delicious secret. Robbie Ann had supposed it was nothing more than that he was extremely pleased to have been chosen as her escort. She had learned quickly that when you were a princess of the royal blood—or thought to be—gentlemen clamored for your company.

But she was genuinely surprised when, once the two of them were alone inside the privacy of his gleaming black brougham, Andrew Forester produced a long slim velvet box. Without a word, he handed it to her.

Inside the box, on a bed of shiny white satin, rested the gorgeous emerald necklace. Robbie Ann stared in wonder as the huge emeralds flashed their brilliant green fire in the shadowy light of the carriage's side lamps. Finally she turned to look questioningly at the beaming, silver-haired Andrew Forester.

"Please accept the necklace as a small token of my appreciation for allowing me the great honor of escorting you to the ball," he said. "Look on the emeralds as my small contribution to your empire, Princess Marlena."

Empire, the devil, Robbie Ann thought without a shred of guilt. *These beautiful babies are staying with me. I've earned them!*

She said evenly, "Oh, no, Mr. Forester, I couldn't possibly—that is, my kingdom couldn't possibly—accept such an expensive gift." She turned her most dazzling smile on him, hoping to high heaven he would insist she keep them.

"Of course, you can, Your Royal Highness. You must. Please. I shall be hurt if you refuse," he said, smiling back at her. He took the necklace from the box, and asked, "May I?"

Without waiting for permission, he carefully draped the heavy stones around her neck. As he fastened the dainty gold clasp behind her head, Robbie Ann raised a gloved hand, touched the round-cut emeralds, and wondered just how many thousands of dollars the fabulous stones had set him back. She wanted to ask but didn't dare. A royal princess never bothered about such vulgar things as price.

Now, as Robbie Ann stood on the wide marble threshold with hundreds of pairs of admiring eyes focused on her, she was quietly scheming how she could keep the gift of the necklace a secret from her entourage. This emerald necklace was hers! The captivated gentleman at her side had given it to her, and she had no intention of parting with it.

No one need ever know. Not Montillion. She would cleverly remove it before returning to the hotel. Not the baroness Richtoffen. She would keep it carefully hidden from the eagle-eyed lady-in-waiting. Not this tall, silver-haired rich man who had handed it to her as casually as if it were a bouquet of spring violets.

And certainly not the true princess, who was, and had been for the past twenty-four hours, mysteriously missing. Lord knew where Her Highness was or when she would turn up. Maybe the princess had finally tired of all this folderol and had taken a permanent powder. Maybe the sheltered monarch had met a rugged charmer and had run away with him! That prospect made Robbie Ann's pulse quicken with excitement. If the real Princess Marlena couldn't be found, maybe she could continue to play this coveted role indefinitely.

Robbie Ann was shaken from her pleasant reverie when the gala's grandly gowned hostess, the aging, arthritic widow Annabelle Boothe, stepped forward with the aid of a cane to greet her guest of honor. Then together the three of them—the stand-in princess, her proud escort, and her happy hostess—moved slowly down the long reception line. Introductions were made. Greetings were exchanged. Respectful guests bowed and curtsied.

Robbie Ann loved every minute of the adulation.

With each hand she shook and each pair of shining eyes she looked into, her guilty joy increased. She knew that she should be ashamed of herself for being secretly glad that the real princess had failed to show up on schedule. The recovered Princess Marlena was to have arrived in San Antonio late yesterday afternoon. But the arrival hour had come and gone and now, more than a full day later, she still had not appeared.

Beside himself with worry, Montillion had told Robbie Ann that apparently the princess had been unavoidably delayed and that she would have to continue playing her role for a few hours longer.

"For as long as it takes," she had said, attempting to look worried, actually feeling quite elated. Then, trying to comfort the distraught, likable factor, she had reminded him, "Now, Monty, you are worrying needlessly. You told me yourself that you sent her bodyguard to Cloudcroft to collect her. What could possibly happen to the princess while she's with him? Not a thing. She's fine, just fine."

Turning about now on the polished dance floor in the arms of her elegant partner, Robbie Ann was grateful to the royal princess. The princess's failure to appear had given her at least a few more hours of this privileged life she had come to treasure.

And, an expensive emerald necklace to boot.

29

A dry, hot wind whistled through the hearty ocotillo. Whip-tail lizards scurried along the desert floor, darting in and out of the dead and dying brittlebush, seeking shade. A red-tail hawk soared over the rising thermals, unbothered by the heat and the wind, above it all. Free.

In a scraggly patch of creosote bush, a bumble bee hovered, its wings blurred in flight as it drifted up to one side, then back. And atop a stark, sandstone mesa, an evil-looking humpbacked vulture perched unmoving, as if he scented death.

Across this harsh, forbidding southern New Mexico desert, two people rode tandem atop a sweating, lathered black stallion.

The man was slumped lazily in the saddle, his hat brim pulled low, his black shirt soaked with sweat under the arms and down his back. Accustomed to riding long hours in both extreme heat and bitter cold, he was unbothered by the soaring June temperature of early afternoon in the desert.

The woman, unused to braving the elements, was so hot and miserable she felt as if she couldn't stand one more minute of the terrible torture. Her hair was damp and sticking to her neck. Her head ached from too many hours under the punishing sun. Beads of moisture pooled between her breasts and dampened her dirty blue shirt. The heat, the dust, the perspiration, prickled her skin, and it seemed there was not a single spot on her entire body that did not itch unmercifully. She felt as if she were rubbed raw all over.

The man and the woman crossing the sunbaked plain had not spoken in hours. When the blazing sun reached its zenith, it had been she who finally broke the strained silence.

"Are we ever going to reach El Paso?"

"Eventually," Virgil had replied, noncommittal.

"That's no answer, Ranger!" Now she was both angry and miserable. "Surely we must be getting close to the city by now."

"We might well have been, if not for your sojourn west with the Apaches," he drawled in his flat Texas twang, which made her long to slap his bearded face. "That little adventure added an extra sixty miles to our journey."

"Well . . . I couldn't help it. It wasn't my fault! It was those impertinent Indians. I told the chief that I didn't wish to go with them!"

"Did you now?" Virgil said with a derisive laugh. "Jesus Christ, woman, they don't call this the Wild West because rules of decorum prevail and laws have weight."

"You should know, Texan, you're the most ill-bred man I've ever had the misfortune to meet. And don't call me woman!"

Virgil shrugged, said no more. Nor did she. They again lapsed into silence.

Now in the searing heat of the early afternoon, there was no sound save the buzzing of the bee, the murmur of flies, the scratching of the perched vulture, and a few sporadic bird cries.

These long intervals of silence, the growing mutual irritation, the constant need to lash out at each other—all were born of an unwanted, undeniable attraction between the two. An attraction that was almost palpable.

Twenty-four hours had passed since they made love in the rainstorm. Since then, they had pointedly tried to stay out of each other's way. But when they had stopped the previous night and made camp, they had accidentally, unavoidably bumped into each other. The brief brushing of body against body was like an electrical shock. One touch was all it took to ignite their simmering passions. Instinctively they began kissing and embracing until, fighting against the growing desire threatening to consume them, one would come to his senses and hastily push the other away.

The first time it had happened, it was the princess who had put a stop to it. Struggling to keep her wits about her, she had torn her lips from his plundering mouth and anxiously pulled away, saying breathlessly, "No . . . please . . . don't. Don't."

Less than half an hour later, when it happened again and she found herself enfolded in his arms with his beautifully sculptured lips pressed to hers, it had been Virgil who snapped out of it. Tingling from head to toe, she had blinked in confusion and disappointment when he abruptly set her back, shook his dark head, released her, and hurriedly turned away.

No fewer than a half-dozen such occurrences had taken place before they finally bedded down—safely apart—for the night.

If they agreed on nothing else, it seemed they were of the same mind on at least one thing.

Neither wished to make love to the other again.

Both were dying to make love to the other again.

Even now, as hot and tired and dirty as they were, lust posed the greatest discomfort. Tensing every time she moved unexpectedly or fleetingly touched him, Virgil was glad she couldn't see the torture in his eyes and know how easily she affected him. His body ached with the overwhelming impact of his desire. His head throbbed from suppressed passion. If he didn't get away from this beautiful temptress for an hour or two, he would crack under the strain.

It was the same for the princess.

She had, from the beginning, been fascinated by the tall, dark, ruggedly handsome Ranger. Mesmerized by the exotic aura of adventure that clung to him. Even before they were intimate, before he taught her the delightful secrets of her own body, she had been physically drawn to him.

She told herself it was only because she had never known a man like him. He was different, a novelty. An original. A tough western loner. A daring don of the desert. Everything about him commanded attention. His dark good looks. His lean, muscled body. His Texas Ranger bearing. His eerily controlled poise—cool as ice and compellingly masculine. What female wouldn't find such a unique specimen powerfully intriguing?

Even royal princesses—she had finally learned—were women first. She had learned it from this erotic man whose animal heat had made her feel for the first time in her life the sweet communion of love, that male-female unity that was the fountain of life. It was somehow rather fitting that it had been this enigmatic Texan who so easily solved for her the mystery of physical love.

Instinctively the princess knew that this man held the key to all her untapped passion. He had taught her a valuable lesson in loving. He had shown her where she most wanted, most needed, to be touched. The keeper of the key, he had expertly unlocked the never-before-opened door of her desire. And once he had fully awakened her, he had come inside that door open to him and had patiently guided her along each delightful step toward total ecstacy. An ecstacy so intense, so pleasurable, so complete, she was sure it would last her the rest of her life.

But the opposite was true.

Now that she knew about such incredible joy, she yearned to experience the earth-shattering magic again. At the same time, she was frightened by such a prospect. Her body was already on fire for him. If he made love to her again, would the heart within her be on fire for him as well?

Worried that the rugged Ranger might make love to her again, and equally worried that he might not, the princess closed her stinging eyes against the burning sun and dry winds and waterless wastes spreading out around them. Certain that this barren desert was the most god-awful place on earth, she offered up a silent prayer that they would reach El Paso soon.

Very soon.

Virgil, scanning the horizon ahead, noticed the dust devils swirling out of the south from Texas and knew what was coming. A sandstorm was heading their way, sweeping across the desert with the aid of its ally, the hot, dry winds.

Virgil drew rein. The princess's eyes opened.

"What now?" she asked, perturbed.

He stood in the stirrups, gazed unblinking at the thickening cloud of golden dust in the near distance, sat back down, threw a long leg over, and dropped to the ground.

Unbuckling one of the scarred leather saddlebags, he told her casually, "There's a little sandstorm heading our way."

"Oh, no! Can't you . . . isn't there something . . . well, that's just all I need!" she said in a huff.

"A little sandstorm's good for the complexion," he said sarcastically. "Just look at my skin."

"Such nonsense. And just why are we stopping? Do you plan to sit here and wait for the storm?"

From the saddlebags Virgil withdrew a rumpled white shirt. The princess recognized the shirt he had been wearing when he took her from the Cloudcroft depot platform. She watched, baffled, as he deftly ripped the shirt up into three strips. He tossed two across the saddle. Then, with his teeth, he uncorked the canteen and poured water onto the largest strip.

He shoved the canteen at her. "Hold this."

She took the canteen and watched as he tied the dampened fabric around Noche's dusty muzzle. He grabbed the other strips off the saddle and poured water over both. He handed her one and told her to tie it securely over her nose and mouth. She didn't argue. When she finished, she looked down at him and involuntarily shivered. With the stark white mask covering the lower half of his black-bearded face and his cold blue eyes lingering on her, he looked like a dangerous desperado.

Through the mask, he said, "Now, move up into the saddle and throw your leg over the horse."

"Why?"

"Just do it."

She did it.

"Now," he instructed, "turn around in the saddle so that—"

"I'm to ride backward?"

"You heard me."

Awkwardly, with his help, the princess turned about so that she was astride the saddle, facing the rear.

She said, "What shall I hold on to?"

"Me," he said, swung up behind her, and immediately put the stallion in motion. The princess had no choice, she wrapped her arms around him. And she didn't object when he drew her legs up over his hard thighs and told her to wrap her feet around his calves. She obeyed. With a long arm clasped firmly around her waist, Virgil drew her closer, so close their masked faces were scant inches apart. His piercing blue eyes pinning hers, his breath hissing through the mask, he said, "Better close your eyes now and—" he reached up, cupped the back of her head, and pressed her face flush against his shoulder, "keep your mouth shut."

Before she could close her eyes the swirling sand spiraled around them. In seconds the storm enveloped man, woman, and beast, the stinging sands blinding them and biting exposed flesh. Her closed eyes burning and watering, the princess clasped her arms tightly behind Virgil's back and snuggled as close to him as possible.

Too close, it turned out.

The princess was certain she was losing her mind entirely when, in the midst of the howling, swirling, stinging sands, while her only concern should have been getting through the storm alive, she found herself stirring and wanting this masked man in whose powerful arms she was enclosed.

With the roar and whine of the wind-pushed sands deafening her and her eyes closed tightly against the growing tempest, all she could think of was that their riding position was so intimate it was almost like making love. Her head was on his shoulder, her masked face turned inward, pressing his throat. Her arms were wrapped around his strong back. Her parted legs were draped atop his spread thighs, her slippered toes curled around his muscular calves.

She realized that he had placed her in this position for her own good. Cradling her against his chest, he could provide the best shelter from the whipping sands with his body.

But, had he realized, she wondered, that with her in that position, it was next to impossible to keep her open pelvis from rubbing against his groin. Ashamed that she could even think of such things at a time like this, the princess could think of nothing else.

While the big black stallion blew and snorted and struggled to move against the thick clouds of sand, the princess gasped and sighed and struggled to keep from moving against the inviting rock-hard body of the Ranger. Her cheeks flushed hot when she realized, suddenly, that she was not the only one who could not sit still.

In subtle thrusting movements, his straining groin began to rise rhythmically to meet each timid touch of hers. At first she thought it was an accident. Like the times they had bumped into each other without meaning to. Soon she knew that it wasn't. Languidly, at first, and ever so gently, he thrust and parried and teased and the princess felt a pleasant pressure against her prepuce.

As the storm grew in intensity, so did their game. Soon, and not so languidly, they began to brush and buck and bump each other in an unorthodox, yet incredibly thrilling, exercise in escalating sexual arousal.

The strange, thrilling game became more than a game when the princess, to her complete shock, began to feel as she had when Virgil made love to her in the cave. That deep, hot yearning, that nameless, helpless feeling that an overwhelming urgency was building inside, that something frightening and wonderful was happening to her.

Virgil knew exactly what was happening to her because the same thing was happening to him. Jesus, if someone had told him yesterday that he was so hot for a woman that he would—with them both fully dressed—climax with her atop a moving horse in the middle of a sandstorm, he would have said they were insane.

He was the one who was insane.

He couldn't let this happen way out here with no way to clean himself up. He wouldn't let it happen. He would give it to her, help her have an orgasm, but he would hold back.

That's what he intended, but it didn't work out that way.

At the height of the roaring, biting sandstorm, the mounted pair clung to each other, pressing and grinding their bodies together, imitating the motions of lovemaking until both reached the pinnacle of pleasure, shuddering in shared release without so much as a single kiss being exchanged or a single article of clothing being removed. At that moment, the roaring, wailing sandstorm reached a loud crescendo, then quickly tapered off and died away.

Virgil's first thought when his heartbeat began to slow was that he couldn't make it the rest of the way to El Paso without a break from this woman. He *had* to get away from this seductive she-devil for a little while, so he could get his head screwed back on straight.

30

By five that afternoon, with the sun still high and hot overhead, the mute, mounted pair had finally crossed completely, west to east, the formidable Tularosa country. Silently, Virgil congratulated himself. He had succeeded in safely transporting a woman down out of the steep Sacramento Mountains and across this parched no-man's-land.

A waterless desert where only the fierce and rugged could live; prickly pear and thorn-covered mesquites, rattlesnakes and tarantulas. She had come through it without injury. He hadn't been so lucky. Fifteen years in the Rangers without a scratch. Three days with her and he had suffered a nail-scraped jaw, a bloodied earlobe, a gouged eye, and broken ribs.

Relief flooded through him as Virgil drew rein among the scattered prickly pears and tall stalks of ivory-blooming yuccas at the base of the jagged Organ Mountains. A far greater relief for him was the thought that this winsome, worrisome woman would be out of his hair and out of his sight for a few blessedly peaceful hours.

The curious princess, now riding behind him again, wondered why they had stopped. She peered over his shoulder to see what he was looking at and almost swooned with pleasure.

"Are we going there?" she asked, speaking for the first time in more than an hour.

Without turning to look at her, Virgil said, "If you can behave yourself and stay out of mischief until morning, we'll spend the night at Tierra del Encanto. Think you can manage?"

"Is it a hotel?" she asked, her eyes focused on the sprawling, two-story salmon-hued structure rising from the foothills of the craggy mountains.

"No. A private home."

As they rode up a long pebbled drive bordered by Texas sable palms, Virgil explained that Don Amondo Rivas, an old and trusted friend and owner of the vast Sunland Ranch, would be more than happy to put them up for the night.

"Who will you tell him I am?" asked the princess.

"Amondo will not inquire," Virgil said. "His manners are impeccable. You will be whoever I tell him you are."

"Then could you kindly tell him that I am—"

"Don't start with that princess nonsense," he cut her off. "We'll keep it simple. You will be Miss Jones."

"What's my first name?"

"Eva." He responded so quickly, it made the princess curious.

"Eva? Is Eva the name of someone you—?"

"There's Amondo now," Virgil interrupted, raising a hand to wave.

Princess Marlena's attention turned to the broadly smiling Mexican who was rushing across the manicured grounds to greet them. A powerfully built man with silver-streaked dark hair, a pencil-thin mustache, black flashing eyes, and the smooth unlined face of a boy, Amondo Rivas seemed genuinely thrilled to see them.

Virgil eased the princess off the stallion and swung down himself. Hastily he tore the sweat-stained hat off his head and held it strategically before him. The princess noticed and knew the reason. He was, she suspected, concerned that his trousers were stained from their early afternoon's carnal calisthenics in the sandstorm.

Her too-large denim trousers didn't give her away, but on the tender insides of her thighs she could feel the sticky residue of her own body's release. They were a shameful, dirty pair, no doubt about it. She only prayed that the immaculate Mexican gentleman coming to meet them wouldn't guess just *how* dirty and shameful.

A young Mexican boy materialized to tend the lathered stallion as the beaming Amondo Rivas reached them, slapped Virgil affectionately on the back, and shook his hand warmly.

"*El Capitán, mi amigo!*" Rivas said, his smile blindingly bright, his dark eyes flashing with delight. "Welcome to Tierra del Encanto! Has been far too long since you last come to visit."

"Good to see you, Don Amondo," Virgil said, then inclined his head toward the princess. "May I present my traveling companion, Miss Eva Jones. Eva, this is my very good friend, Don Amondo Rivas."

"Ah, *Señorita* Eva," Don Amondo said, reaching for her hand, "is a true pleasure to make your acquaintance."

Her first impulse was to correct him, to tell him that she was a *señora*, not a *señorita*, but Virgil shot her a quick "don't do it" look.

She said simply, "The pleasure is mine, *Señor* Rivas."

Don Amondo brushed his mustachioed mouth over the back of her hand and smiled engagingly at her. The friendly Mexican gave no indication, either in word or in deed, that he wondered why she was dressed in soiled men's clothing or why her hair was dirty and tangled. He displayed, as Virgil had predicted, impeccable manners.

Releasing her hand, Don Amondo clasped his own together in a gesture of joy and said, "You cannot know how glad I am to have company!" Addressing the princess, he explained, "I have a big, loud family, but they are away in Chihuahua City. They have been gone for more than two weeks, and the house is much too quiet. I have been so lonely, but now you have come to visit, to keep me company! I hope you will stay several days."

He glanced at Virgil, gently took the princess's arm, and began escorting her toward the imposing hacienda.

"Just for the night, *amigo,*" Virgil said, following.

"No, no, is not long enough," argued Don Amondo. "Soledad and the children are due home tomorrow," he looked over his shoulder, his dark eyes imploring. "Surely you wish to see them, *Capitán.*"

"You know I do. But Miss Jones and I have prior obligations," said Virgil evenly. "We must leave first thing in the morning."

Purposely speaking loudly enough for Virgil to hear, Don Amondo said to the princess, "You must talk to the *capitán.* Persuade him to stay with us a few days. You will do that, won't you, *Señorita* Eva?" She didn't immediately reply. "*Señorita* Eva?"

"Oh, yes, yes," the princess said, embarrassed that she had, for a second, forgotten that she was to respond when addressed as *Señorita* Eva. "I certainly will—" Virgil cleared his throat loudly, "that is we . . . we really must be leaving tomorrow."

"Ah, that is too bad," said Don Amondo. "In that case, you must make *Capitán* Black bring you back to Tierra del Encanto again real soon when you stay longer. Now, come, we go inside."

The huge hacienda was smothered in purple bougainvillea and pink running roses. In the arcaded central courtyard a fountain splashed and someone was strumming a guitar.

A capable staff kept Tierra del Encanto running smoothly, inside and out.

Outside, a platoon of talented gardeners endlessly planted and pruned and trimmed, making the vast grounds surrounding the hacienda a haven. An inviting, shady oasis set squarely between the hot, flat desert and the cool, towering mountains.

Inside, a squadron of polite, cheerful servants kept the many-roomed mansion spotless. Not so much as a single grain of sand or the hint of a cobweb could be found inside the eighteen-inch thick walls. Fresh flowers, changed daily, graced each of the thirty rooms, their pleasing scent mingling with the clean smell of lemon oil that kept the dark woodwork and heavy furniture gleaming.

A skilled chef, lured from a favorite Barcelona restaurant years ago, and a half-dozen kitchen helpers prepared exotic meals in large quantities. And, at least one cook was on call twenty-four hours of the day in case the don or doña or any one of the eight Rivas children happened to have a sudden yen for a hot spicy *chile relleno* or a light, fluffy *sopapilla.*

They all, the gardeners, the servants, the cooks, did their various chores so unobtrusively, they were rarely seen. Never in the way.

In the wide entrance hall of the hacienda, Don Amondo said, extending his right hand, "Come, we will go into the *sala* and—"

Virgil quickly shook his head.

He refused to step foot into that spacious room with its enormous stone fireplace filled with elegant, overstuffed sofas and comfortable chairs and heavy carved tables and valuable art and an ornate piano shipped from Spain.

"As you can see, we're a little dirty."

"Oh, forgive me," said the mannerly Mexican. "I forget myself I am so happy to see you." He looked at the princess. "You would enjoy a nice bath, no?"

"I would enjoy a nice bath, yes," said the princess, already anticipating the luxury.

"*Sí, sí,*" said the don, and snapped his short brown fingers. A fresh-faced servant appeared almost immediately. To her he said, "Consuela, will you please direct the *señorita* to one of the guest rooms and draw a bath for her." He turned back to the princess. "I have daughters of all sizes, *Señorita* Eva. I am confident something can be found for you to wear."

"You're very kind," said the princess.

The don smiled and said, "It is only half past five. You have two and a half hours to rest before dinner at eight."

"Sounds wonderful."

Without so much as a glance at Virgil, the princess turned away and followed Consuela up the center staircase.

On the wide upstairs landing, Consuela turned toward the southern wing, and led the princess down the cool, dim corridor. At the next to the last door, the servant stopped and opened it.

The princess stepped inside the well-appointed room and sighed with pleasure. Tall floor-to-ceiling windows, opening onto an outside landing, looked down on the flower-filled courtyard. The continuous splash of the courtyard's fountain would, she felt sure, lull her quickly to sleep that night.

She turned and gazed at the big, baroque bed. The beautifully carved dark wood headboard soared to a height of three or four feet. At the bed's foot, heavy carved posts rose above her head. A counterpane of shimmering yellow silk was topped with a half-dozen huge feather pillows encased in yellow-and-white silk cases.

The princess, studying the bed, sighed happily. Tonight she would sleep as peacefully as a newborn babe. Alone. She would lock the door against the dark man with whom she had behaved so disgracefully.

The princess already felt better.

Having Virgil Black out of her sight for two and a half hours was exactly what she most needed. In his intimidating presence she couldn't seem to think straight. And, if there was ever a time in her life she needed to see things clearly, it was now.

"*Señorita?*" Consuela broke into her reverie. "Your bath is ready."

"Thank you, Consuela." The princess was already kicking off her slippers and unbuttoning her dirty blue shirt.

The servant said, "While you enjoy your tub, I will lay out several gowns from which you may choose."

Eager to get into that soothing hot water, the princess nodded and hurried eagerly into the bathroom. As large as most bedrooms, the room was embellished in white-and-yellow Mexican tiles. Yellow roses in white porcelain vases sweetened the air. A skylight located directly over the huge white tub brought the outside inside. Bright sunlight, slanted now as the afternoon grew late, streamed down to brightly illuminate half the long tub, leaving the other half in shadow.

Rich yellow carpet covered the floor, and dozens of fluffy white towels were neatly folded and stacked on tall shelves. A freestanding mirror graced one corner of the large bathroom, and the princess learned that once she had stripped and was in the steamy tub, she could see herself in the strategically placed mirror.

She hesitated before climbing into the tub.

It was the first mirror she had seen since her ordeal began. Curious, she turned directly toward the mirror and studied her naked reflection. She hardly recognized herself. Her hair, which had always been her pride and joy, was so dirty and tangled she wasn't sure she could ever get it clean. And even if she did, she had no earthly idea how to dress her own hair.

Twisting a ginger strand around her finger, she slowly lowered her gaze, and it seemed as if she were seeing her body for the first time. She had paid very little attention to her undraped form in the past. She had kept herself slender, but that was only so she would look utterly stunning in the beautiful gowns she favored.

It certainly was not so she would look good naked. That had never made much difference, since no one ever saw her naked save her lady-in-waiting. Not even her late husband, the duke, had seen her totally naked.

Staring at herself now, the princess was interested in her body as she had never been before. She studied the shape and fullness of her breasts, noted that the rosy crests were large and soft and satiny. Her gaze drifted lower to the small waist that every gown she owned accentuated. Smiling, she moved on to the flat stomach and pale thighs. She put her knees and ankles together and was pleased to see that her long, slender legs were near perfectly shaped.

She pivoted, looked over her shoulder, and examined the long, slender back, the rounded cheeks of her bottom. She turned back to face the mirror, intrigued.

As the naked princess carefully studied herself, she felt heat rise to her cheeks. She realized, with a quick stab of fear through her bare breasts, that Virgil Black was responsible for her newfound interest in her unclothed body. She was looking at herself appraisingly, trying to see herself through his eyes, wondering if he had found her pretty when they were naked together. If he walked in the room and saw her now, would he think she was beautiful?

The princess abruptly shook her head to clear it and stepped into the steaming tub. Easing down into the soapy depths, she vowed that as she scrubbed the physical evidence of him from her body, she would wash him of her thoughts as well.

She had, she told herself, been a royal fool. But it wasn't entirely her fault. After all, a dark, dangerous-looking man had kidnapped her against her will, scared her half to death. *He* was responsible. She had read enough about people in similar situations to know that it was quite common for a captive to become dependent on, even trusting of, her captor. That's what had happened to her. She had let her defenses down, and being alone with him in the wilds for so long she had . . . they had . . .

That was behind her. It would be easy to resist him now that they were back in civilization. Already she was beginning to think of him as he actually was: uncaring, unprincipled, heartless. Besides, he was unkempt, dirty, and bearded. Such a man would never have attracted her under different circumstances.

The princess spent those precious hours away from Virgil calmly forgiving herself. Then, quietly lecturing herself, reminding herself of the pressing duties that awaited her. Of the loyal subjects that depended on her. Soon she would be back home at Hartz-Coburg. Safe and comfortable in the cliffside castle where she had been born.

The misfortune that had befallen her here in America would be put forever behind her. She would forget it ever happened.

When eight o'clock came and it was time for her to go down to dinner, the princess was ready for any challenge.

In a perfectly fitting, low-cut gown of delicate white lace over a sky-blue organza underskirt, she felt like her old self again. Beneath the full-skirted gown, she wore brand new underwear of cool eggshell satin, and on her long slender legs were silk stockings. A pair of embroidered velvet slippers were on her small feet.

Her hair was clean and shiny, and it was she who had shampooed it. She was proud of that. It was the first time in her life she had ever shampooed her own hair. She was prouder still of the fact that she had helped the skillful Consuela dress her freshly washed hair. It had been such fun. The two of them had laughed like young girls while both labored to brush, curl, and sweep the springy ginger locks into a fashionable coiffeur atop her head.

With the aid of expensive creams and oils followed by a generous dusting of powder, her slightly sunburned face now looked almost as pale as ever. Lip rouge cleverly concealed her chapped lips; her mouth was again lush and soft.

Pausing on the upstairs landing, the princess drew a deep, relaxed breath. She was confident that her sanity had fully returned. She no longer need concern herself with the lurking sexual danger of Virgil Black. She was not the least bit worried that she might slip and fall again.

It was not going to happen.

The dark, devilish Ranger no longer posed a threat.

31

"Ah, Señorita Eva," said Don Amondo. He was waiting for her at the base of the stairs. "How beautiful you look this evening. *Muy bonito!"*

Smiling at him as she descended the last two carpeted steps, the princess took his offered hand and said, "If I do, it is all thanks to your daughter, Soraya." She touched the delicate lace ruffle of the gown's off-the-shoulder bodice. "Consuela told me the dress belongs to your eldest daughter. I hope she won't mind my borrowing it."

"No, no. Soraya is a very sweet, generous young woman." He beamed with paternal pride as he spoke of his eighteen-year-old daughter. "I hope one day you two will meet."

"I hope so, too."

"Now, come." Don Amondo took her arm. *"El capitán* awaits us in the *sala."*

The don ushered the princess into the *sala* as the desert sun was setting. Lamps glowed brightly, illuminating portions of the spacious room, leaving others in shadow. At the far end of the *sala,* in the shadows, a man stood before the cold fireplace, his back to the room.

"Here she is, *Capitán,"* the don announced.

Virgil Black slowly turned around. He paused, then stepped up into the light. The princess immediately made a misstep, almost stumbled. If not for the don's supporting hand under her arm, she would have fallen.

She had, foolishly, she realized now, expected Virgil to look just as he had when she went upstairs. Nothing could have been farther from the truth.

He stood there, unmoving, perfectly framed by the huge rock fireplace. An elegantly clad, immaculately groomed man who was so sinfully handsome, the awed princess felt as if she couldn't breathe.

The shaggy raven hair had been clipped and washed and brushed straight back from his temples. The bushy black beard was gone. His handsome face was smoothly shaven and glowing with good health. A faint pink line, left there by her scratching nail, curved down his tanned left cheek. His right earlobe was decorated with a tiny healing scab, also thanks to her.

His beautiful eyes were a startling blue in the darkness of his face. His lips, those exquisitely sculptured lips, were turned up in a sexy half smile.

His soiled black shirt and trousers were gone, replaced with a well-cut formal charro suit of midnight black and a snowy white shirt of shimmering silk. A scarf of flaming scarlet was tied around his throat, and in his lapel was one perfect red rose. The short bolero jacket, stretching appealingly across his wide shoulders, hung open down his chest. Through the fine silk of his white shirt she could see the shadowy darkness of crisp curly hair and smooth bronzed skin.

Her knees had gone so weak she could hardly stand, and the only thought running through her mind was that she couldn't wait to have his arms around her again. All her earlier reserve had vanished the instant he turned around.

"Eva, my dear," Virgil drawled, acknowledging her.

"Captain," she managed, wondering if the room really was stifling, or if it was her.

Virgil raised his leaded-bottom liquor glass in salute, then drained the contents, his hooded gaze never leaving her.

The minute he had turned to see her, he knew that he couldn't leave her alone. He *had* to make love to her again. Never had she been more beautiful, more alluring. In the youthful dress she now wore, she looked incredibly fresh and appealingly innocent. She could have been eighteen, so flawless was her face, so perfect her skin, so girlishly slender her body. A wide white lace ruffle, topping the gown's tight bodice, encircled her creamy shoulders, leaving them appealingly bare. That same ruffle dipped low at the center in front. But not low enough. The pale rise of her breasts when she breathed made his own breath catch in his chest. He had to consciously steel himself to remain calm, to refrain from behaving outlandishly.

His teeth were tightly clenched, his jaw ridged. It was with superhuman effort that Virgil Black kept himself from hurriedly crossing to her, yanking that lace bodice down, and burying his lips in the warm shadowy sweetness between her pale perfect breasts.

As the two of them stood across the lamp-lighted *sala* from each other, a silent, urgent message passed between them. It was simply this: *Let's hurry and have dinner so we can make love.*

The don, chattering companionably, never noticed that they only nodded or mumbled acknowledgments to his questions and statements. Don Amondo Rivas was a man who enjoyed talking, so he didn't mind if those to whom he spoke were satisfied just to listen.

"Shall we go in to dinner?" the don finally invited in the same cheerful, conversational tone he'd been using.

"Yes!" Virgil and the princess said in unison.

"Good, good. You are both hungry, no?"

"Oh, yes," said the princess, "quite hungry."

His heavy lidded gaze never leaving her, Virgil said, "Famished."

But once inside the candlelit dining room, the portly don was the only one who ate with gusto. The princess, seated across the table from Virgil, had little appetite for food. She sipped the chilled wine from a stemmed crystal wineglass and pushed the food around her plate with a sterling silver fork. And looked with barely disguised longing at the darkly handsome man across the table.

His carefully brushed hair shone like shimmering black satin in the candlelight, and his lazy-lidded eyes gleamed with a silent sexual promise. The princess had to quickly lower her gaze from his, afraid she might actually swoon. It was then that she noticed, and not for the first time, Virgil's hands. There was both strength and grace in those beautiful hands of his. Such exquisite hands. Lean, tanned hands with long tapered fingers and clean square-cut nails. Deft, dexterous hands. Skilled masculine hands that could ignite incredible heat with the lightest of touches.

Tingling, the princess quickly shifted her attention from Virgil, lest she make a complete fool of herself.

The many-coursed meal moved at a leisurely pace. Throughout, the don did most of the talking. The princess found she was interested in his narrative, because most of his lengthy tales involved Virgil Black, a man with whom she had been intimate but knew little about. Clearly the sunny dispositioned Mexican knew Virgil well and was fond of the stone-faced Ranger.

His silverware poised above his china plate, the don pointed his knife at Virgil and said, "If not for this big brave *Americano*, my precious baby boy would not be here."

Virgil cleared his throat loudly and quickly changed the subject. "So, Amondo, how many new colts did the ranch—"

"*Con permiso, Capitán,*" the don interrupted. "I know you too well. You have never told the *señorita* about saving my son." He turned to her. "Has he?"

"No. No, he hasn't." The princess glanced at Virgil, then back at the don, curious. "Please, you tell me."

The don smiled at the stern-faced Virgil. "You are too modest, *amigo*." To the princess he said, "Doña Soledad, my beautiful wife, says *el capitán* is the bravest man she has ever known."

The princess wanted to hear the story.

The don wanted to tell it.

Virgil rolled his eyes and reached for his wineglass.

Don Amondo laid down his silverware. For a long moment he was totally silent. When he spoke, it was in a low, deep voice that commanded attention. A born orator, he began, "For as long as I live on this earth I will always remember that horrible, horrible day." He leaned back in his chair, made himself comfortable. The princess leaned closer to the table, hanging on his every word.

"It was just a few months ago and I had given my youngest son, Ramon, a gentle mustang gelding for his fourth birthday. Ramon and I were out on the far southern reaches of Tierra del Encanto that cool March morning. I was teaching him to ride, and I knew if we stayed close to the corral, Ramon's older brothers and sisters would come out to watch and they would tease him. You know how that goes."

"Yes," said the princess, thinking that she had no idea, since she had never had any siblings.

"Soledad was very angry with me that morning for not staying close to home. But she is a woman, so perhaps—you will forgive me for saying it—she does not fully understand how easily the pride of a man is wounded. I explained to her that Ramon's pride would be badly hurt if he fell off the pony in front of his brothers and sisters and all the *vaqueros*."

The princess nodded.

"But I digress," said the don, waving a plump brown hand in the air. "Ramon and I were alone and far from ranch headquarters when a band of renegade Apaches ambushed us. I knew what they wanted the minute they surrounded us. My son. My precious son, Ramon." The don shuddered, remembering. "Ramon was torn from my arms and lifted up onto a brave's dancing paint. The warriors took his mustang and my stallion, leaving me afoot. They rode away toward the mountains with me frantically running after them, shouting for them to let my son go. To take me instead. I could see Ramon turned in the saddle, looking back at me, trying very hard not to cry."

The don laughed suddenly and admitted, "My four-year-old son was more of a man that day than his father. He was not crying but his frightened *padre* was. I was sobbing and shouting, and I guess the Apaches found me to be too big a nuisance, because one of the braves turned back and knocked me unconscious with the butt of his rifle."

The don spoke of how the kidnapped boy's mother had had to be sedated, so upset was she. And he told the princess how it had been Ranger Virgil Black who alone rode into the Apache mountain stronghold and bargained for Ramon's life.

Mesmerized, the princess hadn't said a word throughout his fascinating story. She glanced often at Virgil. He was, she could tell, terribly uncomfortable, embarrassed. Which made him tremendously appealing. Most men would have bragged about such a daring feat of heroism.

"I will never," concluded the sentimental Don Amondo, his dark eyes misting, "forget—after staring down that long front drive day after hopeless day—seeing *Capitán* Black come riding up it with my precious baby boy in his arms."

Half-choked up herself, the princess was deeply touched by the revelation. She cast yet another glance at the charmingly ill-at-ease Virgil and tried to picture him with a child in his arms. She couldn't do it. The vision would not come.

A vision that would come and did, was one with her in his strong arms. Instinctively, she knew that it was a shared vision. She knew that Virgil Black was just as eager to hold her in his arms as she was to be there.

"Ah, yes," Don Amondo was saying as he picked up his knife and fork, "we have been through some bad times and some good times together, have we not, *mi amigo?*"

"Mostly good," said Virgil, nodding yes when a servant poured more wine into his stemmed glass.

The don said, "I have the Spanish land grants to tens of thousands of acres contiguous to Tierra del Encanto atop secret aquifers, and El Paso banks have offered Virgil favorable terms to underwrite his own rancho. But he keeps turning me down." He looked at Virgil. "Are we not good friends, *amigo?*"

Virgil nodded, but gave no reply.

"Ah, well, perhaps one day you will change your mind. You cannot be a Texas Ranger forever."

Virgil shrugged.

The don then talked at length of life on the big rancho, telling the princess proudly that all his children were bright and industrious. Each had his assigned chores, and indolence was not tolerated. They were hard workers all, just like their *padre*.

By the time dessert was served, the eager pair seated across from each other were beginning to wonder if the prolonged meal would ever end. Knowing that the golden flan was the last course, both the princess and Virgil devoured the rich pudding with genuine enthusiasm.

"You will have more flan?" asked Don Amondo when all had finished.

"Oh, no, thank you, Don Amondo," said the princess. "Everything was so delicious, I'm afraid I've overeaten."

"You, *Capitán?*" the don asked, smiling.

"No more for me, *gracias.*" Virgil raised a tanned hand, patted his stomach. "It was a superb meal." He pushed back his chair.

"Ah, you both eat like birds," said the don, lifted a silver bell, and shook it. "One helping of flan is never enough for me." A serving girl appeared carrying a small silver tray atop which was a crystal pedestal dish of flan.

As the don enjoyed his second dish of the pudding, he stopped often to tell yet another story. The princess fidgeted nervously. Virgil sat perfectly still, but he kept glancing at a porcelain clock on the long walnut sideboard.

The meal finally ended. The trio left the dining room. In the hacienda's wide entranceway, the princess turned to the stocky Mexican. "It was a lovely evening, Don Amondo. I hope you will not think me rude if I go up. I am so sleepy I can hardly hold my eyes open." She smiled at him.

"But, of course." The don was gracious. "It has been a long day for you. You go now and rest."

The hallway clock chimed the hour of ten o'clock as the princess bade them both good night, lifted her skirts, and turned to the stairs.

"I'm a little sleepy myself," Virgil said, practically holding his breath. "Think I'll—"

"No, no," the don said, frowning, shaking his head. "Not before we share at least one glass of brandy and a cigar."

On the stairs, the princess heard their exchange and prayed that Virgil would turn down the don's invitation. She felt as if she couldn't possibly wait one minute more to be in his arms. She made a tortured face when she heard his calm reply.

Trapped, Virgil said, evenly, "Fine. But only one."

At ten o'clock on that same hot June night, a weary Hantz Landsfelt, Princess Marlena's guilt-ridden bodyguard, stumbled into the El Paso telegraph office.

The clerk behind the counter, a neatly dressed round-faced man with thinning brown hair, looked up. He saw a burly giant with numerous bruises and scratches on his hands and face. The big man was wearing dirty, tattered clothes, and his hair was badly disheveled.

Smiling, the clerk said, "How does the other fellow look, friend?"

"There was no other fellow, and I'm not your friend," yelled Hantz Landsfelt. "Give me a sheet of paper. I must send a wire at once."

"That's what I'm here for," said the clerk, pushing a pad of yellow message paper through the barred window.

In San Antonio, it was just past eleven that night when Montillion, pacing worriedly in the elegant Menger Hotel suite, was startled by a loud knock on the suite's door.

"Telegram," called the delivery boy through the door.

All the blood drained from Montillion's face, and he felt his heart stop beating, then speed out of control. He rushed across the room and yanked the door open.

The slender uniformed young man presented him with a yellow envelope, saying, "I'm supposed to wait for a response."

Ignoring the boy, Montillion tore the envelope open with cold, trembling fingers and read:

MARLENA APPREHENDED BY TEXAS RANGER. SOME KIND OF MIX-UP.

MISTAKEN IDENTITY. MARLENA LIKELY SAFE AND UNHARMED. RANGER BRINGING HER TO EL PASO JAIL. SHOULD ARRIVE ANY . . .

The wire went on to explain how it happened and why. And how he, Hantz, had just arrived in El Paso after a number of unlikely calamities had befallen him. He had, he said, been forced to walk most of the way. In conclusion, the shamed bodyguard asked what he should do next.

"Nothing!" Montillion spoke the word aloud as he reread the telegram.

"What is it, Montillion?" The baroness, tying the sashes of her night robe, had heard the commotion and come into the room.

"The princess," he said. "She's on the way to El Paso."

"Thank God! She's unhurt?" asked the anxious lady-in-waiting.

"She better be!" said Montillion, hurrying to the writing desk to compose his reply.

To the uniformed boy waiting with his hands clasped behind him, Montillion said, "I'll be sending two wires, young man, and I want your word that both will be delivered by midnight."

"Sure thing," said the boy, and when he left he carried two important messages.

One was to Hantz Landsfelt telling him to stay in El Paso, to go straight to the Texas Rangers headquarters and explain what had happened, and then to wait right there for Her Royal Highness to arrive. The second was addressed to the officer in charge at Ranger headquarters in Ysleta.

When the boy had gone, Montillion turned to the baroness Richtoffen, exhaled heavily, and said with relief, "Start packing."

Nodding, she didn't question him. Holding the lapels of her robe together, she turned away without a word.

Moments before midnight, after making her final San Antonio appearance, the ginger-haired, dreamy-eyed actress playing the part of the princess returned to the Menger Hotel. Surprised by all the bustle inside the well-lighted suite at this late hour, her expression immediately changed. A tremor of alarm raced through her, and she gave Montillion a questioning look.

"Good news at last," he exclaimed happily. "Princess Marlena is alive! She's alive and probably unharmed! Isn't it wonderful!"

"Yes," Robbie Ann managed to reply, feeling as if someone had pulled the world out from under her. "Just wonderful," she murmured. Forcing herself to smile, she advanced farther into the room. "I suppose this means curtains for me. Show closed for good. End of the road. Pack up my grease paint and go."

"No, not quite." Montillion smiled warmly at her. "As we speak, the princess is en route to El Paso. So we will alter our planned course. Instead of going from here to Galveston where we were to board the royal yacht for Hartz-Coburg, we will depart for El Paso tonight. Within the hour."

"Where does that leave me?"

"You will go to El Paso with us," he told her.

"Why?"

"In case the princess does not show up as soon as expected, you can continue to play her part. I'm sure I can schedule a rally or two in El Paso and—"

Interrupting, Robbie Ann said, "Monty, has it occurred to you that the Texas Ranger who took the princess might have been looking for me?"

"It has. Yes, it has," said Montillion with no emotion.

Robbie Ann lifted her bare shoulders in a shrug. "And I suppose you expect me to tell you all about it."

"No," said Montillion. "No, not until you're ready." He smiled, and added, "If and when you ever wish to speak of it, I will listen and do my best to understand."

Her brows drawn together, she said, "I . . . I've made some mistakes."

"Everyone makes mistakes," he said, kindly. Then, "I've grown very fond of you." He paused, added, "When all this is over and the princess is back where she belongs, I shall do my best to help you. If indeed you are in some kind of trouble, I'll see if there is anything we can do diplomatically to straighten things out."

She brightened a little. "You'd do that for me?" Then she shook her head and asked, "Why?"

Robbie Ann looked at him with those enormous emerald eyes, so like the eyes of Princess Marlena, and Montillion was tempted to tell her the reason. The real reason. But he did not.

He said only, "My dear, I've just told you. I've grown fond of you and I want you to be happy." Smiling, he said, "You are a beautiful, intelligent young woman, who is, I believe, basically a good, decent person. Perhaps all you need is a new start, a new set of friends. Perhaps Galveston would be better suited to your amazing acting talent. I understand they have several excellent theaters and a large thespian community."

"No kidding?"

"You could travel to the seaside city with us on the royal train. And I could write some letters of introduction for you. How does that sound?"

"Not as good as being princess," she admitted with a sigh, "but better than any other offers I've had lately." Her expression somber, she asked, "If I go to El Paso with you, you won't . . . tell anybody about me? You won't turn me in to the Texas Ranger, will you?"

Montillion looked at the pretty young woman with whom he had spent the past three weeks and felt a deep paternal tenderness toward her.

"No, my dear child. I would never do that."

Midnight at Tierra del Encanto.

Upstairs in the many-roomed hacienda, Princess Marlena paced back and forth before a pair of tall double doors thrown open to the warm June night. A nearly full white moon sailed high in the cloudless heavens, its luminous light spilling across the balcony outside and into her darkened bedroom.

From the flower-filled courtyard below came the tinkling splash of the continuous fountain and the soft romantic strumming of a lone Spanish guitar. The subtle scent of roses mingling with bougainvillea sweetened the still night air. The room's big bed had been turned down, the colorful counterpane removed. Spotless silky white sheets and a half-dozen pillows in lace-edged cases looked silvery in the moonlight.

But the pacing Princess Marlena was not ready for bed.

She was still fully dressed, was still wearing the white lace and blue-skirted evening gown. Her ginger hair was still coiffed sleekly atop her head. When she came upstairs two hours ago, she had waved away Consuela's offer of assistance, assuring the smiling young servant that she was perfectly capable of undressing herself. Which wasn't entirely true, since she had never attempted it and had no idea if she could actually manage.

But she had been so certain that Virgil would follow her up within minutes, and she hadn't wanted Consuela to bump into him and embarrass them all. As it turned out, there had been little danger of that happening.

After Consuela departed, the excited princess had debated whether she should leave the lamps lit or turn them off. She anticipated the minute when Virgil would walk through the door and sweep her up into his powerful arms. She shivered deliciously and decided that the special moment would be more romantic in the darkness. She swept hurriedly around the room and turned out all the lamps, casting the room into a seductive blend of radiant moonlight and cloaking darkness. Tense from head to toe, she had then stood in the very center of the large shadowy room, anxiously awaiting Virgil's gentle knock on the door.

Minutes had passed and he hadn't come. The princess was puzzled. Then an hour had dragged slowly by, and a terrible sinking feeling intensified. Now it was midnight, and two torturous hours had elapsed since she left him and the don downstairs.

He wasn't coming.

Had never intended to come. She had been a silly child to think that he would. Those boldly sensual looks across the table had been nothing more than teasing flirtation. He had made her think he desperately wanted her. He didn't want her. He just wanted her to want him. Another feather in his cap. Damn him for his cruelty.

Facing the inescapable, the princess realized she should get undressed and go to bed. But she wasn't sleepy. She was restless. Confused. Yearning. Disappointed.

Downstairs in Don Amondo's book-lined library, an equally tense Virgil Black swirled the amber contents of his brandy snifter in his warm palm. He flicked the ashes from his second cigar of the evening and glanced—for the hundredth time—at a heavy jade-and-gold clock resting on the don's mahogany desk.

At least a half-dozen times in the past couple of hours, Virgil had attempted to call it a night, pleading extreme weariness. Each time the don had looked as disappointed as a child and had pleaded with him to stay for just a few more minutes.

"Por favor, amigo," Don Amondo had appealed to Virgil. "You come to visit so seldom, allow me to enjoy your company a while longer. It is still quite early. Let me pour you another brandy."

Since he was a guest and Don Amondo was ever the gracious host, Virgil had relented. But he was miserable. Much as he usually enjoyed the don's company, he could think of nothing but the beautiful woman waiting for him upstairs.

If she was still waiting.

Maybe she had grown impatient and had given up. Maybe she had tired and gone to bed, was now sound asleep. Maybe he had read her wrong, and she wasn't really expecting him. Maybe she didn't even want him to come, wouldn't allow him inside once he got there. Maybe he should go straight to his own room and forget about her.

He couldn't do that. The temptation to hold her in his arms was more than he could resist.

". . . so what do say, *Capitán?*" Don Amondo asked as the clock struck midnight. *"Capitán?"*

Snapping out of his desire-induced trance, Virgil realized the don had asked him a question, but he had no idea what.

"I'm sorry," he said, looking sheepish. "What did you say?"

"That I am getting awfully sleepy now myself," Don Amondo said, raising a hand to stifle a yawn. Then he smiled at Virgil and said, "You must be as well. You haven't heard anything I've said for the past half hour."

"Forgive me, *amigo*," Virgil said. "The truth is I am about to fall asleep where I sit."

The don rose. "We can't let that happen."

Virgil came to his feet. The two men walked out of the library and down the wide center hall toward the front of the hacienda. Side by side they climbed the broad staircase, and reaching the second-floor landing, the don, his lids growing heavy, said, "You know your way, don't you? Same room where you always stay."

Nodding, Virgil said, "Good night, my friend."

"Buenas noches." Don Amondo turned down the silent corridor of the hacienda's north wing. The family wing.

Virgil went in the opposite direction, down the southern guest wing. His heart slamming against his ribs, he could hardly keep from breaking into a trot as he walked briskly down the silent, shadowy corridor. When he reached the next-to-last door, he stopped and lifted a fist. But he lowered it without knocking. He felt as if all the air had been sucked out of his lungs.

No slice of light showed beneath the door. She had gone to bed, to sleep. She hadn't waited for him.

Virgil exhaled heavily and turned away. On legs of lead he went on down the hall to the very last door. He entered the familiar room and closed the door quietly behind him. Inside the distinctly masculine room with its dark heavy furniture and stone fireplace and fully stocked bar, a lone lamp burned beside the turned-down bed. Virgil extinguished it.

His eyes narrowed, he moved to the bar in the semidarkness, lifted the stopper of a leaded liquor decanter, and poured himself a stiff bourbon. He drained it in one long swallow and set the glass aside. The straight whiskey burned its way down into his chest, but it was nothing compared to the fierce heat plaguing his body. An invasive, tormenting heat that could not be alleviated by stripping off his clothes.

Grimacing, Virgil impatiently unknotted the scarlet silk neckpiece tied at his throat. The knot undone, he let the colorful scarf hang loose around his neck. He unbuttoned his white silk shirt midway and drew a deep, slow breath in a futile attempt to relax his taut limbs. He raked a lean hand through his night-black hair. He pinched the bridge of his nose. He closed his eyes.

And saw her face.

He opened his eyes and stalked around the darkened bedroom like a caged animal, every muscle in his tall, lithe body coiled as tightly as a watch spring. He silently cursed the bewitching beauty who had gazed so invitingly at him throughout dinner, had led him to believe that she wanted him. That she could hardly wait for the two of them to be alone together.

Virgil stopped pacing, shook his dark head.

She didn't want him. She wanted him to want her. She wanted to tease and toy with him, then turn him down flat. Virgil's innate distrust of women fueled his growing doubts. He had been a fool to think she wanted him the way he wanted her. Damn her to hell! She was beautiful, but cruel. Fascinating, but pitiless. The consummate mistress of deceit.

Virgil stopped pacing, took a cigar from a gleaming silver case that sat atop a drum table, and lit it. Feeling as if he might suffocate, he crossed the room to the open double doors. He stepped out onto the balcony, seeking a much-needed breath of fresh air. He stood in the moonlight smoking the cheroot, cursing himself for his weakness, cursing her for stirring emotions in him that he had, until now, deliberately eluded.

The princess saw him the minute Virgil stepped out onto the balcony, and for a moment she stopped breathing entirely. She watched unblinking as he walked to the railing. She stared helplessly as he stood there calmly smoking a cigar, its hot tip glowing orange in the moonlight.

There was no question but that it was he. That magnificent physique. Those firm masculine features. That inky black hair. He was an arresting figure of a man who would appeal to any woman. To all women. He certainly appealed to her.

Her heart throbbing inside the tight bodice of her off-the-shoulder white lace dress, the princess wanted this man with a deep and urgent longing. Uncertain if he felt the same, she had to find out. She had to go out to him.

The princess drew a quick, ragged breath and stepped silently out onto the balcony and up into the moonlight. Softly, she spoke his name.

"Virgil."

Virgil slowly turned and the princess's racing heart rejoiced. On seeing her, his passionate eyes were instantly aflame with longing.

As she approached him, the princess said, almost shyly, "I . . . it was . . . it's so warm this evening."

In one fluid movement Virgil took the cigar from his mouth, flicked it away, reached for her, drew her into his close embrace, and said, "Baby, it's about to get a whole lot warmer."

34

Before she could respond, Virgil wrapped a hand around the back of her neck, lowered his head, and kissed her. The enveloping hotness of his mouth sucked the very breath from her lungs and made her heart pound alarmingly. When his lips released hers, she felt faint, her knees were trembling, and she clung to him for support.

Virgil swept her up into his powerful arms and carried her swiftly inside her darkened bedroom.

"You *did* come," the princess murmured breathlessly, clinging to his neck. "I thought you weren't . . ."

"Sweetheart, of course I came," he said, inhaling deeply of the perfumed fragrance of her hair. "I wanted to come all this time, but I couldn't get away from the don. I've been going crazy."

"So have I," she admitted, as he lowered her to her feet inside the bedroom.

"Jesus, I've been in agony. From the minute I turned and saw you in the *sala* this evening," Virgil said in a low, husky drawl, "All I could think of was being inside you again."

"Virgil . . . oh, Virgil," she whispered, both shocked and thrilled by his stirring words.

His fiery mouth again covered hers in a kiss so daunting she melted in total surrender. Searing heat enveloped them. Their burning hunger too long delayed, there was no time for civility or restraint. They went at each other in a frenzy of exploding passion, unable to restrain themselves.

Lips anxiously combined in greedy, searching quests, but blazing kisses were not enough. Feverish bodies pressed frantically together, but crushing closeness was not nearly close enough. Roaming hands impatiently sought yielding flesh, but no amount of intimate touching slaked their urgent need.

Without a word, both knew instinctively that taking time to undress before they made love was out of the question. They were far too hot for each other to waste precious minutes disrobing fully. They would have to settle for what burning flesh the other was able to easily bare.

Virgil's lean fingers danced with a wondrous dexterity, sweeping the princess's lace bodice down her right arm to her elbow. His lips fused hotly to hers, he made an impatient groan in the back of his throat, and she instantly read his meaning. She lifted her shoulder so he could slide the lace fabric past her elbow, down her arm, and off.

As soon as her right breast was bared, Virgil anxiously drew her closer, but the princess tore her lips from his and pulled back a little. He knew the reason when her hands lifted to his chest. In seconds she had undone the remaining buttons of his silk shirt, and gazing into his smoldering eyes, she impatiently swept the shirt apart.

But she paused when she saw the clean white tape wrapped around him.

"Oh, Virgil," she murmured, "I forgot about your ribs."

"Forget again, baby," he said, cupped the back of her head, and applied gentle pressure, urging her to him.

He shuddered deeply when, murmuring his name, she brushed warm, sweet kisses to the bared expanse of his naked torso.

"Jesus, sweetheart," he said on deep inhalation of breath, his eyes closed, his heart drumming.

The princess let her open lips glide up over his chest to his throat. She clasped the ends of the scarlet silk scarf hanging loose around his neck and slowly reeled him closer. She tilted her head, opened her mouth, and touched the tip of her tongue to the hollow of his throat. She felt him shudder against her and was thrilled beyond belief that she could so affect him. Her lips traveled up over his freshly shaven chin and settled hotly on his mouth.

As they kissed, Virgil clasped her upper arms and drew her flush against his body. They trembled and sighed into each other's mouths when the princess's bare right breast flattened against his naked chest.

For a fleeting second, that was enough for them. They stood there in the darkness embracing, their arms wrapped tightly around each other, their lips blended in a fervent kiss. Virgil's heart was beating against her bare breast in a rapid, heavy cadence that thrummed through her as if it were her own.

It was Virgil who grew restless, Virgil who wanted more. Much, much more.

Their lips reluctantly separated, and Virgil quickly shifted their position. He urged the princess back over his supporting arm, raised his hand, and cupped the soft, pale breast he had freed. He bent his head, kissed the rosy crest, and heard her quick intake of air.

The princess's eyes slipped closed when his blazing mouth closed over her aching nipple and his lips tugged forcefully. She leaned back in his encircling arm and felt the skirts of her evening gown rising. Felt his deft fingers at the waistband of her underwear. Felt the slinky satin sliding down her thighs. Felt his hand around her knee. Felt him slip her left leg free of the wispy encumbrance.

Virgil reluctantly tore his lips from her breast and kissed her waiting mouth again. A deep, probing kiss that scattered her wits so totally she hardly realized that he was propelling her backward across the room. When they stopped moving and the compelling kiss finally ended, she opened her eyes and saw that he had maneuvered her—not to the bed—but up against a wall where a wide wedge of moonlight illuminated them.

"I want to see you when I love you," Virgil whispered huskily.

The dazed princess nodded weakly and let her head fall back against the wall as he shoved her billowing skirts up out of his way. While romantic guitar music floated up from the courtyard below and the pleasing scent of roses perfumed the night air, she gazed into Virgil's flashing eyes as he wrapped his fingers around the back of her knee and lifted her stockinged leg, urging it up around his back. Her arms clasped tightly around his neck, the inflamed princess came up on tiptoe, slid her bent knee higher, and clamped it firmly against his side.

Which was exactly what Virgil wanted her to do.

His mouth again took fiery possession of hers, and as he kissed her, he slipped his hand between their bodies. He anxiously flipped open the buttons to his tight, black charro trousers and freed his pulsing tumescence. It sprang eagerly toward the inviting warmth of her slender body, settling snugly against her bare quivering stomach.

Virgil ended the kiss, murmuring, "Hold on to me, baby. Don't let me go."

Breathless, the princess tightened her arms around the strong column of his neck. Virgil put his hands to her waist and lifted her a little off the floor, and at the same time bent his knees and crouched down a little.

Then, looking directly in her humid eyes, he held her with one strong arm, ran the tip of his middle finger gently along her swollen cleft. He found her hot and wet and as ready as he. He gripped himself and swiftly inserted his hard, throbbing flesh into her soft wet heat.

Both gasped in ecstasy as he slid easily up inside. Virgil braced his feet apart. He hooked her bent knee over his arm and pushed it up and out, opening her wider so she could take all of him. On fire, the blood scalding through her veins, the princess gasped with joy as he thrust into her, firmly implanting himself in her yielding flesh.

The princess looked into the hot eyes of her dark, enigmatic lover as he filled her so completely, stretching her to accommodate his awesome tumescence. Feeling him throbbing inside her, loving it, the princess realized that in all her years of marriage there had never been one instance that could remotely compare to the electrifying sensations touched off by this dark giant's artful lovemaking.

Panting, gasping, rocking together, the two of them stood in the day-bright moonlight and made hot, impatient love with their clothes half on, half off.

And it was good.

Too good.

After only a few magical minutes, the princess felt herself starting to lose control. She tried to stop herself. She didn't want it to end now. She wanted the sweet elation to last and last. She wanted to stay just this way forever with her lover buried deep inside her, exciting her, pleasuring her. She wanted to remain suspended in this sweet state of building bliss.

But she was far too inexperienced to curb the swiftly increasing pressure. She could feel the intense zenith coming and was powerless against it.

Not wanting the ecstacy to end, she asked anxiously, "This won't be all, will it? You'll give me . . . ?"

"Let yourself go, baby," Virgil reassured her in low, sexy tones. "This is only the beginning. I'll give you as much as you want. *More* than you want."

His whispered words and the rhythmic thrust of his hard flesh in hers sent her helplessly spiraling into the throes of incredible orgasm. His own release beginning, Virgil kissed her quickly, lest her cries of ecstasy carry across the courtyard to the family wing of the hacienda.

When finally the princess collapsed weakly against him, Virgil swept her up into his arms and carried her to the spacious bathroom. There the sated princess was soon enjoying yet another first as Virgil undressed her and himself. He lowered her into the cooling tub of water, which Consuela had thoughtfully filled before leaving, then stepped in and sank down to sit facing her. Without his prompting, she draped her legs atop his, scooted close, and put her arms around his neck.

Through the skylight directly above the large porcelain tub, moonlight poured down as they played in the water, teasing each other, laughing and touching and kissing. They stayed in the tub for a long, relaxing time, taking turns running a soapy washcloth over each other's bodies.

"You're getting your tape wet," the princess said as she washed Virgil's broad chest.

"Doesn't matter. My ribs are fine," he lied. "Why don't you take the tape off for me?"

"I don't want to hurt you," she said.

"Don't worry," he replied flatly. His eyes changed minutely, his words holding a double meaning. "You won't hurt me, baby. I won't let you."

But the princess never noticed. She peeled the tape from his side and gently bathed his bruised ribs. She caught him off guard when abruptly she dropped the washcloth, lowered her head, and tenderly kissed the discolored flesh.

When she raised her head, she smiled at him, and asked teasingly, "Did I make it all better?"

Virgil returned her smile, cupped her cheek, skimmed his thumb over her lips, and said, "For the moment, but you better keep your lips ready. I may need further treatment."

She laughed and playfully bit his thumb.

"You'll pay for that," he warned, pretending anger.

"I'm not frightened."

"You should be." He growled and nipped harmlessly at her bare shoulder. "I bite back."

The princess squealed, shoved him away, and hit at him. He retaliated, grabbing her wrist and shoving her arm behind her. The horseplay soon turned into love play. The frisky punches became tender touches. The glancing jabs became gentle caresses. The benign biting changed to tantalizing kisses.

"Let's go to bed, baby," Virgil said against her temple.

"I'm ready," she eagerly replied.

35

Back in the shadowy bedroom, the princess reached for the nightgown that Consuela had laid out for her. Shaking his head, Virgil took it from her, tossed it aside.

"But I—" she began.

"Won't need it," he finished the sentence. "It's much too hot for nightclothes."

He stepped closer, lifted his hands, took the pins from her upswept ginger hair, and watched it cascade down around her bare ivory shoulders. Awed by the sight of the long, lustrous tresses, he ran his hands through the heavy locks, relishing the feel of the silky hair spilling through his fingers. A muscle jumped at the corner of his mouth. He tightened his grip in her hair and tipped her head back.

He said, "Know what I want?"

She swallowed with difficulty. "Tell me."

"I want to see how all this red hair looks spread out on a white pillow."

"If that's what you want, then that's what I want," replied the princess, surprising herself. She couldn't believe she had said those words. And meant them. She shivered at the realization that she genuinely wanted to please this man instead of only wanting him to please her. She touched his tanned jaw where she had scratched him, and whispered, "Anything you want, Virgil, I want to give you."

More affected by her reply than he would have admitted, even to himself, Virgil abruptly released her hair, picked her up, and carried her across the room to the oversized bed. When he reached it, he stood beside the white-sheeted mattress, holding her high against his chest, desire rapidly heating the blood surging through his veins.

His heavy-lidded gaze locked with hers, Virgil told himself that she meant nothing to him, just as he meant nothing to her. They were after the same thing—a few hours of pleasant sexual diversion. A night of physical pleasure with no consequences.

She, like he, was perfectly willing to play, and neither need pay the piper when it was over. For tonight he would fully avail himself of her considerable charms. He would make love to her until she begged him for more. He would make love to her until she begged him to stop.

He would lose himself in her yielding flesh through the long sultry June night, and enjoy every minute of it. He would take her with infinite gentleness. He would take her with uncontrolled passion. He would, with her easily attained consent, take her any way and every way he so desired.

And when the dawn came, he would have had his fill and no longer desire her.

Virgil put a knee on the mattress and carefully laid the naked princess on the bed, making sure her head was resting on a snowy, silken-cased pillow. He sat down on the bed's edge facing her and meticulously arranged her unbound hair so that it swirled around her head in a huge, shimmering fan of loveliness.

Pleased with his handiwork, Virgil braced an arm across her body and gazed down at her. She was sheer perfection. So slender, so pale, so totally feminine. The stunning red hair, the long, swanlike throat, the soft, rounded breasts tipped with large satin nipples. The flat belly, the riot of ginger curls between her pale luminous thighs. The long, well-shaped legs and delicate ankles and cute baby toes.

But it was more than just physical beauty that made her so utterly irresistible. Despite the life he knew she had led, she looked appealingly innocent lying there below him, lovable and submissive. Her enormous eyes were those of a young, trusting girl. And her slender, pale-skinned body had a virginal, untouched appearance, as if she were actually as clean and pristine as new mountain snow.

Virgil's heart kicked forcefully against his injured ribs as he realized what he wanted to do to her. *Had* to do to her. He was going to make love to her in a way he wouldn't have considered making love to a woman like her twenty-four short hours ago. He was going to love her with his mouth. He had to taste her, to taste all of her, because here in the seductive moonlight on this hot summer night with the plaintive guitar music and the scent of roses stirring his senses, it was easy to pretend that she was as clean and sweet and charmingly naive as she pretended to be.

A skillful lover, Virgil took it slowly, just as if she were actually a modest young maiden who would be shocked and offended if he moved too quickly toward his goal. He patiently wooed her with words and with kisses. He took his time, leisurely stoking the fire in her blood. He kissed and caressed her until she was anxious and trembling. Then he drew her up into his arms and continued to kiss her, to whisper to her, to please and excite her.

Virgil kissed the princess's eyes, her cheeks, her slightly protruding ears.

"You've got the cutest little ears I've ever seen," he murmured, then nipped harmlessly at an earlobe.

"No, I don't," she said breathlessly. "My ears are—"

His lips silenced her. She sighed into his mouth, raised her arms to put them around his neck, but he stopped her. Catching and clasping her wrists together in one hand, he raised her arms above her head and held them there. With his free hand he deftly positioned—one at a time—three or four fat fluffy pillows up against the tall ornate headboard.

Then his hot mouth slid from her lips, moved down across her chin, past the hollow of her throat, and up the swell of her left breast to capture a pale pink nipple. He released her wrists and her arms fell weakly to her sides. A burst of breath escaped her lips when Virgil's mouth enclosed a nipple and he began to suck firmly. Caught up in the exquisite pleasure, the princess hardly realized that as he dazzled her with his tugging lips, he was lifting her up, up and back toward the pillows stacked against the headboard. Gently, Virgil was hoisting her into a kneeling position.

Aware only of the pleasure he was giving her, the princess's hands went into his raven hair, and she whispered, "Darling. Oh, darling."

Sighing with ecstacy, she looked down on the dark, handsome face bent to her. She watched in fascination as his mouth released her wet left nipple and moved to the right one. His teeth raked tantalizingly over the sensitive crest, then his tongue toyed with her before he took her fully into his hot mouth to suck vigorously.

Sensing the level of her arousal was swiftly escalating, Virgil soon released her nipple, let his mouth slide down her delicate ribs. And while he kissed her pale, bare flesh, he continued to lift the princess higher, pressing her up against the pillowed headboard. Swept away on a rising tide of white-hot passion, her eyes now closed, the tingling princess didn't realize that she was now fully standing, her back braced against the soaring headboard.

She might never have realized it if Virgil hadn't said in a low, commanding voice, "Baby, open your eyes."

The princess's eyes slowly opened and she looked around dazed, surprised to find herself actually standing atop the bed, her bare back touching smooth wood, her hips and legs cushioned by soft, fluffy pillows.

"Look at me," Virgil softly commanded.

The princess bent her head, looked down at him, and trembled violently. His handsome upturned face was on the level of her lower belly, and his lean hands were possessively clasping her hips. In his glittering eyes was a hunger that bordered on savagery, and there was an uncommon hardness to his full, sensual lips. The look in his eyes, the dangerous set of his mouth excited her beyond belief. She felt the blood scald through her veins, felt a frightening weakness seize her. She pressed her open palms back against the headboard, needing the support, uncertain how long her rubbery legs would hold her.

Virgil felt his bare belly contract sharply as he gazed at the beautiful woman standing naked and vulnerable before him. Her pale, full breasts were rising and falling with her quick labored breaths, and her flat little belly was quivering and jerking noticeably. Her long legs were slightly parted, offering seductive glimpses of the swollen sweetness shielded by the dense curls. Virgil's heart thudded in his chest.

She looked sweet enough to eat.

Feeling his hot, accessing gaze travel over her body, the princess was suddenly embarrassed, shy. Her weak legs began to buckle, and she started to sag back down to her knees. Virgil stopped her.

"No, baby. Stay where you are. I want to kiss you." The timbre of his voice was low, soft.

"Then you . . . you'll have to stand too if you want—"

"No, sweetheart. I want to kiss you here," he said softly, placing a possessive hand over her, cupping her, gently raking his fingers through the triangle of curls to touch the pulsing flesh beneath. "This is where I want to kiss you, baby."

The princess was appalled. Surely, he didn't mean it. "Virgil, no . . . no . . . ," she murmured, her breath short, her heart pounding.

"Yes," he whispered, and brushed a kiss to her trembling belly. "Let me kiss you, baby. Let me taste your sweetness. If you don't like it, I'll stop."

"Pro-promise?" she asked, short of breath, both incensed and excited by his shocking proposal.

"Promise," he said, as he urged her legs a little farther apart with a gentle hand.

"No, please . . . no . . . ," she whispered, as Virgil leaned to her and nuzzled his nose and mouth in the damp springy curls. "D-don't—"

She gasped as he skillfully nudged the curls aside and kissed her, his smooth lips pressing a brief, tender kiss to the slick female flesh.

"Want me to stop, baby?" he whispered, never raising his head. His coaxing mouth never lifting from her, his furnace-hot breath fanning the flames of her wild desire. "Just say the word and I'll stop."

"I . . . yes . . . yes, stop, please . . . you . . . you must stop." She said.

He kissed her again, opened his mouth slightly, and touched the tip of his tongue to her.

"All right, sweetheart," he whispered, "I'll stop." He turned his head and laid his feverish cheek against her bare belly. "But I wish you wouldn't make me. I want to love you, baby. I want to taste you. You smell so sweet, so clean. Please, let me. Let me. Give it to me, sweetheart. Give it all to me."

The shocked, thrilled princess couldn't resist him. He had her so excited she couldn't bring herself to say no again. She wanted it as badly as he. Shameful as it was, she wanted him to kiss her there. She wanted to feel his smooth, hot lips pressed against that burning, hurting flesh. Even more shameful, she wanted to watch him while he did it.

"Baby?" he whispered, quietly asking permission, already knowing the answer.

"Virgil—" her breath came out in a loud whoosh, "I . . . I don't want you to stop. I want you to . . . kiss me. Oh, kiss me now."

Those were the words Virgil was waiting to hear. He lifted his cheek from her quivering belly, tipped his head back, and looked up at her with blazing blue eyes.

"Sweetheart," he murmured, and slowly lowered his face to her. "I won't hurt you. I'd never hurt you."

He leaned to her, opened his mouth, and again touched her with his tongue. She said his name on an excited sigh and thought she had surely never felt anything quite so stimulating. A practiced lover, Virgil again took it slowly. He gently teased her, doing nothing more than pressing the warmth of his open mouth against her and lightly touching the tip of his tongue to her. He blew his hot breath against her and gave her kiss after kiss of checked intimacy while the mesmerized princess stood there in the radiant moonlight brazenly watching him.

To the awed princess it was powerfully erotic to feel Virgil's mouth and tongue gently touching her while she watched him press his dark, handsome face between her parted legs. His beautiful blue eyes were closed now, his long black lashes fluttering on his cheeks. His dark head was barely moving as he kissed her with incredible tenderness.

As the delicate, restrained caresses continued, the passionate princess found herself longing to reach down, clasp his dark head, and pull him closer. To tilt her pelvis up against his hot face and meld her throbbing flesh more securely with his masterful mouth.

It was all she could do to keep from begging, "Darling, more. Give me more."

She didn't have to say a word.

Virgil knew instinctively when he had gotten her so hot she was dying for even greater intimacy. She began to bend her knees and to involuntarily press her burning pelvis closer to the promise of his mouth. She was, he could tell, ready to be taken all the way. And there was nothing he wanted more than to take her.

"Ah, baby," Virgil whispered and slipped a hand under her buttocks to draw her closer.

He buried his face in her, opened his mouth, and with his tongue began to drive her mad with blinding ecstasy. Soon she was crying out and twisting frantically. Both frightened and elated, she panted and gasped and thought she surely couldn't stand one more second of this shattering pleasure. At the same time she knew that she would die if Virgil took his probing, stroking tongue from her.

As he expertly touched and teased and tasted her, the princess clung to his dark, moving head and ground her groin against him, terrified he would take his loving mouth from her before she . . .

The entire universe was now centered there between her legs where this dark, experienced lover was kissing her. Frantic, her breath coming in shallow little gulps, the out-of-control princess anxiously pressed her pelvis hard against his mouth. And was rewarded with the fiery lashing of his talented tongue. The dazed princess, frenzied with desire, was half-sobbing now, unable to stand still. Wanting . . . wanting. . . .

Attuned to the slightest change in her level of excitement, Virgil knew the moment had come. He held her to him and sank his face deeply into her. He feasted hungrily on her, stroking her powerfully with his tongue until she was thrashing and twisting and calling his name in near hysteria.

The princess felt a frightening tension spiraling higher as her body grew hotter and hotter, especially where he was kissing her. Her fingers frantically clutching his jet black hair, she said his name on a sob, begging him, pleading.

And then it began.

Wave after wave of unbelievable pleasure washed over her, and she cried out, unable to stop herself. The incredible ecstacy continued until she felt as if she would surely scream if it didn't end.

Feeling her potent response, Virgil stayed with her until she got it all out, keeping his mouth fused to her as she shuddered and sobbed and her body involuntarily quivered and jerked.

When the last little tremors had passed, Virgil finally took his mouth from her. Gently he drew her down to her knees. He looked at her flushed face, her bleary eyes, and smiled. His lips wet and gleaming from her fierce release, he kissed her. The princess tasted herself on his lips and was appalled, but his hands began to caress her breasts, her back, her hips, and she soon sighed. He touched her between her legs where he had kissed her and to her astonishment, she felt herself becoming half-excited again. Virgil took one of her hands, placed it on his pulsing erection.

Her slender fingers enclosing him, the princess surprised herself when she said, "You said that from the minute you turned this evening and saw me standing in the *sala*, you could think of nothing but being inside me again."

"I meant it."

She stroked him gently and said, "Wait no longer, my love."

She released him and lay back on the pillows. He nudged her thighs wider apart and eagerly came between. Both moaned with pleasure when he filled her with his hard throbbing flesh.

Gently he moved in her, taking her with unhurried movements, enjoying the feel and heat of her body. For as long as either could stand it, they made love at a leisurely pace, purposely drawing out the joy, making it last. But soon both were wanting more, hurrying to give and to get total ecstasy. Unable to deny themselves one second longer.

Virgil drove into her hard and fast, bringing on the ultimate pleasure both sought. When she began to cry out, Virgil groaned and kissed her to silence them both. She felt his powerful release, and the knowledge she had given it to him took her yet another step higher.

When the intense ecstasy finally ended, they were drained and exhausted. They lay together unmoving, content, their bodies damp and slippery with perspiration. Late though it was, a guitar still played in the courtyard below, the romantic music softly serenading the spent lovers. The sweet smell of roses mingled with the not unpleasant scent emanating from their naked entwined bodies. The moon had risen higher in the night sky, slowly taking with it the luminous light that had spilled across the bed earlier.

When finally the bed and its occupants were swallowed up in the hot darkness, the princess sighed, stirred, and whispered, "Virgil, you awake?"

"Mmmm."

"You better go back to your room before we fall asleep."

"I won't fall asleep."

She yawned. "No? How will you keep from it?"

202 ◈ NAN RYAN

"By making love to you."

Tired and as sated as she was, the princess felt her pulse quicken at his words. Surely he wasn't serious. Even if he wanted to make love to her again, his body couldn't possibly. . . . He wouldn't be able to. . . . That powerful male part of him wasn't capable of . . . of . . .

Or was it?

Not sure how to phrase it, she said, "You're teasing me. You haven't the . . . stamina."

She was surprised to hear him chuckle in the darkness and say, "Come sunrise, you won't be saying that."

36

Brilliant morning sunshine greeted the princess when she stepped into the hacienda's dining room. On seeing her, Virgil and the don came swiftly to their feet.

"Ah, *Señorita* Eva," said Don Amondo, flashing her a wide smile and hurrying to her. "Good morning to you! You slept well I hope?"

Smiling tensely, she allowed the don to usher her forward and, not daring to look at Virgil, replied, "I did, yes, *gracias*. The bed was . . . most comfortable. I feel quite rested and refreshed."

"*Bueno, bueno*," said the pleased don, and pulled out a chair for her.

"Mornin', Miss Eva," Virgil drawled in that flat Texas twang as she slid into the chair.

"Good morning, Virgil," she said, looked nervously at him, and immediately felt her empty stomach do a violent flip-flop.

Blushing profusely, she shook out the large white linen napkin, draped it across her trousered knees with trembling fingers, and hoped the don, now returning to his chair, wouldn't notice how ill at ease she was. Or, how red her face. She vowed that she would not so much as glance at Virgil again. It simply was not safe.

"A good night's sleep has put roses in your cheeks, no?" said the don, drawing her attention back to him.

"Y-yes," she managed, feeling her face growing hotter with the lie.

"If you are to keep them there," warned the don, "you must have a breakfast *grande*!"

Before she could respond, a bevy of bustling servants entered carrying china platters filled with all manner of breakfast edibles, both hot and cold. Fresh fruits were attractively arranged on a bed of chipped ice. Piping hot breads and plate-sized tortillas rested in a cloth-lined basket. There was ham and bacon and thick juicy steaks sizzling in their own juice. Eggs fried and scrambled and boiled. And fluffy golden omelets seasoned with red and green hot peppers.

Platter after platter was passed to her, and to be polite, the princess took small helpings of several dishes. But she wasn't really hungry. Food was the last thing on her mind. She sipped chilled apricot nectar and, unable to help herself, stole covert glances at Virgil.

Lord, he was handsome this morning! He wore a starched white shirt, obviously borrowed from the oldest Rivas boy's closet. The shirt was a might too snug, the cotton fabric straining across his wide shoulders and pulling tautly around his hard biceps. The collar was open at the throat, and the sleeves were rolled up over tanned forearms. His jet black hair was neatly brushed, but an unruly lock fell forward onto his high forehead. His beautiful blue eyes were slightly bloodshot.

She knew the reason.

They had not slept a wink. And she had learned, to her surprised delight, that a healthy, hot-blooded male could indeed make love over and over again in a single night. The slight soreness between her legs was silent testimony to Virgil's incredible prowess.

Less than an hour ago, with the sun beginning to rise, Virgil had hastily gathered up his discarded clothes, kissed her one last time, slipped onto the balcony as naked as the day he was born, and hurried back to his own room.

Just in time.

Not five minutes after he left, Consuela had knocked on the door, and the princess was forced to search frantically for the nightgown she hadn't worn. She had scurried around the room, pushing her tumbled hair out of eyes, before she finally found it under the bed, pulled it hurriedly over her head, leaped back up into the rumpled bed, took a quick breath, and said, "Come in."

A close call.

"*Señorita*—" the don's voice snapped her out of her reverie, "you are not eating. Are you feeling well?"

"Yes, I feel fine," she assured him, nodding, allowing him to place a golden omelette on her plate.

Cutting into a piece of rare, juicy steak, Virgil quietly shifted his gaze to her and shuddered inwardly. Damn it to hell! The long, exhausting night of lovemaking hadn't worked after all. He still wanted her. Wanted her more than ever. Wanted her right now.

God, she looked adorable this morning! Her long hair was pulled to the back of her head and secured at the nape of her neck with some feminine adornment, revealing her cute, small, slightly protruding ears. She wore a long-sleeved white blouse with tight-fitting butter-yellow suede riding breeches and a pair of gleaming brown leather boots. Tied at her throat was a silk bandanna the exact hue of her beautiful emerald eyes. One end of the green bandanna had slipped down inside her blouse, was caught in the shadowy valley between her breasts. His fingers itched to free it.

Virgil made himself look away, instantly angry. And frightened. Scared to death. A few short hours ago he had been so cocky, so certain that a hot night of abandoned lovemaking with this beautiful red-haired witch would put an end to his nagging desire. It hadn't. Far, far from it. Jesus, now he—

"Don't you agree, Virgil?" said the don.

"I . . . pardon?" Virgil had no idea what had been said.

Smiling, the don waved a dismissive hand in the air. "It was nothing important." He frowned then and, looking straight at Virgil, said accusingly, "I know you too long, *amigo*. Something is bothering you. Something is on your mind. Last night you seemed distracted, troubled. Is there anything I can do?"

It was Virgil's turn to lay down his fork and wave a dismissive hand. "Nothing's wrong. Not a thing. I have never felt better in my—"

A loud shout from outside made Virgil stop speaking. More shouts followed, and then an excited servant dashed into the dining room, exclaiming, "They're home, Don Amondo. They're coming up the driveway."

The don quickly came to his feet, tossed his napkin on the table, and said, "Come, *mis amigos*! Soledad and my children have returned at last!"

Breakfast forgotten, Virgil and the princess followed the excited Don Amondo out of the hacienda and onto the broad flagstone patio. Two big black coaches were coming up the pebbled driveway. They rolled to a stop, and from out of the twin coaches spilled eight laughing Rivas offspring along with the serene, statuesque beauty who was their mother.

The don and doña embraced, and she whispered something in his ear that made him color beneath his dark skin.

Then the laughing, happy don was quickly enveloped in a swarm of affectionate children, while the elegant Doña Soledad offered her hand and a warm smile to Ranger Black. The princess almost fainted of shock when Virgil gently raised that small hand to his lips, kissed it, then embraced the handsome Mexican woman, enfolding her gently in his long arms.

When he released her, he drew the princess forward and said, "Doña

Soledad, may I present Miss Eva Jones. Eva, I'd like you to meet Doña Soledad Rivas."

Doña Soledad said graciously, "I am very pleased to meet you, Miss Jones. I am happy Virgil brought you to visit."

"*Gracias*, Doña Soledad," said the princess, smiling.

The older woman, smiling warmly, inclined her well-coiffed head toward Virgil and said, "I do hope you won't mind sharing Virgil for a while." The princess gave her a quizzical look. "See what I mean?" said the doña.

The princess nodded with understanding as the stair-stepped Rivas children, having left their father flushed from their hugs and kisses, turned their attention on Virgil. Surrounding him, the chattering girls all kissed him, the boys shook his hand and patted him affectionately on the back. The youngest of the bunch—tiny, four-year-old Ramon—fought his way through his big brothers and sisters and was promptly snatched up into the arms of a laughing Virgil Black.

The boy's mother and the princess watched as the precious little boy wrapped his short arms around Virgil's neck and unabashedly gave the tall dark Ranger a big kiss. The princess felt her heart squeeze in her chest. She had never been able to picture the tough, hard-faced Texas Ranger with a child. Any more than she was able to picture herself with a baby.

"Ramon loves Virgil very much," said Doña Soledad. "All my children love this big brave Ranger."

Nodding, gazing at the enigmatic man whose hard-planed face had softened amazingly as he held the little boy, the princess allowed herself, for the very first time, to actually think of Virgil Black as a husband. A father. And of herself as a wife. A mother.

The daydreaming princess was swept back inside the hacienda on a tide of Rivases. Place settings were hastily added to the long dining table. Another complete breakfast was cooked. And, for the next pleasant hour, it was like a holiday in the dining room. The big family gathered around the table, sharing the morning meal and the high points of their trip. All the Rivas children were eager to tell their beaming papa of their adventures, and in their excitement, they would interrupt each other and talk two or three at a time. Their indulgent father listened with genuine interest, glancing often at his wife as some silent, secret message passed between them.

The princess looked from one glowing face to another and momentarily envied this big happy family. She had never had a brother or sister, and she realized now that she had missed so much. It was as if she could actually feel the love of these siblings and their proud parents filling every tiny space in this large dining room.

Warmed in the bright glow of all that love, the princess impulsively laid a hand on the arm of the pretty eighteen-year-old seated beside her and whispered, "Soraya, Consuela loaned me your clothes. I hope you don't mind too much."

The pretty young girl laughed and said, "No, *señorita*, not at all. Virgil's *querida* is welcome to anything I have."

"Soraya, you've misunderstood," whispered the princess. "I'm not Virgil's sweetheart."

Soraya started to disagree, but the eldest Rivas boy, twenty-one-year old Arto, pinged on his glass with a fork to get everyone's attention, then told of fighting a young bull on a friend's *rancho* in Chihuahua City. He was hardly finished with his story before the other Rivas children were telling of their varied adventures on the lengthy trip.

Finally interrupting, Virgil said, "Much as I hate it, the time has come for us to leave."

Every Rivas, including little Ramon, protested loudly, begging Virgil to stay on for a few days or at least to spend the night. They were still protesting when the saddled Noche and a gentle bay gelding from the Rivas remuda were brought around to the graveled front drive.

The entire Rivas clan ushered the departing pair out of the hacienda and to the waiting horses.

Speaking loudly to be heard above the din while shaking hands with the don, Virgil said, "I'll see to it that the gelding gets back to Tierra del Encanto."

"Not necessary, *amigo*," said Don Amondo, turning to smile at the princess. "The gelding is my present to *Señorita* Eva."

She opened her mouth, but before she could speak Virgil said, "The *señorita* can ride the gelding when she visits the rancho."

"Virgil's right," the princess said, thanking the don for his generous offer. "When I return to Tierra del Encanto, I will ride the gelding." She smiled wistfully then, knowing that she would never again visit this high desert *rancho* and all the warm friendly Rivases.

Amidst laughter and handshakes and hugs, Virgil and the princess concluded their good-byes. The princess had already mounted the bay gelding when Virgil crouched down on his heels to give little Ramon one last squeeze. Then Virgil came to his feet and affectionately cupped Ramon's dark head, as the little boy wrapped tenacious arms around his leg.

"You must let me go now, Ramon," Virgil said softly. "But I promise I'll come back to see you real soon."

The little boy reluctantly released him, big tears now swimming in his large dark eyes. Doña Soledad diplomatically stepped forward, laid a gentle hand on her son's narrow shoulder, and Ramon turned gratefully into the comfort of his mother's billowing skirts.

The Rivas family stood in the sunshine waving and watching the pair ride away, down the long graveled drive.

37

The mounted pair reached the end of the long drive, passed beneath the tall ranch gates of Tierra del Encanto, and turned south down Ranch Road. In silence they rode, soon leaving the road to skirt the jagged slopes of the towering Organ Mountains as the morning sun climbed higher.

The princess, glancing at the taciturn Virgil, recalled with a rush of pleasure how she'd felt watching this big strong Texan behave in such a tender, fatherly manner with little Ramon Rivas. With the boy in his arms, Virgil Black had revealed an irresistibly appealing, incredibly gentle side to his nature. With the beautiful little child, Virgil had been completely open and giving. Totally unguarded.

He had never been that way with her. Even when he made love to her—as wonderful as it was—she was achingly aware that he was withholding something of himself. That he was more than happy to put his lean, bare body in her hands. But not his heart.

Again the princess experienced that unfamiliar squeezing in her chest as a wave of protective tenderness washed over her. Foolish as it was, she felt a strong yearning to take care of Virgil instead of having him take care of her. To please him, not herself. To stop constantly being the spoiled brat. To start behaving more like the kind, caring Doña Soledad behaved with her husband and children.

The startling realization struck Princess Marlena that here in America, she had gotten a glimpse of how others lived their lives. Those who were not royals, but simply decent, hard-working people. Like the dedicated nuns at Cloudcroft. And the Rivas family. And Virgil Black.

She gave Virgil another sidelong glance and bit her lip. He looked troubled, not happy. She wished she could ease the lines of tension from his handsome face. She wished she could make him laugh the way he had laughed with the Rivases. She wished she could look into his beautiful blue eyes and see the care and affection that had flashed there when he'd lifted young Ramon Rivas up into his arms.

Three full hours into their southward journey, the sun had almost reached its zenith. It beat down with a vengeance from a cloudless sky, and the air was dry, still, and blazing hot.

Virgil knew how badly the princess needed to rest, but he hated to stop. He was afraid of what would happen. Afraid he couldn't keep his hands off her if she lay down beside him. Which would have been all right, if the physical pleasure they shared involved only his body, the way it always had in the past. But it wasn't that way with her. For some reason he couldn't make love to her and then, the minute it was over, forget about it.

Or forget about her.

And that rankled him.

He wasn't used to caring about the women he bedded. To him, from his first encounter when he was a green fifteen, the woman an experienced twenty-six, women had been interchangeable. All alike. The only difference being that some had been blond, some brunette, and an occasional redhead.

But this particular redhead riding alongside him had awakened a new emotion in him, and he didn't like it one bit. He had only to look at her to want her, yet he was sickened by the nagging thought of all the men who'd had her before him. Why should he care? And why, he wondered miserably, did he feel strangely protective of her? Why did his heart hurt when she smiled at him so sweetly?

Virgil closed his burning eyes. He was tired. He was not thinking straight. That's all it was.

It never occurred to him that for the first time in his life he might be falling in love.

Such a possibility had occurred to the princess. She knew, as they rode side by side in silence, that right or wrong, foolish or wise, they were falling in love. She was falling in love with him, and her heart told her, he was falling in love with her.

He didn't know it yet. And she had no idea how it would end. She only knew that she loved this big dark, handsome Texan so much she was even beginning to love this hot, barren, starkly beautiful land he called home. She loved him, and she was going to do everything in her power to make him realize that he loved her as well.

As that truth dawned so clearly while they rode along beneath that hot Texas sun, the princess again turned and gazed fondly at Virgil. He was dozing in the saddle. Bless his heart. He was, she knew, exhausted from making love to her through the long, unforgettable night. Feeling instantly maternal toward him, the princess softly said his name.

"Virgil."

He started, jerked up on the reins, and looked around, instantly alert.

She smiled at him and said, "Shouldn't we stop soon and rest for a while. I'm hot and tired and you must be too."

Reluctantly, he nodded. "There's a secluded cave back in the foothills about a half mile from here where we can nap during the hottest part of the day."

"A nap's just what we both need," she said. And, at the time, she meant it.

But once they reached the cool isolated cavern carved out of the mountainside, they didn't take a nap. They took each other. And they didn't mate wordlessly. For a few glorious moments of bliss they forgot who they were, where they were, and why they were together. Caught up in the rapture, they fervently murmured endearments to each other as though they were actually sweethearts as well as lovers.

After total ecstacy was attained, they lay peacefully in each other's arms, sighing, sleepy, content for the moment. Pressed against Virgil's lean, dark body, the princess looked curiously around the spacious cave.

It was a large shadowy room almost perfectly square. Benches of rock, placed there by nature, were arranged in neat, symmetrical groupings. At the far end of the room, a large square pillar of rock, rising from the smooth stone floor, looked like a bed. Specks of slanted light, sifting through tiny crevices on each side of the room, might have been well-placed wall sconces.

She hadn't noticed any of this before, but now she said in a whisper, "This cave is so . . . perfect. It should have a name."

"It does," Virgil said softly, exhaling heavily.

"Really? What is it called?"

Almost asleep, his eyes closing, he murmured, barely audible, "The Bridal Chamber."

They slept the hot afternoon away.

Virgil awakened first. He looked at the beautiful naked woman asleep in his arms. A tightness forming in his throat, he took a long minute to carefully memorize everything about her, from the contour of her well-shaped eyebrows to the tiny mole on the inside of her left thigh.

Then he kissed her awake and asked her how she'd like to have a nice, invigorating bath.

"You're teasing me," she said, yawning sleepily.

He brushed a quick kiss to her bare belly and said, "Put your pants on, baby. Within the hour you will be relaxing in a cool bath."

They dressed hurriedly and left the Bridal Chamber. Still skirting the mountains, they passed beneath Baldy Peak, then immediately turned and climbed back up the slopes. Just as he had promised, within an hour they had reached Dripping Springs, a labyrinth of refreshingly cool pools created by a spring at the base of the Organ Mountains.

"Such a beautiful place," said the princess, unbuttoning her blouse.

"I thought you'd like it."

"I love it," she said, adding to herself, *And I love you.*

As the sun set they sat naked in a cool, crystal clear pool that offered sweeping vistas of the wide Mesilla Valley spread out below. The princess, resting comfortably in Virgil's encircling arms, watched in awe as the wild, beautiful, cactus-laden land changed colors with the dying of the day.

"It is so quiet, so peaceful here. It's as if we are the only two people on earth."

"I know," Virgil replied. "These mountains used to be called *La Sierra de la Soledad.* Mountains of Solitude."

"How fitting. I could stay here forever."

He sighed. "I was about to say it's time to go."

"Oh, not yet," she protested, turning about in his arms to face him. "First could we . . . have you ever . . . is it possible to make love without us getting out of the water?"

Virgil grinned devilishly. "Come here, baby."

The princess learned it *was* possible. And wildly enjoyable.

Later, when an abundance of brilliant stars winked in the black night sky above, the sated pair were still lolling lazily in the pool. Their heads thrown back, eyes on the heavens, Virgil pointed out the various constellations and told her that when he was a boy, he learned to navigate by the guiding stars.

"By the time I was eight, nine years old, I roamed these deserts and mountains and never once got lost."

Dying to learn more about this man she loved, the princess hoped this was her chance. She said, "You must have been a very smart little boy."

"I won't argue that."

"But I'll bet your mother worried when you went off alone." Virgil's response was a mirthless chuckle. The princess frowned and asked, "Well, didn't she?"

"Sure," he said with the slightest touch of bitterness to his tone, "worried herself sick."

Puzzled, curious, the princess said, "Does your mother—?"

"Enough about mothers," he cut her off, and rising to his feet, pulled her up. His hands at her waist, he lifted her out of the pool. She stood dripping wet on the rocky lip above him. Agilely Virgil sprang up to stand before her.

Pointing, he said, "See that full moon rising? It will light the desert until early in the morning. Let's ride on into El Paso tonight. How does that sound?"

"Sounds fine, on one condition."

"Which is?"

"First we make love in the moonlight."

Virgil reached out, captured her chin, and kissed her gleaming wet lips. Then he knelt on one knee before her, wrapped his arms around her hips, and laid his wet head against her breasts. His breath warm on her chilled flesh, he said teasingly, as if exasperated, "Woman, woman, what am I going to do with you?"

The princess put a hand into his soaked black hair, urged his head back, leaned over, and kissed him soundly. Then she sank down on her knees to face him and, boldly wrapping her hand around his rapidly rising erection, said seductively, "I'll show you what you can do with me."

It was nearing nine o'clock, and the full white moon was bright as day when they reached the sprawling outskirts of El Paso. On a natural rise just north of the city, Virgil abruptly drew rein, pulled up on Noche. The princess nudged her gelding alongside him. Virgil drew a labored breath, turned, and looked directly at her. She smiled and gazed at him as if he'd hung the moon.

He knew then that he couldn't do it. He couldn't take her to jail. He was no longer positive who she really was, but it made no difference. Princess or prostitute, he could not take her to jail.

A vein pulsing on his high forehead, Ranger Captain Virgil Black, for the first time in his fifteen years with the well-trained law-enforcing frontier battalion, made the decision to disobey orders. An action that, he knew well, could end his career.

It didn't matter.

He would rather be drummed out of the corps than to see this woman who had awakened an unfamiliar tenderness in him placed behind bars.

"I can't do it," he said simply, his shoulders slumping.

"I know," she softly replied, reading his meaning.

He exhaled heavily and told her, "I have an old, dear friend who lives near Ranger headquarters. We'll go there, and after you've rested—" he stopped speaking, closed his eyes, opened them, "after you've rested, I'll look the other way while you escape me."

The princess reached out, touched his forearm, and felt the muscles tighten beneath her fingertips. "And if I don't want to escape you?"

"Don't. Don't do this to me," he said without emotion, kicked the stallion into motion, calling over his shoulder, "Come on."

Soon they were approaching True Cannon's modest salmon-colored adobe three miles east of El Paso. Located on a slightly elevated spit of land near the border, the house, which afforded sweeping views of old Mexico and the rugged Franklin range of the Rockies, was at least a half mile from its nearest neighbor.

When the drumming of horses' hooves intruded on the quiet of the summer evening, the silver-haired True Cannon got out of his chair and rushed out onto the porch. He saw the two horsemen riding toward the adobe in the moonlight. Blinking, trying to see better, he made out the set of Virgil's shoulders, the tilt of his head.

At once, True began to smile broadly.

He stepped off the porch and hurried out to meet the pair as Virgil swung down and tethered the horses to the hitch rail. Affectionately slapping Virgil on the back, True nodded and smiled at the princess, waiting for Virgil to introduce them.

The princess swiftly stepped in front of Virgil, put out her hand, and said, "Mr. Cannon, I'm Eva. Eva Jones."

True Cannon glanced at the tall man standing behind her. Virgil shrugged negligently and rolled his eyes. True returned his attention to the princess. Shaking her hand firmly, he said, "Mighty pleased to meet you, Miss Jones. Now y'all come on in the house. We'll tend the horses later."

True Cannon supposed that this red-haired woman calling herself Eva Jones was the thieving saloon singer Virgil had been sent to apprehend. So he asked no questions, just welcomed her into his home and fixed them a late supper.

True was more than a little curious as to why Virgil had brought his prisoner home, instead of taking her straight to jail. But he didn't need wonder for long. Before an hour had passed he knew that they were in love. The knowledge worried True. Her kind of a woman could only lead to heartbreak.

It was not until the princess had retired for the night that True said to Virgil, "All right, son, what's going on here? Come clean. Is she the Queen of the Silver Dollar? Is that pretty little gal in there the thief you were sent after?"

Virgil shook his dark head, rose from his chair, went to the front door, and stepped out into the moonlight. The older, shorter man followed. Virgil leisurely rolled and lit a cigarette. He took a long, deep drag, and released the smoke. True waited impatiently.

Finally Virgil began to speak. Talking softly, he told True all he knew about the woman, laughing hollowly when he concluded by saying, "She refuses to admit that she's the Queen of the Silver Dollar.

Insists on continuing to play some kind of game, to cling to a foolish fantasy. Keeps lying and saying that . . . she's . . . she's . . ." Virgil flicked his smoked-down cigarette away in a shower of orange sparks. "Jesus, True, she swears to God that she's a royal princess. Have you ever heard anything so farfetched?"

"Well, now, Virgil," True said thoughtfully, "that might just be."

"Oh, for God's sake, you don't actually—"

"When I was up in San Antone a couple of weeks ago," True interrupted, "I heard something about a red-haired princess coming out west on a bond tour."

Virgil's eyes flashed in the darkness. His heart beginning to beat double time, he said, "Why didn't you tell me?"

"Didn't figure you'd care," was True's honest reply.

Next morning, as the princess slept, Virgil, feeling haggard and tired, sat down at the kitchen table. True Cannon immediately handed him a copy of the *El Paso Times*. Bare-chested, still half-asleep, in no mood for reading, Virgil gave him a questioning look.

True poured a cup of hot black coffee for Virgil. Then said, "I've got things to do this morning." Heading for the back door, he added, "I'll be back in an hour."

Scowling, Virgil said, "We don't get any breakfast around here anymore?"

True grinned, took his hat from the peg by the door, put it on his head, said, "Drink your coffee and read that paper, son. We'll have breakfast later." His grin broadened and his eyes twinkled mischievously when he added, "That is, if you're still hungry."

And he was gone.

Frowning, Virgil took a drink of the coffee and picked up the newspaper. His half-shut eyes opened wide as he read the front page article about Her Royal Highness, Crown Princess Marlena of Hartz-Coburg visiting San Antonio on the conclusion of a successful bond tour that had taken her to several Texas cities. The newspaper began to dance and vibrate, and Virgil realized that his hands were shaking. He spread the paper flat on the table and read the entire article over again. He was halfway through it the third time when the princess appeared in the kitchen doorway and spoke his name.

Virgil looked up, saw her, and swallowed hard.

Bare-foot, with her hair appealingly sleep tousled, she wore one of True's long-tailed white nightshirts, which reached well below her knees. She was yawning and rubbing the sole of her left foot against the calf of her right leg. She didn't look like a royal princess. She didn't look like a saloon singer. She looked like a cute, sleepy little girl.

She smiled, crossed to him, and looking curiously about, asked, "Where's True?" She came to stand close beside him.

"Gone."

"In that case," she said, leaned down and kissed him quickly, "where did you sleep last night? I missed you."

Virgil didn't answer. Instead, he shoved a chair out for her with his bare foot. "Sit down."

She sat down. He shoved the newspaper toward her. Tucking her wild hair behind her ears, she looked at him quizzically. He shook the paper at her. She took it from him.

"Read it," he said, leaned back in his chair, and crossed his arms over his bare chest.

He stared unblinking as the princess began to read the article. After only a few lines, she stopped, looked up, and said, "I told you and you wouldn't listen." Dropping the paper to the table, she jabbed a thumb toward her night-shirted chest and said, "*I* am the real princess. The woman in San Antonio is standing in for me, pretending to be me." She pushed back her chair and stood up. She came around the table, laid a hand on his bare brown shoulder, and said, "*She* is the woman you were sent to capture. Apparently she looks a lot like me and—"

"Try exactly like you," he cut in curtly.

"Nonetheless, we are two different people. I am Princess Marlena of Hartz-Coburg. I don't know who she is, but I assume that she is the thief you were sent after. My factor, Montillion, apparently chose her for her close resemblance to me, not knowing that she was in trouble. Virgil, it's the truth, I swear it."

Virgil continued to sit there with his arms crossed over his chest, jaw set, not looking at her.

The princess anxiously continued, "This whole thing happened because I got sick. We had been in New York and in Denver and were on the way to Fort Worth when I fell ill. The royal physician said it was a bad case of yellow jaundice. You should have seen me—my face looked like a giant lemon. I couldn't possibly go on with the tour. I was taken to the sanitarium in Cloudcroft and fortunately Montillion found a woman—I'm not sure how—who very closely resembles me so that the tour could go on as planned while I recuperated."

Virgil didn't comment, but she saw the fierce flexing of his jaw, the throbbing of the pulse in his tanned throat, and knew she was finally making headway.

"When you apprehended me at the Cloudcroft train depot, I had just gotten out of the sanitarium and was about to leave for Texas to take my proper place on the tour. But, as you know, renegade Indians had blown up the railroad tracks." She gently cupped his rigid cheek with her fingers. "Please, look at me, Virgil."

He slowly turned his head, looked up at her, and she saw the uncertainty in his beautiful brooding blue eyes. He was, she knew, beginning to believe her, and it was both painful and a relief for him. In a burst of affection, she hugged his dark head to her breasts, bent and kissed his disheveled raven hair, and said, "Don't look so troubled, my love. You believed that you had caught a thief, a bank robber. It was a reasonable mistake. I hold none of this against you." Again she pressed her lips to the top of his dark head.

Virgil gently pulled away from her. "Sit down," he said once more, and when she started to drop onto his lap, he stopped her. "No. Take the chair. We have to talk more."

"Yes," she said, "we do."

They did talk. They talked and talked as they had never talked before. She truthfully answered any question he asked and any lingering doubts he had began to fade as all the pieces of the puzzle fell into place.

Finally she said, "I better get dressed before True gets back."

Virgil nodded.

When she'd left the room, he rubbed a hand over his throbbing temples and wondered how he could have gotten himself into such a sorry fix. And how he was going to get out of it.

39

At noontime, True finally returned to the adobe. He didn't mention the newspaper article. Making only pleasant small talk, he cooked a late breakfast, which the princess and Virgil barely touched. After the meal, the princess, rising quickly from her chair, insisted on washing the dishes.

"Oh, now, sugar, no need for you to do that," said True.

Virgil didn't comment, but he shot her a skeptical look.

"All right," she said, addressing only him, "I admit it. I have never washed dishes in my life. But I don't suppose it is ever too late to learn. So there!"

"Want me to dry them for you?" asked True.

"No, I don't. You two go on. Leave me to my task."

True smiled. Virgil shrugged. They left her alone in the kitchen, and Virgil couldn't believe his ears when she began to hum softly as she cleared the dirty dishes from the table.

Troubled, wishing now that she was really just the saloon singer he had believed her to be, Virgil headed for the front door, telling True to keep an eye on her.

"You going somewhere?"

"Think I'll take a little ride."

"Good idea," said True, knowing where Virgil was going.

He would ride up through the sandstone buttes at the edge of the city and wind his way to the summit of Brizna Peak. Virgil always went to the top of that towering bladelike crest when he was troubled about something or had a tough decision to make or just needed to be by himself. There he knew he could be alone, his solitude ensured by the dangerous trail up which others were reluctant to challenge. Brizna Peak was, and had been since his first trip up at age fourteen, Virgil's favorite place to get away from it all.

The breakfast dishes washed, dried, and put away, the princess looked about at the spotless kitchen, pleased. She was quite proud of herself. She hadn't broken a single dish or scalded herself in the water she'd heated. Maybe tonight she'd try her hand at cooking dinner.

Smiling with the simple pleasure of a job well done, she left the kitchen, went in search of Virgil and True. She found True out on the front porch, seated in a rocking chair, gazing out over the wide valley.

"All finished?" he asked, smiling up at her.

"Yes," she said, looking around, eyebrows lifting. "Where is Virgil?"

"Aw, he just went for a short ride. He'll be back in a little bit."

The princess immediately felt her heart speed. Here was her chance to convince True that she was a royal princess. And, it was her golden opportunity to learn more about the Texas Ranger she had come to love. She sat down in a straight-back chair beside True's rocker and, gazing out at the sunbaked land of old Mexico, said simply, "True, I am not who Virgil told you I am." She turned her head, looked directly at him. Rushing her words now, eager to make him believe she was telling the truth, she said, "I am actually Princess Marlena of Hartz-Coburg and I . . ." She talked a mile a minute, bent on convincing him of her true identity, and finally when she stopped to draw a much-needed breath, the silver-haired True said, "I believe you."

Surprised, she said, "You do?"

"Yes." He grinned. "I'm not as cynical as Virgil. Somebody tells me something, I tend to believe him. Or her."

Relieved, she exhaled, then asked, "Who is the other woman? The one Virgil thinks I am."

"A Las Cruces saloon singer who must be the spittin' image of you, child . . . ah . . . Princess . . ." He stopped, asked, "What do people call you when they get to know you?"

She smiled and said, "Your Royal Highness."

"Oh."

"But you may just call me Marlena," she said. "Now, please go on, tell me about this saloon singer."

"She's a pretty red-haired entertainer who's billed as the Queen of the Silver Dollar. The Silver Dollar's a popular saloon up in Las Cruces. Anyway, three or four weeks ago, an elusive bank robber—a

British fellow—was caught here in El Paso and, under intense questioning, he implicated the Queen of the Silver Dollar as his accomplice. Virgil, against his wishes, was ordered to go up to Las Cruces and bring in the woman."

Nodding thoughtfully, the princess filled in the blanks herself. Montillion had hired the woman to take her place on the tour, so when Virgil reached Las Cruces, the Queen of the Silver Dollar was gone. Then, when he had seen her, the princess, on the Cloudcroft depot platform, he thought she was the missing saloon singer.

"He naturally mistook you for the lady thief," True said, defending Virgil. "He was following orders."

"I know," she said, and then as casually as possible, added, "Virgil is a brave man, isn't he?"

"The bravest," True was quick to reply.

She smiled, nodded. "But not the most talkative man I've ever met."

"He can be a quiet one, all right."

The princess continued to make nonchalant, offhand statements about Virgil, and True, rocking gently to and fro, continued to comment without hesitation.

Soon she said, in the same breezy tone of voice, "Virgil doesn't have much regard for women, does he?"

True Cannon stopped rocking. For a long minute he didn't respond. Then he answered honestly. "Nope. Not since his mama left him in a rundown saloon when he was ten."

The princess's eyes widened in shocked disbelief. "Left him . . . ? I don't understand. What do you mean?"

True Cannon exhaled heavily and shook his head. "I shouldn't be telling you this. Virgil would have my hide if he knew I'd been talking out of turn."

But the princess wouldn't let it go. She wanted to know more. She wanted to know everything. And she was determined to make this kindly silver-haired gentleman tell her.

"Oh, please, True," she said, moving her chair closer and placing a pale hand atop his age-spotted one where it lay on the rocker's wooden armrest. "Won't you tell me all you know? Tell me about *my* Virgil. I *must* know." True didn't fail to notice that she had said "my Virgil." Besides, he could see it in her expressive emerald eyes. She was in love with Virgil Black. Reading his thoughts, the princess looked directly into his eyes and said, "You know, don't you, that I love him?" He nodded his head. "Then, please, tell me about him."

True slipped his hand from under hers, patted the back of her small hand, and said, "If you love him . . ."

"Oh, I do love him. Sooo much."

"Then I guess you have the right to know what's made him the man he is."

True turned his head then and gazed, unseeing, at the wide valley, carefully collecting his thoughts. And he began to talk about the quiet, courageous man he looked on as a son. He told the princess that when Virgil was not quite ten years old, his pretty, fast-living, loose-moraled mother had taken up with an outlaw. She ran away with the desperado, abandoning her only son, Virgil. She left him alone and penniless in an El Paso saloon.

"Dear God." Horrified Princess Marlena raised her hand to her mouth.

"From that night on," True continued, "young Virgil was on his own. A smart, industrious little boy, he supported himself by sweeping up and washing dishes in the very saloon where his mama deserted him. He had no place else to go. No relatives that wanted him. Nobody. He slept on the floor in a back room of the saloon. No bed. No sheets or blankets. Just the bare plank floor."

The princess pictured the frightened little boy left alone with no one to love or care for him. What a contrast with her own privileged childhood. When she was ten years old, she was doted on and spoiled by her father, the king, and by everyone else around her. When she was lovingly tucked in each night, it was in a big feather bed in a well-guarded bedchamber as large as True's entire adobe house.

True went on. "It was a hard, heartless world the boy saw, and so to survive, he became hard and heartless himself. He never had the opportunity to be around decent folks when he was growing up. His world was—from that early age—peopled with gunmen and card sharks and pickpockets and ladies of the evening."

Her heart aching for the lost little boy who was unloved and unwanted, the princess murmured, "My poor Virgil."

Continuing, True said, "Virgil might well have become a bandit himself. But he chose to become a Texas Ranger. Like his father."

"His father? Is his father . . . ?"

"Ranger Captain Charles W. Black was killed in the line of duty. Ambushed by a band of Apaches down in the Big Bend country when Virgil was eight."

True told her that Virgil's decision, at age twenty, to join the Texas Rangers was the best one he'd ever made.

"As far as I'm concerned, the Rangers saved Virgil's life. And, speaking of saving lives . . ."

He went on to tell the princess about the chill autumn day more than ten years ago, when he, True, an aging Texas Ranger himself, had been the only Ranger left alive after a fierce skirmish with a band of bloodthirsty Comanche up on the high plains of Texas.

"They took me to their camp in Palo Duro Canyon where I was held and tortured. I had no chance of escaping so I prayed for death but knew it would be slow in coming. The Comanches do thoroughly enjoy slowly torturing their captives to death. That night Virgil Black managed to silently slip alone into the Comanche camp and rescue me." True smiled then, and said, "I owe the boy my life and no doubt about it. But it's more than that." His smile turned pensive. "The fact that he cared enough about a worn-out old Ranger to come after me is what meant the most to me." He gazed into the far distance, looking back over the years. "I lost my own family a long time ago. Virgil is family to me."

The princess listened, enraptured, as True talked about the man they both loved. His revelations explained so much. Virgil's innate distrust of women was completely understandable. A frightened ten-year-old child heartlessly abandoned by his own mother!

And now she knew that Virgil had believed she was one of those kind of women! How vividly she recalled that first time they had made love. Afterward he had said, "Now we're even. I finally got what I paid for." Dear Lord, the woman Montillion had chosen to stand in for her on the tour was a prostitute that once entertained Virgil! Or had been paid to do so and had reneged on the bargain.

"I've been up since way before the sun," True broke into her troubled musings. "Time for me to take a little nap."

There was one more question the princess had to ask. Even if the answer hurt.

"True, there's one last thing I have to know." She swallowed with difficulty and said, "Who is . . . Eva?"

His gray eyes suddenly twinkling, he said, "Why, I thought you were. Last night you introduced yourself as Miss Eva Jones." He rose from his rocker.

Half-annoyed, she said, "Why, you knew very well I was lying."

"Yes, I knew."

"Who is she? Who is Eva?"

"His mother," True said. "Virgil's pretty, no-account mama was named Eva."

40

That same summer afternoon a westbound train rumbled across the flat, dusty, endless plains of far southwest Texas.

Destination, El Paso.

"I thought you were going to lie down and rest for a while," Montillion said, looking up when Robbie Ann entered the royal day coach.

"I was, but I—" She stopped speaking. Her fair brow puckered as if something was bothering her. She dropped down onto a comfortable overstuffed chair beside the window, glanced out at the monotonous landscape. Thinking aloud, she said, "In only twelve to fourteen hours, we'll be in El Paso."

"Yes," Montillion confirmed. "If nothing unforeseen happens, we should be pulling into the El Paso train station shortly after seven A.M."

Robbie Ann turned from the train window and looked directly at him. "Time is getting short, and there's something I've been wanting to ask you."

"I believe I know what it is," said Montillion. "You are wondering why I picked you to play the part of the princess."

"Yes," she said quickly. "How could *you* know that a woman who looks like Princess Marlena was working in a Las Cruces saloon? I suppose when all is said and done it makes little difference, but I can't help wondering how you—a foreigner—would know where to find me."

Montillion gazed at the pretty ginger-haired woman who looked so much like Princess Marlena. He felt his heart kick against his ribs and wondered, for the millionth time, if he had done something terribly wicked in helping the royal family withhold the truth all these years from this cheated child. Was he, by keeping the scandalous secret, as guilty of wrongdoing as the unfaithful king who had sired her? Was it fair to leave her alone in Galveston and sail home without telling her who she really was?

Astute, Robbie Ann read the troubled uncertainty in Montillion's eyes and knew he was struggling with a decision.

"What is it, Monty?" she said softly, both her tone and her demeanor gently persuasive. "Whatever it is, you can tell me. I'll understand, I will. If you know more about me than I know myself, don't you think I have a right to know, too?"

"Yes," he said finally, "you do have the right to know." Repentant, sorry he had been a party to the underhanded transaction that had robbed this young woman of her birthright, he looked at her and said, "My dear child, I have grown so very fond of you these past weeks and now—" his eyes closed for an instant, "now you are going to hate me."

"I don't hate anyone," Robbie Ann said and meant it. "And I could *never* hate you."

Still struggling with his guilty conscience, Montillion said, "You must understand that what I have to tell you, although quite momentous, unfortunately, changes nothing. And, you must swear to me that you will *never* tell anyone. Absolutely no one."

"Who would I tell?" she said, shrugging slender shoulders. Then, "Besides, I think I've already guessed the deep, dark secret."

"You have?"

She smiled and stated, "You knew my mother. Am I right?"

"No, dear. I didn't. It was your father I knew."

Robbie Ann's green eyes immediately widened, and her lips fell open in surprise. "Are you saying what I think you're saying?"

He shook his head affirmatively. "Your father was the late king Albert of Hartz-Coburg."

Expecting shock, outrage, and anger from her, Montillion was taken aback when Robbie Ann, smiling brightly, clapped her hands with glee. "I knew it! I just knew it!" she exclaimed excitedly. "My mother always told me that my father was of royal descent! That I had royal blood running through my veins, but no one ever believed me! Oh, this is great, this is absolutely wonderful. Wait until I tell Bob that I . . . Oh, never mind him. Please, tell me all about my father and my . . . my—" She abruptly stopped talking. Her smile fled, and she lifted a well-arched eyebrow. "For goodness' sake, this means that Her Royal Highness, Princess Marlena is . . . is . . ."

Nodding, Montillion acknowledged it. "Your sister. The princess is your half sister."

"Well, Lord have mercy!" said Robbie with a loud laugh of sheer delight. "No wonder we look alike."

"It is uncanny. You could be identical twins, so closely do you resemble each other."

"Makes sense," she said, smiling easily. "I never looked the least bit like my mother, so I must have taken after my father." She giggled and added, "Like my father, the king." Her smile suddenly slipped slightly when she asked, "You have known about me all these years?"

"I have," said Montillion, feeling a terrible heaviness weigh down on his heart. "Can you ever forgive me?"

"Ah, there's really nothing to forgive," she said as breezily as if she were discussing the weather. "These past three weeks I've learned enough about all this royal routine rigmarole to know that you were simply 'doing your duty.'" She flashed him a wide conspiratorial smile, and added, "God save the king and all that, right?"

"Correct," he replied, smiling now, relieved that she was not angry. "Robbie Ann, you are a very bright, kind, understanding young woman."

"Yes, well, I'm also a curious one. Now tell me everything. Am I older or younger than my sister? Was there a great big royal stink when I was born? Did the queen know about my mother? Start at the beginning and tell me everything you can remember."

Montillion did just that.

He told her that her mother, Lola Montez, was a young, exquisitely beautiful American actress who was on a prolonged summer tour of Europe when she met the king. He and the queen had been in the royal box at the theater on Miss Montez's opening night.

"The beautiful dark-haired actress immediately caught the king's discerning eye, and he quietly arranged for an introduction. At first Miss Montez spurned his advances, would have nothing to do with him. But he was handsome, rich, and powerful, so he broke down her defenses. He sent flowers and expensive gifts and appeared at the theater every night—often leaving the queen home in the palace—until finally, the lovely actress agreed to a midnight supper.

"It quickly became a serious romance, and Miss Montez, at the king's request, stayed on in Hartz-Coburg when the rest of the troupe left for London. She agreed to take up residence in a little-used royal summerhouse at the seashore down the mountainside from the palace. Soon she was carrying his child. You. When she was six months pregnant, the queen became pregnant with Princess Marlena.

"After your birth, the queen learned of your existence and insisted the king send both you and your mother out of the country, lest her own child's ascendance to the throne be threatened."

Robbie Ann frowned, puzzled. "How could my existence have threatened the princess's right to the throne?"

Montillion hurried on with the story. "Financial arrangements were hastily made with your mother, and the two of you were sent to America with her sworn promise that neither of you would ever return to Hartz-Coburg. And, that no one would ever be told of your true parentage."

Montillion was quick to explain that it had always been quite fashionable and totally acceptable for a sovereign to take a beautiful actress for his mistress. If Miss Montez had not become pregnant, the affair would have gone on for as long as she held the king's interest.

Robbie Ann's green eyes sparkled, and she asked, "Are queens allowed to conduct affairs with handsome young men?"

Montillion colored. "In some monarchies, it has been known to occur."

"You know, the more I learn about the power and privilege of royalty, the more I think I'd fit right in!" She laughed and tossed her head saucily. "Oh, don't look so horrified, I was only teasing. You've spent the last three weeks with me, and I haven't embarrassed you once, now have I?"

"Your behavior has been exemplary. No royal has ever behaved more admirably."

"Why, thank you, Monty." Impulsively she reached out, touched his sleeve, and said, "And thanks for telling me who I am. You don't know what it's like to wonder who your father was. No matter how many times I begged my mother to tell me his name and where he lived, she always refused. She would only say that 'he was a handsome European sovereign with whom she had been madly in love.'"

Montillion pointed out, "She had no choice. Her continued silence was an important part of the bargain that was struck when the financial arrangements were made."

"I understand now. She couldn't tell me." Robbie sighed softly. "And those 'anonymous remittances' that I've received through the years . . . they came from the royal family?"

"Yes. Handled through our agent here in America."

"That's how you knew where to find me. You've kept up with my whereabouts all these years."

"I have. And I've wondered about you more than you'll ever know."

Her somber expression quickly changing, she flashed him a smile as bright as the Texas sun, and asked, "Will I continue to receive my 'anonymous remittances' after this?"

He chuckled merrily. "They can no longer be anonymous, but yes, you will still receive them. And, for giving such a laudable performance these past weeks, you may also keep, as payment for a job well done, the valuable emerald necklace that the wealthy San Antonian, Mr. Andrew Forester, so generously donated to the crown."

Her eyebrows shot up. "Why, I don't know what you're talking about."

"Yes, you do," he said.

And they laughed together.

41

It was late afternoon when Virgil returned to True's little adobe house. The princess was on the porch, waiting impatiently for him.

She rose on trembling legs when he dismounted, rushed anxiously out to meet him, and said without preamble, "True is asleep. But I shall never be able to sleep again until I convince you that I am not who you think I am."

Virgil unhurriedly looped Noche's long leather reins over the hitch rail, then turned slowly to face her, and said, "And just who do I think you are?"

"An entertainer you met in a Las Cruces saloon who took you to bed!"

Virgil gave her a cynical half smile. "And if you are not she, how would you know this?"

"Because, my dearest," she said, impulsively wrapping her arms around his trim waist, "she is the woman my factor, Montillion, hired to take my place on the bond tour. A ginger-haired singer he found in a Las Cruces saloon called the Silver Dollar. A woman billed as the Queen of the Silver Dollar."

Head tipped back, looking up at him, she read both relief and despair in his beautiful brooding blue eyes. Hugging him tightly for a long memorable minute, she released him, then stepped back. "Come with me, Captain."

Virgil followed her. She led him to the porch where they sat down on the steps side by side. Talking rapidly, she told him that she was *not* the Queen of the Silver Dollar as he thought her to be. She was a royal princess and she would prove it. She would send a wire to Montillion and have him come to El Paso at once.

Virgil lifted his arms, raked long fingers through his raven hair, then pressed his temples with the heels of his hands. Exhaling heavily, he gazed at the western horizon where the sun was slipping below the serrated mountain peaks.

Finally, he said, "That won't be necessary."

"Why not? All I have to do is send a . . . a . . . what is it?"

Virgil turned and looked directly at her. "I stopped by Ranger head-quarters while I was out. Your factor, Montillion, has wired my commanding officer, telling him of the horrendous mistake I made. And to say that the royal train will arrive in El Paso in the morning to . . . to—" he paused, swallowed, and his jaw tightened noticeably, "to take you home."

"So you do believe me? You know that I am telling the truth."

"Yes," he said, "I know."

"Oh, Virgil, that's wonderful!" she cried happily, and threw her arms around his neck.

Her forehead resting against his chin, she realized, quite suddenly, that it wasn't so wonderful after all. It meant that tonight was to be her last night with Virgil. An involuntary tremor raced through her slender body. She lifted her head, looked into Virgil's half-shuttered eyes, and saw her own despair mirrored there.

"Oh, darling," she said on a sob, "kiss me."

His tortured gaze dropped to her soft, trembling lips. A muscle spasmed at the corner of his mouth.

But before he could kiss her, True stepped onto the porch, yawning.

"Why didn't y'all wake me? Why, I've slept the entire afternoon away. Now I'll be awake all night. Won't be able to sleep a wink."

The couple seated on the porch steps exchanged quick looks of disappointment. The prospect of having True wide awake until far into the night was frustrating. They needed to be alone. They needed to talk and touch and kiss and . . . say good-bye before tomorrow came.

The princess felt panicky. She didn't think she could bear it if she and Virgil were never to be alone again. There was so much she wanted to say to him. So much she wanted to hear him say to her.

She was in agony as the minutes ticked away and late afternoon turned into evening. When the sun had set completely and twilight settled in, True finally rose from his rocking chair and asked if she would help him cook supper. She agreed and preceded him to the kitchen. Virgil, following them in, took the opportunity to bathe, shave, and change into clean clothes.

When the meal was almost ready, True said to the princess, "You can call Virgil in now."

"Here I am," said Virgil, stepping into the kitchen doorway, filling it with his tall, lean frame.

And taking the princess's breath away. Looking, oh, so handsome in a freshly laundered white shirt and faded, neatly pressed denim pants, Virgil took his place at the table without glancing at her. But she couldn't keep her eyes off him.

His strong masculine presence had never been quite so exciting and potent. Nor had he ever been more good-looking. His jet black hair, still damp from his bath, gleamed in the lamplight as he bent his head slightly to take a forkful of food.

When he picked up a tumbler of iced tea, her attention was drawn to his hands. To those beautiful, brown, long-fingered hands. She felt her breath grow short and her stomach clench. She looked away, silently praying that those lean dark hands would touch her again, all over, at least one more time.

When Virgil finished eating, he complimented them both on the superb meal, pushed his chair away from the table, turned it sideways, and lit a slim brown cigar. Then he sighed, leaning back in his chair, his long body stretched out, legs crossed at the ankles.

He looked totally relaxed and at ease, and the princess felt her spirits sink. How could he be so . . . uncaring? How could he sit there in calm repose while she was so edgy, she was about to jump out of her skin? She was heartsick. This time tomorrow night she would be gone out of his life forever, yet he wasn't at all upset.

She was.

More upset than she had ever been in her life. So miserable the pain was almost physical. The unhappy princess rose from the table and reached for Virgil's empty plate. Her breath caught when his hand shot out and his tapered fingers firmly encircled her fragile wrist, stopping her.

Never releasing his hold on her, he said, "True, think you can manage the dishes by yourself?"

"Been managing for the past thirty years, so I expect I can," said True, his gray eyes twinkling. "Why? Y'all got something better to do?"

Virgil gave no reply. He snuffed out his cigar in an ashtray. Then he came to his feet, drew the princess gently by the wrist around the table to him. He released her wrist, gently turned her about, and with his open hand at her back, guided her through the house and out the front door. Her heart thrumming with anticipation and excitement, she didn't ask where they were going. She didn't care so long as she was with him.

When Virgil lifted her up into the saddle atop Noche, she knew he meant for them to ride tandem. She was glad. She wanted to be as close to him as possible.

Without a word, Virgil unwound the reins from the hitch post, drew them up over Noche's neck, and swung up behind the princess. He wheeled the big black around and galloped him down the narrow, dusty road.

Encircled in his long arms, a foolish smile of pleasure on her face, the princess relaxed against Virgil, loving the feel of the night wind in her face and the solid support of his firm chest at her back. When Virgil put Noche into a comfortable, long-strided lope, she sighed and wished that this ride never had to end. She wished she could spend eternity astride this big, dark, powerful stallion, wrapped in the arms of this big, dark, powerful man.

She wished—sincerely wished—that she were not a royal princess, but was instead the saloon singer he had taken her to be. If she were really the Queen of the Silver Dollar, she could stay there in Texas with him. She could, if she were the saloon singer, spend the rest of her days trying to make him love her as she loved him. As it was, she would spend the rest of her days trying to make herself forget how much she loved him.

When the winded stallion reached the rocky outcroppings of the Franklin Mountains, Virgil drew rein. Snorting and blowing, Noche came to a plunging halt. The princess turned her head, looked up at Virgil's strong masculine profile struck by the moonlight.

He glanced down at her and finally spoke, "I brought you way out here because I had to be alone with you one last time if only for a little while."

"I'm so glad," she replied honestly. "Back at the house, you seemed so relaxed, so totally at ease. I thought you didn't want—"

"Sweetheart, sweetheart," he said, "I wasn't relaxed at all, I was miserable." He smiled then and said, "It was like last night when I couldn't get away from the don. Remember?"

"I'll never forget," she said, smiling back at him.

"You trust me now, don't you?"

"With my life," she answered truthfully.

Pointing, he directed her attention to one of the mountains' jutting peaks. She gazed at a unique spire of rock that rose well above its two neighboring crests. It looked like the sharp, slender blade of a knife.

"You can't see it from here," Virgil said, "but at the pinnacle, there's a smooth, flat mesa about the size of True's front parlor. It's a special place to me. When I'm up there, it's like I'm alone in the world. The trail up is so perilous, no one ever intrudes."

"Can we go up there?" she asked.

Those were the words Virgil wanted to hear. "That's why I asked if you trust me. I want to take you up, but I know how terrified you are of heights. As I said, the trail up is treacherous. So if you'd rather not . . . if you're afraid, I—"

"I'm afraid of nothing so long as I'm with you."

Not trusting his voice, Virgil didn't reply. His heart hurt. And he knew it was going to hurt a whole lot worse tomorrow.

42

Virgil nudged Noche forward, and the responsive mount needed no further reining. The intelligent stallion knew where his master wanted to go. Given his head, Noche immediately began to ascend the rocky face of Brizna Peak.

Trusting his well-trained stallion to get them safely to the summit, Virgil wound the long leather reins loosely around the saddle horn. He slipped his arms under the princess's and wrapped them snugly around her trim midriff.

She sighed, laid her own hands atop Virgil's, and marveled that she had no fear of riding horseback up a hazardous mountain trail at night. Less than a week ago she would have been sick with terror. But that was before she met Virgil Black. In Virgil's arms, she had never felt safer.

His noble heart pumping, lungs expanding, the stallion labored up the steep stony slope. The trail spiraled into and around impassable cracks. It went up, up, up over five hundred feet of steep-sloping solid, slick rock. If the stallion took a misstep, if he started sliding, they would fall to their deaths below.

Muscles straining, sharp hooves dislodging loose rocks, Noche carefully ascended the dangerous serpentine trail almost to the top. The tired stallion halted when he had walked as close to the top as he could. The rest of the trail up was a dark, spiraling path cut between a corridor of giant boulders too narrow for him to navigate.

Virgil swung down and reached for the princess. She stood close behind him in the thick darkness while he unbitted the black and loosened the saddle cinch. From behind the cantle, he unstrapped a blanket, tossed it over his left shoulder.

Then he reached behind him, took the princess's hand, and drew her along after him up the pitch-black path, cautioning as he went: "Turn sideways here" and "Duck your head" and "Watch it, there's a chasm here you must step over."

When bright moonlight greeted them, the princess knew they had reached the summit. Once at the top, Virgil immediately knelt and spread the blanket at the center of the smooth mesa. The princess, experiencing none of her usual aversion to heights, stood close to him, mesmerized by the incredible 360-degree view from this lofty lookout.

"Virgil," she murmured, "we're up so high. We must almost be in heaven."

He rose, stood up behind her, clamped an arm around her waist, and said truthfully, "As near as I'll ever get."

Spread out far below, the lights of El Paso and Juarez twinkled like glittering diamonds tossed out on a bed of black velvet. Dark looming mountains marched north to south, their towering monoliths the natural western boundary of the sister border cities.

Virgil gave her a few minutes to enjoy the spectacular scenery, then he said, "Come. There are some things I want to say to you."

They moved to the spread blanket, sank down to their knees, and sat back on their heels, facing each other.

The princess reached out to touch him, but he stopped her. "No, don't. Don't touch me. If you do, I won't be able to think." She nodded, understanding, and placed her hands on her suede-trousered thighs.

Virgil drew a long breath and said, "First of all, you'll never know how terribly sorry I am that . . . that . . ."

"You mistook me for the Queen of the Silver Dollar."

"Please, sweetheart, don't prompt me. And don't interrupt. For once let me do the talking and you keep quiet, okay?"

"Okay," she said, contrite.

He started over. "You have no idea how sorry I am for the indefensible mistake I made in apprehending you. You tried to tell me who you were, but I wouldn't listen. I was arrogant and intolerant and cruel. You have every right and reason to hate me. I've done you a terrible injustice and I wish there was some way I could right all the wrongs, but I—"

The princess could keep quiet no longer. "There is a way."

"There is?"

"Yes. You can truthfully answer one question for me."

"Fair enough."

"Do you love me? Even a little?"

"I do," he said without hesitation. "I love you, Your Highness. I love you and I'll never stop loving you."

"Oh, Virgil," she said, lunged up onto her knees, and threw her arms around his neck. "I love you, too. I love you so much it hurts."

"I know," he said, putting his arms around her. "I know, sweetheart. Unfortunately, the fact that we love each other changes nothing. No matter how much I love you, you're still leaving tomorrow." He pressed her close against him. "Aren't you?" He held his breath, hoping she might say no, knowing that she wouldn't. Couldn't.

Against his shoulder, "Yes. Yes, I am leaving tomorrow. I have no choice. You understand, don't you, my love?"

Virgil exhaled heavily, lifted a hand to stroke her hair. "Sure I do, baby. Sorry, I mean, Your Highness."

She pulled back to look at him. She gazed into his tortured blue eyes and said, "Make love to me."

She saw the muscles in his smooth tanned throat constrict. With difficulty, he spoke. "I can't do that. I can't make love to a royal princess."

"I *am* a princess, but I'm a woman first." She tightened her arms around his neck. "*Your* woman. Make love to me, Virgil. Please."

"Jesus, I can't resist you," he said truthfully.

"Don't even try," she replied, unbuttoning his white shirt. They quickly shed their clothes and stretched out naked on the blanket beneath the twinkling stars. There was a trembling in the princess's pale thighs and a quivering in her breasts when Virgil laid a gentle hand on her stomach. He studied her through the long black lashes that curved down to his olive cheeks. His passionate eyes aflame with love and longing, he gazed at her, knowing—in that instant—that for as long as there was the breath of life in him, his heart would belong to this ginger-haired princess who could never be his.

The princess laid a pale hand on his dark chest and softly said his name, shattering the last remnants of his self-control. He swept her into his arms and kissed her. They kissed and sighed until both were anxious and ready for total possession. Virgil put his hands to her narrow waist, stretched out on his back, and lifted her astride his hips.

He said in that flat Texas twang she so adored, "I want to lie here below and look at your beautiful face while I make love to you."

He took her hand, drew it to his lips, kissed its soft palm, then drew her slender fingers—one at a time—into his mouth and gently sucked and licked them until they were wet. Needing no instruction, she wrapped her gleaming fingers around his throbbing erection and guided the smooth hot tip up inside her.

They both gasped with growing elation as she slowly lowered her body on his, sliding sensuously down on that rock-hard phallus of pulsing male power. When he was securely inside her, stretching and filling her, she began the age-old rolling of her hips as if she had done this a thousand times before.

She hadn't.

She hadn't even been aware that lovers mated in this position, but she knew right away that she liked it very much. Her hands gripping his ribs, she leaned down for his kiss, then straightened once more. Rocking and grinding her bottom against him, her movements met by the rhythmic upward thrusting of his seeking pelvis.

They looked into each other's eyes as they made love there on that windswept summit beneath the stars and above the glittering lights of the two desert cities. Both realized, as they surged and pressed and sought total fulfillment, that this divine coupling was much more than just a sexual union. It was spiritual as well as physical. It was that wonderful mating of soul and body experienced by only the lucky few who have known true love.

Both cried out when they climaxed together. The sounds of their ecstacy carried on the night winds to echo throughout the eroded towers, pinnacles, and rocks balanced on pedestals.

Collapsing atop Virgil's slick broad chest, the princess stayed with him still inside her for a long peaceful time, reluctant to move, to release him, to let him go.

When her heartbeat had returned to normal and she could breathe easily, she began to talk, to tell him about her life in Hartz-Coburg. She told him about her arranged early marriage and said she had respected but not loved the duke. She had married out of duty. After the duke's death, there had never been another man in her life. She talked about her parents, the king and queen. She filled him in on anything he might wonder about, and when she had concluded, she said, "Now, my love, it's your turn. I know so little about you. Tell me about your life, your loves."

"You are my only love," he said.

She lifted her head, looked at him skeptically. "Now tell the truth. I would suppose that you've had lots of women before me."

"Sure, I've had a lot of women," he admitted. "But, I've never loved a woman until you."

She liked his answer. But there was one last little thing she wanted to know. Walking her fingertips over his chest, she said, "Was one of the women you've . . . ah . . . had . . . the . . . the Queen of the Silver Dollar?"

"No."

"No? You wouldn't lie to me, would you?"

Virgil chuckled and admitted, "I fell asleep in her bed before . . ." He shrugged bare shoulders. "I swear to you that I never laid a hand on her."

"Good," she said, pleased, then laid her head on his chest and murmured, "Tell me about your parents."

To her surprise Virgil needed no further coaxing. He spoke fondly of the brave Texas Ranger who was his father. He told her that Captain Charles W. Black had died a hero.

"I was just eight when he got killed," Virgil said, "but I remember him well. He was a big, kind, easygoing man who was affectionate and brave and I was very proud of him."

"I'm sure you were," she said. "And your mother?"

"A pretty, high-spirited woman with an infectious laugh and a zest for living. I lost her, too. When I was ten."

"I'm sorry," the princess said, touched that he chose to say nothing unkind about the woman who had given birth to him.

When True had told her about Virgil's mother deserting Virgil when he was a child, her first question had been, 'Virgil told you about it?' To which True had replied, "Lord, no, to this day Virgil's never said a word about her, even to me. The bartender at the saloon where she left Virgil told me about it."

Pretending she didn't know the truth about the mother who had callously deserted him, the princess said now, "Do you look like your mother?"

"No," Virgil said. "But I look a lot like my father."

She detected a note of relief in his tone. She knew why. With a mother like his, he was glad to know that her lawfully wedded husband actually was his father.

They continued to talk easily, to reveal more of themselves to each other. To kiss and sigh and make lovely memories to store up and sustain them through a lifetime apart.

They lay in each other's arms and vowed never to forget a single thing about this beautiful starry night together.

Sighing, gazing into the flashing eyes of her godlike lover, the princess said softly, "The poet said 'There is a moment in every life which is never surpassed.'"

She sighed and hugged him when Virgil said, "This is that moment."

At *El Paso's busy downtown* train depot, Virgil and the princess slipped out onto the wide wooden platform to be apart from the others. Under the broiling afternoon Texas sun, they stood looking into each other's eyes, making strained small talk, painfully conscious that this was their final farewell.

Once they said good-bye, they would never meet again.

As much as he loved her, Virgil felt as if he hardly knew this stunning woman who, dressed once again in her own regal clothes, looked every inch the royal princess. Already it was nearly impossible to picture her in the those tight yellow suede riding pants she'd worn only yesterday.

And had eagerly shed last night atop Brizna Peak.

It wasn't just the finery that made her seem a stranger. She was back amid all the trappings of royalty. The gleaming royal railcars awaited her on the tracks. And just inside the crowded terminal, her factor, Montillion, her lady-in-waiting, the baroness Richtoffen, and her bodyguard, Hantz Landsfelt, were at her beck and call.

Through the open terminal doors, came the first boarding call.

"It's almost time," the princess said.

"Yes, I . . . wait, I almost forgot." Virgil reached into his pocket and withdrew a clear pint bottle. "*Una poco donacion,*" he said, handing it to her. "A little gift."

Curious, the princess took the bottle. "The white sands!" she exclaimed happily. "You *did* get me some of the precious white sand. You knew how badly I wanted it and you . . . you. . . . Oh, Virgil," she looked up at him like an excited little girl, "you couldn't have given me anything that would mean half as much to me." She swallowed past the growing lump in her throat and said softly, "Thank you, darling. Thank you so much."

"You're very welcome, Your Highness."

Clasping the glass bottle as if it were priceless, the princess dropped one of her spotless beige gloves.

"You dropped a glove," Virgil said, stooping to pick it up.

He started to give it to her. She put out her hand to take it. But he withheld it. "I'll keep it, sweetheart," he said, tucking the glove into his shirt pocket, "So I'll have something to remember you by."

"Yes, of course," she said, her heart aching. "Keep it and . . . think of me . . . sometime." She tried to smile, failed.

"Every day of my life," he said, and in the fleeting expression she saw in his beautiful blue eyes was the revelation of a soul in torment.

It was gone in an instant, and she thought that, although they had come from two different worlds, they were, in some ways, very much alike. She had been trained from childhood to conceal suffering and to suppress all signs of emotion. He had trained himself from childhood to conceal suffering and to suppress all signs of emotion.

His eyes were dry and so were hers.

The second boarding call came.

"Oh, God," he said, "this is hard."

She stepped closer, laid a hand on the gleaming silver star on his chest, and said, "I love you. I will always love you, my darling."

Virgil took a deep breath, touched her pale cheek with gentle fingers, and said, "And I love you, Your Royal Highness."

She swallowed anxiously, then swallowed again. "You could come with me. I could give you a title."

"Princess Marlena," he smiled sadly and said, "I already have a title. Captain, Texas Rangers."

Her heart breaking, she nodded, knowing he would never leave the Rangers.

Wishing he could kiss her, knowing he could not, Virgil squeezed her small hand one last time, then stepped back as her royal entourage surrounded her and hastily ushered the princess on board.

With True at his side, Virgil Black stood on the depot platform and watched the train with its royal railcars carry away the love of his life. While the princess waved a gloved hand for as long as she could see him, the Ranger's hands remained at his sides, his fingers curled into fists so tight his short nails were cutting into his palms.

"You shouldn't have let her go," True said. "You'll never find another like her."

"No, I don't suppose I will," drawled Virgil. "I don't run into too many royal princesses in my line of work."

He turned quickly and walked away so that the older man wouldn't see the mist of tears in his eyes.

When the depot had been left behind and the train snaked slowly eastward, the princess, fighting back the tears she refused to shed, turned her head, looked out the window.

Montillion, concerned, inquired respectfully, "Your Highness, are you all right?"

"Yes, I . . . it's just . . . this American desert," she said, looking longingly out the window of the royal coach, "it has toughened my muscles, but softened my pride."

"We better close the window," Montillion said, "looks like a west Texas dust storm is forming to the south."

She turned, smiled, and repeated what Virgil had said to her that day they got caught in the sandstorm, "Why a little sandstorm is good for a girl's complexion."

Montillion frowned, puzzled. "I'm afraid I don't understand."

"I was teasing," she said, turning back to the window.

When the slow-moving train began to pick up speed at the outskirts of the city, the princess was still staring out the window, looking back.

"Forget something?" asked Montillion.

"I wish I could," said the princess. She turned to look at her factor with big, sad eyes. "I can't. Oh, Montillion, I love him so. I wish I were not a princess. I wish—"

"Do you really mean it?" Montillion interrupted. "You would be content to stay on in America with your Ranger?"

"I would gladly give up the throne for the man I love," she said, and unable to fight back the tears any longer, buried her face in her hands and began to sob.

Montillion looked with love and pity on this remarkable young princess he had known since birth. He drew a deep breath and said, "Perhaps there is a way."

The princess looked up at him with round, tear-filled eyes. As quickly and succinctly as possible, Montillion told her exactly the same incredible story he had told Robbie Ann earlier. At the conclusion of the tale, he said, "And she's right here on the train with us. Stay right where you are."

He hurried away, returning seconds later with Robbie Ann in tow. The two young women stared at each other, speechless. Then they fell into each other's arms crying and embracing and talking at the same time.

"You look just like me!" said Princess Marlena pulling back to gaze at her half sister.

"You're prettier," said Robbie Ann.

"No, I'm not. Did you get my awful ears?"

"Did I ever!" Robbie Ann tossed back the right side of her hair. "Look for yourself."

"You did!" squealed the princess, and the sisters went into fits of laughter.

"There's not much time," Montillion reminded them.

"He's right," said Princess Marlena, stepping out of Robbie Ann's embrace but continuing to cling tightly to her hand. Eagerly, she asked, "If I chose to stay on in America, would you take my place on the throne?"

Robbie Ann looked from the princess to Montillion. "Would that be possible, Monty? I mean . . . we all know that I am . . . well, you know."

"That doesn't matter," Montillion assured her. "Our country is a forward-thinking, modern kingdom. An illigit—a Morganic offspring can ascend to the throne, just as he or she could in say, Scotland."

Robbie Ann's wide-eyed gaze returned to her newly found half sister. "Montillion's telling you the truth," the princess assured her. "So you see, you wouldn't be taking my place on the throne. It is actually *your* place, since you were born before me."

Nodding, thinking, Robbie Ann said worriedly, "But I'm wanted for robbery."

"Not in Hartz-Coburg," said Montillion. "Our only trick is to get you out of the country as quickly as possible." His brow furrowed then and he asked, "But what about your accomplice? That fellow the paper calls British Bob? He means something to you, doesn't he?"

"He's my latest affliction," said Robbie Ann with self-effacing charm and a smile.

"Could you bear to leave him?" asked Princess Marlena.

"You mean would I give Bob up for the throne?" said Robbie Ann, laughing merrily. "Quicker than you can say 'Your Royal Highness'!" Then, looking at Montillion, she said, "But I would hate to see Bob go to prison."

"That's no real worry." Montillion dismissed any lingering concern. "I'll send a telegraph to Hamilton Fish, the American secretary of state. He can be convinced to show your gentleman friend leniency."

Shaking her head, Robbie Ann again turned to Princess Marlena. "You're sure you want to do this?"

"Very sure. And you?"

"I've never wanted anything more in my entire life," said Robbie Ann.

The sisters hugged again, and the princess said, "I'm so sorry about all those years we—"

"Let's just be glad we found each other," Robbie Ann said into Princess Marlena's ear. "And promise you will stay in touch with us."

"I promise," said the princess, then turned eagerly to Montillion. "Now, Montillion, quickly, please, reach up and pull the cord. Have them unhook this coach from the rest of the train."

Montillion shook his head. "Sorry, my dear, but this is the *royal* coach. All I can do is have the train stop so that you can get off."

And with that he pulled the cord, and the moving train began to slow. When it came to a full screeching stop on the tracks, the princess hugged Her Royal Highness Robbie Ann one last time. She dashed over to the cushioned seat where she'd left her bottle of white sand. She snatched up the bottle and bolted to the door.

Her sister said, "Is that all you're taking with you?"

"It's the only thing I want," said the starry-eyed Marlena.

Then, laughing, she hugged Montillion and murmured, "Monty, dear loyal Monty."

She stepped down off the train, threw her slender shoulders back, and walked all the way to True's house. The sun was setting when she reached the little adobe.

True and Virgil were out on the porch when they spotted her coming up the narrow dirt road in the gathering twilight.

"What the . . . ?" muttered Virgil and came to his feet. "Jesus, it's . . . it's. . . ."

He stepped off the porch and started running, his heart pounding in his chest. The tired, happy princess ran to meet him. Tightly clutching her bottle of white sand, she leaped into his outstretched arms, and Virgil swung her around, exclaiming, "You've come back! Baby, you've come back to me!"

"Yes, yes, yes," she said, "I couldn't leave you. I couldn't!"

"Thank God," he whispered into her ginger hair. "I don't want to live without you. *Can't* live without you, Princess."

244 ◆ NAN RYAN

She kissed him soundly and said, "I don't like that title anymore. I don't want to be called princess."

"What do you want to be called?" he asked, swinging her up into his arms and carrying her toward the adobe house where the smiling True was clapping his hands with glee.

Her slender arms looped around the strong column of his neck, the princess looked into the Ranger's shining blue eyes and said, "Mrs. Black. Mrs. Virgil Black."